On Solid Ground

by Keith R. Clemons

To Jackie
For love of God and country

GEORGE COLTON
PUBLISHING

George Colton Publishing, LLC.
For information email:
GeorgeColton@att.net

Churches, schools, charities, and other not-for-profit organizations may acquire George Colton books by writing to the above attn: Ministerial Markets Department.

This book is a work of fiction. The characters, incidents, and dialogues are products of the author's imagination and are not to be construed as real. Any resemblance to actual events or persons, living or dead, is entirely coincidental.

Published by George Colton Publishing LLC

Clemons, Keith R. 1949-
    On Solid Ground / Keith R. Clemons -- 1st ed.

Library of Congress Control Number: 2018955938
ISBN   978-0-9731048-6-8

Printed in the United States of America

First Edition

18 19 21 22 23 24 25– 10 9 8 7 6 5 4 3 2 1

Acknowledgements

To Linda Anderson, Sandy Roberts, Kathleen Moore, and, last but definitely not least, my wonderful wife Kathryn, who willingly gave of their time and energy to help me prepare this manuscript for publication. And to my daughter Melody, who always amazes me with her fantastic cover designs. Bless you ladies, one and all. I couldn't do it without you.

Soli Deo Gloria - To God Alone the Glory!

Dissimilarity

Day is day and night is night
They're never quite the same
Except within that moment when
The dawn and dusk remain
For as twilight fades to darkness
And dawn returns to light
One cannot discern which one
Is day and which is night.

And distant too are wrong and right
Though close like night and day
When truth once held as black and white
Melds into muddled grey.
As absolutes are compromised
When wrong is viewed as right
There's no discerning darkness from
The dimming of the light.

Keith R. Clemons

Prologue

A few yellow lights emanated from the windows of homes on both sides of the street. Garbage collectors were working at the end of the alley banging trash cans against the side of their truck. A dog, threatened by their arrival, barked incessantly. As usual, Stan was up before the sun broke the horizon, but the edge of the earth now held a blue iridescent glow that wasn't there when he'd first tossed his blankets aside. He had polished his shoes and was sitting on the edge of the bed slipping them on, listening vaguely to the TV droning in the background.

It was a morning news program and the talking heads were pontificating over the announcement made by Senator Charlotte Weise that had web blogs and Twitter feeds buzzing.

The coffee maker *beeped* three times, letting Stan know a fresh pot was ready. He could smell the aroma of the coffee wafting into the room. Stan grabbed a tie from the rack and spun it around his neck, slipping the knot up under his collar and pulling it snug. The TV was in the living room, but standing in front of the closet mirror he could see it from where he stood, only the picture was reversed. He swept his hand through his hair, smoothing it in place and reached for his navy blue herringbone coat to complement his tan slacks and light blue shirt. The tie was midnight blue with tan stripes, bringing it all together. He hobbled into the kitchen to fill his travel mug glancing at the TV screen from the side. It was a

KEITH R. CLEMONS

close-up of Senator Charlotte Weise.

"I understand there's always been a negative side to using the term socialism," she said. "But I just felt the time was right to step up and let my constituents know where I stand. It's obvious they appreciate the work I do. I mean, after all, my base is so strong no one wants to run against me. But I've always upheld social values and social justice. I want to create a world of greater tolerance and equality for everyone. And I'm not alone. A recent poll found that four out of every ten adults prefer socialism to capitalism, and among millennials the number is significantly higher. The time has come to tell it like it is. I want to be a part of creating a new, better America…"

Stan sipped his coffee, but took it in too fast scalding his tongue. He jerked the cup away, swallowing fast and stepped back to avoid what dribbled on the floor. He was fanning his face with his hand as he set the cup down. Charlotte, a socialist, *who would've thunk it?* He sucked on his tongue, smiling awkwardly at his own humor. His eyes went back to the TV.

"Well Chad, it's either political suicide or pure genius. I guess we'll just have to wait and see."

"I don't think it'll be a problem," the morning show's co-host responded. "She's right about her popularity. Her constituents will continue to vote for her. They like what she stands for. They won't switch their vote. And she's right about America changing. Most young people believe in social justice, and the aging population, who may hold a more conservative point of view, become fewer every year…"

Fewer every year? Stan thought. *Oh, he means because they're dying. Too bad, because there's wisdom in those gray heads.*

Previous generations saw the negative side of socialism. They knew instinctively, whether they believed in Christ or not, that God was essential to America's well being. A socialistic worldview, whether democratic socialism or autocratic communism, generally

2

disparaged the existence of God and a godless world could never be a better place in which to live.

Stan started for his library but stopped. He didn't have time to look it up. Besides, he already knew what it said. Karl Marx, the architect of modern socialism, had written, "The first requisite for the happiness of the people is the abolition of religion." In his view, religion was a placebo used by the weak to cope with an insufferable world. It was nonsense. God had placed a shadow of Himself in every human soul, a likeness that prompted men to seek Him out. What atheists failed to realize was that along with the removal of God, came the elimination of moral restraint which always led to a nation's decline. A more biblical worldview, proved by history to be true, was that righteousness exalted a nation.

Stan held his leg as he stooped down, ignoring the ache of his old war wound, the last vestige of his service to his country. He would probably die of old age before that pain left his body. But they'd said he'd never walk again and they'd been wrong about that, so they might be wrong about the pain too. He wiped the coffee until the napkin became sopped and then used the counter to pull himself up. Reaching for another, he dropped it to the floor and swirled it around underfoot to clean the rest.

As a key to the fulfillment of prophecy, socialism was inevitable. Relinquishing the rights of America to the United Nations, the tearing down of national borders and the growing use of digital currency were just harbingers of a day when all nations would give up their national identities to become nation-states serving a centralized government. Stan grabbed the counter and held his leg out straight, stooping over to pick up the soiled napkin. He grimaced as he tossed it in the trash. The planet would fall under the authority of a leader who controlled the world's economy through a common currency—*that no man might buy or sell, save he that had the mark...or the number of his name*—at least that's what Bible said. He grabbed his travel mug and screwed on the lid.

A cardinal, bright and red as the morning sun, was chirping in the tree outside his window. "Hey little fella, I guess you needn't stress out over what's to come, eh. Lucky you."

The Bible also said that about that time Christ would return to judge the earth for its iniquity. Stan picked up the remote, shut off the TV and with coffee in hand headed for the door. He prayed he would be on the side of Christ at His coming, not caught in the entanglements of some new world order.

Rachel collected her computer and cell phone, putting one in her pocket while hanging the other by a strap over her shoulder. Just a few new toys. It made her feel good to know she could buy them. A year ago she'd had nothing, now it appeared she had it all: a full scholarship to Northwestern and the prospect of a job managing the campaign office of Senator Weise. She inserted her key into the lock to secure the door and made her way down the hall to the staircase because it was closer than the elevator. She wanted to be on the shore of Lake Michigan before sunrise.

She walked across grass lit by streetlamps, the cool dew sloshing up on her flip-flops. She might've worn shoes, but she didn't want them getting filled with sand. She held the strap of her computer, pleased with the purchase. Her expenses were paid by her scholarship and, much to her surprise, she'd already received her first check, ostensibly to purchase books. She'd decided to also use it for the two things she needed most, a phone and a laptop.

Her foot caught a ridge, tossing her off balance. Her computer case swung forward but she caught it, bringing it back to her side. She hadn't bought a fancy computer, she'd survived this long without one; so anything that let her type and surf the web was enough. She was thrilled to find her dormitory had Wi-Fi and now used the computer mostly for streaming news programs and watching the History Channel. Not so her phone. She had for the longest time wanted to be able to take pictures, so she made sure her smart phone had a good digital camera, which meant her phone cost about twice as much as her computer.

Night insects were swirling in the light from the lamps along the path. She rubbed her arms to warm herself. At Campus Drive she veered right and crossed the road to the access point of North Beach.

She stepped onto the strand and slipped her flip-flops from her feet so she could feel the sand squishing between her toes. The morning air smelled like the sludge that backed up against the block wall of the southern shore. She hadn't noticed it before, but maybe it was stronger in the morning before the sun rose and burned off the odor. The light on the horizon was already a faint purple and growing brighter by the minute. She needed to hurry. She reached for her six inch tripod, the one with rubber legs that could clamp onto almost anything. It was the only phone accessory she'd bought. She headed for an outcrop of rock where she hoped the tripod's flexible feet would be secure. Slipping her computer from her shoulder and placing it on a flat surface, she attached the tripod to her phone and positioned it on the rock facing the Eastern shore. There, she was done and all set up. The sun had yet to lift its hoary head.

She had a meeting scheduled with Senator Weise that afternoon. She couldn't stay on the beach too long. As soon as she got her sequence of pictures she would run back to the residence to shower and change. She wished Ms. Rosen, her former guidance counselor, could be there to introduce her. The idea of walking in unannounced to meet with someone she didn't know, especially someone of Senator Weise's status, was unsettling. What if they didn't get along? She'd still have her scholarship, but she'd have to find another job. Last night while surfing the web she'd come across a podcast with a clip of Senator Weise announcing she was a socialist.

The purple curtain was fading, the edge of the earth now bathed in red. The sun would be up in less than a minute. She looked into the digital screen but it was black. There wasn't enough light to see anything yet.

Rachel wasn't sure where she stood on the issue. She'd once won a debate arguing the benefits of socialism over capitalism. Ms. Rosen would have told Senator Weise about that, which probably went in her favor. The trouble was she'd looked at the issue from both sides and wasn't convinced socialism was necessarily better.

The sun's crest had just surfaced. She tapped the camera button on the phone and set it to take one picture every ten seconds. The sun would be up in a few minutes and she would have a series of photographs showing its rise, symbolic, she thought, of the rags to riches story of her life. A gust of wind hit the shore nearly knocking the phone over. She grabbed the tripod's legs and held them in place while using her free hand to sweep the hair from her eyes. It really didn't matter, if being a socialist elevated her in the eyes of Senator Weise, then she would be a socialist.

Now the only thing missing in her life—was her father.

One

STAN SAT at his desk gazing out the window of Power Advertising, the firm that bore his name, only right now he wondered if owning his own business was such a good thing. His personal haze was every bit as real as the one he saw hovering over the skyline of Chicago. He tapped the desk with this finger holding the document up to read. *This is nonsense.* He reached for his phone and pushed the intercom button. "Bruce, can you come into my office for a minute?"

A few minutes later Bruce, his creative director and second in command, stood at the door leaning on the frame for support. He tapped the wood lightly with his knuckles. "You wanted to see me?"

Stan waved him in, indicating he should take a seat. He handed the document over. "You know anything about this?"

Bruce received the folio, glancing at it quickly. "What is it?"

"It's a lawsuit alleging I discriminated against some friends of yours, a couple of guys opening a new gay club. They said you recommended me."

Bruce was shaking his head.

"I declined their business," Stan continued. "I had to. They weren't asking me to advertise a new product, which I would've been happy to do, they wanted me to promote their club, which was like asking me to endorse their lifestyle. Now I get this lawsuit

claiming I discriminated against them for their sexual orientation."
He looked sharply at Bruce. "Did you know about this?"

Bruce curled his shoulders, folding into himself. He read a few
paragraphs and turned the page, his fingers trembling. He looked
up and shook his head. "No, no, I know nothing about this. You
have to believe me boss. Whenever someone asks me where I work
I always brag about this place. I tell everyone how great it is to work
here and how open and understanding you are. These guys must've
heard me talking and got the wrong idea. I...I...I'm sorry, but I
don't know anything about it."

Stan swiveled his seat to the side, staring out the window. It was
a vapid day full of wet heat. He ran his fingers through his hair,
feeling the moisture in his scalp. This wasn't the first time they'd
declined to do business with someone. There had been others
whose business ethics weren't in line with his Christian beliefs. He
turned back to Bruce. "This whole thing is frivolous. These guys are
out to silence anyone who objects to their way of life. If they could
they'd have me tarred and feathered and run out of town."

"Boss I...I don't know what to say. I saw the names on the
complaint but I don't know them. They're probably just two guys I
met at a club. I wasn't meaning any harm, I wouldn't do that. I'll ask
around and see if I can find out who they are. Maybe I can explain
and get them to drop the whole thing."

Stan's eyes went to the flag standing in the corner of his office.
The America he knew was quickly becoming a memory. "That
would be great Bruce, that would be great. I don't have the money
or the time to fight a thing like this."

It was after seven o'clock. Most of his staff had already
straightened their desks and packed their briefcases and gone home.
Only a few working on projects with short deadlines remained. He
should be at the mission handing out food with Bishop Samuel.

That's where his heart was, following the command of Christ to feed the poor, but instead Stan sat alone in his office mulling over how such a suit might affect the business and what that might do to their bottom line. Darkness had fallen on the city, in more ways than one. He couldn't fathom being sued for refusing to promote the way a certain group of people chose to live. He tossed the document on the table.

The world had gone crazy. God created them male and female—*period!* Stan didn't buy the theory of evolution, but those who did would certainly acknowledge that what they called natural process had resulted in two distinct genders. But not today, today people were being told their genetic makeup didn't matter, it was their thoughts and emotions that made them who they were. A man could be a man, or a woman, or be transgender, or be gender-neutral, or be gay, or if he wasn't sure, be undecided.

Stan leaned back, his hands gripping the arms of the chair. If a man were to tell his psychiatrist he thought he was a dog and then get down on all fours barking and start biting the psychiatrist's ankles the psychiatrist would have him committed. But if a man were to tell his psychiatrist he thought he was a woman, and then put on makeup, dress in women's clothes and go around kissing other men, that would be viewed as perfectly normal. Such nonsense. All it took for a man to know he was a male was to stand naked in front of a mirror.

Stan picked up the lawsuit and flipped through the pages. And he was being sued because he chose not to advertise something that was not only prohibited by God but throughout history was antecedent to every great nation's fall. The matrix had to have somehow become inverted because surely he was living in an alternate reality. That was the only plausible explanation. He reached for the phone. It was time to call his lawyer.

• • •

Satchel walked the grounds picking up gum wrappers and cigarette butts. The air was warm, the sky clear. The only thing preventing him from enjoying the morning were the rolls of razor wire on the fences surrounding him. But if everything went as it should, that would end today.

Each morning for the past ten years he'd woken cursing himself for being so stupid. He'd been careful to not commit crimes that carried heavy prison time and then gone and blown it all in one reckless act.

The trial had been a fiasco. He didn't have money to hire an attorney, so he'd used a court assigned public defender, a man who couldn't care less that this was his first offense or that the shooting had been an accident. He hadn't planned to use the gun, it was just a prop, something to intimidate the man behind the counter. None of that came up in the trial. It had been a slam dunk for the prosecutor who walked away with kudos and pats on the back for getting the judge to dish out one of the longest sentences for a first offense on record. The judge had incentive. Illinois had just passed a law demanding longer sentences for crimes committed with guns. Prior to that, most first offenders were given one to three years. He, on the other hand, had received six.

But that was just the beginning of his woes. You would think, in a facility where every move was monitored, that getting into trouble would be difficult, but that discounted his temper. It wasn't long before someone cut in front of him in the food line. They had words, but when the man brought a food tray down on Satchel's head, Satchel put him in the hospital, a crime for which Satchel was sent to isolation. Another man tried to change the channel while Satchel was watching the Chicago Bulls getting creamed by the Celtics. Already emotionally charged, he'd sprung from his chair and exploded into the man like a bull. The man's jaw had to be wired shut, forcing him to take food through a straw. Once again Satchel ended up in isolation. His reputation for violence earned him extra scrutiny. When Skinhead Jack tried to stick him with a shiv the guards were quick to respond. But not quick enough. Jack ended up receiving a transfusion for the loss of blood and narrowly escaped with his life. It was a clear case of self-defense, but Satchel was taken to court where he got another four years tacked onto his sentence.

Afraid his escalating crimes might prevent him from ever leaving prison, Satchel had signed up for an anger management class. It helped some, but his response to conflict was instantaneous. When rage bubbled up inside him, he blew like a volcano. No amount of self-help gobbledygook could keep the lava from spewing out.

Then the first letter from Rachel had arrived. She'd let him know she was in school and doing well; but being around so many kids whose parents drove them to school, took them to football games, and attended PTA meetings, had awakened in her a need to know her father. She'd told him about Mr. Morris, and Mr. Purvey, and Mr. Crenshaw; but they were just foster parents, not her own flesh and blood. She'd said she wanted to become better acquainted with her real father. She felt there was a natural bond in that.

The effort she'd taken to track him down, surprised him. She had gone to the school library and used the computer to surf the internet for Illinois State correctional facilities. From there she was able to access the lists of inmates housed in each. She had searched half a dozen before she'd found his name, Satchel Carter, in the Dixon correctional facility. Her foster parents didn't own a cell phone. They had a landline, but would not allow her to use it for long distance calls. That led her to write. The prison's website let her know that all inmate mail must be received in a plain white envelope and be printed on standard sheets of paper and would be read before being passed along, but she didn't care about that. She was writing to let him know she wanted to reconnect.

Satchel had sat on his cot reading that first letter with his shoulders heaving, afraid his cellmate might notice and make him for a fish. He'd choked back his emotions and let nothing show but it had killed him. He made a point of making sure to read all subsequent letters only when he was alone. Each one made his eyes well up, and the lump in his throat hard to swallow. It was difficult to imagine his daughter, after all he'd done, wanting to establish a relationship with him.

It had put him on the path to rehabilitation. He began seeking advice from the prison chaplain, the end result of which led him to the conclusion that his anger stemmed from his belief that no one gave a hoot whether he lived or died. His life was a meaningless series of events that served one singular purpose—survival. Only now he found he had a daughter who cared about him, and the chaplain said God loved him; so to Rachel he began writing letters, and to God he began to pray.

Rachel wanted to know everything. She asked him to tell her what life was like in prison in full detail from the jumpsuits they wore, to the cameras monitoring their every move. He told her of his daily routine, how he was required to make his bunk and keep his cell clean, how everyone had a job that enabled the smooth operation of the facility; from laundry detail, to being part of the kitchen staff, to library duty, to outdoor maintenance.

Over the years she had stopped calling him Satchel and started calling him dad, something she confessed was awkward for her at first. He vowed to do everything in his power to become a good citizen and work toward an early release.

It had paid off. He was going home—*today!* After ten years he was finally being set free and truth be told, he was scared to death. He had nowhere to go, no money and no job, and as much as he was determined not to ply his former trade, he didn't know what else he could do. He had to survive until he could find work.

First and foremost he wanted to find Rachel but he didn't know where to start. The last letter he'd sent had been returned with a message scribbled across the front that read, "No longer lives here!" Rachel had apparently moved on to go to college and hadn't yet sent him her new address. In hindsight, perhaps it would've been better to let her know his release date, then she might've sent her new address with greater urgency. Maybe he could ask the warden to forward his mail. The only problem was, he didn't know where he would be living.

It still bothered him, though she never brought it up, to know that as a parent he should be providing for her education, or at least her basic needs. He was chagrined at the thought of a time when he'd told her she didn't need school. Now she was writing that she'd received straight A's. His little girl was a genius. He wrote back to tell her that by all means pursue that education. He reinforced the thought by letting her know he himself was taking a course in commercial cooking and hoped, once he got out, to be a short order chef.

Satchel stuffed a scrap of paper into his bag and turned around. His pulse quickened. He was being approached by three men. His throat constricted cutting his ability to swallow. He knew what was coming. It was about Skinhead Jack saving face. Jack had let him know the only way he was leaving the prison was in a box. The movement was quick, but as a pickpocket Satchel was accustomed to slick moves. Jack's hand had seemed empty before but now it held a piece of hard plastic, honed sharp, with the sun glinting off the blade.

Satchel felt an anxious bolt of electricity course through his veins. It was three against one, not bad odds considering two of them were scrawny, at least compared to him, and he'd beaten Jack before. He could take them. He clenched his teeth, his jaw set firm, his fists solid as balls of iron. They were within a few feet of him. One good lunge would draw blood.

"Told ya, skank, you ain't leaving. Not on your own two feet."

Others around the yard were starting to take notice. They moved in creating a loose circle around the fight.

Satchel took a step back, readying himself. It was his fight to win—*what about Rachel?* If he ran he'd be labeled a coward. Jack drew his hand back ready to thrust the blade into Satchel's gut. Satchel sucked in his breath glancing at those surrounding him. He would leave today, either through the main gate—or in a box. *Okay, I'm a coward.* He turned, and shoving the spectators out of his way, ran like a cockroach on hot cement.

Two

T HE WARM morning had melded into a hot afternoon, but Satchel refused to give up his coat. He felt ridiculous hanging around shantytown in a suit and tie but it was all he had. He'd been picked up for pickpocketing, thus his reason at the time for wearing dress clothes, and he'd worn the suit throughout the trial hoping to look respectable. When he was ultimately convicted, not for pickpocketing but robbery and assault with a deadly weapon, he'd been taken in a van to Dixon. There he'd traded his business attire for a prison jumpsuit, which was why the suit was returned to him when he checked out. He doubted his other clothes still existed. His former landlord wouldn't have held onto them all these years. He could feel the sweat rolling down his chest. He raised his arm to see if he was getting ripe. Thankfully, he smelled fine.

He stood at the curb admiring the dirty streets and the traffic that polluted the air. Horns honked and lights blinked and aluminum cans cluttered the gutter, and he had never seen anything so beautiful in his life. He felt like a child. He wanted to run and tag the nearest light pole and turnaround and run back again but his legs were too old for that. Didn't matter, he felt like it anyway. The place he was heading for was just ahead. He picked up the pace.

He'd been given a list of halfway houses that took in ex-cons and helped them integrate back into society. He chose this one because he'd been here before. The food was good, the beds decent, and they made you feel welcome, at least that's how it had been the last time he'd stayed here. He approached the door. The paint was lime green, cracked and peeling like a lizard shedding its skin. The doorknob was tarnished brass. He reached up and rang the bell. It took a few minutes. Satchel stood at the doorstep subconsciously shuffling his feet until he heard a click and saw the door handle starting to turn. He took a step back.

"You!" he said.

"Me?"

Satchel felt his chest tighten. *That face*—a face his mind had conjured up so many times it was as familiar as his own—was the last he'd expected to see. That face had peered at him all through his trial, and for years after that while lying on his bed staring up at the ceiling. And now it was right here glaring at him.

"I…I think I've got the wrong place." He took a step back and feigned glancing up at the sign. "Yes, sorry about that, mate." He turned to go.

"Wait."

Satchel paused, looking back over his shoulder.

"Satchel? Satchel Carter?" The man held up a note reading from it. "No, this is right, I've been expecting you."

"Look, I don't want no trouble. It's better if I go." He extended his hands out with the palms open as though trying to show he wasn't carrying a weapon. He felt the heat of the day compacting under his suit, rills of perspiration streaming down his chest.

"There's no trouble."

Satchel shook his head and slipped a finger under his collar to vent the steam building inside his shirt. During his trial he'd examined the man's face, certain he'd seen it before the robbery. Now he knew where. He swallowed but his mouth was dry. "Look here, mate, you know me, I'm the bloke what shot you. I think it would be better if I went someplace else."

Stan took a step back opening the door wide. "Nope, this is the place. You're right where God wants you."

They were seated across from each other at one of the long tables in the dining room. Satchel had removed his coat and laid it over the back of a chair. He took a sip of the coffee he'd been offered. This bloke was weird, sitting across from the chap what shot him and didn't seem bothered at all. He took another sip and set the cup down, the overhead fans creating rings on the surface of his coffee.

"So what are the rules? I know you got rules, everyone does."

The man was dressed in blue slacks and a white open-collared shirt. Satchel remembered seeing him years ago while serving food. *The gimp with a limp.* The man stretched his legs out front of him and folded his hands in his lap. "Yes, I suppose we do. We have to maintain a certain amount of discipline. Like we expect all our guests to be in by ten o'clock. We don't allow alcohol of any kind, or smoking inside the building. You're also required to be looking for a job and to provide us with copies of the applications you fill out. This isn't free long-term room and board. We want to help people get back on their feet, not be taken advantage of. In your case, I expect you to begin work tonight."

Satchel lifted his head raising an eyebrow. His cotton shirt felt itchy but he refused to scratch. The overhead fans, whirling like the blades of helicopters, kept the air circulating, making it cooler than outside.

Stan let go of his foot and leaned forward with his elbows on his thighs, his hands clasped between his knees. "All of the men who stay here help out in one way or another, either by cleaning or painting or serving food. The folks at Dixon provided us with a summary of your background. I saw where you took courses in cooking. That's good. It's something we can use around here. Meal preparation starts at four o'clock. The kitchen's right there," he said flipping his thumb over his shoulder toward the far end of the room. "Come a few minutes early so I can introduce you around. Providing you don't poison anyone," Stan smiled, "we can put your experience on your résumé and perhaps provide your future employer with a good reference. That's about it. Long as you keep the rules, your free time is your own."

Satchel nodded slowly. "Count on it. I was a pickpocket, not a car thief. I'm not into heavy crime. And I never hurt no one..." he paused looking at Stan's chest. "...I mean...that was the only time I ever used a gun. I'm not like that. Anyway, now I got a chance to turn things around. I'm putting all that stuff behind me. I'm a changed man."

Stan hooked his thumbs in his pockets and leaned back in his chair. "Oh? How's that?"

"I don't know. I'm just being good, that's all."

"Do you think you can be good on your own?"

"What do you mean? Yeah, I guess so, sometimes. I mean I ain't perfect."

"No one is."

Satchel shuffled in his seat. A gray shorthaired cat hopped down from the windowsill and trotted across the floor heading for a water bowl in the kitchen. Satchel's eyes followed it causing Stan to look back over his shoulder to see what had caught Satchel's attention.

"He's a stray but we feed him and let him in when it's cold, kind of a house pet."

Satchel thrust his bottom lip out and grunted. He folded his hands and leaned forward with his elbows on his knees. "Thing is, I have to. I have a daughter what I haven't seen in a while. I'm doing this for her."

"Why is that? Why not for yourself?"

"Look, it is what it is. I've never been anything but a thief. But this little girl of mine she's like, I don't know, some kind of honor student or something, the furthest thing from me a dame can be. She goes to school, gets good grades, and even though I messed her up, she still wants to see me. She forgave me, know what I mean? I ain't been the same since."

"That's the first thing you've said that makes sense. Forgiveness. That's God's gift."

"Huh?" The cat meandered over, sat beside the chair and reaching his paws up, hopped into Satchel's lap.

"You were forgiven by your daughter and look how that made you feel. Just imagine how good it feels to be forgiven by God?"

Satchel began scratching the cat's ears. It was purring and rubbing its head against his shirt. "I, uh, yeah, I kind of figured you'd be like that. I came here a few times when I was on the street. I heard you preach. Look, I mean no disrespect but I already got religion. I mean, while I was in the slammer I started to pray. I even asked for God's forgiveness, but I figure it was more about getting things off my chest, you know, like confession is good for the soul and all that. Truth is, I'm not even sure God exists."

"But if He does?"

"If He does, I think we're good. I mean there's a whole lot worse than me. I mean I never killed no one..." He looked up at Stan and realized what he said. "I mean I never intended to...and you're still alive. It could've been worse."

"Thank God. Yes, it could have been, but the fact that I lived doesn't make your actions any less criminal. Fortunately God doesn't judge us on the severity of crimes we commit. The only thing He judges us on is whether or not we accept His forgiveness."

Satchel took the cat under its front legs and set it on the ground. It tried to jump up again but he blocked it with his hand. "Sorry, cat, I ain't into kitties." Then he looked at Stan. "Okay, I get it. I'm trying. Anyway, if you've gone over everything, can I get you to show me to my room? I'm a bit tired and if you want me to work tonight I better get some rest."

19

Satchel lay on a single bed with his hands folded behind his head staring up at the ceiling. Dust motes inhabited corners like tiny clouds on a gypsum sky. His breathing was audible as he let out a sigh. Several more beds were stationed around the room. Most would be filled by nightfall, though it wouldn't be as crowded as in the winter when it became difficult for the homeless to sleep on the streets.

The stairway leading to the second floor reminded him of his apartment at Chen's. Another thing he'd screwed up. He'd never find lodging as cheap as that, and being a short-order cook didn't pay all that much. Chen was the one who needed salvation—imagine wanting to play with a little girl…Satchel felt his gut wrench. He had accommodated Chen with his own daughter. He bit his lower lip and tried to relax, his stomach twisting like a washcloth being wrung dry. His life had been one screw-up after another. "Forgive me…" The thought hit him that his uncertainty about God might just be his undoing.

Stan took the elevator to the top floor of the Winston building. The men standing beside him were holding briefcases and dressed in suits, making him glad he had donned his tie and slipped into his coat before driving over. He'd removed them because he thought wearing his professional gear might make someone who'd just served out their sentence, uncomfortable. And then his guest, Satchel, had showed up in a suit and tie—*go figure. Of all the gin joints in all the towns in all the world, he walks into mine.* The Lord does work in mysterious ways. Stan's lips formed an upside down smile. The idea that a man who shot him would end up a decade later asking for his help was bizarre. But that was God. There was no question in Stan's mind that God had sent Satchel to him for a reason. He approached the door. The brass plaque on the wall read, "Livingston and Stone—Attorneys at

Law." He went in and approached the reception desk. "I have an appointment with Mr. Stone, two o'clock."

The woman ran a pink fingernail down her appointment book. Her brunette hair was short and styled in swirls that masked her narrow face. A faint wisp of Versace Eros lifted from her clothes. "Yes, I have it down. Just have a seat and Mr. Stone will be right with you."

Stan turned, looking for a place to sit. The office was similar to his own, paneled in dark wood with paintings on the walls and windows looking out over the Chicago skyline. The air outside was heated and saturated with moisture that smelled of impending rain. Another man sat on a small reception sofa thumbing through a newspaper while waiting to be seen. That left the wing back chair. Stan hoped the other guy was there for Mr. Livingston. He looked at his watch, he didn't have much time. He needed to be back at the shelter by four o'clock to get Satchel acclimated. He swiped a copy of National Geographic from the coffee table and took a seat, keeping his legs out straight to reduce the strain on the muscle of his thigh as he paged through the magazine.

"From apes to humans: understanding our evolution." Stan looked up and huffed a sigh, letting the air out through his nose. He liked National Geographic when the stories were about other places and cultures, and like everyone else, he loved the photography, but modern science had come up with so many reasons why evolution didn't work it boggled him that they still printed this stuff. He glanced down and read the article's first sentence, "It may seem a little humbling to learn that our human genetic blueprint is ninety-eight percent the same as that of our distant relative, the chimpanzee…" *Yeah,* he closed the magazine and tossed it back on the table, *and our genome is ninety percent the same as mice, but we don't look like them so no one's suggesting we come from rodents.* It was naive to assume similar genetic architecture automatically meant common ancestry.

A young man with short cropped hair and a two-day-old beard approached Stan. "Mr. Powers, Mr. Stone is ready to see you now." He turned and led Stan down the hall to a corner office and ushered him in. Stan heard the door close behind him.

Arthur Stone rose from his seat and walked over, extending his hand. "Good to see you Stan," he said. He was taller, but not by much. His grip was firm but not overbearing, and with a physique that suggested he'd just stepped off a rowing machine, looked much younger than his sixty-eight years. He had medium-brown hair with just enough gray around the temples to look mature. His face was long with a steeply inclined nose and deep set eyes that looked out at the world from beneath heavy brows. He turned and sat at a corner table, inviting Stan to do the same. The office wasn't ostentatious. The walls weren't filled with law books, nor were there photos of Arthur Stone shaking hands with celebrities and heads of state. It was merely a functioning workspace. Stan liked it that way. "You mentioned a lawsuit," Art said.

Stan pursed his lips. His elbow was on the arm of his chair. He opened and closed his fist several times. "Seems like I've got myself a bit of a situation."

"How's that?"

He clasped his knee with his hands and slid his wounded leg out straight. "About a month ago two guys popped into my office and said they were opening a new club and wanted me to handle the promotion. Turns out they were opening a gay bar. You wrote out charter. You know it prohibits advertising anything that appears unseemly so I was forced to decline. I referred them to a couple of competitors I respect and we said goodbye. That was it. There was no hostility, at least not that I could discern, but then today I received this." Stan handed Art the envelope he'd been holding.

It took a few minutes for Art to peruse the document. His lip jutted out with a frown. He let the folio slide back onto the table and held it down with the flat of his hand. "Unbelievable," he said, shaking his head. "You know you're not the only one going through this?" He tilted his head up slightly so that his eyes, staring out from beneath the shelf of his brow, looked dark and somber. "Christian bakers and photographers and caterers are being asked to do gay weddings, and the Supreme Court has yet to make a definitive decision about whether they have the right to refuse. Unfortunately, the lower courts are consistently siding with the plaintiffs, and since we live in a blue state, I'd say your chances of winning this thing are slim to none."

"What about that baker down in Colorado, the one that refused to make a cake for a gay couple's wedding? Didn't the Supreme Court rule in his favor?"

"Not quite. The Supreme Court said that the Colorado Civil Rights Commission had overstepped their bounds when they derided the baker's religious beliefs, so their ruling was overturned. The issue of whether or not a Christian business can refuse to provide a product or service to a gay person has yet to be decided. Knowing the political climate here in Illinois, I think it's a safe bet that you'll lose this case. You want my opinion, I suggest you go in with an offer to settle this out of court. Going to trial would be a lot more costly, and as I said, you'll probably lose. Of course, you can always appeal, but ultimately I think you'll have to take it all the way to the Supreme Court, which would take years and loads of money. Anyway, that's my advice, take it or leave it. Either way I'm not the right man to represent you. You need a trial lawyer. If you want, I can provide you with a recommendation."

Stan's eyes furrowed in, his mouth agape. "You're saying no?"

"I'm saying this firm focuses on corporate and tax law. We settle most of our suits through negotiation. Our battleground is the boardroom, not the courthouse. These guys want to make a point. They want to paint you as a bigot and see you publicly humiliated. You dared to suggest that the way they live might be wrong and they're going to take you to task for that. If you want to fight this thing you're going to need a good trial lawyer."

It suddenly occurred to Stan that he was getting the same rebuff he had given Kosner and these two gay men. *Sorry, but I feel I'm not the right one to do this for you.* What goes around comes around. But he wasn't ready to give up. Following the example of Kosner, he brought the flat of his hand down and smacked the table. *Whack!* A piece of notepaper flew off the table. "That's exactly right and it's because you're right that I want you to represent me. There are probably a few good lawyers out there who understand what this is really about, but I'd be hard-pressed to find one. I need someone like you, someone who knows the issue and knows me and knows why we need to win this thing. And as for you not being a good trial lawyer, this is a civil suit, not a criminal case. I think you're selling yourself short. You're a negotiator and a good negotiator looks at all the facts and determines the best way to bring everyone together and solve the problem. You may have to negotiate with the plaintiffs and the judge, but I think from what I know of you, you'll do fine."

Three

RACHEL TRAVERSED the campus being careful to stay on the sidewalks and not get her feet wet. The lawn sprinklers were whirling throwing misty rainbows into the air. She was wearing light leather slip-ons and needed to keep them dry. It was important to look professional at her interview. First impressions were lasting. Her outfit was a one piece blue jumper with full-length legs but no arms, like a classy form of bib overalls. Her hair flowed behind her in waves like a river reflecting the yellow sun. She stopped at the corner. A little red hand was blinking warning her not to cross the street. She pushed the button on the lamppost and waited till the hand morphed into a man walking. She headed off campus to Sheridan Road and turned right. According to Ms. Rosen, she only had to walk about a mile and she would come to the building that housed Northwestern campaign headquarters of Senator Charlotte Weise.

She was told she couldn't miss it, but she checked the note just to be sure she hadn't passed it already. The address she wanted was still about a block down, probably where the long black town car was parked. The sun warmed her shoulders, which were already tan from her walks along the beach. Her bronze skin had small freckles dotting her upper arms and back. As she drew closer she could see a man in the driver's seat, but he didn't acknowledge her as she peered in so she turned back toward the front of the building. It looked to have been an old wholesale office supply company that had gone out of business. The big paper posters in the front windows now advertised the re-election of Charlotte Weise, Senator. She considered knocking but this wasn't a home, it was a place of business. Her heart pattered softly in her breast as she reached for the knob.

The place was rather stark. There was a desk just inside the door with a chair and a lamp. All around the walls were tables with corded phones and computer terminals. She envisioned the room full of students making calls and thought it odd that in this day and age they wouldn't use their cellular devices. But then the calls couldn't be billed to one account. Rows of cabinets were mounted over the tables. One door hung ajar letting her see the reams of paper and stacks of pamphlets inside. A copy machine sat in a far corner with several pieces of paper sitting loosely in its tray.

"Hello?" she said hopefully loud enough for anyone inside to hear.

"Come on in, I'm back here." A woman's voice came echoing down the hall.

Rachel headed on back, noting that the linoleum flooring was scratched and dirty. She could hear her feet clapping as she walked down the hall looking to the right and left into each room she passed. They seemed pretty much the same as the front entry, filled with tables and chairs and the occasional desk. Only one room was different. It seemed to be a meeting room as it contained only one long table surrounded by several chairs. At the end of the hall, in the last room on the right, she stepped into what was more like an office. It too had a desk, but it differed in that there were several waist high bookcases and filing cabinets, but no workstations.

The woman seated behind the desk rose and shook Rachel's hand. She was short, probably about five-foot-four, and wore a stylish blue outfit composed of a blue skirt and jacket over a white blouse. Her face was thin, keeping with the rest of her body, and she had high cheekbones that appeared to be dusted with rouge, but the makeup didn't hide her wrinkles. Her hair was short and gray, sticking straight up on top and her hazel eyes were as puffy as canvas water-bags. The pink lipstick she wore had been applied over chapped lips that looked flakey, and when she smiled her teeth were stained yellow. Rachel couldn't tell if it was from smoking, or too much coffee.

"I'm Charlotte Weise," she said. "And you must be Rachel. My, you look lovely. I think our party is sometimes accused of having a bunch of old hags running the show. And I have to admit there's some truth to it. We feminists grew up in an age when beauty was frowned upon. We wanted to make the point that it was our minds that were important, not our bodies, but I think we've overplayed our hand. It's time to change that image. Please have a seat."

Rachel didn't know how to respond to such a statement. She sat down in one of the chairs facing the desk, folding her hands in her lap.

"I've heard a lot of good things about you, Rachel, but there's also a lot I still don't know. Your guidance counselor is a good friend of mine. She tells me you've excelled academically. She also informs me that you did it the hard way, that you come from a foster home that provided little support."

"It wasn't so bad. We didn't have much money, so I didn't get a lot of things other kids received, but as long as I did my duties I was left alone. I had plenty of time to study."

"Yes, and I hear you put that time to good use. I'm told you landed yourself a scholarship here at Northwestern," she winked, "Northwestern is my alma mater too, and I can tell you that's no small feat. But what I don't know much about is your politics. If you're going to work with me we have to see eye to eye on the issues. I spoke with your teacher, Vivian, but she couldn't offer me much in that regard, other than to say how you won a statewide competition debating the benefits of socialism over capitalism, and how important it is to you to put an end to poverty." Charlotte paused giving Rachel time to respond, but Rachel said nothing so she resumed again. "I don't know whether you know it or not, but I'm a socialist, so I'm glad you won that debate. I want a world where everyone shares equally in everything, where no one is king or pauper. No one with money, or power, or good looks should be viewed as better than anyone else. This world has had enough of that, and it's time for change.

"We're trying to raise up a generation of young people who understand that all humans need to be accepting and tolerant of each other. We've had enough of racism and bigotry. This is what socialism embraces; the kind of world where every person can live by the dictates of their own conscience without fear of criticism or recrimination. Are we on the same page here? It's one thing to want to help the poor, but that's only part of our mission. You have to be ready to fight for the rights of everyone, and especially those who so often get looked down upon by the social elite."

Rachel wasn't sure she aspired to join the "revolution" as some of her high school peers called it, but Ms. Weise's ideas sounded good so why not?

"Of course," Rachel said. "If we're going to save this planet we have to learn to get along. Everyone knows that."

Charlotte smiled. "Most of the kids on campus are like-minded and believe in what I'm trying to achieve. These are the kids you need to recruit." She reached into the desk drawer and removed a folder, placing it on the desk. "This is a list of students who have worked for me in the past. Many of them have graduated since the last time I ran for office. You'll have to replace these with new blood. But most of the others will be happy to help out again.

"I'm giving you this because you need to start recruiting now, even before the semester starts. I'm a fairly popular incumbent, so right now it looks like I'm running unopposed, but we can't rest on our laurels. November's still six months away and who knows what will happen between now and then. If I'm going to win, I'll need a strong team behind me and I want you as part of it. Together we can make a difference." Charlotte rose from her chair and stood, extending her hand again as though letting Rachel know the interview was over. "It's been a pleasure getting to know you, Rachel, but you know how it is, once you enter politics your life is not your own." She paused to look at her watch. "I have a caucus meeting in an hour so I have to be going. Okay, this is your office now. The file's on your desk. I suggest you begin calling people right away. Now if you'll follow me to the door I'll give you the key and show you how to use the alarm."

Warm air swept into the room the minute they stepped outside. Rachel had felt the stifling heat throughout her interview. The small boxlike room was a veritable oven. She'd worried her forehead was starting to glisten. Apparently the building's air conditioning unit hadn't been turned on yet. She'd have to see about getting that done.

Senator Weise's driver popped out and came around to open the door the minute she started down the sidewalk. Rachel gave a quick wave as the senator climbed into her car. The window came down and Charlotte tipped her head out, "We're expecting big things from you, Rachel. Don't let us down."

Rachel turned back, closing the door behind her. Where had she heard *that* before? Seemed like all her counselors and advisers were expecting her to be a huge success. Now all she had to do was live up to their expectations. *No pressure.* She traipsed down the hall and turned into the office—*her office*— she could only imagine what prestige that carried. Would other students gladly subordinate themselves to someone so young and inexperienced? She reached for the file on her desk and walked around to sit in her chair. Only one way to find out. She opened the page to the first name and picked up the phone to dial. One ring…Two rings… Three rings…

"Hello this is Beth, I'm not here to take your call right now. You know what to do...leave a message."

"Hello Beth, this is Rachel Carter. I'm a student at Northwestern and I've just been hired to manage the campaign office for Charlotte Weise. She gave me a list of names to call and since you're one of the people that helped out last time I was wondering if I could get you to volunteer to help us again. The number here is 847-491-0837, please give me a call."

Rachel set the phone down, her heart thumping loudly. She opened the desk drawer and found a box of tissues and began dabbing her forehead. It was much too hot. Until just recently, she hadn't owned a cell phone, and calls made from the landline in the Crenshaw home had been few and far between, so she wasn't really great at talking to people on the phone. Now she was faced with the prospect of having to call dozens of people she'd never met and convince them to work for her for free. Washing dishes would be easier, though it might pay less. She wiped her eyes with the palms of her hands and stopped to read a poster mounted on the wall in front of her.

Imagine there's no heaven
It's easy if you try
No hell below us
Above us only sky
Imagine all the people
Living for today...

Imagine there's no countries
It isn't hard to do
Nothing to kill or die for
And no religion, too
Imagine all the people
Living life in peace...

Imagine no possessions
I wonder if you can
No need for greed or hunger
A brotherhood of man
Imagine all the people
Sharing all the world...

You may say I'm a dreamer
But I'm not the only one
I hope someday you'll join us
And the world will live as one.

John Lennon circa 1971

The song had been written before she was born, but it was famous and she recognized the lyrics. John Lennon was part of the Beatles, a group that had skyrocketed to fame during the psychedelic sixties. It was easy to see why this particular song was mounted in a position where the person sitting at this desk could read it. The words called men to put aside their lust for possessions and the greed that prevented them from sharing all things in common; it decried the nationalism that had fueled so many wars and denied the religious ideology that divided the world into so many factions.

The problem was the author of the song, Mr. Lennon, had earned millions for his work but failed to divide up his wealth and share it with everyone else. It was hypocrisy to say all men should share all things in common and then squirrel away your own belongings and keep them to yourself. Still she could understand why Ms. Weise would want to read these words daily. They encompassed everything she believed.

She bit her lip and picked up the phone again, placing the cool plastic of the headset against her forehead before dialing the next number on the list. One ring…two rings…three rings… "Hi this is Bobby Bobble-head and if you don't know that's not my real name then you have no business calling me…" Rachel quickly looked at her notes. The name was Robert Donnelly "…Otherwise please leave a message."

"Hi Robert, this is Rachel Carter. I've just been hired to manage the campaign of Charlotte Weise. She's running for the Senate again and gave me a few names to call. You're on the list. I was hoping you'd be willing to volunteer again. The number is 847-491-0837. Please give me a call." Again she put the phone down, her heart still pounding but not quite as hard as before.

Rachel took a deep breath and let it out slowly. *What if she couldn't reach anyone? What if everyone refused to help?* She pulled the drawer open and rifled her fingers through its contents until she found a rubber band. The back of her neck felt moist. She pulled her hair up, twisting and folding it over and fixing it in place with the band to keep it off her shoulders. She paused, holding the receiver on her desk in both hands as she took a deep breath, then picked it up and dialed again. One ring…two rings… "Hey, this is Yolanda, what's up?"

Rachel snapped forward in her chair. "Oh, hi Yolanda. Glad I caught you. Have you, I mean, would you be willing to volunteer to help Charlotte Weise get elected again? She's running for another term. She asked me to call a few people that helped out in the past and your name was on the list."

"Oh, sorry, I can't. I graduated last year. I took a job in Des Plaines so I don't live in Evanston anymore, but you can tell Charlotte I'll be voting for her, that's for sure."

"Oh, I understand, well, okay, I hope it goes good for you there. And thank you for your vote. Bye."

Rachel grimaced, realizing she'd been too abrupt. Her heart began pounding again. She didn't know how to handle rejection. She slumped back into her chair still holding the receiver in her hand. On her way over she'd thought, *how hard can it be?* She was starting to believe it would be very hard but she was determined. Others had done this job and apparently had done just fine. She would too. The receiver started beeping loudly in her hand letting her know she needed to place it back on the cradle. She pushed the button cutting the line and waited a few seconds before letting go. She picked it up and heard the dial tone again. Her eyes went to the list, Susan Waxman was next. She punched in the number and placed the phone under chin, leaning back in her chair. The phone was answered on the first ring.

"Hello."

"Oh, hi. Is this Susan?"

"Yes."

"Hi, uh, this is Rachel Carter. We've never met, but I'm working for Charlotte Weise and I was asked to call you to see if we could depend on you to help out with her re-election this year."

"Charlotte's running again? So soon? Wow. You bet your sweet bippy. I'm in. That girl's done more to promote women's rights than anyone I know. You just say when and where and I'll be there."

Rachel placed the phone back in its cradle and breathed a sigh of relief. Maybe it wouldn't be so hard after all.

It was after six when Rachel placed the phone on the hook for good. She remembered how angered the Crenshaws became when people called in the evening and especially around dinnertime. They hated having one of their game shows interrupted by someone trying to sell vacation packages. She vowed not to make that mistake.

While making calls, she had gone through the drawers of the desk and found the usual items; pens, notepaper, stapler and hole-punch as well as boxes of paperclips and pads of sticky notes. The two bottom drawers held hanging files, some empty but others filled with papers and notes from campaigns past. The biggest find, however, was an envelope with her name on it. In it she discovered a credit card wrapped in a handwritten note from Charlotte.

> Rachel, use this card for your monthly expenses. Please hold onto your receipts and try to keep expenditures under five hundred a month, which should be enough to keep the office running smoothly on a month-to-month basis. Any special projects, like the printing of business cards and brochures, or special events will need to be approved by me in advance.

> Wishing you great success,
> Charlotte

Wow, it sounded like Senator Weise had expected to hire her all along, and that the "interview" was just a formality. It was one of those times when she felt like someone, or some thing, was moving her like a pawn on a chessboard, which was fine as long as she didn't get nicked off by another player.

She'd only taken one other break from her calls. About an hour in she found herself needing a rest, just a moment to clear her head and stretch her legs. The room across from hers was the only one she hadn't seen. She found it filled with several roundtables surrounded by chairs with a small refrigerator, microwave and kitchen sink. *The lunchroom.* On the counter was a coffee pot. The credit card was to be used for office expenses and she knew from instinct that the fuel required by people manning phones was coffee. She checked the cupboards above the sink but they were empty. She would make sure to buy some before heading back to her room for the night. Coffee had to qualify as a business expense, *didn't it?*

The day was spent by the time she locked up. Setting the alarm was a bit unnerving. Charlotte said she had only fifteen seconds to get the numbers right or all hell would break loose, but it hadn't been a problem. She walked away satisfied that all-in-all, it had been a good day. She hiked up her dress and slid off her shoes so she could feel the cool grass under her feet. Placing the shoes in a shopping bag, along with the tin of Folgers coffee and a box of Krispy Kreme donuts she'd purchased at the 7-eleven, she turned into the splendor of Northwestern University. The sky glowed yellow with afternoon light. Pigeons scratched for seeds on the campus lawn and seagulls circled in the air. A wind off the lake had cleared out the haze, leaving a few cumulus clouds bouncing on the eastern horizon. Perhaps she'd have enough time to grab a book and head down to the beach.

She didn't have a benchmark by which to measure her success, but she felt good about what she'd accomplished. She had called thirty-six people and found five ready to start immediately. They would join her in the office first thing in the morning to develop a strategy, and then together they would call the rest of the names on the list. But first they would do a meet-and-greet in the boardroom. She squeezed the bag of coffee and donuts, making sure they were still there. She had to get to know the people who would be working for her. She wanted their input. They had, after all, done this before and she had much to learn.

Four

S ATCHEL WAS doing his best to keep things moving. He was grilling burgers on a flat iron stove that sizzled and popped with grease. He wiped his brow with his sleeve and continued flipping the burgers as fast as he could, one at a time, row upon row, until two dozen circles of meat had been turned. Then he went back to the beginning and started again. Behind him, other parolees were slicing tomatoes and emptying bags of lettuce into huge bowls. To his right, another man was laying out buns on the racks of an oven, toasting them to a golden brown.

Satchel used a hand towel to mop his forehead again, then scooped the grilled burgers onto a large tray, piling them high, and turned to place them on the counter. It was the epitome of being a short order cook because as fast as he could get the meat off the grill the men in line devoured them. *Hungry buggers,* but he understood. Years ago he had stood in that line himself waiting for a bowl of soup just to warm his insides. Now he was the one helping others and he had to admit it felt kind of good.

Old Samuel was sitting on a stool preaching up a storm. Hell fire and brimstone for those who refused God's grace. He wondered who actually owned the place. Seemed like the black dude with the white goatee did most of the preaching, but Mr. Powers was always there cooking and cleaning and making sure everything else got done. Right now he was in the back stacking steamy hot plates fresh from the dishwasher. He turned around. The kitchen area was steeped in smoke. Small shards of beef left on the griddle continued to burn. He stepped into the vapor and began peeling discs of sliced ground beef, filling the grill to capacity. He was finding it hard to keep up with the chap beside him. Toasting buns took less time than cooking meat. "Where's the beef!" the man chided, citing a Wendy's commercial from the 1980s. Satchel tried to ignore the remark but he shot a quick glance at Mr. Powers, hoping he hadn't overheard. He didn't want Mr. Powers thinking he couldn't handle the job. The raw beef sizzled as he flattened each piece with the spatula. How many more did he have to make?

He chanced a look out the door to see how long the line was, but he couldn't see around the corner. All he knew for sure was that the last man hadn't yet reached the door. Seeing the men in that line was creepy. He understood the difficulty of shoving one's pride into a corner to accept charity. A few of them deserved it. They'd traded their lives for a needle and a bottle of wine. Not him. He prided himself on not being a street person, which is why he always tried to maintain an apartment for himself. He didn't beg, nor did he steal. He was a professional pickpocket, more of a magician using sleight-of-hand, *now you see it now you don't,* than a thief. A few of the faces he'd seen were so gaunt he could imagine how this might be their last meal.

"Quit gawking. These buns are cryin', where's the beef?" The man turned to him with a big grin shining out of a short beard. Satchel felt a burning inside but refused to give it place. He turned back to the grill, sipping in his breath while counting to ten.

He flipped another row of burgers, watching the grease snapping in the cloud of steam. Short order cooks didn't make much, but hey, neither did pickpockets. At least they made enough to pay the rent and utilities, with a little left over for food and clothes. He'd find a job soon enough, if he just kept looking, and he was determined not to give up. Chicago had tons of restaurants.

And he wouldn't need a car. The subways could take him just about anywhere.

He did have to wonder though, if he hadn't connected with Rachel would he have returned to the life he'd had before? It was an interesting question, and one with an easy answer. *No.* If he hadn't connected with Rachel he'd still be in prison for putting skinhead Jack in the ground. Either that or Jack would've shanked him and he himself would be food for the worms.

"I got two dozen buns waiting for meat. Are you going to cook or what?"

It was all she wrote. Satchel swung around taking the guy next to him by the throat. Trays, utensils and plastic cups went flying all a clatter as he doubled the man over shoving his face into a serving bowl of potato salad. "You watch your mouth," he said, as he drew his elbow back ready to bring the man's head up and put his fist through it like a melon. But the room had gone silent. The line had stopped moving, the homeless had stopped eating and those serving were gawking in disbelief. Stan hobbled over grabbing Satchel's arm, dragging it back to spin him around.

"What the heck?"

Satchel froze. His victim pulled his face from the bowl and grabbed a towel, shrinking away with bits of potato salad clinging to his beard.

"Outside, Satchel. Now!" Stan yelled, his finger stiff, pointing toward the door.

Satchel scowled, his eyes burning with rage, but he didn't argue. He pulled the string of his apron releasing the bow in the back and flipped it over his head tossing it to the floor. His jaw was clenched so tight his cheeks were turning red. Hamburgers continued sizzling on the grill as he pushed through the line, elbowing people out of the way with Stan close behind.

"Think you're tough, is that it? Someone comes at you and you smash their face. That's not how we do it here."

But Satchel's rage hadn't subsided and someone had to pay, gimp or not. Ignoring the wound that had given Stan a permanent limp, he charged forward with his head lowered like a battering ram. *Ooffff,* and he and Stan went sprawling to the ground. Stan rolled away and, getting up on his good foot, stood bracing his leg to steady himself while Satchel scrambled to his feet.

"Feel better now? Think you can get that anger under control?"

Satchel tightened both fists and stepped in to plant one in Stan's kidney while bringing the other up under his jaw, but Stan's military training came back like an instinct. He twisted to the left avoiding the kidney punch and brushed Satchel's fist aside using his good knee to slam him in the groin. Satchel doubled over, sinking to the ground. He teetered, planting his palm on the sidewalk to support himself, then swung around and took Stan by the knees, lifting him. Stan winced in pain and began pounding Satchel's head and back with both fists. Satchel struggled to his feet and blindly dove forward, slamming Stan's back into a lamp post. The post shook. The glass vases at the top rattled.

The men in the line formed a circle as dollars began changing hands. It was clear that the new chef had a good thirty pounds on Mr. Powers, but they were taking even odds. It was good theater and they'd seen the play before. Cons always had a beef with someone. And Stan was ex-military. It was funny how men who were too poor to feed themselves always found enough money to place a bet.

Satchel held on as they moved around the post causing Stan to fall backward pulling Satchel off balance. They tripped over the curb and fell into the street. A screech of tires, horns blaring, and a curse from an irate driver. "Get out of the road you..." *Honnnnnnnk* "...idiots!"

Satchel had hoped to fall on Stan and pin him to the ground, but Stan struggled to his feet again. He raised his fists in a boxer's pose waiting for Satchel to right himself. Satchel bounced up,

39

bruised but not broken. He wiped his mouth with a thumb, finding blood where his jaw had scraped the pavement. "You want a piece of me? Come on." He wiggled his fingers to pull Stan in. "Bet you been dreaming of this for years."

Stan lowered his fists, rolling his head around on his neck and rotating his shoulders like a boxer loosening up. "I don't want anything from you, Satchel. Except maybe better behavior." He dropped his fists, "I'm going back inside. Maybe you should walk around the block and clear your head."

Stan spun around and stepped up on the curb again, but Satchel wasn't through. "Don't turn your back on me, mate." He lunged forward and dove into Stan sending them crashing to the sidewalk with Satchel on top. Stan twisted around and planted his good foot in Satchel's chest kicking him hard enough to remove the air from his lungs. Stan staggered to his feet and stood waiting for Satchel to get up. Satchel was still trying to catch his breath as he stumbled forward, loosely flailing his fists. Stan countered and Satchel's nose erupted into spurts of blood. He brought his hands up to cover his face and fell to his knees. Applause erupted from the crowd.

"Anger's not the answer, Satchel. You need to figure that out." He reached out to take Satchel under the arm to lift him. "Can one of you men give me a hand getting him on his feet? I think he's had enough for one day." Then he leaned into Satchel's ear and said, "If you're strong enough to stand, we still got about fifty men to feed and I could use the help."

Satchel stood at the grill deftly flipping burgers, determined to finish his shift. He owed them that, and he wanted to do enough to justify grabbing a meal for himself before leaving. He had to leave, he knew that; there was no way he could stay after all that had happened. The man whose face he'd slammed into the bowl hadn't returned. Fortunately, he'd already cooked enough buns for everyone in line. It looked like there might even be enough for a few extra he could stuff into his pocket. He didn't know when he might eat again.

Men go through their whole lives trying to be good and screw it up every time. That's what the preacher said, and he knew it was true. If it wasn't for Rachel, he'd be trying to scam a ticket back to England. It might've been better if he'd never come, but the temptation had been too great. *Just a bit of luck.* The man had been gorging on fish and chips at an outdoor pub and had carelessly laid his jacket over the back of an empty chair. It was just too easy. All Satchel had to do was stumble along like a drunk, bump into the chair and fall down, taking the jacket with him. Transferring the man's wallet from the jacket pocket to his own was a piece of cake. He'd dusted the jacket off, picked up the chair and laid it over the back and with profuse apologies had stumbled off. He didn't know until later that he'd scooped up not just a wallet but a passport and airline ticket. The plane was leaving Heathrow at eight bound for America, giving him plenty of time to get a forger he knew to put his picture on that passport.

That was almost twenty years ago, though he'd wasted ten of them in jail, and now he couldn't leave. He had a daughter. He stacked the burgers on a tray and turned, placing it on the counter. The men were still straggling in. He hoped there was enough. He turned back to the stove and began scraping the flat iron with the blade of his spatula to clear the remaining food residue. The bits of charcoaled beef were corralled and scooped into a waiting steel bucket. He turned down the burners, wiping his hands, and removed his apron, this time hanging it on a hook next to the grill. The counters were already being cleaned by the men responsible for serving, including Mr. Powers, who was aggressively wiping the stainless steel bowls with a towel.

He walked into the next room where a clatter of dishes and cutlery rose in the steam of the men washing dishes. The cat was consuming bits of burger from a bowl on the floor, but it had to jump aside when one of the dishwashers backed up with an armload of plates. This was how he imagined a restaurant worked; each man knowing his job and doing it. He would find a job, and then he would find Rachel, and maybe, with her help, get his life back together.

It wasn't like it was his fault. He wanted to control his anger and he'd tried, he really did. He let the first few remarks slide but there came a point where he'd snapped. He couldn't control it because he didn't have time to think about it. He couldn't count to ten, or take a deep breath, or do any of the other exercises they taught him to do, because he was already going crazy before he realized what was happening. How do you control that?

He went back to the dining room, taking a plate from the stack at the end of the counter. The last of the guests were already being fed. Only the staff remained. He tried to do a headcount to see how far the burgers would go. There were a dozen burgers and five staffers left to be fed. If each, including himself, took two it would mean he would have to leave empty-handed. But everyone might not eat two so there might be extra. At least he could eat now so he wouldn't go away hungry. He paddled mayonnaise and ketchup onto the buns, placed two burgers on top, covered them with lettuce and tomatoes and sandwiched them together. He moved further along, bypassing the potato salad even though he was hungry and knew he should eat, but he'd smashed a man's face in there and it somehow didn't seem right. He did scoop a handful of crisps onto his plate and at the end of the counter filled a paper cup with coffee.

He turned around, staring into a room that was now almost empty. The clamor of men eating was notably less. The old black preacher was putting away his guitar. He wore alligator boots and had a large cross hanging from his neck. He'd been playing that guitar for as long as Satchel could remember, long before he'd been sent to jail, but no one ever listened. And he'd preached the same old sermons, but no one listened to those either.

Satchel made his way to an empty table and sat down. He picked up one of the burgers, food he hoped would last a few days. It looked small in his big hands. He took a bite, relishing the fruit of his labor. In prison, a typical evening meal was a slice of bologna, a piece of white bread with a pat of butter, and a scoop of coleslaw, the minimum amount of nutrition required by law. Next to that, this was a king's feast. He took another bite letting the juice of the burger mingle with the ketchup on his tongue before swallowing. He glanced back over at the counter and saw the serving crew filling their plates. Didn't look like there'd be much left over.

"Mind if we join you?"

Satchel's head snapped up. Two men stood in front of him with burgers on paper plates. They didn't wait for his answer but scooted back the chairs and sat down, placing their plates on the table.

"I spoke with Brother Samuel while you were resting earlier," Stan said. "There's a restaurant he knows of that's going to need a new chef. Just a small family business, but the owners are getting older and they've had their son filling in. But he's now back in school trying to get a law degree so they have to do all the work themselves. It's a bit too much for them and they mentioned to Samuel how they were going to have to hire some help. Problem is I was all set to recommend you and then, well, you know, I can't send you to them and have you blow up like that. Samuel says they're not quite ready to hire someone yet, so what I'm recommending is that you use the interim to prove yourself." Stan took a bite of his burger looking across the top of the bun to gauge Satchel's response.

"You gotta be kidding," Satchel said.

"About what?" Stan's eyebrows raised. He pulled the burger away from his mouth chewing. "*Uhmmmm,* I don't know what else is on your repertoire but you sure make a good burger."

"You saying you want me to stay?"

"Why not? You and I had this discussion earlier."

"What discussion?"

"About forgiveness, remember? Christ has forgiven me, but He requires that I also forgive others. In this case that's you."

"Me too." It was the man whose face Satchel had shoved into the bowl of potato salad. "Actually, I need to ask your forgiveness."

"What?"

"I shouldn't have gotten in your face like that. I was out of line. I'm sorry."

Satchel rolled his eyes. "You blokes are bloody daft."

Stan looked at the other man and chuckled. "Daft? You mean nuts? No, not daft, just forgiven."

Bruce approached the building with the same fluttering in his chest he'd had before. Maybe Mr. Powers didn't deserve to be sued, but there was only so much he could do. It was the third club he'd visited, and probably his last, at least for the night. The sign over the door read, "Rainbow Lounge," in multicolored letters. He'd always liked this place, though he didn't frequent it now as much as he did when he was single. His partner didn't like to dance, which was sad because Bruce loved spinning and gyrating under the lights. There was so much energy there, so much indulgence, so much—*fun*.

He squeezed through the door, hoping to sneak in unnoticed. He wanted to find a table where he could sit and just observe, but it wasn't to be.

"Bruce sweetie, where have you been? I haven't seen you in like, forever. Oh you dear boy you really shouldn't stay away so much. We really miss seeing that cute little bum of yours out on the dance floor. How is Donnie anyway? Did you break up, are you orphaned, is that why you're here? I know he never liked this place. That's so sad."

"No, Donnie's fine, we're still together." Bruce tried looking around the man hoping to find what he'd come for. The room was filled to capacity with men huddled in groups of twos and threes and, as far as he could see, every table and chair was taken. "You'll have to excuse me, I'm looking for someone."

"Ohhh, it's like that is it. Out for a little something on the side." The man laid a thin long fingered hand on Bruce's arm and leaned in to whisper. "Don't worry, I won't say a thing."

"No, it's not like that. Never mind. Excuse me." Bruce stepped around the man and melted into the crowd. He was looking right and left, staring at the faces and getting a few winks and nods in return. It almost made him wish he was single again.

The stage lights came on, revealing a buxomous woman standing in front of a microphone. She was tall and thin, wearing a long blue sequined gown and three inch stilettos. Her platinum blond wig was piled high and adorned with three blue feathers that shimmered and quivered as she turned. She took a step forward and when she did, the slit of her gown parted revealing her long, well-tanned legs. Her mouth was full and red, but when she brought the microphone to her lips her inflexion was that of a man.

"Hi boys," she said, her eyelashes fluttering long and dark.

"Woo-hoo, hi ya babe." Cheers and whistles and catcalls erupted throughout the room.

"I have a special number for you tonight, one I know you're going to like because I wrote it myself and it's just for you." Her words were whispery and smooth as she walked over to a karaoke machine and pushed the button to play. She stepped back, rotated her shoulders perpendicular to her audience, dipped her head and winked.

"Atta girl."

"Sing it babe."

"Woo-hoo."

Bruce continued through the crowd. The entertainer began her number in a low contralto meant to sound seductive. He didn't see the couple he was looking for, but he was pretty sure he would recognize them if he did, or at least one of them. He made his way to the back and began weaving through the tables. The music may have been seductive but it was also loud. There was no point in finding them if he couldn't carry on a conversation. He ended up at the bar and, well, when in Rome… "I'll have a diva daiquiri," he said to the bartender who approached with a napkin in hand, which he laid on the counter. *Why are the bartenders always so cute?* The man was thirtyish with curly brown hair and a buff jaw. He was wearing tan slacks and a white shirt with the collar open down to the second button. In any other setting you might think the man was an actor, or a model, but not necessarily gay.

Men on either side, who'd parted to let him in, turned his direction.

"I've seen you here before, haven't I?"

Bruce turned, nodding. "I used to come all the time," he said.

The bartender returned, setting the cocktail on the napkin. "That'll be eight dollars, ice cream," he said. He placed his hands on the bar with his palms turned out, smiling impishly.

Bruce blushed, flattered the man found him attractive. He reached for his wallet and removed a five and three ones, thought about it for a second, slipped them back into his billfold and removed a ten, laying it in the man's hand. "Thanks," he said.

He picked up the ruby colored drink, peeling the wet napkin away as he took a sip through the straw. *Ummm,* not bad. It was his favorite drink, but he'd had two already, one at each of the other bars he'd visited, so this would have to be his last. Each one had been different, varying in the amount of rum, sugar and lime used but this bartender had gone further by adding strawberry schnapps, and a real strawberry crowned the rim of the glass. *You got to love a man like that.* He turned and swished into the crowd.

He didn't know how many gay bars there were in Chicago,

probably quite a few, but this one, and the two he'd been to already, were the only ones he knew how to find without looking up an address. He'd promised Stan he would look into it, not spend his life in the process. He took another sip. This was his best shot. It was where they'd hooked up before. They were good people. Once he explained, they'd want to drop the lawsuit. It was the right thing to do.

He ventured on around to the other side. The noise in the room was escalating as those who wanted to carry on a conversation were forced to increase their volume while the performer, wanting to be heard, seemed determined to drown them out. His heart began to flutter. *There.* It was them, he was sure of it, sitting at a table that seated four. He walked over and squeezed into the booth.

"Hi guys, remember me?"

Both men turned to stare at him. The one on the right began to nod. "Sure, about a month ago, you were here with your partner, what was his name, Danny?"

"Donnie," Bruce corrected. "But that's right. We joined you at a table because Donnie didn't want to dance and he was tired of standing."

"Yeah, that's right. Sorry, but I forget your name."

"Bruce."

"Hi Bruce, it's lovely to see you again. Is Donnie here or are you on your own tonight?"

"I'm alone. Donnie had to work." Bruce took a sip of his drink and set it down using his finger to wipe his lip.

"Ah, too bad. He was fun. So you're all alone tonight? Well, I must say you do look gorgeous. I love that shirt. Is it silk?"

Bruce brought a hand up fingering his collar, "no, just polyester but does have a nice feel. I, ah, I'm embarrassed to say it but I've forgotten your names as well."

"I'm Marty, and this is Thomas." The man on the right leaned in to rub shoulders with his partner then lowered his voice to whisper, "Be careful, Thomas is in a bit of a snit tonight, putting a damper on all my fun." He gave a girlish flick of his hand as if to say, I'm just kidding.

Bruce shook his head. "Marty? Of course, how could I forget that? Whenever you got cute, Thomas called you, smarty. Smarty Marty, I remember that now."

"I've asked you not to do that," Marty said, smacking Thomas playfully on the shoulder.

Thomas swatted Marty's hand away. "You're too sensitive. It's just fun."

"Sorry," Bruce said. "I didn't know it was a touchy subject, but I'm glad I found you two. I was hoping to ask you a favor."

"Us?"

"Yeah, well, remember the last time we met we were talking about our jobs and you said you were opening a club and I told you I knew a really good agency that might help you promote it. My boss said you stopped by and talked about it but he felt it wasn't right for our agency and now you're suing him."

"Damn straight." Thomas's demeanor changed, his eyes bristling, his lips, that a moment ago held a bemused smile, were rigid. "That sucker dissed us. You'd think in this day and age he'd be smart enough not to do that." He leaned back crossing his arms as if to say don't challenge me.

Bruce leaned in with his arms folded on the table, but pulled back when he realized the table was wet. He began wiping himself with a napkin. "I know, that's what's so strange. He's one of the nicest people I know. I mean, he might have a few rough edges but don't we all? He didn't mean to offend you, and I know he regrets what he said."

"And you're saying this because?"

"Because you're suing him and he's a nice guy. He doesn't hate anybody, and especially not gays. If he did I wouldn't be working there."

"Good point. Why are you?"

"Why am I what?"

"Why are you working there? I mean here's a guy who says opening a gay bar goes against his conscience. That's out and out homophobic." Marty was looking on shaking his head, but Thomas plowed on. "Gender discrimination's illegal. Guys like that need to be taught a lesson."

"But why? He's not out to hurt you. He doesn't care if you open a bar, he just doesn't want to be part of it himself. Didn't he give you names of other places you can use?"

Marty took a sip of his peach Margarita and set his glass down, wiping his lips with a napkin. "I was saying that too, Thomas. You know I was. He didn't sound like a man who hates gay people. You know I said that. I wish you hadn't filed that lawsuit. We need to get along with straight people."

Thomas's eyes narrowed as he looked at his partner. "Shut up," he said, then looked at Bruce again. "Your boss make you come here and say that?"

The tranny on stage was belting out her latest song building to a crescendo. Bruce leaned forward again raising his voice to be heard. "No, this is my idea. He doesn't even know I'm here."

"Well you can go back to your office tomorrow and tell your boss I'm suing him for everything he's got. And I'll win. There isn't a judge in the world that wouldn't see this as gender discrimination, and that's illegal. The good news for you is, I'll probably end up owning the place and then you can work for me."

Stan looked at his watch. Two a.m. He was trying to sleep but the heat was insufferable and his mind was wound like a spring. The fan at the foot of his bed whirred away, but it was just circulating hot air, bringing little relief. He kicked the sheet off rolling over for the umpteenth time. There was too much to think about.

He rolled onto his back interlacing his fingers across his stomach. There was no point in worrying about it. It was God's problem. He pulled his pillow out from under his head and began pounding it, then stuffed it under his chin. His eyes were closed but burning. Would he ever fall asleep? He turned onto his side, repeating the routine he'd been doing for the past four hours.

The fan kept whirring and the joints of the old house creaked, but that hadn't bothered him before. He was usually a sound sleeper. Air-conditioners made noise too. Who's to say it would be any better? Retrofitting an old house with the necessary vents was expensive. The money could be put to better use.

Maybe this whole thing of not being able to sleep was God's way of trying to speak to him. *What is it you want me to do, Lord, I'm listening.* He brought his knee up and rubbed his shin where it had been bruised when he struck the curb. He was getting too old for fights like that. If Satchel was going to be a threat to others, maybe he shouldn't let him stick around. Yet he couldn't cut him loose because he believed he'd been sent by God, and if God wanted him there, who was he to argue?

He flopped onto his side. All this tossing and turning was ridiculous. He should just get up. He rolled back and raised himself on his elbows, his hair buffeted by air from the fan. Were they actually going to sue him simply because he viewed homosexuality as a sin? It was a personal belief. He hadn't condemned their lifestyle in public. They had come to him. He'd only expressed that he couldn't in good conscious promote what he believed was wrong. This was America. How had it ever come to a place where standing for one's beliefs was viewed as a crime? He lay back and rolled onto to his side. His leg was throbbing, but it wasn't keeping him awake; it was his thoughts. He tossed the covers aside and sat on the edge of the bed. If he wasn't going to sleep, maybe he should look for something to read.

He pushed himself up and limped to the kitchen, his bare

feet padding on the cool surface of the tile floor. He found a glass in the cupboard and went to the refrigerator to fill it with ice. Cold water might help. At least it would bring his body temperature down. He headed for the living room holding the glass to his cheek. The wet condensation felt good. Light from a streetlamp shone through the window illuminating the shadows. Several cars were parked along the street. He could see the net used by neighborhood kids for playing street hockey sitting on his neighbor's lawn, along with an overturned bicycle. *Something to read.* His Bible and a newspaper were on the coffee table. He picked up the Bible and turned on the lamp, flipping the Scriptures open.

The problem started right there in Genesis when man first chose to do things his own way. Or perhaps even further back when Satan, in his vanity, rebelled against God believing his wisdom and beauty to be superior to that of his Creator. That's where the battle lines were drawn, Satan against God. Satan saw a chance to neutralize God by using man's natural tendency to question God's authority—*"Has God really said?"*—and since that time man had come to question God on almost everything.

Stan shut the Bible and set it aside. The room was stuffy, and carried an air of mothballs and creosote. He considered going back to the bedroom for the fan but he didn't want to get up. His head fell back against the cushions. A billion tiny pricks of electricity buzzed through his body. There was no way he was going to sleep, and thinking about the fall of man only increased his frustration.

Had God said He created the heavens and the earth? Man knew better. The universe was a cosmic accident and man, by accident, created himself.

Had God said He knew every child in the womb before it was born? Man knew better. A fetus was just a blob of tissue to be tossed aside at man's discretion.

Had God said for a man to lay with a man as with a woman was an abomination? Man knew better. A man's desire to sexually join with another man resulted from normal physical attraction.

And on, and on, with man trying to thwart God at every turn.

Stan used the palms of his hands to massage his temples. It gave him a headache just thinking about it. If only men could see that rebellion against God doesn't turn out well. Satan's fate was a foregone conclusion. *"And the devil that deceived them was cast into the lake of fire..."* But that was his decision. God had given him free will, just as he gave all his created beings. Milton described it in his epic poem, *Paradise Lost,* when he said Lucifer decided it was "better to rule in hell than serve in heaven." Not such a great choice when you consider that eternity has no end. Such would also be the fate of those who followed him, whether unwittingly or not.

Stan shook his head and slumped deeper into the cushions. *Even so, come quickly Lord Jesus.*

It was all part of living in the last days. It wouldn't be long before every knee would bow and every tongue confess Christ as Lord. He glanced at the Bible on the table, its gold edges looking gray in the subdued light. That was the conclusion of the matter. In the beginning God created, in the end God would destroy. He would establish a new heaven and a new earth wherein the lion would lie down with the lamb and there would be no more war, no more death, no more crying, and no more pain.

Stan rubbed his arms chuckling to himself, *it's sweltering outside and I've got goosebumps.* He picked up his glass and took a long slow drink, then held it up to the light admiring its clarity. All this gobbledygook about man destroying the planet was just naïve. Man might pollute the air with greenhouse gas and glutt the oceans with too many plastic bags, but man would never destroy the planet because that was God's prerogative. Man should be ecologically responsible; but his mission on earth was not to save the planet, but to save souls from perishing. When that time came, God wanted as many as possible to enjoy His re-creation—the new heavens and new earth.

Stan took another sip of water and tried closing his eyes. He placed a hand over his forehead, a hand that felt cool from handling the wet glass, but his temples continued to throb. He had hoped reading would make him relax. Instead he found himself more agitated. His eyes fell on the newspaper. That wouldn't help. Even in the dim light he could read the headline, "Weise Campaign Rolls On," and beneath that a subtitle that read, "Thousands attend rallies in show of support."

Forget reading the article, it would only further his depression. Charlotte Weise stood for the very things he'd just been thinking about. She was among those who took pleasure in challenging God. She openly advocated for a woman's right to kill her unborn child. She wanted men and women to decide for themselves how, and with whom they would enter into sexual relations; and perhaps most scary, she wanted a world free of religious constraint. She was pushing for a new world order where nations gave up their national identities to become the vassal states of a global government. Only then, she claimed, could there be an end to war.

Stan sighed. His anxiety was growing into a full-blown headache. World peace wouldn't come until Christ established His kingdom as foretold by the prophet Isaiah, *"and they shall beat their swords into plowshares, and their spears into pruning-hooks: nation shall not lift up sword against nation, neither shall they learn war anymore."*

But that was a day yet future; Stan had to live it in the here and now. The world was in rapid decline, but there wasn't much he could do about it, other than oppose it, which he knew he would. The question was how? It was something he'd been mulling over for months, but what could one man do? His eyes went to the newspaper. Charlotte Weise was one person and she was doing something. She was making great strides to advance her cause and, whether she knew it or not, she had prophecy on her side. Ultimately global governance would be established and, at least for the short term, would prevail. He shook his head, rebuking himself for letting such things fill his head. It wasn't going to help him sleep.

Five

RACHEL PUT the phone back in its cradle. *Oh for Pete's sake,* of course Mr. Murphy wants a tax receipt, everyone wants a tax receipt. She made a note to tell the caller to always assure the person they were speaking with that they would receive a tax receipt. *Whew,* she sat back with her hands laced over her stomach trying to catch her breath.

She had to get her report finished before going home, but the phone never stopped ringing and the interruptions kept coming. She leaned forward, staring at her computer trying to figure out where she left off.

The Brookshire's, fifth line down, third column in, her finger tracking the spreadsheet. There it is, they gave fifty dollars. Add a note that they're not to be called again for at least six months. She finished typing and let her finger drop to the next line. They had to keep stringent records about every donation made, the amount, the date and demographic information about the donor. Those who declined to give were still asked for their vote and a tally of their commitment had to be kept as well.

Riiinnnnnng…riiinnnnnng…riiinnnnnng. Rachel bit her lip, shaking her head as she reached for the phone. "Hello, this is the Weise campaign. How can I help you?"

"Oh, hello. This is Ellen Dawson. I was called last week for a donation and I just want to say, it's wonderful work you do. I gave a hundred dollars, but this morning I got called again and I was just wondering, did you get the check I sent? I mean, I wouldn't ask but I thought maybe my check got lost in the mail. Is there any way you can look into it for me?"

"I'm sure it's nothing like that. Sometimes names end up being entered into our system twice. That's probably what happened. Two of our callers probably each had your name on a different list. I apologize for the inconvenience." All the while Rachel was speaking, she was scrolling through her computer trying to find Helen Dawson's name so she could assure her the check had been received, but she didn't see it. "I'll try to find your check and get back to you to let you know it's been received. Uh, is there anything else?"

"No, nothing, I just want to make sure my check's not lost…"

Rachel wrote Mrs. Dawson's name and number on a scrap of paper and hung up the phone. People had so little regard for her time. It would be okay if each person were the only one that called, but the calls just kept coming and the time she gave each one just kept adding up. She reached for her coffee but her mug was empty—*again.*

She got up, placing a hand on her lumbar to ease the stress. Too many hours of sitting. She balled one hand and wrapped it in the other and raising her elbows rotated to the left and then back to the right. That felt better. Grabbing her mug she headed for the coffee room, but took a detour down the hall just to see how things were going.

The office hummed with activity. Each room she passed held half a dozen volunteers making calls. The chatter of the voices and the hum of the copy machine and printers were music to her ears. It meant goals were being met. Charlotte had called to commend her for receiving so many voter commitments and donations this early in the campaign. They were off to a good start, but they had to keep the momentum going.

Not so long ago she'd been an orphan living on the streets eating garbage from a dumpster. But she'd determined that wasn't going be her fate. Now she was enrolled in one of the most prestigious colleges in the land and managing the campaign of a political dynamo. She still needed to connect with her father. She'd used the office phone to call the penitentiary so she could apologize to him for not writing, but was told he'd been released. She pressed her hand into her lower back again. The pain had been increasing for some time. *Just stress.* It would go away as soon as they got through this. The fatigue would lessen as soon as she allowed herself time to rest. There was simply too much to do.

She felt a hand take her arm and pull her around. "We really need to audit these lists, they're so outdated it's unbelievable. I just called three dead people in a row. I know some of them might have died recently but not all. I had one guy tell me his wife had been dead for three years. You should be telling everyone to mark dead people off the list so we won't have this problem next time."

Rachel sucked in her breath, grasping for strength. Leadership was a heavy burden, but she bore it well. Maybe it was the fact that she was tall so that even some of the young men were forced to look up to her. Or maybe it was her posture; she always carried herself with her shoulders back and head held high. Or maybe it was the fact she rarely smiled so that people understood she took this job seriously. Whatever the reason, she had earned the respect of her peers. She was the go-to person for problems, but that meant carrying the weight of everyone else's burdens along with her own.

The man confronting her was about her height but grossly overweight. He wore loose-fitting jeans and a baggy sweatshirt in a vain attempt to hide his burgeoning stomach, and his feet were covered with a pair of dusty sandals with the buckles undone. His unruly hair was sandy blond with bangs that kept falling in front of his eyes. He kept one hand ever in the process of pushing them back on his head. His eyes were small, like two olives on a plate.

"That's a great idea, Ron. I want you to bring that up at our next staff meeting. We're always looking for ideas to make the office run more efficiently. Keep up the good work." She gave him a light pat on the shoulder and proceeded to the lunch room.

She wasn't surprised to find it empty. It wasn't the lunch hour, and her volunteers weren't prone to coffee breaks. They were an industrious group on a mission to get a very important candidate into office. She placed her cup on the sink and filled it with the last dregs in the pot. An hour before, she'd been there and supposed that someone else would come and take what was remaining. Then it would be their responsibility to make a fresh pot. No such luck. She dumped the sodden coffee filter into the trash and reached up to the cupboard for another. It seemed like she was the only one who ever made coffee. The bag was on the sink, Starbucks brew, expensive but the preferred choice of her crew. She placed the new filter into the coffee basket and unfolded the foil bag, filling it with two full scoops.

How strong to make the coffee had been one of the first arguments she'd had to settle. Some liked their brew black as espresso, others wanted it nearly transparent. They settled on a compromise—two level scoops. That was generally dark enough to please the concentrated drinkers, and for the others she'd bought a teapot so they could heat water and dilute their brew.

She filled the machine with water and clicked it on. Hopefully the coffee would help ease the soreness in her back. Caffeine was known to do that. How many cups had she had today? Three, no, four, she forgot about the one she'd had at home. Her home coffee maker was one of the best investments she'd made. She couldn't start her day without coffee, though she hated heading down the hall every time she needed to fill the pot with water. Now she was considering the purchase of a microwave. Eating out was expensive, and the student hall didn't serve meals during summer break.

She was dreading the day she would come home and find her

privacy invaded by a roommate. She enjoyed living alone. She liked the solitude. It gave her time to think. She had enough problems throughout the day. The evenings were her own, and she cherished the downtime where she could just read and relax and not have to talk to anyone. Fortunately, the start of the new semester was still two months away. She didn't need to worry about it until then. She took a sip and headed out the door but had to stop abruptly to avoid bumping into a young man on his way in. Her coffee splashed over the side of her cup onto her hand. *Awhhwhhh,* she screamed, as the hot liquid seared her skin.

The young man, equally surprised, reached for her arm to steady her but she jerked away, setting the cup on the counter with a loud clunk, fanning her fingers, *Awhwwww!* "What are you doing?" She held her hand and hurried to the sink to rinse it under cold water.

"Sorry. Sorry, I didn't mean…I just came around the corner and you were there."

"Well slow down and be more careful."

"Yes, of course, sorry." He grabbed a paper towel and began mopping up the coffee on the sink, wiping her cup dry and setting it down again, then stooped over and began mopping the floor. He too was a freshman, a first-year student looking to make an impression. He had that innocent naïveté of someone who hadn't yet experienced the world and was stumbling through life with the awkwardness of a bird afraid of leaving the nest. He wore blue slacks and hard black leather shoes with a white shirt and blue V-neck sweater. He rose and set the sopping towel on the counter. His hair was a fop of loose dark curls atop a straight narrow face, his lips were thin and rose-petal pink and a pair of thick black glasses surrounded his eyes.

Rachel knew his story. He had spent far too much time talking about himself during their interview, how his parents were both lawyers and wanted him to be the same. When called, they had readily donated to the cause, and then sent their son over to participate in getting Charlotte reelected. He had never met Senator Weise, didn't even know who she was, and considered himself to be somewhat apolitical; but he was willing to dive in and do whatever needed to be done and, as far as Rachel was concerned, that made him right for the job.

"Sorry, Scott, I don't mean to be critical, I wasn't looking either," she said as they headed out the door together. She glanced back over her shoulder. "Weren't you going in there to get something?"

"No, I was looking for you. We have a problem..."

Satchel shuffled his way through the city, noting the way things had changed. He remembered this being a neighborhood where small businesses thrived. What happened to the shoe store, the bakery, and the pawn shop? The Chinese laundry had been replaced by a laundromat with dozens of whirling machines. JoJo's Pizza was gone too, now just an empty shell with graffiti painted walls. Sad because his daughter had made her way kicking and screaming into the world in that eatery and to see it in such poor condition didn't seem right. The poverty seemed epidemic. He glanced down the street at a half dozen formally prosperous enterprises which now sat like empty carcasses left to rot in the sun. It seemed the long hand of the slum was reaching out to claim more territory.

He stopped at the corner, but didn't wait for the light to change. There was hardly any traffic on the street. No wonder there were more people at the mission these days. At least it made his job secure. He wasn't getting paid but he did get free room and board, and as long as he could control his temper he might have a real job in a few weeks.

He had to put up with the Bible studies. They didn't force him to attend, but the evening study took place in his dorm where a group of men circled chairs and read out loud, and in the morning the study was in the dining hall adjacent to the kitchen where he was working, so ipso facto he was forced to listen. It was a small price to pay.

Some of the teaching wasn't all that bad. This Jesus bloke had always seemed like a bit of a wimp, but he was finding that sometimes the appearance of weakness was just a disguise for strength. He'd turned the other cheek the day Skinhead Jack had come at him with a shiv on his last day in prison. Seemed like a jolly good idea at the time, and it worked bloody well. But other than that he'd never run from a dusting, ever, not since the day he'd beat down Clay Goodayle in the high school locker room. He wasn't looking for a fight, he'd just gone in to see what there was of interest. The rugby team was out on the field, but they'd had to change into their uniforms so it stood to reason their wallets would be left in the pockets of their regular clothes. It was disappointing to find most of the lockers secured but when in frustration he slammed his fist into Clay's cabinet the combination lock popped open. He had just pinched the wallet and was going through it when Clay appeared at the door, a shadowy figure backlit by the sun.

"What're you doing, mate?"

Satchel froze, unable to speak. The wallet in his hand was wide open revealing several pound notes. The air around him swirled with the aroma of sweat and soiled socks, but it occurred to him what he was really smelling was fear.

Clay walked over, a full head taller than Satchel, oozing sweat and feral energy. He slammed a flat hand against the locker with a bang, leaning in to remove the wallet from Satchel's fingers. "I believe this is mine."

"No worries mate, I found it on the floor, I was going to return it. I was just heading out to give it to you."

"No, you weren't. You're a bloody thief."

Satchel tried to duck under Clay's arm, but Clay grabbed his collar and slammed him against the locker, the sound of crashing metal reverberating through the room. "You're daft if you think you're leaving without paying."

Satchel saw the perspiration on Clay's lip, the eyes cold as stone, and the throbbing temple at the side of his neck. He tried to push Clay's hand away. "Excuse me, I've got to be going."

"You're not going anywhere, mate." Still holding Satchel by the collar, Clay wadded his fist ready to turn Satchel's head into mush, but self-preservation kicked in and Satchel, acting on instinct, slammed his fist up under Clay's breastbone causing him to stumble back.

For a second, Clay's face went blank, the act of being hit totally unexpected, but then his face began to burn and his eyes to steam and his lips tightened into a knot. He drew back, ready to deliver his coup de grace full strength, but Satchel ducked and Clay's fist went into the locker with such force it left a dent in the metal the size of a softball.

Awwww! Clay took hold of his wrist, the useless hand flopping limply. "You son of a…I think you broke me hand. I've got a season to play... You little pissant, I'm gonna…"

But Satchel knew it was over. Clay couldn't do anything with a broken hand. Satchel squeezed around him walking toward the door but stopped, turned around, and said, "Tell your mother her little boy hits like a girl," and walked out.

That was the first time he'd ever had to defend himself, and he had crushed his opponent without breaking a sweat. It occurred to him that his only real enemy was fear, once that was dealt with he was free to act. Whether he won or lost didn't matter, the point was to stand and fight. Only now, as he thought about it, he realized maybe that view was jaded. He'd taken the man's property and inflicted an injury that would keep the school's star fullback out the rest of the season. How could he justify that? Up till now he'd always assumed that it was Clay's fault, that he had brought it on himself, that he would've been fine if he just hadn't poked the bear. Now he wasn't so sure.

Satchel hooked a finger under his collar and pulled his shirt away from his chest, swallowing. Saliva hung in his throat like a knot. Too much humidity. The sky had grown shadowy like someone had dropped a net of gray gauze over the city. Pieces of paper danced along the gutters in the wind.

He had already come to the conclusion that stealing was wrong, he wasn't going back to jail, not for any reason. But the anger part, the part that, right or wrong, made him answer a challenge, that part he wasn't so sure about. Was it because he was strong, or because he was weak? It was easy to lash out and pummel someone. It took real strength not to fight back.

It was hard to reconcile what was going on inside. He was ready for change, even before, when he'd promised to do it for his daughter, but he questioned whether saying a few words into the air could make any difference. That whole scene in the room last night, where the man started to blubber and beg forgiveness, and all those other Bible thumpers surrounding him with arms wrapped around his shoulders, it was inane. He couldn't be party to that. Still, when it was three a.m. and he was still laying there staring at the ceiling with his hands folded under his head, he'd figured what could it hurt to try. He didn't need to tell the others. If there was no God, he'd see no difference and even if he saw a difference, it didn't necessarily mean there was a God. It could be just a bunch of feel-good psychobabble. But it was worth a shot, so he'd gone ahead and done it. If God forgave him, fine, and if he didn't, fine, he'd find some other way to get a grip on his anger.

He glanced up at the sky. It had turned a dark grayish-green. They were in for a storm. Clouds were coming in fast with pulses of lightning flickering in the hot air. The morning had begun sunny but humid enough to make his T-shirt wet before he had traveled a few blocks. Now he wished he'd picked up a hooded windbreaker before heading out. Large drops began dotting the sidewalk. He skipped and broke into a slow run. He could always ride out the storm under the shelter of an abandoned store, but the overpass was just ahead and he thought he could make it without getting too wet.

It wasn't likely he'd recognize any of the people there. It had been ten years. Most of the weaker ones would have died, and others would have moved on. He doubted anyone would remember Wren, or the little girl he'd fathered so many years ago, but he had to ask. He had nowhere else to turn.

Child services hadn't been any help. They claimed once Rachel became an adult, they'd closed the book on her case and lost track of her. He could tell they were lying. He'd never been convicted of mistreating her, but they knew about it. They weren't going to let him anywhere near his daughter.

The rain was heavy now, his feet splashing through puddles, getting wet. It was the wrong day to wear tennis shoes. The canvas absorbed water. He did, however, appreciate the free wardrobe. The clothes weren't really his, but as long as he found something on the rack that fit, he was welcome to wear it.

He reached the cement viaduct and turned right. Water was coursing down the center like a river. Blotches of color loomed ahead. Talk about change. The place where a few bums and winos used to sleep off a drunk was now a full-fledged tent city. He slowed his gait as he reached the overpass. Who were all these people? He wandered through the maze checking out the faces of the forlorn and weary but recognized none. Where had they come from? One thing remained the same. Wood pallets were stacked beside the oil drums scattered throughout the area. Smoke rose from the barrels. Satchel assumed the fires were for cooking. No one needed to keep warm in this heat.

The tents were tattered and old, their once bright colors of orange and blue and green now faded. Sheets of plastic covered several, probably to keep the rain from seeping through holes. No one paid attention as he wandered through the camp. They were used to strangers coming and going. In fact, most seemed embarrassed and looked away when he tried to examine their faces. A woman ducked to exit her tent, a small head held to her breast. *A child?* The place smelled of stale wine and human waste and someone was living there with a child? The ground was littered with broken bottles and discarded syringes. It wasn't safe. No wonder so many ex-cons found themselves back in jail. The slammer was better than this.

As soon as it stopped raining he would head back. There was no point in asking these people anything. Half of them looked like the walking dead and the other half looked like they soon would be. An old timer was sitting in the dirt by himself picking at the scabs on his arms. Maybe he'd been around long enough to remember. Satchel walked over and sat down, realizing the minute he did why the man was sitting alone. The air around him reeked of urine, feces, and body odor. His hair was dusty, not gray, but the carved lines of his face were deep and the bags under his eyes were rimed with pink flesh. His clothes looked like they'd been soaked in water and rolled in dirt, and then soaked and rolled again and the process repeated many times. The man reached out a hand so thin it looked like the claw of a bird.

"Got a cigarette?" The man's eyes were vacuous like holes drilled into a piece of wood, and his beard looked like a Brillo pad that had scoured too many pots and his teeth, at least those that remained, were as yellow as an old pair of dice. But Satchel thought he recognized something familiar about the voice. "Freddie?" He said.

Stan stared out the window. The rain pelting the glass sounded like a bucket of water poured on a sheet of tin. The sky crackled as lightning bolts lit up the downtown core. He checked his watch, then swung his feet around and got up to turn on the TV. Thank God the rain hadn't flared up earlier. It would've ruined his announcement. Hollywood heartthrob, Mitch McCullum, appeared on the screen with a mouth full of veneered teeth selling the brighter white of his favorite toothpaste. Well, *duh*. Stan hoped he'd never have to put that kind of campaign together for a client. He reached for the remote to turn the volume down. He wanted the evening news.

He went back to perusing the monthly financials. Things were looking good, sales up eight percent over the previous quarter, which was unusual because the summer months often brought lower sales. Advertisers generally held back knowing a good percent of their customers were away on vacation. They were ahead of the curve, at least for the moment.

He held the spreadsheet up, running his fingers through his hair as he leaned back. But would it be enough? The columns showed the appropriate distribution of funds for building lease, employee compensation, insurance, office supplies and contingencies. And in spite of his accountant's objections, he always made sure they set aside enough to keep the soup kitchen going. It was a tax write off, but truth be told it was his real reason for keeping the agency alive. Only now he'd been called to a new mission and he wasn't sure where he'd find the money for that. A lot depended on how much this lawsuit was going to cost.

He slid the spreadsheet into a drawer and leaned forward. "Come in," he said. acknowledging the tap on his door.

"Hi boss, got a minute?"

"Sure Bruce, what's up?"

Bruce treaded lightly into the room, taking a seat in one of the chairs. He was wearing a pair of narrow pointy-toed shoes with gray slacks and a white shirt with the collar open down to the second button and the cuffs rolled back on the sleeves. Stan could see he wore a crucifix on a silver chain underneath the shirt. He crossed one leg over the other and said, "Remember when I said I'd try to talk to those guys who filed that lawsuit?"

Stan put his pencil down and leaned back in his chair.

"Well, I met with them last night," Bruce paused, waiting for his boss's reaction, but Stan just nodded. "Well, unfortunately, I have some bad news. Thomas, he's the beefcake in the relationship, his partner Marty is more of a Lacy, but Thomas is saying he's going to take us down." Bruce shifted in his seat with his hands interlaced over his knee. "I tried talking him out of it but he wouldn't budge. His partner, Marty, was nice about the whole thing. He wouldn't mind dropping the suit at all, but not Thomas. He thinks you're a bigot, even though I told him you're definitely not. He wants to make an example of you."

Stan's bottom lip slid out, his hands resting on the arms of his chair as he rocked back. "I already spoke to my lawyer. I found out this morning that a court date has been set, so I guess there's not much we can do. We'll just have to let it play out and see what happens. But thank you for trying." He leaned forward again. "I am glad you dropped by. There's something I want to talk to you about."

Bruce shifted in his seat again uncrossing his legs and pulling on his pants to straighten the material. "Oh, what's that?"

"I'm thinking of taking a leave of absence. You're my second in command, so I may need you to run things for a while."

Bruce sat up, his elbows resting on the arms of the chair; his eyes wide like he'd just been slapped. He raised a hand. "You can't be serious, what about…"

"Don't worry, I'm not dropping off the planet. I'll be here if anything serious comes up, but I want you to take more responsibility for meetings and client management…" Stan looked up as three other people thundered into the room.

"Turn on the news," Beth said, her hands flicking in front of her trying to hurry them along.

"It's on channel seven," Jeff said. "Turn up the volume. Quick or you'll miss it."

A picture of Stan standing on the dais in front of City Hall appeared on the screen. He was surrounded by reporters, each pushing their microphones forward, trying to get in his face.

"Mr. Powers, what prompted this decision?"

"Mr. Powers, I understand you run a small Chicago business. What's your experience with politics? What do you bring to the table?"

"Mr. Powers, are you running on the Republican ticket, or as an independent?"

The television shot switched to the reporter in the street. "Little is known of Mr. Power's politics, whether he leans right or left, or why he's jumping into the race at this time, but we'll be digging into this further and have more for you as the story develops. Back to you Marjorie."

The scene changed to the ABC eyewitness newsroom where Marjorie Wilkes sat at the anchor desk. "Well I guess you heard it here first, independent businessman Stan Powers has decided to toss his hat into the senatorial race. So far Charlotte Weise has run unopposed. I'll bet this comes as a surprise. What you think Zach?" Marjorie said, tossing the ball to the reporter on the street.

"I'm not sure, but one thing is certain, Senator Weise is a very popular candidate. Mr. Powers will be running as an underdog. It will be interesting to see if he can pull it off. This is Zach Taylor, reporting from City Hall."

The scene switched back to Marjorie at the anchor desk. "Indeed it will, Zach, indeed it will. In other breaking news…"

Stan pointed the remote at the screen and clicked the off button. "I was hoping to tell you about this before you saw it, but the time slipped away and frankly I'm still trying to settle into the reality of it myself. Okay, I know you've got a lot of questions but if you bear with me, I'll try to get them answered."

"What are you doing? You can't run for office. You've got an agency to run," Julie burst out.

"I know that, but you don't really need me. Most days I just sit in my office crunching numbers. You guys do all the work. I know this will take a large part of my time, but I plan to still be involved and when I'm not here Bruce will be in charge, just as always."

"Clients expect to see you at meetings," Julie retorted. "To them you *are* the agency. It's your word they want to hear when we promise the job will be done on time and on budget."

"That's only true when we're trying to land an account. You always handle the day-to-day meetings, and I'll be there to support you when you need me."

"With all due respect," Jeff joined in. "I think you're freaking nuts. You know how popular Charlotte is? You haven't got a chance of winning. You'll just end up wasting everyone's time."

"You're right, Jeff. I don't plan on winning. You all know my politics, you know I don't agree with the direction our country's going. I want to do something about that. I may be a voice crying in the wilderness, but someone has to say something. With Charlotte running unopposed there's only one message out there. I just thought it might be nice to have someone offer a different perspective."

"And who's going to pay for it? You told that reporter you're running as an independent. Without party support you'll end up paying for everything yourself, in which case your message won't get very far."

"What I told that reporter was that I hadn't spoken to the GOP. This whole thing came up last night when I couldn't sleep. If I meet with GOP leaders and they like what I have to say maybe I'll get their support, but I've decided to run whether they support me or not. And as for my message not getting out, I suspect media censorship will have more to do with that than lack of money."

"You're making it awkward for us," Jeff said. "I think I speak

69

for everyone here when I say we like you as a boss, but we don't necessarily see eye-to-eye on a lot of the things you believe. Are you going to fire us if we don't vote for you?"

"I hope you know me better than that. Each one of you makes a unique contribution to this team. Your employment here is not contingent upon agreeing with me on anything. As long as you faithfully continue to perform your duties, you'll always have a place here."

"Yeah right," Bruce said, folding his shoulders in to rub his arms. "As long as you own the agency, but your point of view could cost us that too."

Stan glared at Bruce, his lips taut and his eyes narrow letting Bruce know he didn't appreciate the comment. "I've made my decision, and I'm not going to back down. Now, I suggest we all get back to work and attend to the business at hand."

Bruce rose from his chair and left the room followed Beth and Jeff, but Julie stayed behind.

Stan leaned in and picked up his spreadsheet to continue his analysis but looked up when he saw her still standing there. "Yes?"

"Permission to speak freely?"

A light smile formed on his lips at her use of military protocol. He rocked back slipping his hands into his pockets and crossing his feet at the ankles. "Of course. What's up?"

"You say you're a Christian. Didn't Christ teach us to feed the poor? That's all Senator Weise wants to do. She just wants the rich to give a little of what they have to make sure people don't starve. What's wrong with that?"

"Nothing. I just don't agree with the way she wants to do it. Christ tells us to take care of those in need, and we must do that, but he didn't tell the Roman government to step in and steal from the rich and give to the poor. He gave the command to the people themselves. Christ wants every decision we make to be of our own free will. He won't force men to do anything, not even serve Him.

He wants us to willingly take care of the poor, if not out of our love for our fellow man, at least out of our love for Him. When we're forced to do it, or do it begrudgingly, we're not showing His love working through us, we're just doing what we have to do. By the way, this romantic notion of Robin Hood stealing from the rich and giving to the poor is mistaken. Robin Hood didn't steal from the rich, he took the tax money the government unjustly collected and gave it back to the people. There's a lesson in that."

Julie's face fell into a pout. "That's okay as long as the rich do heir part, but most often they don't. They live in extravagant houses and drive luxury cars and then fly their pollution producing planes to Paris for dinner and don't care one bit that poor immigrant children live in small houses, often with multiple families sharing food and expenses just to get by. We have to end poverty somehow. Forcing people to do what's right might be the only way. I know you say you're against things like abortion…" Julie glanced back over her shoulder to make sure Bruce wasn't listening, "…and homosexuality, but there's nothing you can do about those things. Even if you made them illegal again, people would continue doing them just as they did before. There's no point in trying to do anything about that, but at least we can try to end poverty because that's something nobody wants. Wouldn't that be the more Christian thing to do?"

Stan shook his head. He'd heard the argument before. He knew Julie, as an unbeliever, wouldn't relate to what he was about to say. "I'm sorry, Julie, but even with all your best efforts, you won't be able to end poverty. Christ said, 'The poor you will always have with you,' so unless you know something He didn't, poverty is here to stay. The truth is, Christ didn't come to save the poor, though he commands us to help whenever we can; He didn't come to save the planet, though He expects us to be responsible stewards of His creation; He didn't even come to save the Jews from an oppressive government, though they wanted Him to. Christ came to save

71

sinners. We know abortion and homosexuality are sins so I, as a Christian, cannot stand with any political party that seeks their advancement. Poverty is egregious, but fortunately no one is going to hell for being poor. Christ died to save men from the very things Senator Weise wants us to approve. I'm hoping to do what I can to show a better way."

The downpour ended as quickly as it came. The storm moved off to the west but a few raindrops still drizzled the ground. The sky now displayed white billowy clouds filigreed with light.

Satchel towered over the almost comatose body of Freddie who remained on the ground like an inert pile of soiled laundry.

"Come on Freddie, get up, I'm taking you with me." He was breathing through his mouth. The putrid air might be saturated with germs.

Freddie didn't acknowledge him. He remained in his crouched position staring straight ahead like he was seeing something no one else could see.

"Got a smoke?" he said to no one in particular.

While sitting beside Freddie, Satchel had noticed the puncture marks. So much caked on dirt made them hard to see but they were there; little welts the size of pinpricks, ruby red. Freddie had sold his soul for a needle and a bottle of wine.

"Come on, Freddie, you need something to eat." This time when Freddie didn't speak, Satchel reached down to take his arm but Freddie shook him off.

"Nooooo," he said

"Come on, I just want to help."

"Don't need no help."

"Yes you do, Freddie, you do need help. Remember that soup kitchen, the Daily Bread. The preacher down there will fix you up."

Freddie looked up, his jaundiced eyes as yellow as his teeth.

He extended an arm that looked to be all bone and pointed to his muscle with a finger. "Got some juice?" He cackled, but his words came out through chapped lips, dry as desert air.

"Yeah, come on mate, we'll get you fixed up."

Suddenly Freddie's disposition changed. He stared at Satchel like he was seeing a vision, or a ghost. This time when Satchel tried lifting Freddie to his feet Freddie didn't resist. Satchel held his breath, placed his arm around Freddie's waist and started walking.

The after five crowd bustled through the streets of Evanston. Cars changed lanes and crisscrossed in front of each other in an effort to get home. *Beep, beep, beeeep.* Rachel made her way across the park. She was thankful the rain had stopped. She hadn't thought to bring an umbrella. Dozens of tree branches were scattered across the grass, brought down by the heavy wind. Several young black men were raking leaves from the dark loam of the garden. That was one thing she wanted to fix. College should be affordable for everyone. These young men shouldn't have to spend the rest of their lives with blisters on their hands. Her foot sunk into a soft spot and she pulled it back, leaving her shoe behind. The grass was soggy with thin layers of water lying in patches of low ground. She balanced on one foot and plucked her shoe from the sod, placing it back over her toes to slip it on. A gust of wind sent her hair swirling around her face. She pulled it back and held it against her neck with her hand.

She paused, stretching to relieve the tension in her back. It had been a hectic day putting out one fire after another. The biggest, of course, was the news that Charlotte now had competition. They had spoken on the phone, but Charlotte reassured her that this man was a nobody from nowhere and was likely only using the announcement to garner his ten minutes of fame. In any event, the late entry from Hoosierville didn't stand a chance. She encouraged

Rachel to double down on her efforts to raise money and not to give it another thought.

Another gust of wind lifted her skirt, forcing her to let go of her hair so she could hold it down. She needed more clothes. She didn't have enough to get through a week, and doing laundry more than once a week encroached on her reading time. A flash of memory took her back to the Salvation Army where she and Freddie, and later her father, had bought clothes for practically nothing. She would have to go online to see if there was a Salvation Army in Evanston.

Right now her stomach was calling. The restaurant she liked best was only a few blocks off campus, a small eatery owned by an elderly couple who always smiled and treated her like family. It was only open till seven. She glanced at her watch. She had plenty of time. It was just down the street.

A car wooshed by spraying street water into the air. Rachel drew her hands to her shoulders and turned her back but the spray hit her anyway. It wasn't much but it did dampen her skirt and blouse. *Snap crrraaaaaack!* Her head jerked around to see a large oak come down in the front yard of an old gabled house. The bushy head of the tree landed on the columned portico with a loud *wafump.* Rachel held her hair back with one hand and her skirt with the other until the gust passed.

Scott was in a tizzy, worried about how competition might impact their efforts. Maybe she wasn't being fair. She'd been concerned too, at first, but then she'd spoken to Charlotte, and Charlotte had put the matter to rest. By now, most of her volunteers would have heard about it. She needed to calm their fears. She would prepare a statement and read it at their morning staff meeting.

The house on her right had been turned into a family restaurant. It was low key, barely discernible from other houses on the street, though most of those had become businesses too. If she hadn't been told about it, she wouldn't have known it was there. A single plaque on the door was all the advertising they used. The sign read, "Mama's Home Cooking." This was where she would eat. She took the steps up onto the porch, reached for the door, and stepped inside.

"Ah Rachel, honey, welcome back. Come'ere, give Mama a hug."

Rachel reciprocated wrapping the short plump lady in her arms. The woman's smooth black skin held a sheen that Rachel suspected was produced by the warm kitchen. Her face was round, her eyes like black buttons and her hair, styled in a short Afro, shined like platinum.

"I keep telling you, you're much too skinny, you come right on over here and we'll fatten you up." The lady took Rachel's hand and led her to a small round table in the corner. "You sit right here and I'll go fix you a cup of coffee." She turned and walked away, the ancient hardwood floors squeaking under her feet.

Rachel looked around, enjoying the ambience. There were pictures on the walls, prints only, none of them expensive, but well framed and hung straight. A fireplace graced one wall and while it was too warm to be lit, Rachel fancied the day when winter came and the comfort it would bring. A wood plaque etched with the words, "Give us this day our daily bread," was resting on the mantel. It made her wonder if Mamma was religious, though it was a common phrase so Rachel couldn't be sure.

All the tables and chairs were mismatched like they'd been assembled from several garage sales, but that only added to the restaurant's charm. Beside each table was a basket filled with newspapers and magazines. Rachel reached down and lifted out a newspaper to read while waiting.

Mama was already pouring her coffee as she unfurled the paper. A man's smiling face stared back at her. Her eyes darted up to the lady, her fingers cupped over her mouth, "Oh," she said.

"Something wrong, dear?" Mama continued to pour.

"Yes, no, I mean…" But there *was* something wrong. She knew that face. It was, *him*, the man who, as a child, she'd seen standing over her mother's body, a face that was ineradicably etched into her brain, only now she knew his name.

Six

THE HUMIDITY was back with a vengeance. Heat radiating through the hazy clouds absorbed into their clothes resulting in a musty sweat that saturated them to the bone. Satchel kept his arm around Freddie, one putrefying step after the other. The combination of perspiration, urine, and fecal matter was almost intolerable. There's a point where caked on dirt and sweat cancel out a person's smell, but not so with Freddie. Holding onto Freddie was like sticking your face into the bowels of a dead skunk. Satchel was sure he hadn't had a bath in months, and the further they walked the more rancorous his odor became.

They passed one vacated premise after another, the rooms inside strewn with newspapers, upended trash cans, scattered litter and soiled mattresses. Some had holes in the walls leveled by gangs releasing their frustration, and all contained graffiti—the new art deco. The alley seemed innocuous as they made their way from one side to the other, until a man popped up from behind a trash bin wielding a knife.

"Give me your money, your watch, your wallet, everything you got, and be quick about it. I don't want to have to stick you." The man stopped short, waving his hand in front of his face, *phew*.

Satchel turned, facing him, incredulous. "You're off your trolley, mate. Do we look like men what have fat wallets? Get out of here. I got no time for this."

The bandit wavered for moment, then brandished his knife, waving it around again. "I'll cut you, I swear."

"What, with that? You couldn't poke a frog with that. Now be a good chap and take off before I make you eat dirt."

But the man wasn't listening. He lunged forward taking a swipe, but the arc of the knife fell three inches short of hitting anything.

"Bloody hell!" Satchel caught the hand and squeezed till it dropped the knife, then he spun the man around planting a foot in his backside sending him sprawling to the ground. "There's a mission right down there," he said, pointing. "I suggest you try it. They got good food and maybe you'll find God." He reached down and picked up the knife, sliding it into the pocket of his denims. He took Freddie by the arm and continued down the street as though nothing had happened.

He could see Freddie was dying. The rotten teeth, yellow skin and hollow bones were indicative of a slow wasting away. Getting Freddie to the mission probably wouldn't make a difference, but if ever a soul needed saving, this was it. He hoped the preacher was up to the challenge.

Satchel scratched a place on his cheek where it itched. His behavior boggled him. He could've wrapped that kid into a pretzel and plopped him into the dumpster. He didn't know he was capable of mercy. And Freddie? He could easily walk away and leave Freddie to die. If ever he needed proof that he was changing this was surely it. This thing with Jesus was making him care. Not that he'd had some kind of miraculous conversion, it was just that he was seeing things through a different set of eyes. Just last night the men in his Bible group had read where Jesus embraced a leper, not considering what it might do to Himself. Satchel, had closed his eyes and thought, *man, what a chump.* But here he was, being a chump for Freddie.

They stumbled through the door. Satchel half believed they'd toss Freddie back onto the street. Who could blame them? Freddie's smell alone polluted the environment. The men worked hard to keep the dining hall clean and germ-free, and here he was bringing a ninety-eight pound bag of bacteria inside and setting him in a chair. Satchel tried to pull away but Freddie clung to his arm. Looking up through yellow water-soaked eyes he said, "Man, I need a fix. You...you promised."

Satchel swept his arm free and looked down on the hopeless lump of humanity. "No, I said they'd fix you up, not give you a fix. Can I get you something to drink, water, milk, I think we've got some soda?"

The overhead fans spun like plane propellers, but they just recycled the already hot air and redistributed a smell that was so bad even the cat stayed away. The room had to be near eighty degrees and yet Freddie's body was trembling. He tried to bring his eyes up to meet Satchel's but it seemed they were weighed down. They closed again. "I...I know you." he said, as though recognizing Satchel for the first time.

Satchel knelt down, looking Freddie in the eye. "You do know me, mate. A long time ago. We used to hang together under the bridge. Remember? I had a little girl, Rachel. Her mom used to turn tricks in that old warehouse by the lumber yard. You remember her? You know where she is?"

Freddie kept his arms wrapped around himself, still shivering and trying to keep himself warm. "She's dead."

"Right. You got it. But not her, the little girl, the one you said made you lots of money. Do you know where she is?"

"I need some junk, man. You gotta help me."

"Sorry boys, we don't open till five. You need to wait outside till then."

Satchel looked up. The old black preacher had entered the room carrying his guitar. He walked over to the small stage and set the instrument on its stand, the strings sounding a discordant note. He was wearing denims with alligator boots and a white dress shirt with the sleeves rolled back on the cuffs. Around his neck hung a shiny metal cross the size of a man's fist. He brought a hand up to scratch his bald head. "I suppose if you're hungry I might find something in the refrigerator."

Satchel raised himself off his haunches. "That's okay preacher, I can get it myself. I'm your new cook but, sorry, I guess we haven't had the chance to meet."

The preacher was over six feet tall and thick in the chest, a trim piece of meat without an ounce of gristle. He turned and came back toward Satchel, extending his hand. "Then I guess it's time to fix that. Name's Samuel, or Bishop Samuel to those in my church," he winked and brought a hand up to cup the side of his mouth like he was sharing a secret, "they kind of get a kick out of using highfalutin titles, but between us Samuel's just fine." He was smiling, his eyes bright as obsidian and his mouth a purple leaf split down the middle exposing rows of virgin white corn. "I heard about you. Seems you put on quite a show for the folks the other day," and when Satchel started to protest, raised his hand and said, "This is a house of mercy. I'm not your judge, He is." He raised his index finger and pointed to the ceiling.

"Sorry, I guess I got off to a bad star…"

"Like I said, I'm not your judge. Couldn't judge you if I wanted to. I don't even know your name."

"Satchel, like a ruddy sack or bag, and, no, I don't know why my parents stuck me with that moniker."

"Satchel it is. And this is?" The preacher stooped over to shake Freddie's hand.

Freddie ignored the gesture. He kept his arms wrapped around himself, continuing to quake.

Samuel was standing right next to Freddie but he didn't seem put off by the smell. In fact, he seemed oblivious to it. Takes some special gift to do that. "That's Freddie," Satchel said. "I think he's going cold turkey. I think he needs to detox. That's why I brought him here. I heard you got programs like that. I thought you might be able to help."

"I see. That's not something we handle here, but my church, Christ's Holiness, has a program they can put him through, if he's interested.

"He is."

"All right then, Samuel said. "Help me get him upstairs and we'll give him a bath before we take him over."

The headquarters for Charlotte Weise's campaign was in a monolithic structure on Wacker Drive in the central part of the city. The fifty-one story building was one of the tallest in Chicago. It was a blue glass edifice known for the ceiling design of its lobby where a person could stand gazing up at what looked like the bottom of a circular staircase with a bank of lights spanning each step. It was pricey real estate, with marbled floors and cultured plants, but Charlotte argued she needed it because she was a corporate watchdog. This particular building housed corporate giants like Deloitte, Wells Fargo Capital, RR Donnelley and Bloomberg, firms in the top one percent. As the people's champion, she needed to keep an eye on such corporate entities to make sure they gave back in proportion to what they stole. When asked how she justified wasting so much taxpayer money on such posh office space, she pointed out that she was doing it to save the environment. The building had a sustainable design certified LEED-CS Gold by the U.S. Green Building Council. On a personal note, she loved looking down from her office on the forty-second floor at the ant size cars and pedestrians on the streets. She was lord and protector of the little people.

The office was a maelstrom in upheaval. Aids sat at computers trying to discover everything they could about this man, Stan Powers. No detail was to be overlooked, and the more questionable the content the better. Sadly, all they'd been able to conjure up so far was that he was a decorated war hero, a former US Navy SEAL wounded in battle, who had come home to start his own business, a reasonably successful advertising agency.

Rachel ran through the lobby, not stopping to admire the interior trees which to her looked like they'd been trimmed to resemble toilet brushes, or the lights that bounced off the marble floors at her heels. She pushed the elevator button, paused to wait for the door to open, and hopped inside glancing at her watch. She was already five minutes late and Charlotte disdained tardiness. She still had to cover forty-two floors.

The elevator doors opened and she rushed out, looking for a sign to point her in the right direction. She began her sprint down the hall. She was dressed to look smart but the hair she'd pinned on top of her head to be professional was falling down and her goodwill supplied briefcase was banging her knees. She stopped just outside the door to smooth her jacket and straighten her dress. Then she took a breath and walked in with the cool composure of a yoga instructor.

She was greeted by a receptionist in the outer lobby who asked her to sit down and wait. She did, but she couldn't relax. The foyer was small, containing only two chairs, thickly padded and covered in soft burgundy leather. What would they do if a delegation arrived? She looked at her watch again, knowing each passing minute only made her look worse.

The interior door of the office opened and the receptionist waved her in. "They're in the board room waiting for you," she said. "This way."

The receptionist led her back to a room filled with a dozen or more people all seated around a long table. Talk about being on the spot. The double doors behind her closed as she stepped inside.

Everyone was staring at her. Was she supposed to say something?

"Um, hi. Sorry I'm late. I had to take the subway in from Evanston and then I had to catch a taxi and, the traffic, well, this is Chicago."

From the end of the table Charlotte looked up and caught her eye. She gave a flick of her wrist and said, "Since you haven't been here before, I'll overlook it, but next time leave a little earlier. Keep in mind that all these people have busy schedules and waiting for you isn't on their agenda. I'll save the introductions for later. Please take a seat so we can get started.

Rachel saw only one empty chair and squeezed around the table to take it. She felt the weight of two dozen eyes on her as she took her seat. It seemed like the dress code was casual. She had dressed professional. She would remember that next time. A yellow legal pad and pen sat in front of each person. She set her briefcase beside her chair. She probably wouldn't need it. She glanced around to see if she was still being observed, but most of the eyes had gone to Charlotte who was now standing at the head of the table.

"Okay, I think you all know why we're here. First I want to assure you that I don't consider Mr. Powers to be a threat. I'm the incumbent and that goes in our favor, and our poll numbers are very good, but we can't just assume he won't be a problem. The newspapers are already calling him the underdog, and people love to root for an underdog, so we have to plan our strategy carefully and see if we can't take this man down before he has the chance to do any damage. That won't be easy. I have a team of aides out there looking to find dirt on this guy, but so far they've come up with nothing. I'm not going to pretend someone could say the same about me. Politics is a dirty business and I'm sure I've made enemies. The public is very sensitive to accusations of misconduct and though I've always done my best to treat everyone fairly, there's bound to be someone out there looking for a chance to stick a knife in my back. Last thing I need is for this to become a contest about ethics."

As she listened to the preamble, Rachel's eyes began to burn. She brought her fingers up, rubbing the bridge of her nose. "You'd better hope it does," she murmured.

"What's that?" Rachel hadn't meant to be heard but Charlotte picked it up. "You have something to say?"

"No, it's nothing. I just don't think Mr. Stan Powers is a paragon of ethics. Everyone's got skeletons in their closet."

"Uh huh, well I hope you're right, uh, Danny?"

The attention of the people around the table turned to a young man with his hand raised.

"I don't think you've got a thing to worry about," he said. "People are smart enough to know every good politician has to bend the rules sometimes. You stand on your record. Your efforts to improve our black neighborhoods, your bill to get corporations to pay for the mess they've made of our environment. And there's no greater champion of women's rights. No one even knows what Mr. Powers stands for. Heck, probably doesn't even know himself."

A spurt of chuckles and guffaws danced around the table.

"All right, that's enough, let's not dismiss the man until we know what he's about. Ellen?"

Ellen lowered her hand, dropping it to the table. She began picking at a cuticle. "Has anyone looked at his taxes yet? You said he's a businessman. Don't all businessmen try to screw the government out of paying their fair share. Seems like that might be a good way to get him. Look at what happened to Al Capone..."

More giggles from her peers.

Ellen looked up sharply, "No, I mean it. He was a mobster, but he was squeaky clean until they nailed him for tax evasion. I'll bet this guy has cheated the government somewhere. What if we go after him on that?"

The boy sitting beside her looked over smirking. "First of all, there's something called privacy. You can't just go look at someone's tax records. You'd need a court order."

"Okay, let's keep it light. We're just throwing out ideas, and by the way, Ellen, that's a good one. I might know someone over at the IRS who can do a little background check for us. Who knows, maybe they'll even call for an audit. It never looks good to be audited while running a campaign. Jonathan, you had your hand raised."

"Yeah, I think I have an idea. It relates to what Danny said about Mr. Powers not having a platform. I think we should arrange a debate, not next month but right now. I think you should call Mr. Powers and congratulate him on his candidacy and then suggest that it would be, as a way of introducing him to the public, a great idea to have a debate. You know, let the voters know where each candidate stands on the issues. This dude's politically naïve. I expect he doesn't know the first thing about how to handle a moderator's questions. He'll be tripping all over himself. You'll crush him, make him look so bad he won't want to show his face in public again."

That might work, Rachel thought. *Catch him off guard and humiliate him.* She pushed against the edge of the table, squirming in her seat to get comfortable. She was too young to have back pain. She tried to relax, discreetly taking in a couple of slow deep breaths but the throbbing didn't stop. It was causing her to lose focus. She needed to pay attention. Having that man in office would be a travesty. She was determined to see it never happened.

Samuel was singing. His deep baritone voice gurgled like water poured over gravel.

> "I am not skilled to understand,
> What God has willed what God has planned,
> I only know at His right hand,
> Is one who is my Savior."

"Pass the soap, there, Satchel," he said, as he poured water on Freddie's chest to loosen the caked on dirt. His giant three inch metal cross clanked against the tub as he leaned in to scrub.

> "I take Him at His word indeed,
> Christ died for sinners, this I read,
> For in my heart I find a need,
> Of Him to be my Savior."

"Now Freddie, if I had known how much work this was going to be, I might have reconsidered. You got more dirt than a greased cat in a dustbin. Darn soap just soaks in. Can't even get it to lather. Satchel why don't you grab that shampoo and wash Freddie's hair?"

The bathroom floor looked like someone had hosed it down. A half dozen bath towels were wadded on the tiles soaking up the water but a constant cycle of waves splashed over the tub's edge with every twist and turn Freddie made. He was fighting them and though he had little strength, he was effective in keeping them from getting him clean.

> "That He should leave His place on high,"
> And come for sinful man to die,
> You count it strange, so once did I,
> Before I knew my Savior."

Satchel kept one arm around Freddie's chest, holding him up as he soaped his hair. He didn't want to squeeze too tight. The boy was fragile. Apply too much pressure and he might break. Stripping Freddie's clothes off had sickened him, like watching a film about one of Hitler's death camps. Freddie was nothing but loose skin wrapped over a collection of brittle bones. The boy was slippery and used the soap to his advantage, twisting around onto his stomach sending more water over the tub's rim onto the floor.

"That's good, let me get his back." Samuel began rubbing Freddie's backside with the bar of soap. The water was the color of sludge. "That was a good first attempt, but we have to do it again." Samuel reached his hand down under the water and pulled the plug letting the tub drain. He didn't seem to notice that his clean white shirt now looked like it'd been dragged through an oil spill. The mucky water gurgled and swirled as the tub emptied. "Keep him down for me Satchel, don't let him climb out."

"*Noooooooo*," Freddie flailed his arms, looping around to sit up again. "I don't like it…"

"We'll be done soon," Samuel said. "We're going to clean you up on the outside, and then were going to take you to a place where they'll show you how to get clean on the inside." He reached for the hand shower and washed the muck away, then reset the plug, and began filling the tub again.

> "Yes, living, dying, let me bring,
> My strength, my solace from this spring,
> That He who lives to be my King,
> Once died to be my Savior."

They had debated giving Freddie a shower but figured it was likely he'd just ball himself up on the floor making washing him impossible. And there wasn't enough room in the stall for three people. At least in the tub they were able to get him somewhat stretched out, only they hadn't planned on him kicking so much. *Water, water, everywhere and not a drop to drink.* Another wave came crashing over the side landing in Satchel's lap. Satchel and Samuel were both fully dressed, but even though Freddie was the one taking the bath, they were fully soaked.

Satchel didn't have to wonder whether or not Samuel sang in the shower. Of course he did. The man sang all the time, and especially at every service, but he was pretty sure no one listened.

He certainly hadn't. Now, somehow, words he'd never considered before were replete with meaning.

> "Amazing Grace, how sweet the sound,
> That saved a wretch like me.
> I once was lost, but now am found,
> Was blind but now I see."

Satchel uncapped the bottle of shampoo, pouring two tablespoons into his large palms and slapped them down on Freddie's head. It was time for a second attempt. Samuel looked up and winked, "That's good, brother, we don't want to baptize this boy without a laying on of hands."

"What's that all about, anyway? Baptism, I mean. What's it supposed to do?"

"It doesn't *do* anything. It's just an outward show of our commitment to follow Jesus. It's symbolic. You stand there, having confessed your sin, and having received Christ as your savior, and you say, now I'm dead to sin. So you get immersed in the water as a symbol of being buried, and you're brought up to symbolize you're alive again with a new life in Christ. You should try it sometime." Samuel launched into another verse of Amazing Grace, his voice even louder as he slapped water over Freddie's body rinsing it clean.

> "Through many dangers, toils and snares,
> I have already come.
> Tis grace that brought me safe thus far,
> And grace will lead me home."

"Take it easy Freddie, we're almost done."

"*Noooooo, muphhh,* stop it," Freddie gurgled as Satchel held the hand shower over his head to rinse his hair.

"I think we've got it," Samuel said, pulling the plug on the drain. "Might as well use that thing to do a final rinse. Here Freddie, let me help you to your feet." Samuel reached down, taking Freddie under the arms and pulled him up, holding him steady while Satchel hosed him off. "We'll have to see about getting you some fresh clothes," Samuel said. He reached for a towel and began swabbing Freddie. "Freddie, I need you to bring your foot up over the tub. That's it, be careful, it's slippery. Now, the other one," but Freddie was off balance and his foot slid out from under him causing him to stumble backward. Satchel caught the fall and lifted him up out of the tub. He was light as a doll. Freddie cupped his hands over his man parts and stood dripping water on the floor. His jaw was trembling.

"Whew, what a mess," Satchel said, sliding a towel around on the floor with his foot to mop up some of the water.

Samuel looked at his watch. "We still need to comb his hair and get him dressed but I'm thinking it's too late to get him over to the shelter tonight. Let's clean up this mess and square Freddie away. Then I think they're expecting you to help down in the kitchen and I have to preach. You feed their bodies and I'll feed their souls and perhaps," he said, placing his hand on Freddie's head, "Freddie will get the blessing of both."

Seven

STAN SAT at his desk staring out the window, trying to catch a breath between calls. He brought his pen to his mouth, biting the tip. It was much ado about nothing. It wasn't like he was running for president or leaving the country. The buildings across the street obstructed his view, but the sky between them was flamingo pink. The earlier storm had dissipated, leaving gulls circling on the afternoon breeze. The days would get longer as they headed into summer, which was good. The extra daylight hours would give him more time to conduct evening rallies. A pigeon landed on the brick sill of the window, cooing and preening itself but saw movement inside and immediately flew off. Stan swung his chair back around and with his pen sandwiched between his fingers, began tapping the desk. The phones had been ringing incessantly. Clients were worried about the future of their accounts, friends called to either congratulate him or suggest he was out of his mind, and national and local news media wanted to schedule interviews. He'd gone from 'nobody wants to know me,' to 'everybody wants to know me,' in a matter of minutes. Stan had never received so many calls.

He rotated his shoulders, his shirt clinging to his back. The storm had left a dampness that made the room feel musty. It smelled like it always smelled after a heavy rain, like a building left to rot in its own decay. The thirteen floor brick structure was hailed as a modern skyscraper when it debuted back in 1911, but the passage of time had taken its toll. It had been renovated and upgraded several times, but for all of that, when wet weather seeped into its pores, it smelled old.

Stan reached out and clicked on his lamp. He had never been given to spontaneity. The whole idea of jumping into a race without much forethought was completely foreign. One minute he'd been trying to figure out how to handle a man like Satchel, and the next he was thinking about how to change the world. It had something to do with the picture in the newspaper. Ms. Weise seemed so aloof, with an air that suggested the election was in the bag. He disagreed with almost everything the woman said and the idea that she would be swept into office unopposed, just didn't seem right. The more he thought about it, the more convinced he became that someone had to do something; and that that someone was him.

He turned back toward the window and looked at his watch. That's why the calls had stopped. It was after seven, the media would assume he'd closed up and gone home. Sunlight fringed the edge of the buildings turning them into silhouettes. Seagulls coming in off the lake fluttered in the sky like paper kites twisting and turning on a breeze. He had the feeling that his one sleepless night would soon become many.

He pulled himself up and went to the window. The problem wasn't his commitment, he'd made the decision and he would follow through; the problem was that he didn't know what he was doing. He didn't have an organization behind him, he didn't have financial support, and he didn't have a campaign manager or a speechwriter or a team of people making calls.

He, of all people, knew the power of advertising, but he didn't have the money to launch a serious media campaign. He was an unknown, going up against a woman whose face was seen every day. She was a media darling. You couldn't drive down the highway without seeing one of her billboards, or pick up a newspaper without reading about her in an article, or watch TV without seeing one of her ads. Her face was as recognizable as Hillary Clinton's and Michelle Obama's, both of whom were born in Illinois and would certainly endorse her. Now the reality was sinking in and he was starting to realize just how dumb this idea was. The musty room was making him feel the way he felt when he'd hid in his grandma's closet as a boy, claustrophobic.

Deep in his gut he had the feeling it wasn't his idea at all. God frequently put ideas into the minds of men. Joseph's brothers came up with the idea of selling him to a few Ishmaelite traders, but later when Joseph confronted them from the power of Pharaoh's throne, he implied it wasn't their idea at all. "You meant it for evil," he said, "but God meant it for good." If it was God's idea, Stan didn't need to worry.

The sun moved out from behind the building, blinding him. He brought a hand up to shield his eyes and turned his back to the window, facing the interior of the room. The design on the floor was of twelve yellow rectangles separated by window frames, with his own shadow standing in the center like a man shrouded in light—the American citizen, the average Joe. He removed his jacket, laying it over the arm of his chair, and walked over to the flag. That's why he was doing this, for God and country. Somebody had to do something. His country was in decline, a country he had fought for, and almost died for, and if his country was worth fighting and dying for, then certainly it was worth standing up for.

It was not lost on Stan that in 1776, the same year America framed its Declaration of Independence, a Scottish historian, Alexander Tytler, published *The Decline and Fall of the Athenian Republic*. While his purpose was to measure the ancient population of Athens, the document became a template for understanding the formation and subsequent abolition of governments. From Egypt to Israel to Persia to Babylon and Greece and Rome. Each one had followed a cyclical pattern that led from bondage to faith, from faith to great courage, from courage to liberty, from liberty to abundance, from abundance to selfishness, from selfishness to complacency, from complacency to apathy, from apathy to dependency, and from dependency back to bondage again. It was a cycle that spanned so many generations, it seemed as constant as the rise and fall of the sun.

Stan couldn't speak to other nations whose cultures had been consumed by the flames of history, that was for historians more learned than he, but he did know something about Israel. Their rise and fall was documented in Scripture. Mr. Tytler's conclusions fit them to a T. And the same was true of America. It was ironic that about the same time America was forging a new democracy, five thousand miles away in Scotland, Tytler sat down to write: "A democracy cannot exist as a permanent form of government. It can only exist until the voters discover they can vote themselves largesse from the public treasury. From that moment on, the majority always votes for the candidates promising them the most benefits from the public treasury, with the result that a democracy always collapses over a loss of fiscal responsibility, always followed by a dictatorship."

Stan figured America was at the place in the cycle that led from complacency, to apathy, to dependency. America had lost its fiscal responsibility and politicians, in seeking more votes, had promised more than the public treasury could afford. The result was a spiraling debt which would ultimately lead to financial collapse.

America had been gambling at this table for many years. With tens of trillions of debt, she was propelling herself toward fiscal disaster which, if Tytler's thesis was correct, would lead to a collapse and eventually, subjugation. Only this time it would be under the hand of a world dictator known to those who followed Bible prophecy as the "antichrist," and from everything Stan could see the man was soon to be revealed. Stan stepped away from the flag giving it a salute, *long may she wave.*

Rrrriiiiiinng. Stan shook himself from his thoughts. They were at it again. Dang thing just wouldn't stop. *Rrrriiiiiinng.* Why hadn't God called him to be an evangelist? It would make the job a whole lot easier. At least then people would come to hear his message; *rrrriiiiiinng,* and he wouldn't have to take it to the streets. He went back to his desk and pulled the receiver to his ear.

"Stan Powers," he said.

"Mr. Powers, this is Charlotte Weise."

Stan felt his heart choke. Goosebumps rose from a chill that didn't come from the overhead fan. He subconsciously rubbed his arm. "Senator Weise, to what do I owe the pleasure?"

"I just thought I'd call and congratulate you on your decision to run for office."

"Oh. Thank you. I guess." His response was hesitant and guarded. It was like a sixth sense, the feeling one had when they were in the crosshairs of a sniper.

"No, seriously, politics is a rough game. Anybody willing to try their hand at it deserves to be congratulated. I don't believe we've ever met, have we?"

"No, I don't believe we have." *What's she leading up to?*

"Well, I'd like to fix that."

"Pardon?"

"I had this idea. Why don't you and I get together and have a debate? I'm sure there are a lot of people out there wondering who you are. Truth is, I wonder myself. This might be a really good way for you to introduce yourself to the public and share your ideas. You and I probably have different political views. Here's the thing, I had some time scheduled for a local interview but the host took ill and they called to cancel. Since they've already put the interview in their listings they've offered me the time to use any way I see fit. The slot is already paid for. We have the studio for an hour, and since I think it would be to my advantage to learn what you're about, I came up with the idea of a debate."

"What's the catch?" Stan was thinking of the old cliché, *when something seems to be too good to be true, it probably is.* He kept the phone to his ear and began pacing, the light from the window glinting off the polish of his shoes.

"No catch. Just show up. The moderator will ask us each a series of questions and the audience will come away with a better understanding of where we each stand on the issues."

Stan straightened himself, easing the pressure on his leg while struggling to understand the motive behind her making such an offer. If they were just going to ask him questions he supposed he could handle it. He did want to get his message out, even if it was only on a local station, but…"I don't know. I should probably focus on hiring a political strategist or a campaign manager and let them deal with these kinds of things."

Charlotte sighed, but Stan couldn't tell if it was out of frustration or disappointment. "All right, I understand. No harm in asking. I just thought you might like the opportunity to introduce yourself and tell the public what you stand for. Don't say I didn't make the offer."

Stan reached up and rubbed his chin. It did sound like a good idea. And it was free publicity. "No, I think you're right. Let's do it."

"Now that's the spirit. I'll have one of my staff call to set up the date and time…"

Stan turned away from the phone all of a sudden feeling like he was back in the jungle with his feet sinking in quicksand. It wasn't always the obvious enemy that killed you, sometimes there were fire ants and jungle cats and snakes. If it seems too good to be true, it probably is. His bowels felt jittery like tiny fish swimming in his gut. It was only a debate. All he had to do was answer questions. What could possibly go wrong?"

Satchel wanted to keep an eye on Freddie, but there were too many distractions. He had to remain in the kitchen moving about from one station to the next making sure vegetables and potatoes and meat were being cut and made ready for the broth, and Freddie wandered about, refusing to sit still. They got Freddie dressed and down the stairs and sat him in a chair beneath an overhead fan in hopes of keeping him cool, but Freddie was restless and wouldn't stay put. He had gotten up several times, walking around the room, rubbing his arms, twisting and turning like a curled autumn leaf dying on the end of a branch. The gyrations didn't ease his suffering. Pain deep in the bones, so common to heroin withdrawal, was nearly impossible to kill.

The main thing was to keep Freddie from going outside. He'd already been through the building trying to bum cigarettes from everyone. Smoking wasn't allowed in the mission so Freddie had come up empty, which made him even more jittery. It seemed like bumming a smoke was more important to him than getting a fix. Satchel didn't even remember Freddie smoking before, but the testimony of his rotting yellow teeth affirmed he'd been a heavy smoker for some time. Men were already lining up for the evening meal. Satchel could hear their conversation building on the other side of the door. If Freddie snuck out while Satchel had his back turned it was likely he wouldn't come back.

Satchel wasn't even sure the culprit was heroin. He hadn't seen the substance, just the track marks on Freddie's arm. Addiction followed any number of drugs on the street. It didn't have to be smack, it might be OxyContin, Vicodin, morphine, codeine or fentanyl; there was a veritable smorgasbord of choices. Dope was available to anyone desperate enough to seek escape through dissociation, and many came in consumable packets that didn't require a heated spoon and needle.

It was the hopelessness, not the opioids, that was the problem. The drugs were just a bandage to cover feelings of emptiness and despair. Satchel had been there. He'd always prided himself on how he'd avoided the trap of injecting his arm with chemical cures, but the alcohol he drank was used for the same purpose, so he wasn't any better. Everyone was free to choose their own poison. He wished he could make Freddie understand that drugs and alcohol weren't the answer. The boy needed God. Satchel stopped stirring, broth from the long handled spoon dripping into the pot, his thoughts catching him off guard. Was that really how he felt? Funny how the God he didn't believe in had climbed into his head and taken up residence there.

He began stirring the pot again, making sure the brown gravy didn't stick to the bottom of the pan. Steam rose from the bubbling brew. He slipped his hand into it bringing it to his nose. The sweet smell of savory broth rose in the air, *ummmm*. The whole room smelled good, even with Freddie in it. And Freddie was like a new man. His odor, dissolved in the bath water, had been funneled down the drain. Now maybe Samuel could work some magic and get him clean on the inside too. Satchel glanced at the stage where Samuel was sitting on a stool tuning his guitar, *plunk, plink, plank, plonk*. The Reverend, or Bishop, or whatever he called himself had changed clothes but still looked the same. He still wore a white long sleeve shirt with the collar open. Satchel could see his metallic cross glinting in the light.

"You about ready for the meat and potatoes?" Satchel turned and smiled at Davis, the man whose face he'd shoved into a bowl of potato salad. He nodded, "All good," he said.

Davis scratched his beard and then picked up a bowl of steamed potatoes, carrots and onions and plopped them into the pot simmering with Satchel's broth. The packages of meat were precooked. They didn't have time to simmer the stew for eight to twelve hours to make everything tender. The meat, potatoes and vegetables were made ready to assemble so the stew could be ready to eat in minutes. Satchel's contribution was that he'd taken the waxed cartons of broth and added his own spices to provide additional flavor.

"There, just let that simmer fifteen or twenty minutes and we're good to go." Satchel wiped his hands on a towel and took off around the counter to go visit Freddie. "How you doing, mate," he said.

Freddie was sitting down. His knees were drawn up under his chin and his arms wrapped around his legs with his feet on the chair's seat. "I'm hurtin', man. I need something," he said. His jaw was quivering like he was sitting on a block of ice.

"I know mate, I know. You gotta put up with it for the night. Come tomorrow we'll get you in detox."

Freddie looked at him, his eyes watery and vacuous as sinkholes filled with rain. "I'm not going to make it."

Satchel placed his hand on Freddie's shoulder squeezing it reassuringly. The rotator cuff under his skin felt like a golf ball. "Just hang in there. You'll do fine."

From the stage, Samuel strummed a few chords, his hand sliding up and down the neck of his instrument. The old Gibson looked hacked, its pegs were tarnished, its lacquer chipped, and the frets were worn almost to the wood, but the music that flowed from its box sounded like it came from another realm. Samuel hummed along for a few seconds then he broke into song, his voice gravelly but smooth, like water gurgling down the drain.

> "Just a closer walk with Thee;
> Grant it, Jesus, is my plea;
> Daily walking close to Thee,
> Let it be, dear Lord, let it be…"

The door at the front of the building flew open. A silhouetted figure squeezed through the men already lined up outside. "We'll be serving in about fifteen minutes," Stan said. The mutters from the crowd tapered off as the door closed again. "Sorry I'm late. I got hung up at the office. Actually, I left the office on time but there was a gaggle of reporters waiting for me outside and I couldn't get by without answering their questions."

Samuel set his guitar down and picked up a pencil which he clamped between his teeth as he shuffled through the notes on his music stand. "I understand why you think you gotta do this, but it sho ain't gonna help us," he said, without looking up.

"Now don't start. I already told you I'm not forsaking the mission." Stan removed his suit jacket, laying it over his arm. He hooked a finger in his collar and undid the button, pulling his tie away from his neck. "About the only time I won't be here is when I'm called out of town. This mission will always be my first priority. Now if you'll excuse me, we'll be serving in about fifteen minutes and I still have to change."

Stan felt a trickle of sweat running down his chest. The fans were working to circulate the air, but it was laden with moisture and hard to push around. They managed to generate a lot of noise but did little to cool the room. Satchel was seated at the table with someone Stan didn't recognize.

"Hey Satchel, dinner about ready?"

Satchel struggled to get up, bumping the table as he scooted his chair back. A saltshaker toppled over leaving a white trail of tiny granules as it rolled. Satchel reached down and with a broad hand swept them off the table. "Yeah, we're good, I got it simmering on the stove but I need to go stir the pot. Freddie, you hang in there."

"Who's this?"

"Yeah, uh, this is Freddie. He's an old mate of mine, from before. Freddie's kinda going through a hard time right now so I'm lookin' after him."

"He's going through withdrawal." Samuel stepped down from the stage and walked over to join the group. "He's got the heebie-jeebies but it ain't too bad. I've made arrangements for him to start rehab tomorrow."

"What about tonight?"

"About that. I can't put him with the other men. You know how it is, it's worse with some than others, but long about two or three in the morning he could be climbing the walls. All right by you if we put him up in your changing room? Just for the night."

Over by the kitchen counter one of the servers, Manny, was looking at his watch. His eyes flicked to the door. Stan raised his wrist to check the time. "Look guys, it's time to open up. I still have to change. We'll have to talk about this later."

The room was a cacophony of noise. Voices rumbled, feet stomped, chairs squeaked, silverware clicked and pots and pans clanked as more than a hundred men took part in a feeding frenzy that reminded Satchel of puppies squirming to find their mother's teat. Samuel was on stage singing, but as Satchel looked out over the room he could see no one was paying attention. He'd never listened either, partly because of the noise, but mostly because he hadn't wanted to hear the message the songs were trying to communicate. Too bad. He actually wanted to hear them now.

Samuel swung his guitar down, placing it back in its stand. He reached for his Bible and held it up, its gilded edges shimmering in the glow of the tungsten light. "Now you boys ready to hear from the Lord?"

A few eyes in the crowd lifted from their plates and one man actually scooted his chair back and folded his arms and stretched his legs out in front of him like he was ready to pay attention, but the vast majority just kept swilling their stew. It made Satchel want to go bust a few heads but he held back. Nobody listened to Jesus either.

"How many of you boys know my Jesus?" A few furtive hands went up around the room but they dropped back quickly. "Well I'm gonna tell you about Him. My Jesus was a crazy man. Did you know that? That's right, just plain crazy. I mean, what would you say if I came out here and told you that I was the Way, the Truth, and the Life, that you can't get to Father God except through me. You'd say I was crazy, right. Well, that's what Jesus said, 'I am the Way, the Truth, and the Life,' Crazy right? Just plain crazy. He stood by the tomb of Lazarus and He said, 'I am the Resurrection and the Life, he that believes in Me shall never die,' and then He raised that po' man from the grave. Can I get an amen?"

Satchel was stirring a stainless steel pot with a long handled wooden spoon, his eyes on the crowd but no amens were forthcoming. He glanced to his right. Stan, or Mr. Powers, as most referred to him, was working right alongside pouring one stock pot of stew into another. He worked with a limp, like a former street person, or someone born with a handicap, but Satchel figured him to be high on the organization's food chain because all matters of importance were referred to him, yet he wielded a knife, broom and pot-scrubber just like everyone else. His fresh change of clothes, denims, tennis shoes, and a camouflage T-shirt, were covered with a white apron that was now stained with broth. He put the shiny, chrome-like barrel down and wiped his hands on the apron looking over at Satchel as he smiled, but Satchel turned away. Toward the back of the room Freddie was wrapped in his arms, pacing back and forth.

"My Lord Jesus said, 'He that believes in Me, though he were dead, yet shall he live'. Some of you boys out there are dead already. You just don't know it. But Christ said I have come to give you life. And not just in heaven, neither, un uh, but here on earth. He said He came to give you life more abundantly. Can I get an amen?"

Old Samuel was preaching up a storm, his black head looking like a charcoaled matchstick. He tromped around on the stage flailing his Bible, waving it high, the gravel in his voice pouring out like peals of thunder.

"But brothers you've got to do something to get this life. You've got to acknowledge that you need it, that you're sorry for all the wrongs you've done and that you can't make it on your own. Then you've got to ask for it. Christ gives it freely to anyone who asks. He said, 'he that cometh to me, I will in no wise cast out', but you've got to come. I'm asking you to do that right now. Christ said, 'come to me all you who are weary and heavy laden and I will give you rest.' That's rest from all your problems, brothers. You got problems with alcohol? Leave 'em at the feet of Jesus. You got problems with drugs? Leave 'em at the cross. You come down here right now, come right down to the stage and bow down and kneel before Jesus. You ask God to forgive you and He will! And you trade that body of death for a new body full of life and not just life now, but life forever in heaven. Glory to Jesus!"

Satchel had the strangest feeling, like iron particles caught in the field of a magnet, he felt an urge to go fall on his face before God and beg forgiveness, but he looked around the room and no one else was moving. He didn't want to be the only one. Hadn't he already done it the other night in his bedroom? Wasn't that enough? Why make a public spectacle of himself? He turned around and carried his pot of stew over to the vat and poured in the remainder. They would save it for another night. He carried his pot to the kitchen and, leaving it for the dishwashers to take care of, went back to his place at the counter.

"Come on brothers, this could be your last chance. You might die tonight. What are you waiting for?" But the words were lost on the crowd. Several men got up and made their way outside pulling their cigarettes from their pockets before they reached the door, while others continued to shovel food into their mouths without lifting their eyes to Samuel.

"Jesus is calling you right now, and if you say no, he might not ask again. Come on now, get up out of your chair and come down here and receive Jesus…"

Samuel's gaze froze, his face showing an element of surprise. His mouth formed an O as his hand jutted out with his fingers curling in toward himself. "That's it, brother, that's right, you come on down."

Satchel's eyes followed Samuel's to the back of the room where he caught a flicker of movement. A wraith soul staggered forward. Light was glittering off the tears streaming down his cheeks. He stumbled through the tables and chairs with men shrinking back out of his way. At the foot of the stage he crashed to his knees, burying his face in his hands. Samuel knelt down beside the willowy figure, placing a big arm across his back as the man began to sob. Satchel couldn't believe what he was seeing.

It was Freddie.

Eight

THE SERVICE concluded without fanfare. Men rose silently from their places and gathered their paper plates and napkins, their chairs screeching on the floor as they made their way to the exit. A rapidly filling plastic tub stood by the door to collect their trash, though there was probably as much on the floor as in the bin. Satchel caught the sour smell of each man as he passed by, the sweat trapped in their glands after several days, or even weeks, without a shower. Bishop Samuel stayed at the front with Freddie. They remained hunched over like two mushrooms growing through the floor. Samuel was whispering quietly to Freddie as Freddie's shoulders continued to heave.

Satchel remained in the kitchen. He had his duties to perform, the leftover stew had to be put in the refrigerator, the bowls emptied and the counters wiped down. Two men wandered through the tables tossing the remaining paper plates and cups into trash cans lined with black plastic bags. A third man went around filling salt and pepper shakers, and straightening tables and chairs. Satchel wanted to hear what the preacher was saying to Freddie, there might be something he needed to know, but he didn't want to intrude. Freddie might be getting some things off his chest that were personal.

Steam rose from the kitchen where the men scrubbed pots and pans. Someone tossed a towel at Satchel and said, "Don't just stand there, help dry." Satchel started to say something about his being the cook and how it wasn't his job, but he saw Mr. Powers mopping the floor and thought better of it. He walked over and picked up a large stainless steel vat and began wiping it inside. He stepped two feet to the right to get a better view of the preacher and Freddie, but just as he did, they both turned their heads to look at him. He turned away ignoring their gaze.

The last diner left the building around eight o'clock. Stan set his mop aside and went to lock the door. He flicked off the lights and killed the fans in the dining hall. The men in the kitchen finished putting things in the cabinets and polishing the stainless steel counters and Satchel took the last pan from the drainer, wiped it dry, and put it away.

Satchel felt a hand on his shoulder. He turned and saw Davis staring at him with a clamshell smile stuck to his face. The man was always smiling and, though Satchel was at a loss to explain why, it irritated the bejesus out of him. "Hey Davis, what's up?"

"Several of us are going upstairs to have a Bible study. Want to join us?"

Satchel dried his hands and tossed his towel into a laundry basket. "Sorry mate, I'd love to, but some other time." He tipped his head toward Freddie. "That boy over there is going through a hard time. I think he's going to need me tonight."

Davis wiped a hand across his mouth and brought it down to stroke his beard. "Yeah, look at that. That's so cool. What's the dude's name?"

"Freddie."

"Right, well, tell your friend, Freddie, the boys and I will be praying for him." Several of the other staffers were already clomping up the stairs. Davis patted Satchel's shoulder, "We'll be praying for you, too." Then he went and joined the others with his boots hammering the wood.

Earlier Satchel had seen Stan make his way up the stairs, but now he came back down, favoring one leg over the other, dressed in his suit again. He walked over to Samuel and with his coat laid over his arm leaned down to say something in his ear.

The room was sweltering. Satchel swept his hand across his head, his thin hair feeling wet to the touch. He didn't think it had been any cooler when the fans were going, but it certainly seemed warmer now. A bead of perspiration dropped off his nose falling onto his shoe.

Stan straightened himself and headed for the door, letting himself out. Samuel's eyes came up and met Satchel's. He gave a light tip of his head indicating that Satchel should join them. The room was in shadows, the only light coming from the stairwell. They were the last ones in the room. Satchel made his way over, bumping through the tables. He scooted a chair out and started to sit down but Samuel was already beginning to stand, bringing Freddie up by the hand. His white goatee stood out like cotton pasted to black construction paper. "Let's get Freddie upstairs and squared away," he said. "This could be a long night."

Satchel had to practically carry Freddie up the stairs, but it was no effort. Freddie felt like a stick figure carved from balsa wood.

Bishop Samuel had his key out unlocking the door. He threw it open and stepped aside so they could enter.

The room was small; no more than ten-by-ten in size, with what looked to be an old army cot along one wall. There was a dresser sitting under a window devoid of curtains. The view looked down on the alley below. The closet couldn't have held more than a few suits of clothes.

"We call this the prophet's chamber. It was originally meant to be used by guest speakers when they came to visit, but we haven't had any of those in a long time so now it's mostly used by Mr. Powers. He has his own place in the suburbs but sometimes when the meetings go late he stays overnight, and then he has to have somewhere to change and get ready for work in the morning.

"He the one that owns all this?"

Samuel frowned. His white eyebrows scrunched in, squinting. His hand came up to grab his cross. "Nobody owns this place, except the Lord." His voice sounded like he was chewing on rocks. "We have a Board of Directors that oversees our operation and we're supported by a number of local churches that give us money to help feed the poor, but this is God's work. Stan's church is very involved, and he himself is a big contributor, both of time and money, which is why he's here most every night, but we're an independent mission."

Satchel still had his arm around Freddie, but the boy was shivering. He saw a folded blanket on the edge of the cot. He picked it up and unfolded it, and draped it over Freddie's shoulders. "What do you mean, 'Stan's church?' I thought you and Stan's church was the same?"

"Good lawdy no. I preach over at the Holiness Church on the south side. Ours is primarily a black congregation. When I preach people get excited. It's nothing like what you seen here tonight. I got people jumping up and down shoutin', 'Praise the Lord' and 'Praise God' and the 'Amens' roll like thunder, but not everyone can handle preachin' like that. Stan, he's a Baptist, and Baptists are generally more sedate." He winked and said, "We call 'em pewsitters 'cause they like sittin' in the pew nice and orderly without saying much. Only the preacher talks and he speaks quietly, in kinda hushed tones. They're a bit boring for my taste, but that don't mean we don't both read the same Bible and worship the same God."

Satchel walked Freddie over and sat down beside him on the edge of the cot. "How you doing mate? You okay?"

Freddie looked up, his eyes empty as tin cans. "I hurt," he said.

"Where does it hurt?"

"Freddie continued shivering in spite of the blanket. He was looking straight ahead but didn't appear to see anything. "Everywhere. It feels like someone's flayed my skin open and is

107

using pliers to squeeze my bones." His shoulders started to quake and his chest to heave. He pushed down on the mattress and tried to stand, "Sorry, I need a bathroo…" He tried to bring a hand to his mouth but it was too late. The surging from his stomach swelled and ejected onto the floor. He stood with his hands on his knees his head dangling between his legs, drooling. He wiped his mouth with the back of his hand. "Sorry I…I shouldn't have ate."

Satchel looked up to find Samuel but he was already gone. He returned a few seconds later with a mop and metal bucket on wheels and began cleaning the mess. "Don't you feel bad about a thing, Freddie. Ain't nothing we ain't seen before."

Freddie tried to nod but upchucked again his drool dripping into the pool of vomit "I hate this," he said.

"Don't worry about it. It's just your body wants more dope, but we're not going to give it any, are we?"

Freddie's stomach continued heaving but there was nothing left to expel. Samuel just kept cleaning, sweeping the wet mop back and forth and rinsing it in the bucket of water until the floor was clean. Then he disappeared again. The wheels of the metal bucket could be heard clacking down the hall. When he returned, he held a glass of water in his hand. He held it out to Freddie. "Here," he said, "take a drink."

Freddie took a sip but handed the glass back shaking his head. Samuel set it on the dresser and helped Freddie ease back down onto the bed. There wasn't a chair in the room. Satchel wondered if Samuel tried to sit on the cot whether it would be strong enough to support the three of them.

Samuel got down on his knees and put his arm around Freddie pulling him in close like a child. "Freddie you gave your heart and life to Jesus tonight. You're His problem now. He's going to take care of you; I promise you that. It won't be easy, it never is, but we're gonna trust and pray and I know my God is going to give you the strength you need." Samuel brought his head back to gaze at

Satchel. His eyes were white and veined like marble. It looked like they were pleading. "What about you, Satchel?" he said.

"Me? What about me?"

"Freddie thinks you're an angel."

"What?"

"You know, a huge being, usually with a sword, sent by God to communicate a message."

"Bishop, I've been called a whole lot of things, but no one's ever called me an angel."

"Well that's what Freddie said. He thinks you're the real McCoy. He said when you were standing over him you had this glow surrounding you and he heard God say, 'Go', and he said he knew he had to go with you or he was gonna die. That's why he let you bring him here, and why he came forward tonight. So, if you're not an angel, what are you?"

"Excuse me? I'm not sure what you mean. I'm nothin', preacher, I'm nothin'."

"Exactly. You're just a mortal soul in need of salvation, just like the rest of us. Freddie has given his heart to Jesus. He's a child of God now, and God's gonna to take care of him. But I haven't heard you say you've taken that step. You want to help Freddie, that's good, but Freddie really needs God's help, and so do you."

Satchel's lips puckered in a pout. He folded his arms over his chest and leaned forward, staring at his feet. He shook his head. "I don't know how all this stuff works, Bishop. I kind of did something the other night, but to tell the truth, I don't know exactly what it was. The other guys in the room were praying, and I told God if he gave me a reason to believe, like if He could show me how to control my anger, I'd give it a shot and see what happens. And He did, too. At least I think He did.

Samuel placed a hand on Satchel's knee. "You know, we don't all say the same prayer the same way, but God knows our heart. If you asked for God's help, then you admitted that you can't do it on your own. That's what God wants to hear. He hates our pride. He hates it when we think we've got it all figured out, or think we can do it our own way and don't need His help. But you're not like that, you cried out to Him. The Bible says, 'they that call upon the name of the Lord shall be saved.' Now, the name of the Lord is Jesus. You gotta come through Jesus. Did you do that Satchel? Jesus said, 'I am the way, the truth, and the life, no one comes to the father but by Me.' You heard me preach that tonight. You gotta go through Jesus. Once you do that, as surely as you're bound to this planet right now, you'll be kingdom bound when you die. Did you do that Satchel? 'Cause it's important that you do it in Jesus name."

Satchel didn't look up, but nodded in affirmation.

"Glory to God. Thank you Jesus!" Samuel raised his hand and stood, the smell of vomit still saturating the air. Someone was tapping on the door. He went to answer it. It was Davis wearing a smile big as a half moon.

"Hey bishop, *uh*, us guys were praying in the other room and, well, we all felt like the Holy Spirit was telling us we should be in here praying with you. Okay if we come in?"

Samuel took hold of Davis' arm, pulling him inside. "You know better than to ask. Get in here."

Five men filed into the room. Satchel recognized all of them as workers he'd seen in the kitchen, men with beards and tattoos and greasy hair that looked like they'd be more at home on a motorcycle that in a church. Satchel stood and so did Freddie. The men began laying hands on their shoulders, heads, and backs, anywhere they could reach out and let them feel their touch.

Samuel raised his hand. "Glory to God! Glory to God! Give God the glory! Amen! Amen! Amen!"

To say the rest of the night passed without incident would be a distortion of fact. Freddie still had the shakes, still had the urge to vomit, still had a deep aching in his bones, but now he had a group of men willing to work with him to see he made it through the dark hours unscathed. No one mentioned the putrid smell. Freddie was thankful for that. Thankful too that no one seemed to think his heebie-jeebies were anything more than something he had to work through. He couldn't sleep, no matter how hard he tried, and the men couldn't stay up all night, so they established a schedule with each man volunteering to spend one hour with Freddie. They stood by his side, when necessary walking him around in circles, at times sitting with him to talk things out, and always praying without ceasing. Satchel and Samuel were the only ones who never left the room. Each of the other men after completing their shift went back to their beds to catch a few hours sleep. Freddie was exhausted but he must have had toothpicks propping his eyes open. He simply couldn't get them shut.

They had brought up several pots of coffee from the kitchen along with muffins, granola bars, and other snacks. By the time light began filtering through the window Satchel was enjoying a buzz. His eyes felt strained and itchy, and he had to stretch to ease the tiredness in his back, but he was fully awake. As the sun came up and light filled the room they received word that someone in the kitchen was making them breakfast. They helped Freddie downstairs and into a chair and passed him a bowl of cream of wheat. For Freddie, bland was the special of the day. No one wanted to see his stomach become active again. Satchel piled bacon on his plate along with three eggs, three slices of toast and two pan-size waffles.

Samuel had disappeared to go take a shower, but he was out now wearing blue denim jeans, his alligator boots and a white shirt. The shirt matched the color of his small goatee. He sat down in front of Satchel holding a cup of coffee with steam rising from the brim. "I just got off the phone with the opioid treatment facility. They say we can bring Freddie over anytime, so as soon as you're finished eating I'll bring the car around." Satchel took a sip of his coffee and nodded. There were only two others in the kitchen. Most of the men had elected to sleep in, but the five of them joined hands before leaving and prayed that the detox would be a success.

Satchel helped Freddie out the front door and found Samuel waiting in the car. It was a white 1960 Cadillac Eldorado convertible with the top down. A once swanky model, it had wire wheels, whitewall tires, and fins large enough for a sailboat. Had it been in good condition it might have been worth some serious coin, but the metal was fringed with rust, the paint oxidized and the tailpipe was spitting blue smoke. When Samuel hit the gas, which he did every so often to keep the engine from stalling, the whole thing rumbled like a speedboat.

Satchel put Freddie in front on a cracked leather seat with the wadding showing through. He got in the back on the driver's side. Samuel sped away spinning up dirt from the curb. It was one of those days when it felt good to be alive. The sun dominated the sky, daring the clouds to take purchase in its dominion. The breeze combing through Satchel's hair smelled sweet as the buds of an evergreen, and the warmth that splayed across his arms bore witness to a life, or perhaps a spirit, that had been reborn. He had never felt so free—not because he was outside the prison—it was a freedom he felt on the inside. Something had released his soul to take flight. He lay his head back and looked up into a blue cloudless day. *Absolutely cracking.* He wondered if his mate, Freddie, was getting this. He had experienced the same spiritual awakening but somehow he still seemed bound. His eyes looked straight ahead but they weren't blinking and his face was void of expression. It might be a week or more before Satchel could judge whether or not Freddie had actually returned from the grave.

Samuel's arm was hanging out the window, his white shirt tousled by the slipstream of the car shone brightly in the sun. The air resounded with his vocal cords bellowing at full strength.

"All hail the power of Jesus' name,
Let angels prostrate fall.
Bring forth the royal diadem,
And crown Him Lord of all," he sang.

Something welled in Satchel's chest making him want to sing too, but he didn't know how.

They were traveling through neighborhoods Satchel was familiar with, but the further they went, the more the scenery changed. It was obvious they were heading deep into the south side of Chicago, a place he usually avoided because the crime rates were so high. He felt apprehensive. The Chicago papers were full of stories about innocent bystanders being shot by gang members in a turf war. They drove block after block where his and Freddie's were the only white faces he saw.

"Let every kindred, every tribe,
On this terrestrial ball,
To Him all majesty ascribe
And crown Him Lord of all."

Samuel's voice boomed off the walls with the message that all men were brothers. Every kindred and every tribe were one in the body of Christ.

Satchel could dig that. If the Bloods and the Crips were to face-off and start shooting at each other and Satchel was taken in the crossfire, so what? They couldn't kill him. He was heaven bound. *Smashing that!* Oh, what a glorious day.

The boat motored down streets where the buildings were covered in graffiti and had metal bars over their windows. Dust and rubbish lined the curb. Alleys were swollen with stained mattresses and toppled shopping carts. A kid with a baseball cap sitting backward on his head, and jeans so low the cuffs were frazzled from being dragged on the ground, stood on the sidewalk by a stack of used tires probably pinched from a car. He was holding a sign made from a cardboard box and written in felt pen that read, "$25/esh are all for for $75." Satchel doubted he was really selling tires. He probably had drugs stuffed in the rims.

Samuel pulled to the curb in front of what Satchel hoped would be a hospital but instead looked more like an abandoned store. A paper sign, curled and yellowed by the sun, was taped inside the front window. "Opioid Treatment Center," it read, and below that, "Free Clinic."

Samuel swung his door open and planted an alligator boot on the road. "This is it," he said. He stepped out, his three inch cross sparkling in the sun.

Satchel pulled himself from the car and hiked around the nineteen-foot long vehicle to collect Freddie. He popped the button and heard the hinges creak as he pulled the handle back. The three foot wide door scraped the sidewalk as it opened. He got Freddie out and standing, then took his arm to steady him. Samuel came up taking Freddie's other arm, and they escorted him inside. The reception area was neat but the carpet was worn. Dirt ground into the pile apparently defied steam cleaning. The walls, with their orange-peel texture, were flaky and in desperate need of paint. A black woman with an ochre-colored Nairobi cap sat behind a bulletproof sheet of glass. She slipped a few forms underneath a gap at the window's base. "You'll need to fill these out," she said, her voice muffled behind the thick glass. "And we'll need to see some identification for insurance purposes.

"We don't have insurance."

"No, I mean our insurance, in case something goes wrong."

Samuel sat down beside Freddie and began filling out the paperwork, but most of the questions were about the patient's medical history and Freddie didn't have one. He didn't have an address or phone number or a regular doctor to contact in case of an emergency. He didn't know if he had an appendix or not, whether he had high or low blood pressure, or a heart condition, he only knew he was still alive and the rest didn't matter because it had nothing to do with his drug addiction. Samuel did his best and made sure Freddie signed the wavier absolving the clinic of any and all malpractice. He ended up passing the papers back through the window with more blanks than lines filled in.

"Thank you," said the lady in the burnt-orange hat. Her multicolored blouse had poufy shoulders that ballooned out from her portly frame, and her large hoop earrings swung back and forth when she turned her head. "Just have a seat and someone will come and get you." She reached out her hand to retrieve the papers, a dozen silver and copper bangles dangling from her wrist.

Satchel picked up a magazine and began flipping through the articles, then leaned over and nudged Samuel's shoulder.

"Look preacher, if you gotta take off, I don't mind. I mean you got your church to take care of. I can get Freddie checked in and walk back from here. It's no big deal." He paused and thought about what he'd just said and how it would mean walking several blocks through neighborhoods he was unfamiliar with, among a strata of people he didn't completely trust and realized he didn't care. Whether he lived or died didn't matter anymore, though he would like to see Rachel, so maybe there was a good reason for staying alive.

"No sir. The Lord has put this boy's soul into my hands and I aim to see it through. 'Sides, mine's a small church; only about fifty people. I'm not a full-time pastor. I prepare my sermons on Saturday, and give them on Sunday and the rest of the week I'm free to work at the mission. And that's the way I like it."

A door opened and another black lady beckoned them inside. "Please come on back gentlemen, we're ready for you now." She wore a red suit with matching red lipstick and a uniform pair of red pumps. Her blouse was white, accented with a string of red beads. Her glossy black hair looked like it had been ironed flat and curled under her chin. A row of bangs hung down to just above her eyebrows. She held the door wide, admitting them into the back of the office, but when she closed the door she locked it behind them. "Just for security," she said. "The sign on the door says we're an opiate treatment center so people think we keep drugs here. We don't, but that doesn't stop anyone. Once they think you have drugs, they'll come at you any way they can. We have to keep things buttoned down pretty tight. I take it you already met Akira at the front desk. My name's Jennifer Mitchell," she said, holding out a hand with fingernails painted the same color as her dress.

Satchel took the hand and reciprocated. "Satchel Carter," he said.

Samuel kept his hands folded in front of him and smiled broadly. "You already know my name, Miss. Jennifer, but this one is Freddie," he said, patting Freddie on the shoulder. He's the patient. I don't believe I know Freddie's last name."

Satchel shook his head. "Me neither. That's how it is on the street, no last names."

Freddie remained silent, either unwilling or unable to volunteer the information.

Jennifer smiled, then turned and led them down the hall into a small room with a table and four chairs. "Please have a seat," she said. "I just need to go over the process with you so everyone understands what to expect. Our purpose here is to get the drugs out of Freddie's system. It's a process called detoxification." She picked up a dry marker and went to a whiteboard, drawing a profile of a man's head. "The human brain is full of receptors." She drew a bouncy line in a circle to resemble a man's brain and filled it with dots to illustrate the receptors. "Now normal healthy endorphins attach themselves to these receptors," she began drawing circles around the dots, "and these endorphins give us energy and make us feel good. The problem is when you take opioids you overload these receptors with huge quantities of artificial endorphins." She circled the small circles with even bigger circles, "giving you a surplus of good feelings. You enter a state of bliss like nothing you've ever felt before. And as your brain acclimates to this feeling it wants more, but because you've been feeding yourself artificial endorphins your natural supply has stopped being produced, so when you come off your high you're left with no endorphins at all, and subsequently can't feel good until you take more drugs. It's a downward spiral because the more drugs you take the more your brain craves the feel-good feeling which means you have to take more and more opioids to get the same high."

She snapped on the cap of her dry marker and used it to tap the table, making sure she had their attention. "Another problem is that because they're attached to your receptors the opioids stay in your system. The first three or four days after you stop taking them you don't notice much difference because the residual opioids are helping you maintain a mild feel-good sensation. But after a few days this sensation wears off and the longer you go without replenishing your endorphins the more critical your need becomes and pretty soon you find yourself in a pit you can't crawl out of.

"This is where you have to be strong, Freddie. A lot is up to you. All too often people leave after the fifth or sixth day without completing the program. They can't handle the lack of endorphins. They feel like they have to do something to get them replenished so they leave and a few days later the police show up asking questions. Then we hear stories about how they broke into a house and stole a TV, or prostituted themselves because they had to do something, anything at all, to fix the bad feeling."

She looked straight at Freddie. "I want you to know this upfront because we're here to help, but much depends on you. We have a very high success rate with those who want to become drug-free. Is that what you want? Because if you don't there's no point in even starting the program."

Freddie glanced up, the drooping folds of flesh under his eyes looking like raw meat. He nodded.

"Good. Now I'm given to understand you've already been off heroin for several days. That makes our job easier because you're at the point where the craving usually becomes unbearable and yet you're here instead of on the street trying to find a fix. By now your body is probably feeling a lot of discomfort. We can help with that by giving you naltrexone, just a small dose, but it stimulates the good feeling your body craves and helps us bring you down gradually. I would estimate that in another five to seven days your body should be completely cleansed of opioids."

She looked at Samuel, then at Satchel, and then at Freddie again. "But that's just the start. You can walk out of here drug-free but that doesn't mean you're cured. There's an old cliché, once an addict, always an addict. There will always be that something in your brain that cries out for the feel-good feeling you once craved. You'll have to fight it every day for the rest of your life. You'll need to get counseling to keep you from having a relapse. We'll put you in touch with several groups that work like the AA to give you support."

She placed her dry marker on the table and looked from Satchel to Samuel again. "Gentlemen, thank you for getting involved. I'm sure Freddie appreciates all you've done, but we'll need to take it from here. If you want, you can schedule visits, but for the most part we want Freddie to concentrate on getting better, and frankly sometimes having friends and family around can be a distraction."

Samuel looked at Satchel, his large white eyes acknowledging that they were being dismissed. Samuel thanked Mrs. Mitchell and gave her a shoulder hug, then placed his hands on Freddie's head. "God, this child is yours now. You gotta take care of him. I'm not telling you what to do, you know what needs done better than I, but I am asking you to show some mercy and grace and bring this boy back to us with his body made as clean as you made his spirit last night. In Jesus name, Amen!" He turned, dropping his big hands to Freddie's shoulders looking him straight in the eye. "Go with God, Freddie, go with God and He'll go with you."

They watched as Jennifer took Freddie's arm and led him down the hall, then they turned to take their leave, bounding outside into a glorious day.

Jennifer showed Freddie to a small apartment. It was furnished with a bed and a table with one folding chair. A second chair with padding and wraparound arms sat in the corner facing a small TV that was mounted high on the wall. The remote was on the table. Freddie peeked into the bathroom and saw a thirty-six inch shower, a commode with rust stains around the bolts, and a single sink, also stained with rust where iron-rich water had dripped from the faucet.

"This will be your home for the next five to seven days," she said. "We have a small library of books and magazines down the hall. You can bring them back to your room, or you can watch TV. Meals are served at eight, noon and five o'clock. Following each meal you're required to attend a group session with one of our counselors. This is an open forum where we encourage participants to discuss any issues or problems they may be having." She looked at her watch, "Lunch isn't for another few hours, but I expect you to be there and I want you to attend the session afterward. You need to start meeting some of our other guests. Sometimes finding a friend to encourage you makes all the difference. We also have two full-time counselors on call twenty-four seven who can come and visit anytime you need someone to talk to.

"Since you were brought here by Bishop Samuel, I assume you're affiliated with the Holiness Church. We have a full-time chaplain on staff as well as volunteers who will come and pray with you at your request. If the pain becomes unbearable please press that button," she pointed to a device mounted on the wall over by the bed, "and a nurse's assistant will come and see what we can do to help. It takes as much as ten days to get the drugs completely washed out of a system, but you've already been without heroin for a few days so with you it should take less. If you stay with the program and make it to the finish, when you leave you'll be clean. Then it's up to you whether or not you stay that way."

Nine

RACHEL FELT like she was walking on a sponge, each footstep sinking into the lush carpeting. Everything smelled new, like the interior of a new car, or the way it smells when you sit on a piece of new furniture. The boardroom table, an immaculate slab a rich red wood, shone under the bell shaped lampshades of three fluorescent bulbs that hung by cords from the twelve foot ceiling. The windows were wall-to-wall. She wanted to step up and take a look at the city below, but she didn't dare. She didn't want to draw attention to herself. From where she stood she could see only sky. The wall opposite the window was taken up by an eight foot mural showing farm laborers working in the field, smiling as they plucked grains and fruits from miles of rolling hills with a cityscape of tall towers looming on the distant horizon.

Rachel raised her eyebrows as she moved around the table. She had to bear in mind that this wasn't just Charlotte's campaign headquarters, this was where the congresswoman worked year-round. She probably had to entertain heads of state and needed nice furniture and art to make a good impression.

Rachel glanced at her watch. She had time to spare. She'd given herself two hours to get there, instead of one, and had arrived forty-five minutes early. It had given her time to grab a latte from a nearby Starbucks and wander around the lobby enjoying the architecture and cultured plants.

She had waited until fifteen minutes before the meeting was scheduled to start before going upstairs. She didn't want to seem too anxious, nor have any chance of being late. She'd been ushered in and found a half-dozen other people already seated around the table. She shook her head discretely. How long had they been there? She hadn't seen any of them making their way through the lobby, though she'd watched. She wanted to know what arrival time was deemed appropriate by everyone else. Still, the table was only half full. Others would arrive shortly. She wasn't the last.

She placed her briefcase on the floor and, because she'd earned the right of selection, took a chair situated more in the center of the table. She had doffed her business attire for blue jeans and a white V-neck sweatshirt with a huge number 51 silkscreened on the front, and the word, "NORTHWESTERN," printed above in serif caps. Her hair was pulled back in a ponytail and, keeping with the casual motif, she wore flip-flops on her feet.

The standard yellow tablet and pen were positioned neatly in front of her along with a copy of what looked to be an agenda. The items were sitting on mirror images of themselves reflected by the table's high gloss shine. She smiled at her colleagues, nodding without saying anything because she couldn't remember their names. Instead she reached for the agenda and started to read but discovered it wasn't an agenda at all, it was a biography of Mr. Powers: his place and date of birth, where he'd gone to school, his years in the military, his Purple Heart and other accolades, his religious affiliations, with a note that said he might try to fly the morality flag but they had separation of church and state to counter that—*morality flag? Bull! He was one of mom's best customers.* What a clown—his marriage to a woman who died of unspecified causes and the fact that he never remarried. *Yeah, tricking with mom while married, woohoo!* The outline also included the fact that he was currently being sued by a gay couple for refusing their business, (this item was underlined and followed by three exclamation points), and a rather lengthy story about his saving a young black girl during the holdup of a gas station convenience store. She checked the date of the article. Apparently it had happened more than ten years earlier, about the same time he'd murdered dear old mom.

Several other members of the team were ushered in. They took their seats and immediately struck up conversations with their friends. Rachel envied them. It was obvious they'd been around Senator Weise longer than she. While walking through the lobby she had considered how the money spent on such high-end office space might be better spent on feeding the poor. Maybe they were ignoring her because they sensed she wasn't fully on board. One young man cupped his hand around his neighbor's ear and said something secretive, which caused both people to glance at Rachel and burst out giggling.

Charlotte entered the room and took a seat at the head of the table. Her hair was short and disorderly, though Rachel could see it was styled to look that way. She wore a blue business suit with a white blouse that had frills that draped down from her neck in a V. She opened a folio and removed a few sheets of paper which she placed on the table. Then she interlaced her fingers, and with her hands locked together, put them on top of the papers to hold them in place. Her eyes traveled around the table, "Good, I'm glad to see everyone's here," but they stopped when they landed on Rachel. "Ms. Carter, what is that you're wearing?" she asked.

Rachel felt her heart skip and her skin tighten like paper. "Me?" she said pointing to herself. "Jeans and a sweatshirt, why?"

A few chirrups broke from her colleague's faces.

Charlotte rose from her seat and leaned over with her knuckles on the table. "And what does your sweatshirt say?"

Rachel saw others starting to snigger, though it appeared they were trying to hold it back. She looked down her shirt, pulling the material out with her fingers. "It says Northwestern. It's where I go to school."

"Would you say you're proud of your school, Miss Carter?"

"I don't know, I suppose so. I mean I haven't really started yet. I'm waiting for the new semester."

"And why are you proud of your school? Is it because they have a high standard of academic achievement, or because they have a great football team? Or maybe it's the social life?" Charlotte had been pacing, but she turned to look directly at Rachel. "I understand some of those fraternities throw a good party."

Rachel folded her arms and squirmed in her seat, trying to get comfortable. "I'm not sure what you're getting at. Have I done something wrong?"

The Congresswoman shook her head and began to walk around the table with her hands behind her back. "Rachel, I don't care what you wear to these meetings. You want to wear a sweatshirt, go ahead and wear a sweatshirt, fine by me. You want to come topless and express how you're free to not wear a shirt like your male counterparts, that's okay too. But that thing you have on is not just a sweatshirt; it's a symbol of something. That's a football jersey, and football is the one thing I deplore about Northwestern. I went there, you know, it's my alma mater and I think it's a great school, but it focuses too much on football and football communicates all the wrong values. Football is all about competition and that's one thing we need less of, not more. All competition does is give one person the ability to say they're better than someone else. How are we going to demonstrate the equality of all mankind when we take a bunch of jocks out onto a football field and have them beat each other up to prove one group's superiority over the other? It's a disgusting game, one that subliminally infers that men are superior to women because women are," she brought her fingers up and made air quotes, 'too weak' to play such a game. And it teaches that violence is the way to get ahead; just push everyone else aside and run over people and you'll reach your goal. I won't have it, and I ask you kindly not to wear your football jersey in this office again." She looked around the table. "Don't you laugh. You've all been through this before. Every year we find someone who doesn't know my feelings on this. And Rachel, since you're new, I'm going to overlook it this time, just as I did your tardiness last week, but that's two strikes, let's not make it three."

"Yes ma'am," Rachel said. She felt deflated. She'd only wanted to fit in. It was like someone had burst the balloon of her good intentions, spewing them into an atmosphere of ill will.

Charlotte went back to the head of the table and took her seat. "Now let's get down to business. Each of you has in front of you as much information as we've been able to gather on Mr. Powers, and I think it's going to be a slam dunk." She brought her fingers to her lips covering her mouth. "Oops, did I just slip and use a sports analogy…"

There was a flurry of laughter around the table.

"Now, in case some of you haven't heard, Mr. Powers has accepted our invitation to have a debate, which is why I asked you all to come back on such short notice. The date is set for next week so we don't have much time to analyze his weaknesses and develop a strategy. I want to thank Jonathan for coming up with the idea. Sorry, I know you thought we should do it sooner, but we had to schedule the airtime and that's the earliest the station could squeeze us in. My call blindsided him though, caught him totally off guard. I doubt he'll have time to prepare, so thank you Jonathan." She put her hands together applauding softly, and the rest of the group joined in.

"I also need to compliment our intelligence team for what they've come up with. Apparently our Mr. Powers isn't much on social media so we couldn't find anything really nasty to use against him, but as you scan this document, I think you'll see there's enough. And don't let this thing about his being a Navy SEAL dishearten you. I know there's a certain demographic that finds patriotism attractive, but they're a small group. Nationalism is a thing of the past. The world is tired of one nation bragging about how much better they are than everyone else. 'My button is bigger than your button.' Give me a break. We've done a ton of polling in this area and one thing comes through loud and clear. People are tired of guns and war. The world wants peace and it's up to us who have studied and learned and possess the gift of intelligence, to give it to them. We're going to paint Mr. Powers as fearful and ignorant. We'll portray him as a hawk with his finger on the button. A man who's only claim to fame is that he's killed a whole boatload of innocent human beings. Our position will be that the world is changing and we're in the forefront leading the way to lasting peace. Mr. Powers is about to walk into a firestorm that will make his time in Iraq seem like a walk in the park."

Stan had arrived at the office just as the sun was cresting the horizon. The sky was translucent and yellow as a lollipop held up to the light. He carried his coat with him, not wanting to wear it because of the heat, but knowing he might get called into a meeting and need it later.

He had let himself in, made a pot of coffee, and gone back to his office to read the newspaper, closing the door behind him. There would be a nonstop trickle of people knocking on his door the minute they found out he was there. He wanted to enjoy his self-time for as long possible. He could hear them now, the phones ringing, the copy machines whirring, the low drone of conversation, but he wasn't ready to face them yet. By now they would have come up with a whole new list of reasons why he should bow out of the race, not the least of which was that they all loved Charlotte Weise. He wasn't ready to defend his position yet.

He rubbed his eye with a knuckle and yawned. Sleep had eluded him again, which was becoming a habit, only this time he'd refused to get out of bed. He'd done that once before and look where it got him. The house had sagged and groaned like an old man with sore bones, keeping him awake. That's what he liked about his cell phone, he could turn it off. A constant barrage of reporters trying to get a scoop would only have added to his insomnia. Unfortunately, the same didn't hold true for the phone on his desk which was blinking red when he arrived. He'd made the mistake of pushing the button and found more than a dozen requests for interviews. The Chicago Sun-Times, the Tribune, the Defender, the Crusader, the Reader, and Newcity, all wanted to tell his story. Conservative talk radio WIND and WCPT progressive talk wanted him live on air and all three network affiliates wanted to know where he would be appearing next. It only stopped when his answering machine's cache got full and couldn't take anymore messages. *Lord, what have I got myself into?*

He rotated in his chair, swiveling around to face the window. The sky was now a pale yellow, more like vanilla pudding. He'd slipped into his coat because the air conditioning unit was keeping the office on the cool side. He got up and went to the window, folding his hands behind his back. A few seagulls circled the building across the street while pigeons nested on cement ledges and swallows darted in and out of their mud domes on the roof. The cars below were in their usual commuter logjam piling up at the light. Dozens of pedestrians scurried from one side of the street to the other before the light could change. He knew there was no real chance of it happening, but what if he won? Would he be able to govern so many people with so many different points of view? You can't please all the people all of the time. And if elections were won by the candidate who offered the most freebies then they'd be sorely disappointed in what he had to offer. He was wasting his time.

He turned around, acknowledging a knock at his door. Nothing lasts forever—especially peace. "Come in," he said.

His receptionist stuck her head in. "Oh, I'm glad to see you're here. I didn't know." The scent of her Obsession perfume floated through the air. He shouldn't be able to smell it from where he stood but he wasn't about to tell her that. She thought it made her sexy.

She opened the door wider. A man in a brown shirt stood behind her. She stepped to the side allowing him to enter. "You got a letter. I asked the courier to leave it with me but he says it's registered and you need to sign for it."

"Sure, I'll take it."

The man entered the room holding a large bubble envelope. He held it out to Stan. The warm weather had him wearing a summer version of his brown uniform, shorts and a short-sleeved shirt emblazoned with the familiar gold UPS logo. His kinky blond hair was down to his chin and he maintained a full beard and had a tattoo inked on his neck of a shield with crossed rifles that said, "Field of Valor, Iraq 2003." Stan tried not to notice the prostheses located where his foot should have been. He took the letter, signed the digital signature panel and handed it back. "Thank you for your service," he said.

The man tipped his head, turned around and saw the bullet riddled flag hanging on the wall. He paused for a second, saluted the flag, and turned back to say, "And thank you for yours."

Stan nodded and began opening the letter as the man made his exit. He pulled a sheet of paper from the envelope, scanning it quickly.

"Anything important?"

Stan shook his head. "It's information about our trial; date, place and time. My lawyer informed me about this already but I guess this is the official notice." He folded the letter again and smacked it against his palm and tossed it in a drawer.

"You want me to close the door?"

"No, that's fine, leave it open."

"You've got a few reporters hanging around outside. Do you want to see them?"

Stan grimaced, raising his eyebrows in exasperation. He folded his arms across his chest. "No, not right now. You'd think they'd get the idea that this is a place of business, not politics. We have work to do." He turned back toward his desk, signaling to the receptionist that he was through, but as he did his eyes went to the flag. "Wait!"

The receptionist spun around, leaning against the door with her hand on the knob.

"How many did you say there were?"

"I don't know. I didn't count, maybe five or six."

Stan puckered his lip and nodded. "I guess that's not too many. Show them into the boardroom."

Stan waited in his office while the group was being seated. He wasn't sure he was doing the right thing, but if he didn't say something they would likely continue camping in the hall and that wouldn't be good for business. Giving interviews was part of politics. Might as well get a few done all at once.

He entered the room to find five people, three men and two ladies, seated around the table. Two were ethnic, a black man and an Indian woman, which might make some of what he had to say difficult. It was so easy to be misunderstood. They busied themselves setting up their recording devices and tablets. He waited until he had their full attention and then said: "Mind if we dispense with the introductions? You all know who I am and I'm sure I'll get to know each of you over time, but for now if you could just leave your business cards with my assistant that would be great. I'll have to be short because this is my place of business and we have clients coming and going all the time. I'm here to work, not start a campaign. I know you have a lot of questions, I respect that, but I'd rather not answer them right now. I just thought I'd invite you in to let you know a little about what you can expect from me."

The Indian woman, wearing a bright yellow business suit with a coiffure of short black hair, raised her hand. "Just one question before you start, please," the audacity of which brought a few chuckles from her peers, "I need to know, please, how you spell your name? We would not want this to be wrong, am I right?"

Stan joined in the mirth, the corners of his mouth curling into a smile. "That's Stan, S-T-A-N, Powers, P-O-W-E-R-S."

The woman used her tablet to write it down. "Thank you."

Stan nodded and began to pace while doing his best to keep his leg straight and hide his limp. He turned and let his eyes come to rest on each person seated around the table for just a second. "I suppose you're all wondering why I've decided to get into politics. I guess the best explanation is this. I just had a young man in here. You probably saw him leave; you would've noticed because he was missing a foot. A good man who's not letting life's difficulties get in his way. He's got a job, he's working, he's not sitting around complaining about how unfair life is. The man's a patriot, a veteran of Operation Iraqi Freedom, a man willing to give a part of his own body to help others enjoy the freedom we all take for granted. I fear there aren't too many like him today.

"We used to be a country where the majority of young men were like that. Our country was known for its goodness. You could leave your house unlocked when you went out, or leave your key in the ignition when you went into the supermarket. Most folks went to church on Sunday and young people said, 'yes ma'am,' and 'yes sir,' out of respect. Our flag was held in esteem by our citizens, and was welcomed around the world. Other nations looked to us for assistance which we freely gave out of our abundance."

He paused and, perhaps for effect, leaned forward with both hands on the back of a chair. "Our politics were different, too. We had different parties with different visions for America, but if we didn't like who got elected, we didn't riot in the streets and use profanity to express our disappointment. We had respect for the office and hunkered down to wait knowing we'd get another chance in four years."

Stan let go of the chair and stood straight, shoulders back, drawing in a deep breath which he exhaled slowly like a long sigh. "It pains me to see how far we've strayed in so short a period of time. Today, America the good leads the world in violent crime. Think about all the school shootings. We didn't have them back in the 1950's. And it wasn't because there weren't any guns. We had just come out of World War II. Army surplus stores sprouted up across the country and any kid who wanted could walk in and buy a gun without filling out a form or getting a license, but he didn't take it to school and shoot his classmates, he took it out to the field behind his house and shot tin cans. The biggest problems schools had back then were kids running in the halls and chewing gum.

"But then came the 1960's and everything changed. In the name of freedom we decided to cast off the moral restraints of previous generations. We decided to unleash the bonds of our sexual behavior. 'If it feels good, do it,' we cried, and when someone got pregnant we pushed for abortion laws to dispense with the inconvenience. We used chemical stimulants to free our minds and take us to a higher plane of understanding. We took prayer out of schools so we wouldn't feel guilty or feel like we were being judged. We stopped telling kids they were creations of God and started telling them they were accidents of nature. Now a shooting takes place and we question why God would allow it. We've kicked Him out of our schools and then when tragedy happens, blame Him for not being there to protect our children."

A few of the reporters shifted uncomfortably in their seats. One man reached for his recorder picking it up as though checking to make sure it was on. Another stared out the window and the Caucasian woman brought a finger up to bite her nail. Stan felt the room getting warm. He slipped out of his coat, placing it over the back of a chair.

"I tell you, we're headed in the wrong direction. America has the highest murder rate in the industrialized world. Right here in

Chicago, one or two people get shot every day. Our country is suffering from an opioid epidemic that killed seventy-two thousand people last year. Teen suicides are at an all-time high. Just last year forty-five thousand people took their own lives because they had no purpose, no meaning, no reason to go on. Sexually transmitted diseases are rampant. Twenty million new cases of gonorrhea, chlamydia, and syphilis are reported each year. Distributors of pornography make over fifteen billion dollars annually, not counting Internet sales which is where they get most of their money. And you wonder why Isis and Hezbollah and other radical terrorist organizations call us the 'Great Satan.' It's not because they see the Bible as inferior to the Koran, it's because we refuse to live by what the Bible says, and they see our ignoring God's laws for what it is—evil."

The female reporter stopped biting her nail and waved her hand in front of her face as though fanning away the smell of manure. Across from her, a male colleague caught the gesture and rolled his eyes in agreement. Stan continued on.

"America used to be a place where heroes, like that young man, were honored. Today we don't honor heroes, we honor celebrities and sports figures. We don't want honor, we want fame, and then we watch as our sports heroes with million-dollar contracts refuse to stand for the flag because they feel America disrespects them for not being white. They fail to see it's America that gives them the freedom to attain the success they've achieved and that the same opportunity is available to everyone regardless of the color of their skin.

"People say they want to change America. They say we need free education, free housing, free medicine, we want a new social order where there are no rich and poor, but we ignore places like Venezuela where socialism has brought total economic ruin." He glanced around the table and saw his audience fidgeting and heard at least one audible groan. "Okay, that's an extreme example, but practically every socialist country is in a mess. People aren't flooding their borders to sneak in, they're fleeing their borders trying to get out. They want to come to America, where we have the greedy one percent. Why is that? It's because socialism doesn't work. We need to think more like John F. Kennedy who said, 'Ask not what your country can do for you, ask what you can do for your country.' That's the nut of it. That's the kind of change I'd like to see. I'd like us to return to a moral and decent America. Some would call that regression; I call it progress in the right direction."

Stan looked at the assembled group. They were slouched in their chairs. No one had taken notes, perhaps because they depended on their recorders, but batteries die so you'd think they'd want to write down something just in case. He brought his wrist up and glanced at his watch. "I guess that was a bit of a tirade. Sorry, you caught me in an emotional moment but that's all I have to say for now, so if you'll excuse me, I have a business to run."

A hand shot up. It was Bill Murphy of the Chicago Tribune. "Mr. Powers, just one question. You seem good at exposing America's problems, but how do you plan on fixing them?"

Stan sighed. He lifted his jacket from the back of the chair and slipped it on. "I don't. It's not up to me. I think our country has forgotten that we're a government *of* the people, *by* the people, and *for* the people. We forget the, *of the people*, and *by the people*, parts and tend to think our government exists only *for the people*. Our forefathers wanted us to be self-governed. My goal is to wake people up and show them that our future isn't in the hands of the government, it's in their hands. They alone will decide whether to continue heading in the direction we're going, which will ultimately lead to our destruction, or choose a different path. I think the American people have it in them to do what's right. We may be racing for a cliff, but we've still got time to turn things around."

Ten

STAN SANK deep into the pillows of the sofa. His slippers, corduroy with a fleece lining, were loose from years of wear and barely clung to his feet. He had them propped up on the coffee table with his tablet open in his lap. His finger swiped the glass, turning the page. He tried to focus on the article but his mind was too distracted. He couldn't recall what he'd just read. The weight of it was pressing in on him; the fluffy overstuffed cushions acted like a black hole sucking him in. He shook his head trying to snap out of it.

He could hear boys playing ball hockey in the street. Their wood sticks were scuffed and splintered, old enough to belong to a World War II vet. Their net was homemade, a sheet stretched over a chicken-wire cage, and their ball looked like a tennis court reject. Their voices were muffled, yet distinct. "Pass it to me. I've got a shot. Over here," they yelled, as their feet thundered across the asphalt rink. Out the window he could see a mother pushing her baby in a stroller while trying to keep up with her three-year-old who was barreling down the sidewalk on a tricycle. Children were the future. He would like to give them a bright one, but it didn't look like they'd give him the chance.

He glanced at the screen again. He wasn't ready to surrender, but he sure had cause. He was like a king standing on the parapet of his castle overlooking the assembled armies of his enemies, a force a hundred times larger than his own. The first round had already been fired, a salvo that shook the walls of his fortress.

BACK TO THE FUTURE
Toss your computer, Powers wants a return to the 1950's

U. S. DECADENCE FUELS ISLAMIC TERRORISM
Isis set to destroy America because we ignore the Bible

REPUBLICIAN SAYS DEMOCRATS ARE RIGHT!
Stan Powers quotes JFK to justify platform

It was hard to look at the newsfeeds without wanting to hurl. He glanced back out into the yard where the children were laughing and playing, innocent and unbeguiled. Who would they grow up to be, purveyors of truth, or the source of subtle lies? It was fake news. The reporters had taken his words and twisted them to suit their own purpose. How could he go out and face the public when they were looking at him through a distorted lens? The articles he read were fabrications. They'd taken his words out of context, added innuendo, and drawn conclusions he never intended anyone to make. What happened to journalism? Good reporting, the five W's and an H: who, what, where, when, why, and how, used as the basis of a story before delivering the facts. Personal opinion was left outside the door when the reporter sat down to write. Not now. None of the articles he'd read fit that criteria. Journalism today seemed to be a, 'make it up as you go,' proposition.

He'd invited five reporters into his office, and not one of them got it right. The overwhelming armies of the enemy had struck the first blow, but not a mortal one. He would rise and meet their challenge. The debate was just a few days away. It would be his chance to clear things up. Live television didn't lie. People would hear firsthand what he was saying. He needed to find a strategist, someone to get him out on the campaign trail making speeches. Live presentations would be far more effective than interviews.

Stan pulled himself from his thoughts. His phone sat ringing on the coffee table. He slid his notebook off his lap and reached out, but was barely able to grab it before falling back into the cushions. The black hole was sucking him in. He rubbed his back trying to relieve the stress. All morning he'd been getting calls from news journals wanting him to comment on the stories, but he didn't know anyone he could trust to report what he said accurately, so he'd ignored them all. His eyes glanced at the call display. It might be the office needing something. The call was from a Ralph Sanderson. He knew Ralph, he'd contributed to his campaign when he ran for a seat in the house. Why would he be calling? His thumb swiped 'answer' as he brought the phone to his ear.

"Stan Powers."

"Stan, this is Ralph. I don't know if you remember me but…

"Of course I remember you. I've been keeping track of your efforts. You're doing a good job there in Washington. I hope you keep it up."

"Well, thank you. Listen, the reason I'm calling is that you've come to the attention of the GOP. You know we don't have a candidate to run against Senator Weise. Her popularity's so strong no one wants to challenge her. But I guess you've decided to do that. Am I right?"

Stan struggled forward in his seat, his thoughts still weighing him down. He pushed his hand into his lumbar, trying to straighten himself. "Yes, I kind of stepped into it by accident, but the news is out so yes, I guess I'm in the race."

"That's terrific. Glad to hear it. I just want you to know the GOP is behind you. We may even provide financial support. We're not making any promises, not right now, we still need to learn more about you, but we'd love to send Ms. Weise packing so I'm pretty sure you can count on our help."

Stan glanced at his computer, the dreadful stories staring back at him. "Did you read what they said about me in the papers this morning?"

Ralph chuckled. "I wouldn't worry about that. In fact, the worse you look in their eyes, the better you look in ours. We've all been through it before."

"I appreciate that."

"Well listen, I've got to run. I'm due in the House in five, just passed under the rotunda while we were talking. Magnificent building. Remind me to have you here as my guest. I'd love to show you around. Anyway, gotta go. I just wanted to let you know our thoughts."

"Thank you, Ralph. Any support you can give would be most appreciated."

"I'll let the boys know we have your ear. Okay, I won't keep you. I know you're a busy man. Keep up the good work and hopefully we'll get together soon."

Stan set his phone down and closed his computer. Grabbing the arm of the couch he pushed himself to his feet. He had no reason to feel weak. This was only the first skirmish in a war that had just begun. He placed both hands on his hips and with his fingers massaging his lumbar, leaned back and stretched. The kids outside were on his lawn chasing a dog that had run off with their ball. "Go that way." "I got him." "He's under the bush." Oh, to have that much energy. It was time to end the pity party. Those kids were the future. They needed protection. He would do it for them.

The usual breakfast for guests staying at the mission was a bowl of cereal. Not for Satchel, he went straight for the bacon and eggs. Why not? He was the cook. The others probably didn't want to bother with the mess. *Such a small price to pay.* The bacon sizzled as he dropped two slices of bread into the toaster. He cracked the eggs, separating the shells until the gooey stuff dropped onto the hot frying pan. *A man needs a good breakfast.* He waited until the whites were done and then flipped the eggs over and waited another minute before using his spatula to heft them onto his plate. The bacon hissed and sputtered on the grill. He grabbed up several slices setting them beside the eggs and waited for the toaster to pop. Laying the spatula aside he took the lightly-browned bread and buttered it and headed for the dining room.

The folding tables were lined up straight, the way they'd been left the night before. He pulled back a chair, set his plate down and went back to get his coffee. *No muss, no fuss, no hassle.* Nothing left to do but the dishes. Two men at the far end of the room sat hunched over bowls of cereal, a box of Cheerios between them. It was silly not to make a good breakfast. He went back to his table and set his coffee down. The overhead fan made ripples on the surface of the liquid. He took a sip and dug into his eggs.

Looks like another beautiful day, he thought, glancing out the window. The sky and the other side of the glass was a hazy blue. *Bah, bland as porridge.* He grabbed the shakers of salt and pepper and dusted his eggs, then took a chunk of bacon into his mouth. Rachel was probably up by now sitting in some other part of the city eating a breakfast just like this. Aside from hiring a private investigator, Freddie was his last hope of finding her. He wondered what Freddie was eating this morning. He should check in on him, just to make sure he hadn't bailed on the program.

A pair of boots came thundering down the stairs. He looked up and saw Bishop Samuel scratching his goatee as he headed for the kitchen. Satchel plowed more eggs into his mouth and watched as Samuel walked over to where he was sitting.

"Mind if I join you?"

Satchel waved his hand at a chair. "It's a free world, mate." He picked up a slice of bacon with his fingers, shoved it in with the eggs and spoke while chewing. "Glad you're here, Bishop. I wanted to ask you something. I know it's only been a few days, but do you think it's too early to pay Freddie a visit?" Another thought occurred to him. He'd been thinking about walking to the clinic, but if he could entice Samuel to go, he might hitch a ride.

"Nope, matter of fact I don't. Soon as I finish my coffee I'll be going over there myself. Just to see how he's doing." The old pastor's voice sounded like gurgling water, like a person would hear sitting on a rock by a stream.

"Think I could tag along?" Satchel asked.

"You could, but I doubt you want to."

"Bugger all. Why not? I'm the one what got him into it."

"The lady who owns the restaurant Mr. Powers told you about, the one who might need a cook, she called this morning. She says her husband is tired of doing everything himself. It's too much for him. She called to see if you were available. She'd like you to start right away."

Satchel's head snapped up. "You mean you got me a job?"

"It's not a guarantee. She wants to interview you first. I told her I'd send you over this afternoon around three. I have the address." Samuel slipped two fingers into the pocket of his shirt and pulled out a small scrap of paper. "I drew a map here on the back but it's easy to find, less than a mile from the subway station." He passed the slip over to Satchel. "She'd like to see you soon as possible. I know it's short notice but when opportunity knocks you gotta answer."

Satchel ran his fingers over his scalp feeling more skin than hair, then picked up his mug and held it out. "That's smashing, mate. It downright takes the biscuit. You can count on me. Only, if you don't mind, could you tell Freddie I'm sorry. Send my regards and tell him I'll be out to see him soon as I can."

"I'll do that." Samuel placed a broad hand on the table and pushed himself up. His white shirt had the cuffs folded back at the wrists, his denims were cinched with a rodeo buckle, and his boots, a glossy yellowish-green, looked like they'd just been polished. His chrome cross rocked back and forth as he stood. He reached for his wallet and pulled out a few bills, laying them on the table by Satchel's plate,

"What's that?"

"Transit money. You have to take the subway to get there." He raised his coffee and took a sip. "I think I'll pour the rest of this into a travel mug and take it with me." He placed one hand on Satchel's shoulder, closed his eyes, and raised the mug to heaven. "Lawd give Satchel here the right words to say so his interview will go well today. Thank you, Jesus. Amen."

Samuel took the same route to the clinic he'd taken before, down through the darker part of Chicago's south-side. Addicts, prostitutes and gang bangers clustered around each other defiling the streets. They were easy to spot. A dealer stood with his back to a laundromat wall. His foot was propped up against the bricks, his pants hung low on his hips, there were dark shades hiding his eyes and he wore more gold chains than a sultan king. His bodyguards kept their heads swiveling right and left, checking to make sure he was safe. Indeed a fallen world. Samuel pulled to a stop at the light. The car's top was down. It felt good to have the sun warming the top of his head.

Three working girls were standing on the corner wearing glitzy halter tops and miniskirts that barely covered their butts. Their lipstick was heavy, their eyelashes long, and their wigs webbed with hairspray. One broke ranks and came over, her glossy stilettos clicking on the pavement. She propped her elbows on the door of Samuel's car and leaned in with her arms folded. He had to turn his head to keep her breasts from poking his nose. "Hey Reverend. Don't 'spose you'd like a little company?"

"Hi Doreen. Don't you look nice? I'll bet your mother would be proud. I was just thinking about you the other day. I haven't seen you in church lately."

"Maybe it's because I don't go to church."

"Maybe you should."

"Maybe I will, but not today." The light turned green.

"You take care of yourself, Doreen. Make sure you don't wait too long. God is patient but he won't wait forever."

Doreen stood back as Samuel stepped on the gas. The huge caddy lurched forward, leaving her fanning away the blue smoke. He raised a hand, waving as he drove off. He knew this part of town well. He'd grown up here. He'd been one of those gang bangers. He'd worn the bandana and defended his crib. He knew how these people thought, how most of their actions were merely a response to life's misery. He wished he had billions of dollars to give. He'd love to shower them with money and put food on the table to improve their lives, but it would be a temporary fix. When the food ran out they'd be back on the streets. They had to want it enough to get it for themselves.

Samuel was fourteen years old when he learned that lesson. He was a proud high school dropout, already running drugs for Johnny Jaxs, a man he revered whose life had come to an abrupt end. The guns had cracked with bullets pinging off the walls as windows shattered and people scattered. When the smoke cleared, young Johnny was lying in the middle of the street in a pool of his own blood. Samuel had stood over the lifeless body, the eyes still open staring at nothing. What good was all the cash he'd collected, the fancy car he drove, and the jewelry he wore, now? Samuel's decision that day had changed his life forever. He'd gotten out and stayed out, and the only thing stopping any one of these people from doing the same thing was the will to do it. Up ahead a car pulled to the curb. A young boy, probably only seven or eight, leaned into the passenger-side window and popped back out with a wad of cash. Would they ever learn?

He braked to a stop in front of the clinic and got out, closing the door with a heavy metal thud. *Too many drugged out people, too many dying every day.* He stepped onto the curb and trundled across the sidewalk with his alligator boots crunching grains of sand as he reached to open the door.

The receptionist asked him if he had an appointment.

He said, "Morning, Akira. No, I wasn't sure I needed one."

"Just a minute," she said. The dress she wore had a nice floral print, a mint green with lavender flowers, but it draped her body like a sack with holes cut out for her head and arms. At least a dozen strings of beads dangled from her neck. Her hat looked like an Arab turban and was also lime green, matching the color of her dress. She went around the corner to open the door.

"Come on in, Reverend, I'll take you back."

Samuel followed her down the hall, her broad hips almost brushing the walls on either side. They stopped when they reached an open area that resembled a community center filled with couches and chairs, and ping-pong and billiard tables. People were milling about, some sat in chairs reading while others huddled in small groups conversing.

"I don't see him. Wait here, I'll check the library." The woman turned and walked away disappearing down the hall for a moment, but she returned without Freddie. "He's not there either," she said.

"Who are you looking for?" They turned to acknowledge a man with long greasy hair, a patch over one eye and small pointy goatee that made him look like a pirate.

"Freddie, no last name."

"I know Freddie. I saw him a few minutes ago. I think he's with Angela. Maybe they went to her room."

"Boys aren't supposed to visit the girl's rooms." The receptionist huffed off with Samuel in tow. They turned down a hall with rooms on both sides, most of them with their doors open. She had to turn to the side to let several people pass by. About halfway down she stopped at a closed door. She paused for a moment then opened the door and went in without knocking. "I was told you were in here. Freddie we have a rule about men going into women's rooms."

Freddie sat on the edge of the bed with his hands folded in his lap and his shoulders hunched forward. He began wiping his hands on his pants, trying to get them clean. "I'm sorry, it was only for a minute."

"It's my fault. I wanted to show him my..."

Samuel walked in, interrupting the woman mid-sentence. He stopped short, surprised by what he saw. Freddie had gotten a haircut and a shave. His skin was lighter where his beard had been, but the color had returned to his face. A different man. He almost looked healthy.

Freddie scratched behind his ear and then under his arm. He looked at Samuel but not into his face. His eyes were focused on the center of his chest. "Uh, Bishop, I didn't expect to see you so soon."

"Hi Freddie. You look good. How you makin' out?"

"Can we take this out to a more public place?" Akira interjected.

Freddie got up and slipped by the receptionist, followed by the girl he was with. She looked to be about forty, a bit older than Freddie who Samuel judged to be in his late twenties. She was whispery thin with a gaunt face and hollow pockmarked cheeks. Her hair was a dirty blond that hung to her shoulders like fine strands of wire.

Akira turned to Samuel. "I'll leave you with them," she said. "I have to be getting back to the front."

Samuel followed the group down the hall. When they came to the community room the receptionist turned left while Freddie and Angela turned right. The couple was holding hands as they went to an empty table and sat down.

Samuel walked over and pulled back a chair, joining them. "How you doing, Freddie?"

Freddie brought a hand up to scratch the back of his head and then scratched his cheek. "Fine, I'm fine." He wrapped his ear with a finger and ended up tugging on the lobe.

"You feel the need to use? I mean, I imagine it's pretty hard about now."

Freddie was wringing his hands unable to look at Samuel. He looked at his feet instead. "Sure, but me and Angela, we talk each other through it. Sometimes she gets desperate and I talk her down, and sometimes she has to save me. She's not going to let me use."

"Strength in numbers. That's good. Are you still calling on God? You know He's there when you need Him."

Freddie folded his arms, leaned forward, and began rocking back and forth. "Yes, but He sent Angela. Like she's an angel, you know? Like Angela means angel, right pastor?"

Samuel glanced at Angela but her eyes averted, fluttering around the room like two birds in a cage with no place to land. "You never know who God's going to use," he said.

Satchel's feet were killing him. He was wearing the tennis shoes he'd taken from the wardrobe closet because he'd thought they'd be comfortable, but now they pinched his feet and his arches hurt. His heels felt like hot lead. He regretted his decision to walk from the mission in Fuller Park to the main subway loop downtown. It would have been better to detour to the Orange Line and take that to the downtown core, but he'd been walking all his life and figured a direct route to the Red Line was better. He'd miscalculated. The twenty blocks he'd estimated turned out to be more like forty. By the time he trundled down the stairs into the subway station he felt like he was walking on blisters. He stopped at a kiosk to get a token and arrived at the gate just as the northbound train was leaving. He sauntered to the track hoping the next one would be soon. He needed to get off his feet.

The station felt musty and smelled like burning electrical wire. He raised an arm, sniffing to make sure he was okay. This meeting was important. He was determined to land this job. He needed to earn enough money to find Rachel. Down the track a light came into view. Another train rolled in but not the one he wanted. The Red Line didn't go as far as he needed, but the map showed he could transfer at the Howard station to the Purple Line, which would take him the rest of the way.

The crowds lining up along the track were growing thicker. He'd been here before as a pickpocket moving through the masses to see if he could spot an easy mark. It wasn't a terrible location, but he preferred working out in the open because in here he had to keep a constant eye out for the police. They patrolled the stations, where on the streets they were few and far between. Plus in the business district people seemed to have more in their wallets.

A scrubby man in a wrinkled suit shuffled through the crowd passing out leaflets. Satchel always refused them, but when the man pushed one into his hand, he held on. The bold headline across the top read: "Are You Going to Heaven? You decide!" It was a gospel tract. Any other time he would've tossed it into the trash, but this time he slipped it into his pocket. He would read it while on the train.

The floor at his feet began to rumble. He looked to his right. Another train emerged out of the tube. It was the Red Line going north. The train came to a hissing stop. The doors opened and Satchel clambered on shoulder to shoulder with people who bumped and jostled him on every side. He pushed through the crowd to grab a seat. The doors closed and the train took off again with half the people left standing. He wanted to lay his head back and rest but he couldn't. A pregnant woman who seemed to have nine month's worth of baby in her belly, was holding the bottom of her stomach to ease the strain on her back. He got up and offered her his seat, taking hold of the metal chrome bar to catch his balance—*standing again*. This whole thing about being a Christian was weird. He wasn't chivalrous. It was something completely foreign to him, something only a few days ago he would never have thought to do. The realization that a change was taking place in him left him flummoxed.

The train began to slow. It hissed to a stop and with a squeal the doors opened again. The sign said, "Chicago Station." About a dozen people got off giving Satchel the chance to find another seat. He pushed his feet out in front of him and lay back, closing his eyes but squinting so he could still see enough to make sure they hadn't taken on another pregnant lady. They hadn't. He crossed his arms and nodded off. There's something about wheels rumbling underneath a train that, like a gentle massage, makes you relax. Satchel didn't wake up until the intercom announced they'd arrived at Howard station. He lurched forward, jumping to his feet. This was the last stop on the Red Line. If he hadn't been jolted from his sleep he would have still been on the train when it reversed itself and headed back into the city. He headed for the doors, exiting at Rogers Park.

Satchel followed a young blond lady across the station to the Purple Line transfer. She was tall and thin, and wore her hair in a ponytail. He couldn't see her face, but guessing by the way she carried herself, her purposefulness and poise, he'd say she was attractive. Rachel was blond like that. Pretty, too. As soon as he saved enough money, he'd hire a service to locate her.

The northbound train was waiting on the track, its doors were open but they wouldn't be for long. He willed his aching feet to move faster and boarded just in time. The doors closed behind him with a *whoosh* and a *clunk*. He found a seat and dropped into it without problem. There were fewer people on the subway at this end of the track, so plenty of seats were available. He slipped the gospel tract from his pocket and settled in to read. *Am I going to heaven?* Good question. He opened it. Inside the writer had summarized three verses of scripture. The first was Romans 3:23, which said that all men were sinners and unable to meet God's expectations. The second, Romans 6:23, said that sin resulted in death but that eternal life could be found in Jesus; and the third was John 3:16 which stated that belief in Christ was required for salvation. In a nutshell the pamphlet just reinforced what Samuel had told him. Satchel sighed. *Just checking,* he thought as he stuffed the pamphlet into his pocket again.

The train rumbled down the tracks. The total ride from the loop downtown to the end of the line took just over an hour. He was afraid if he fell asleep this time he might not wake up, so he forced himself to observe his surroundings. The blond girl was three seats in front of him. He could see only the back of her head, her ponytail hanging over the seat. She picked up her briefcase and pulled it into her lap removing a computer. Satchel stared out the window taking in the scenery. The above ground track was nice because it offered something to look at. In his mind he went over the questions he thought the restaurant owners might ask and how he would answer. Samuel had been very clear. "Just be honest," he'd said. "They know about your past, so don't hide anything." How could they hire someone guilty of shooting someone else? Then he remembered Stan was the man he'd shot and Stan was the one recommending him for the job. Go figure.

The wheels squealed to a stop. People grabbed their belongings and struggled to their feet, ready to get off. The girl in front of him closed her briefcase and stood, heading for the door. He followed her outside into the warm afternoon sun. She turned, exposing her profile. He was right, she was attractive, make some bloke a bloody fine wife. She headed in one direction. He looked at the map he'd been given. Not the direction he was going. He took off in the other.

• • •

Rachel walked down a series of steps and turned toward the Northwestern campus. She swung her briefcase out, letting the momentum carry her forward, and let it ease back, stepping lightly. It was a glorious afternoon. Maybe she should take advantage of it. Charlotte had ended the meeting early. They knew so little about the man, they'd come to the point where they were repeating the same things over and over. The only new information came from the newspapers. That alone was enough to put Charlotte in a good mood. They examined each article, underlining and putting asterisks beside important points. At least now they knew who they were dealing with. The man stood convicted by his own words, every bit as bigoted and narrow-minded as Charlotte had said. Charlotte wasn't perfect, mind you. She had her quirks, like thinking football conflicted with her socialist ideals. That was just plain silly.

Rachel raised her hands and tried skipping, but her briefcase threw her off balance. She straightened herself. She was a representative of Senator Weise. She should act more mature. Charlotte was a mixed bag, that was obvious. Some of the things she espoused seemed duplicitous, like making a show of distaining competition and then competing with Mr. Powers for a seat in the Senate. Wouldn't she be showing her superiority if she won? And she'd let everyone know she planned to recuperate at her condo in Hawaii when all this was over. That took money. Didn't equality mean her entire staff should be rewarded with a Hawaiian vacation? And if she was sincere in wanting to improve the lot of her fellow man, shouldn't she sell that condo and give the money to the poor?

Rachel had struggled to understand the benefits of socialism. All her classmates seemed for it, but she wasn't sure. She'd been the captain of her high school debate team. They had an unblemished record, defeating not just the schools in her district, but also sweeping the regional finals and were on their way to the state championship. Some genius had come up with the topic, "Capitalism vs Socialism, an economic model." They were told not to discuss social justice, that had too many tendrils running in too many directions for a one hour debate. This was strictly about which system provided the best economic health for a nation. It was too bad because socialism's economics seemed to falter under scrutiny. Social justice was much easier topic to defend. Her classmates weren't demanding strict socialism, anyway. They wanted something called, "democratic socialism," wherein socialism and democracy were combined into a hybrid, but when she drilled further down she found proponents of that idea only saw it as a stepping stone to a day when full socialism could be legislated.

She did her best nonetheless. It was the event her teacher, Ms. Gessner, had invited June Brewster to attend and largely why she was enrolled at Northwestern today.

Rachel had argued that socialism could create the kind of utopia mankind had sought since the beginning of time, where everyone could live cooperatively, all working toward the greater good and sharing equally in its reward. In her argument she'd shown how allowing a few corporate executives to make decisions affecting millions of people with the sole purpose of increasing their own wealth was disingenuous. How much better to allow the people themselves to run the companies in which they worked so they could make decisions that benefited everyone equally. She'd praised the mantra, "From each according to his ability to each according to his contribution." Government's role was to manage the overall business strategy to ensure equitable distribution of materials and resources.

To make sure she knew how her opponents would respond and how to answer their objections, she had studied the subject from both sides, but about halfway through discovered she was starting to favor capitalism. She became convinced those defending it had a better chance of winning. It came as a surprise when her team was awarded the championship. She found out much later that several members of the group defending capitalism were themselves in favor of socialism and didn't have the heart to argue against something in which they believed.

Her own doubt began with the realization that people aren't inherently cooperative. People always differed on how things should be done, how the company should be run, and what was in the best interest of all concerned. Regardless of the situation, when you have two people discussing an issue you're bound to come away with three different opinions. Arguments were bound to ensue, personality conflicts to arise, and disgruntlement to settle in. It was the nature of the beast. She also considered that truly motivated people might lose the incentive to work because there would always be someone getting the same amount of pay that refused to contribute equally. Entrepreneurship and innovation would suffer, leading to a decrease in the number of products that might otherwise be developed.

Her opponent had given several good examples of how profit driven capitalism worked, but one in particular struck home, probably because so many of her classmates used Apple products. He'd mentioned how if Steve Jobs had worked under a socialist government, he might not have been able to save the company he'd founded. By the end of the third quarter of 1997, under the leadership of John Sculley, Apple had lost a billion dollars and was looking at insolvency. When Jobs was brought back, they had fifteen products on the market. Jobs fired three thousand people and cut Apple's product line down to four. A socialist government would likely have viewed the employees as more important than profit and prevented him from making such cuts, thus dooming the company to bankruptcy. Instead, by putting profit first, the company not only survived, it thrived and became one of the richest companies in the world, employing about fifty-thousand people in the US alone.

The point was not lost on Rachel.

When she'd argued for socialism, she used Norway, Sweden and Denmark as glowing examples of socialist countries where the state provided healthcare, education and pensions to improve their citizen's quality of life. She hid the fact that her research also revealed that in all three countries sixty-five percent of the wealth was held by ten percent of the people who, like America's one percent, were in lockstep with capitalism. The ninety percent didn't feel the need to accumulate wealth because the government cared for their needs, so there was no incentive to be entrepreneurial.

She'd withheld a list of countries that had embedded socialism into their constitutions: Algeria, Angola, Bangladesh, Guyana, Mozambique, Portugal, Sri Lanka, Tanzania, and Venezuela, because their governments were either corrupt, insolvent, or both, and as such were detrimental to the image she wanted to project. When countries like Russia, China, Cambodia, Vietnam, North Korea and Cuba were used to illustrate socialism, and the hypocrisy of murdering millions of their own citizens to impose a government that claimed to be "for the people," she'd argued that those were communist countries, run by dictators, not the citizens, and could only be used as examples of socialism run amok. She pushed from her mind the thought that, like the capitalist one-percent she was disparaging, the socialist leaders of these countries had created centers of wealth and power around themselves while their outlying citizens were impoverished and left without hospitals and schools.

She'd won the debate, but had gone home questioning whether she was right. She was confused. In her heart she decided one political system was probably as corrupt as another and that the best course of action was to remain neutral.

There was one thing she and Charlotte agreed upon however, and it superseded all else. Mr. Powers could never be allowed to take office. Rachel picked up the pace, not skipping but doing a hop-step that expressed her exuberance. For a moment she thought about taking the rest of the day off, maybe grabbing a good book and sitting by the lake to read. They weren't expecting to see her back at election headquarters until the following day. But she shook the idea from her head. Hers may be only one small cog in a much bigger wheel, but it was incumbent upon her to do everything possible to make sure that man never got elected.

Satchel took the few steps up to the porch, the wood boards stretching under his weight. The screen door was closed, but through the mesh he could see people inside. When they said he'd be working in a restaurant this wasn't what he had in mind. He let himself in and flinched when the spring-loaded door slammed behind him with a metallic *twang*. He looked around at the wallpaper, the framed pictures, the mismatched collection of tables and chairs. It was midafternoon, about halfway between lunch and dinner, so only a few patrons occupied tables. Satchel turned around to see if he could find the owners and nearly bumped into a woman who had approached from behind. She was large and black and looked somewhat like the picture of Aunt Jemima printed on pancake boxes.

"Welcome, sugah. Can I help you find a seat?"

"No, thank you, but if you work here, you could direct me to the owner."

"That would be me, sugah." She made the second syllable of the word sound like gah, like she hailed from the south, sug-gah.

"Blimey, my mistake." Satchel said extending his hand. "The name's Satchel. The lads over at the mission sent me here to look at a job."

"Oh. Just look at you, such a fine big man. Just what we need and honey, I love that accent. Where do you come from?"

"Originally, England, but I've been here long enough to call this my home, though I'm not a citizen yet."

"Well you just come on over here and sit down. Let me get you a cup of coffee and we'll have us a talk." She put her arm through Satchel's and guided him to a table. The chairs were old but they looked sturdy. He sat with his arm up picking at a cuticle. She returned a few minutes later with his coffee in one hand and several packets of cream and sugar in the other. She set them in front of him and took a seat herself. "So you were a jailhouse cook," she said.

"Not exactly. I was in the slammer, but I didn't work in the kitchen, which is a good thing because you wouldn't want to eat the kind of stuff they fed us. Truth is, while in jail I went to school to become a chef. I've learned how to fix everything from eggs to the chicken that laid them. And I know my spices. I got a special knack for mixing one seasoning with another to make things taste special."

"Now don't you go thinking you're going to spice up Mama's chicken. No one gonna do that. No sir. My recipe's fine as it is."

"Sorry, I didn't mean…"

Mama slapped his arm and took his hand in both her own. "I was just funnin' with you honey. My recipe is good, but there ain't nothing in this big wide world that can't use improvement." She stared into his eyes. "Know what? I like you. You got a good honest face. I've decided. You want the job it's yours." She squeezed his hand.

Honest face? He could feel the moisture in her skin and the calluses on her fingers. "So that's it?"

"Unless you don't want the job. Only pays three-fifty a week, but it comes with room and board so all your housing, utilities, and food expenses are paid. That's around fourteen hundred a month to do with as you please. The bedroom's upstairs. I kinda like the idea of your staying here so you can watch over things at night."

"What about your husband?"

"What about him?"

"Doesn't he get a say? We haven't even met."

"Don't you worry about him. No suh, un-uh, like they say,

153

'When Mama ain't happy, ain't nobody happy'. He just leaves me alone to make these kinda decisions."

"Okay, when do I start?"

Mama looked at her watch. "Honey, we got customers gonna be coming in here startin' about four o'clock. We got less than an hour to get ready, so how 'bout you just get your sweet backside into that kitchen and we'll get things started right now."

Eleven

STAN WAS in the green-room having his makeup done. The room wasn't green. He wasn't sure why they called it that, but it was where he'd been asked to wait until they needed him on stage. As a rule Stan avoided social media. He was clueless about the Twitter buzz the debate had created. He'd thought they'd be in a television studio with an audience of maybe thirty or forty. The pulse of the crowd was audible. His waiting room was well removed from the main conference stage, but he could hear the throbbing of the crowd even from there.

Charlotte had set the venue; the Murdoch Room at the historic River Roast. He hadn't raised any objections, though as he passed through the conference center, he had to ask who was paying for all this. They weren't serving food, but the room alone must have cost a fortune. He did learn from the coordinator that Charlotte was hosting a cocktail reception for a few of her most prodigious supporters after the debate.

It was unnerving to arrive an hour early and find the room nearly full with lines of people standing outside waiting to be seated. He hadn't given any more interviews, but the media had been issued a press release and had run with the story. Apparently people were interested in what he had to say, or maybe that was his ego talking. They were probably there to see Charlotte. The media had shown up in droves. The first three rows of the room were for journalists, and all along the back wall TV crews were positioned to record every word.

The whole thing was a bit unsettling. When he originally spoke to Charlotte she had mentioned a slot she had prescheduled which she was generously offering to share with him. Walking through the main hall he had seen cameras from every network affiliate, plus a few local channels. The debate was short notice. They couldn't all be broadcasting live. It would mean an interruption of their regular programming schedules. And if they weren't going live it meant they would be editing what he said and featuring clips on their news programs. The *editing* part bothered him because once again it meant they could slant things the way they wanted without regard for what he actually said.

He was looking for someone to tell him what to do and where he should be when a voice in the crowd exclaimed, "Isn't that Mr. Powers?" and pandemonium broke out. The room flooded with questions. Reporters jumped up, cameras started strobing, and microphones were poked into his face. Someone grabbed his arm and pulled him out a side door hustling him into the room where he was sitting now.

His makeup artist was leaning over staring at him. He pushed Stan's hair back and dusted his forehead with a soft bristle brush. "The light in here is awful. How am I'm I supposed to make you look good when all I see are shadows. Not even a full mirror."

The man dusted Stan's cheek with a fine powder. "Just to reduce the glare," he said. Stan tried to refuse the lipstick but the man cautioned that his lips would look white on TV and make him look ghoulish. "Everyone needs just a touch," he said. Stan's sandy blond hair was naturally wavy. He didn't need hairspray but the man used it anyway. He held up a mirror for Stan to see. "There, you look a hundred percent better, don't you think?"

No, not really, he thought. What Stan saw in the mirror was a painted clown, but he understood the need to add color and reduce glare for the cameras, so he let it go. "Yes, that's fine, I appreciate it." The man was only doing his job.

"All right then, I guess I'm done. Stay here. They'll come and get you when they're ready." The man tossed his brush, mirror, hairspray, and makeup into a large black purse. "Ta, ta," he said, slinging the bag over his shoulder as he headed for the door.

The room they'd put him in was small, maybe twelve by fourteen, and normally used for business meetings. There were dents in the carpet indicating where the feet of a long table had been. A dozen upholstered chairs were lined up against the walls. The pictures were nicely framed but obviously commercial reprints. One wall had a whiteboard mounted on it and a cart with a projection system had been pushed into a corner. The vent overhead hummed with a flow of air keeping the room cool.

Stan began to pace hoping to work off the tension he felt. It hurt when he held his leg straight, but he was determined not to let his limp show. He shook his arms and arched his back straightening himself. He hadn't done much public speaking, though he had been called upon to give a presentation to fifty members of the Ad Council at an industry tradeshow and that had gone well, but this was different. He was told the main conference room seated over three hundred and judging from what he'd already seen, it would be full. Add to that the pressure of looking into television cameras knowing he was really speaking to millions. He didn't need to be nervous, the Lord was on his side, but that didn't change how he felt. He pulled his shoulders back and tried breathing deeply as he navigated the room.

The door, which had been left ajar, swung open and a young man with a name tag that read, Kyle, beckoned him with a hand. "They're ready for you now, Mr. Powers. If you'll just come with me."

Stan kept his shoulders back and his posture straight, keeping his limp to a minimum as he followed the young man down the hall to a door leading into the conference center. They stopped to allow a young woman to exit before going in. She was tall and lithe and wore her blond hair swirled up on top her head in a bun. She stopped abruptly, her bright blue eyes drilling into his. A hand came up to cover her mouth. "Oh!" she said. Then her eyes averted and she ducked away. Stan watched her scurry down the hall without looking back.

He turned and followed Kyle into the main convention center. "Wait here while I go check the schedule. One station is going live so we have to start on time. I'll be right back," he said. He turned on his heel and walked across the room to the other side to confer with a woman wearing a headset. She was holding a clipboard and began flipping through the pages. Stan looked over his shoulder at the audience. Every seat seemed to be taken, with dozens of people standing along both walls. Members of the press, seated in the first three rows, were wearing large badges with their names in bold so they could easily be identified. Kyle was heading back. Just behind him Stan saw Charlotte Weise and a cadre of her staff standing on the other side of the room. Someone motioned to her and she started up the steps to her podium.

"I'm told it's time to get you onstage," Kyle said. He led Stan up the three stairs to the top of the recently constructed platform and positioned him in front of a lectern. Stan gritted his teeth, ignoring the pain of trying to bend his leg naturally. "We need to do a sound check, just say something into the mic."

Stan knew whatever he said would be heard so rather than sound foolish he merely said, "Testing, one, two, three, test." A man in the back waved his hand signaling that the audio level was acceptable." Charlotte was asked to do the same but when she went to her podium she looked at the crowd and with a smile said, "My, what a lovely turnout we have here tonight. I want to thank you all for being here." Her voice was both friendly and welcoming. The guy in the back raised his arm again and she took a step back.

The moderator came up the steps holding a wireless mic. Kyle leaned over and said "I have to leave you now; they're ready to go. See the guy back there holding a tablet, watch him. In a minute you'll see his hand go up and he'll do a countdown with his fingers; three, two, one, and then he'll point at the moderator and you'll know the cameras are going live. Good luck."

Stan took a long slow breath to calm himself. *Look at all those people.* He wondered once again if they were there to see him, Charlotte, or both. His eyes roamed the crowd. It was hard to see with the camera lights in his eyes, but he found the group he was looking for, the parolees from the mission, tattooed and bearded and not particularly an image he needed to be associated with, but he was glad they were there all the same. A few of them waved to get his attention and he nodded in recognition. They'd let him know they wanted to attend, but it would have taken a herculean effort to get everyone fed and the place cleaned up in order to make it on time.

He saw the floor manager's hand go up and begin the count. When they reached "one" the lights on several of the cameras turned red and he knew they were live.

A master of ceremonies, wearing a black tuxedo and starched white shirt with pearl buttons, stepped into the spotlight. He brought a handheld mic to his mouth and said, "We're thrilled to have you with us here tonight at the River Roast Convention Center in beautiful downtown Chicago where in just a few minutes Senator Weise of the great state of Illinois and her challenger, Mr. Stan Powers, will debate the issues facing America today. We'll begin by asking each of our speakers to spend just five minutes summarizing their vision for this great state, and by extension all of America. This will be followed by questions from a panel composed of Ms. Natalie Grimes of ABC, Milton Hauser from CBS, and Jerry Blackwater from NBC. So without further delay," the MC turned toward Charlotte, "I'll begin with our Senator, Ms. Charlotte

159

Weise. Senator, please spend a few minutes sharing what you hope to do for us in Washington."

Charlotte stepped up to the podium and with a smile as big as Chicago leaned just a little toward the mic and said, "Thank you, Chet." Then she looked out over her audience and began a monologue she'd rehearsed a thousand times.

"Ladies and gentlemen, it is a great pleasure to be here representing the great state of Illinois and to share with you a little about what I believe the future holds. Those of you who know me, know I've spent most of my political life fighting for social justice. America's past is overshadowed by a dark cloud of bigotry and intolerance but we mustn't let that be our legacy. We need to put behind us the sins of our past, the sin of bigotry, the sin of greed, the sin of intolerance, and move forward into the light where, as it states in our Constitution, all men are truly considered equal." A flurry of applause erupted from the room. "We want a world of equal opportunity, where skin color, gender, sexual orientation, and religious beliefs are never considered when someone applies for a job, or tries to get a loan, or gets pulled over for a speeding ticket. Where fair wages are paid to all our workers, even those doing jobs no one else wants to do. Where women are free to choose whether to have a family or a profession. And where those choosing a profession are able to advance in their careers without fear of sexual harassment." The cheers around the room grew a little louder. "Our nation should not be a nation that elevates one belief system over another. America was founded on freedom of religion so that all faiths can coexist equally, which includes the right to be an atheist or unbeliever if one so chooses. We want a world with a safe environment for our children, where they breathe fresh air, have clean water to drink, and where they and their parents can choose to visit any number of thriving national parks when it's time to take a family vacation. We want to enact programs to take care of the poorest among us and make sure their children are clothed and fed and given good schools to attend. We want to make sure those who have come from around the world to participate in this great nation are made to feel welcome, because we know every one of us has an immigrant in their background somewhere..."

Stan listened, trying to calm the palpitations of his heart. There was nothing new in her speech but it would be hard to counter. Who in their right mind would be against social justice? Everything she said sounded right. He looked up at the cameras. Several were pointed at him, probably there to catch his reaction. He smiled pleasantly keeping his eyes fixed on Charlotte as though paying rapt attention. The room was getting warmer. He felt perspiration breaking out on his forehead and considered which would look worse, being caught looking like he was sweating on camera, or caught with a handkerchief wiping his brow. Either one could be interpreted to mean she had him squirming.

Satchel kept one eye on the TV and his other on the food he was preparing. He placed a miniature loaf of bread on a plate and filled two bowls with salad. The television was tuned to the debate. Mama had let him know she voted for Congressman Weise in the last election, but she knew Stan personally and supported the mission so she was conflicted. When Satchel mentioned how he hated to miss the broadcast she'd brought a small portable television from home and set it up in the kitchen.

"Now that's why I'm a Democrat, honey. You never hear a Republican talking about taking care of the poor or people of color like me."

Satchel put a scoop of steamy mashed potatoes on one plate and a tinfoil wrapped baked potato on another with a side of sour cream and butter. "I see good intentions," he said. "But talk is cheap. Before my time in the slammer, I used to hustle on the streets of Chicago. I go away for ten years and come back and I don't see a lot of change. Not from Democrats or Republicans. I hear a lot of promises. But frankly I see more poverty on the streets today than I did before I went to jail. Why is that?"

Mama wiped her hands on her apron and busied herself filling a wire basket with packets of salad dressing. "So you're Republican. No use denying it. Mama can always tell a Republican, especially when they come into my restaurant. I can tell just by the way they look at me, like this is slave owner's kitchen and it's my place to serve their food. Now don't get me wrong, sugah, it's not that I don't like Mr. Powers, I do. It's just that Senator Weise is for the little people, not the corporate crime bosses. You're one of us little people, so you should be voting for her too."

Satchel took a ladle, scooped up a pile of peas and put them on the plate next to the baked potato and chicken. On a plate with mashed potatoes and Salisbury steak he put a ladle of green beans. "I'm no Republican. I'm not even a citizen so I can't vote, but frankly I don't see any of them being much good. I'm just saying I hear a lot of talk but see very little action. But Mr. Powers there, he puts his money where his mouth is. I don't care what party he represents. He's down there feeding the poor every day."

"Uh huh, sugah, I'm with you there. That's the reason I wanted to watch." Mama picked up the plates and headed for the dining room to serve her guests. "I admit he's doing a mighty fine job here, but I gotta think about what's best for the country," she said as she disappeared around the corner.

The moderator thanked Charlotte and turned to Stan. "Mr. Powers I confess we know very little about you, which is something I hope we can change tonight, but I do have a few things worth mentioning. Most notably, it appears you're an American hero. A retired Navy SEAL who earned a Medal of Valor and a Purple Heart during a tour overseas, and back on the mainland saved the life of a child by taking a bullet during a holdup attempt in a Chicago suburb. I want to say that's very commendable. You also own a small business called Power Advertising. That's about all we have. I think there are a great many people in this audience, and perhaps even across the nation, who are interested in learning more about you, so please, sir, share with the people out there what you hope to accomplish if you get elected."

Stan placed both hands on the podium and looked into the camera. "Thank you, Chet. And thank you Senator Weise," he glanced over at Charlotte, "for giving me this opportunity to share my vision for America. The first thing I'd like to say is that we really don't have a reason to debate. All those things you said you wanted are the same things I want, and I'd wager most Americans want, a pure and just society where everyone is viewed as equal and treated fairly. So I guess what we need to debate is not what we want, but what is achievable, and what's the best way to accomplish what we set out to do."

He turned his attention back to the audience, letting his eyes roll through the crowd. "I'm sure many of you out there read the articles recently printed about me. I want you to know I take exception with much of what was said, but one thing I did agree with was that, unlike my fellow candidate, who just stated America's past is dark, I see America's past as being a shining example of good. No, I'm not saying we're perfect. The years we spent facilitating subjugation and slavery are shameful. We have much to answer for. But I can say that for the past two centuries, nations around the world have looked upon America as being a shining light on a hill. At least that's the way it was until around the 1960's."

Stan eased the pressure off his leg and tried to relax. He would lose his audience if he got fired up and came on too strong. He took a slow breath. "Most of you know I'm not a politician, but I am a student of history, and if you read history you'll find this country wasn't founded by politicians, it was founded by farmers

163

and inventors and merchants, regular people like you and me. Their stated purpose was to keep government from interfering in people's lives. But they knew that could only be accomplished if people were willing to be governed by a higher authority. As John Adams said in 1735 'Our Constitution was made only for a moral and religious people. It is wholly inadequate for the government of any other.' The founders of our nation expected men to live by the Ten Commandments. They reasoned that if men answered wholly to the laws of God, there would be little need for government. Their assumptions proved correct. America grew to become the richest and most powerful nation on earth.

"Now, don't make the mistake of thinking our forefathers were limited in their perspective and couldn't know what life would be like in modern times. They knew exactly what would befall our nation if it ever turned its back on God. I'll give you an example. In 1776, the same year of our nation's founding, Edward Gibbon, in his classic work, 'The History of the Decline and Fall of the Roman Empire,' showed how in the latter days of Rome, life became cheap. Abortions were routine, and unwanted children were left by the side of the road to freeze to death. By the time Justinian came into power, homosexuality, bestiality, pedophilia, and drunken orgies were commonplace. On top of that, regulations had increased to where manufacturing became almost impossible and taxes on trade were so great the economy stagnated. You'd think Rome would know better because they'd conquered Greece only after it had fallen into similar disrepair. There was no end to the immorality and licentiousness that surrounded people of that day.

"Sadly, it's easy to see that America is now on that same path, perhaps not as far along, but we're heading the same direction. We've seen tremendous change over the past fifty years. I wager most elderly folks around the country, people who grew up watching 'Ozzie and Harriet' and 'Father Knows Best,' scratch their heads and wonder what happened. It's simple. We've taken God out of American life. Until the 1960's we honored our nation's founding fathers by acting like a religious people. We had prayer in our schools, Bible studies were encouraged on campus, and the pews of most churches were full on Sunday mornings.

"Our decline began when we took prayer out of schools and replaced God with evolution. Now schools that were once safe havens for kids are fraught with venereal disease, teen pregnancy, drugs, and guns. If anybody wants to know what happened, that's where it started. Just like with Egypt and Israel and Babylon and Greece and Rome, our movement away from law and order, discipline, and yes, God, has brought us to the place where we now call acceptable, things we once counted as evil. There's a scripture in the Bible, Isaiah 5:20, that says, 'Woe to them who call evil good and good evil.' That's us. We call all forms of evil good, our wanton promiscuity, the murder of our babies, the legalization of drugs, our immoral lifestyles. One day, like every great nation before us, it will lead to our demise.

"So if I'm elected and sent to Washington my purpose will be to sound a warning, to wake the nation up to bring us back to our knees before God. Because I know, and I believe, as said by Abraham Lincoln and '...as proven in history, those nations only are blessed whose God is the Lord.'

Thank you."

There was scattered light applause throughout the building but most people looked confused. No one knew quite what to say. That's not how politicians were supposed to talk. An evangelist, a pastor maybe, but not a politician.

Mama had stepped into the kitchen to get a pot of coffee but got caught up listening to Stan's speech. "Okay sugah, you got me. That's one Republican I could vote for. I'm not saying I will, mind you, I'm just saying he's got the right idea. Yes suh, we don't want

God in school no mo'. I used to live on the south side and I knows how bad the schools are today. And I also knows what they were like when I was young. And I don't care whether you believe in God or not, the idea of having God in school is the best thing you can do to keep things orderly. You read the Ten Commandments at the beginning of the day, then you pray, and you let the kids know that God's watching. You better believe kids act a whole lot different 'cause they know if they don't shape up and fly right they could end up in hell. They don't teach that no mo', un uh. Kids today think they can get away with anything, but not if God's watchin', no suh. These kids got to know when they leave this life there's another one comin' and if they die they may not like what's waiting for them on the other side, un uh, no suh." She grabbed the pot and headed back into the diner to refresh her customer's coffee.

"Natalie, you had a question, I believe for Senator Weise."

"Yes, thank you, Chet." The reporter from ABC smiled pleasantly and shuffled her notes. She looked at Charlotte. "Senator Weise, you've been in office for twelve years now and here in Chicago we haven't seen an appreciable reduction in poverty. By extension I would think the same holds true for the rest of the country. I know this is one of your campaign hot buttons. How can you assure your voters that you have a plan to win the war on poverty?"

"Thank you Natalie, that's a terrific question. I believe we've made great strides to end poverty. It has always been one of my strongest resolves. I think the people in this room as well as the viewers out there watching on television will attest to my efforts to bring affordable housing to those needing a place to live. Our efforts have increased our national welfare funding by thirty-two percent over the past few years, and our federal food stamp program now has an annual budget of seventy-four billion to feed the poor. Now

I'm not saying the system is perfect, or that there's not a lot more to be done, but I believe to say there's been no appreciable reduction in poverty is unfair.

"Here's the real situation. Currently about fifteen percent of our population lives below the poverty line. That's way too big a number because it represents about fifty million people. But this country also has a great number of wealthy people, the one percent whose annual adjusted gross incomes exceed five-hundred thousand. Our challenge is to help the rich people give more of what they have to help the poor. Rich people may only compose one percent of the population, but they hold forty percent of the nation's wealth. If you look at my track record you'll see how hard I've worked to get bills passed that redistribute some of that wealth from those who don't need it, to those who do.

"Now before I get criticized for being a Robin Hood that steals from the rich and gives to the poor, I want to make it clear that I don't begrudge rich people anything. I understand the argument that they've earned their wealth and deserve to keep it. But how much wealth does one really need? You can only buy so many boats and houses and cars. There comes a point when every wealthy citizen must realize they've been disproportionately blessed and should with great gratitude willingly provide for those less fortunate. Unfortunately, altruistic people like that are rare so we, as a government, have to give them a nudge to help them do what's right.

"If I'm elected I promise to continue these efforts until our society of haves and have-nots aren't separated by so great a divide."

Chet, the moderator, nodded appreciably and turned, looking back at the panel. "All right then, Milton, I understand you have a question for Mr. Powers."

"Yes indeed, thank you Chet." Milton looked at his card for moment then raised his eyes to Stan. "Mr. Powers, you spent your whole preamble criticizing our country for being ungodly. It might surprise you to find that per capita America still has more churches and more people who say they believe in God than any other nation on earth, but there are also those who believe that science and knowledge are preferable to believing in the supernatural. So my question is how do you plan to represent the vast number of people who don't agree with the idea that God should have a place in America?"

Stan leaned into the podium, shifting his weight to ease the pressure on his leg. "I'll answer that question, but before I do, can I address something Ms. Weise just said?" He looked at the moderator and Chet gave him a nod.

"By all means, go right ahead but you only get two minutes total so be quick."

"Thank you. Senator, you just took ownership of the nation's housing projects. You touted them as a victory in the war on poverty. The fact is, some of those projects have become the biggest slums and most dangerous places to live in the nation. I would argue that's because you can't throw money at a problem to fix it. Lyndon Johnson declared the war on poverty in 1964, and since that time we've spent fifteen trillion dollars fighting this war, yet today poverty is just as great as it was then, perhaps even greater. I don't deny that we need programs to assist those in need but as you pointed out, the real problem is with the heart of man, at least that's what you indicated when you said most rich people need to be nudged to help the poor. What they need is a change of heart. The Bible speaks more about poverty than almost any other topic, but it always puts the burden on men to help each other, not government.

Let me give you an example, and forgive me if this one strikes close to home. According to public records you own two houses; one here in Chicago and one in Georgetown at the nation's capital, and you also own a condominium in Hawaii. Your personal worth is over two-point-five million. Do you need three houses? Why not give one, or maybe even two, to families in need. There are plenty of people who have no place to live, while at any given time you have two houses sitting vacant. And why aren't you taking some of that money you've got in your bank to buy food for the hungry? According to public record, you give less than one percent of your income to charitable organizations. You were right when you said people of wealth sometimes need a nudge to do the right thing. I think you need to be pointing that finger at yourself, as well as a lot of others on The Hill. Take, for example, the leader of your party. She has a net worth of close to fifty million, money primarily earned by her investment banker husband. Why isn't that money being used to feed the poor? If the party you represent truly believes that money can solve the problem, I recommend you all dig deep into your pockets and turn this problem around."

A camera caught Charlotte's face. Her expression was flat and void of color. The sparkle that moments before had shone in her eye had been extinguished. A wave of murmurs rolled through the audience.

"Now to answer your question, Mr. Hauser. I can accept that you and many others don't hold the beliefs I do. That's your right. But I suggest we all take a look at history because, as you know, those who fail to learn from history are destined to repeat it. Historians throughout the centuries have concluded that the collapse of every world power was preceded by the abandonment of morality, and morality goes hand-in-hand with godliness. George Washington in his farewell address said, 'Of all of the dispositions and habits which lead to political prosperity, religion and morality are indispensable...' The link between a nation's morality and its prosperity, is indisputable. America existed as a moral nation for a hundred and fifty years and we prospered. Out of our abundance we became lenders to every nation. Now we are in moral decline and find ourselves saddled with unimaginable debt while we borrow from everyone else. Washington went on to say, 'and let us with caution indulge the supposition that morality can be maintained without religion.' Religion and morality are two sides of the same coin. The problem in America today is that we no longer want morality. We want to be free to live any way we choose, so we cast off the restraints of religion and thus find ourselves in that precarious position of being on the very edge of collapse. You ask how I would serve you as a non-religious person. My answer is this, I would ask you to do what Charlotte asked of the rich, give up some of the rights you think you're entitled to for the good of everyone else."

With the exception of a soft glow given off by a single nightlight, the community center was dark. Angela had her feet up on the couch with her arms wrapped around her knees rocking back and forth. A large clock on the wall sounded a *tic-toc* with each passing second.

"I don't think I can take it. I'm going to quit. I need a fix—now!"

Freddie, sitting beside her, put his arm over her shoulders. "No. You can't do that. We're gonna make it. You're just having a bad day. Let's talk about something else. Tell me about your family. You said you called your mom and dad. What did they say?"

Angela used the back of her hand to wipe her nose and then combed her fingers through her brittle hair. The faint glow of the nightlight was producing a halo effect. "They want me to come home. I haven't been there in twenty years. I hadn't even spoken to them, but my counselor said I needed to call those I've hurt to make amends." A tear escaped her eye but she wiped it away with her palm.

"So what did they say?"

There was a long pause—the ticking of the clock filling the void. *Tic-toc, tic-toc, tic-toc.* Angela sniffed and wiped her nose again. "They said they love me." She looked at Freddie. The dim light cutting across her face caught in the creases, making her look even older. "Talk about too little too late. They should've said that a long time ago 'cause it sounds kind of stupid now. Especially coming from my old man who used to beat me just for kicks."

Freddie's grip on her shoulder tightened. "Oh God, did he... I mean, were you raped?"

Angela shook her head and planted her face against her knees. Her tears were flowing freely now. Her mouth was wet as she spoke. "No, nothing like that, but I remember coming home drunk one night after he'd told me I couldn't go out and he grabbed me by the wrist and dragged me down the hall to my room and beat the tar out of me." She continued rocking back and forth making it difficult for Freddie to keep his arm across her shoulder. He pulled back and she sniffed. "I guess what he really did was put me over his knee and spank me. But he spanked me hard and it hurt. I was humiliated. He treated me like a child. I was fifteen years old."

"Yeah, my old man used to beat me too. I'm not never going back there."

Angela raised her head off her knees but she was still looking down. She used her finger to pick at a loose thread that had become unraveled from the couch. The smell of pizza from someone's dinner still hung in the air. "Maybe you should." She looked over at Freddie. In the low watt light her red eyes looked to be pooled with water. "My parents don't hate me. I don't think they ever did. We just couldn't get along. But it was nice to hear them say they love me. You should call your parents. They're older now, maybe they've changed." She looked down as she continued to loop the string around her finger. "Besides, when we get out of here I've got nowhere else to go. I have to go home. If I go back to the streets I'll end up using again. At least you've got that church to go to."

"It's not a church, it's a place that feeds people, and I don't know if they'll let me stay or not." Freddie crossed his feet, uncrossed them, and crossed them again. He began wringing his hands in his lap. "I…I don't know, I was kind of thinking maybe we could stick together. Maybe I can find work or something. We could look out for each other. Like you said, I'm through with living on the streets and I don't got no home to go to. That door is closed. I don't never want to see my old man again."

The moderator, Chet, had tossed the ball to Jerry Blackwater from NBC. Of the three journalists, Jerry was the one that made Stan the most uncomfortable. So far every question he asked was designed to make Stan look bad. Why would anyone want to know if he paid his employees equitably? It had nothing whatever to do with the issues at hand. It was simply a ruse to catch Stan off guard and have him admit publicly that he paid his female employees less than he paid the men for the same work. Fortunately, outside of himself, the person in the firm who took home the most money was his account executive, and she was a woman. And he paid all his writers and artists the same. Jerry was looking at him now. He seemed to be smiling, but Stan couldn't tell by the contour of his lips whether the smile was malevolent or mischievous. The rhythm of his heart increased. He was in trouble either way.

Jerry held his card up to the light as though making sure he understood the question before asking it. "Mr. Powers, you referenced homosexuality several times tonight and in each case insinuated that it was immoral, yet you insist that you're not homophobic. You claim your stance is, live and let live. I doubt that's true, so here's my question. Is it true that right now you're being sued for refusing to do business with a homosexual couple?"

Stan grimaced, but corrected his face quickly because he was on TV. It was bound to come up sooner or later. In fact he was surprised it hadn't come up before. "Yes, Jerry, that is true, but not exactly in the way you framed the question. I would never refuse to do business with a gay person. The truth is, I employ a gay man in key a senior position on my firm. He's my creative director and one of the finest people I know. I knew he was gay when I hired him and I respect him highly, not for his chosen lifestyle, but for his work, which is exemplary. He knows my views and we get along fine. One of the beautiful things about America is that we can agree to disagree. But as to why I'm being sued, it's because the gay couple that came to me asked me to promote a gay club. Now if they had come to me asking that I advertise a new can opener, or something else they'd invented, I would have gladly taken them on as clients. But promoting their club would mean designing a campaign that enticed men to enjoy a behavior I believe is unhealthy. In essence I'd be putting my stamp of approval on it, so I declined. I gave them a list of other advertising agencies I thought would be happy to have their business and we let it go at that. Why they're suing me now I really can't say. I guess we'll have to wait till we get to court to find out.

As to why I believe homosexuality is bad for society, it's just that historically it's been at the forefront of every nation's decline. More importantly, every major religion defines homosexuality as sin; Christianity, Judaism, Islam. Now I doubt the leaders of these religions sat down at a table one day and decided to make homosexuality taboo. There's something much bigger going on, I call it God, you call it whatever you want, but there's a spiritual dimension that sees…"

"Oh for crying out loud! I've had enough of this." Charlotte was glaring at Stan her face red and flat as a clay plate. "I feel like I'm standing up here debating Hitler. Never have I seen such bigotry. You keep talking about going back to the past. Now I know why, because back in the 1940s, Hitler was stuffing homosexuals into gas chambers. That's the world you want. I want no part of this. Having a dialogue with such evil only degrades my office and that's something I refuse to do. Now if you'll excuse me." Charlotte turned and walked off the stage while strobes popped and cameras zoomed in on the action.

It would make a great morning headline.

Twelve

THE REID bar was buzzing with conversation, a subdued polite chatter perhaps, but buzzing nonetheless. The thirty invited guests and their significant others stood in small clusters holding their half-filled cocktail glasses while nibbling on Chick Pea Tapenade and Yellowfin Tuna Tartare as they waited patiently for Charlotte to make the rounds and greet everyone personally. Men were dressed in casual fashion with collarless jackets and designer shoes, while the ladies were in bejeweled evening gowns and wraps, mostly black, with an occasional splash of rose, or purple to give the room color.

Charlotte refreshed her martini and, holding the crystal vase with her fingertips, sidled up to a group she hadn't acknowledged yet. Her own dress, of course, was blue, the party color, the one she'd worn on stage because she didn't have time to change. Her nails and lips were painted pink and her streaked, salt and pepper hair had that styled-disheveled look she was famous for, though most of the pictures of her were from an earlier day before her hair began to gray, or she had to hide the laugh lines crinkling her eyes, or the creases surrounding the corners of her mouth. She was pleased with the turnout, and pleased in particular that most people saw her indignation as a coup.

"I can't believe what that man said. I would've walked out too. I've never seen such an open display of misogynistic, racist, and homophobic rhetoric. To think such bigotry still exists in America. They should lock the man up before he does someone harm."

Charlotte took the comment for what it was. Mrs. Rand was defending her honor. "What concerns me," she said, "is that there are others out there just like him. It certainly shows our education of the country has a long way to go."

"I'll drink to that," Mrs. Rand said, lifting her Manhattan before bringing it to her lips.

Charlotte took a sip of her own drink, winked, and moved on to the next group. She had to be careful. Too many toasts and she wouldn't be able to walk. She'd been at this for an hour already and was beginning to feel tipsy.

"Hi Jim, so nice to see you and Helen again."

"Hi sweetie. Glad to see you're still on your feet." Jim Stewart leaned in to kiss the Senator's cheek. "You sure gave them hell out there."

Charlotte pulled away, but only slightly. She couldn't afford to be caught on camera and have it look like inappropriate sexual contact. Jim was still standing too close. His deodorant's springtime freshness was overbearing. She pushed him back with the flat of her hand and then feigned to be admiring his tie. "Oh, real silk. I like a man who's not afraid to wear silk. I only said what had to be said. Powers was making a fool of himself. One of those macho rednecks who's too stupid to see he's digging his own grave."

"You got that right. You already had the election in the bag, but if you ever doubted it, not anymore." Jim raised his glass in a salute.

"Thank you, Jim. I appreciate your support. Now, if you'll excuse me, I have to circulate and try and catch everyone before they leave."

A server stopped and replaced the martini in Charlotte's hand with a fresh one even though her glass was only half empty. A toast was being raised, the glasses tapping each other with the unique ring of crystal. She took a sip repeating the process over and again.

She was used to it. She'd done it a thousand times, always with the goal of securing large donations, but it was taking its toll. She paused to look around the room. Her focus was fuzzy. The police chief was there, and the mayor. What would they do if she started to stumble or simply passed out? Teddy, CEO of Dunnigan and Frisk, one of the state's biggest law firms; Jim, president of Harcourt Brace Publishing; Bill of Standard Oil; all the movers and shakers of Chicago would witness it happen. Thank God she hadn't allowed the media to attend this soirée.

"Charlotte, I hate to say it but we have to be going. The hors d'oeuvres were spectacular. A fine reception. Thank you." Roland took her hand warmly giving it a squeeze.

Charlotte let go, but left her fingers resting on his forearm lightly. "Thank you, Roland. I'm pleased you and your wife could make it. And thank you for your generous contribution."

"No, no. Not another word. I do, if I might be so bold, have one piece of advice."

Charlotte took another sip, trying to look interested, but knowing she didn't really want his opinion. Everyone wanted to offer her their advice—and everyone expected her to take their advice. She brought the drink away from her lips. "Oh, what's that?"

"What Mr. Powers said about you personally giving to the poor. You need to get ahead of that. The whole room went quiet for a minute. It seemed like you'd lost your audience. I found it a bit disconcerting."

Charlotte took a final sip and set her empty glass on a nearby table. "It was pure nonsense Roland, you know that."

"Yes, I know it, and you know it, but some of those folks out there may wonder. You need to do something big, something that shows the people how hard you fight for the poor. Maybe set up a statewide clothes collection, or sponsor a food drive or something. Anyway that's just my opinion; take it for what it's worth."

"I will, and you know I value your opinion." She picked up

another glass and raised it high, tipping her head in a thank-you, goodbye, gesture, then turned and saw her campaign manager. His eyes were focused on Roland's back, watching him go. He glanced at Charlotte and nodded as if to say "he's right," but his smile was vague as though he was still processing what the man had said. She walked over and melded into another group of guests. She didn't want to discuss it now. Okay, maybe Roland was right. It was the one time her opponent had her on the ropes. She wanted to celebrate, but the force of his argument kept her from declaring total victory. She regretted not having the presence of mind to turn it around. She should have asked how much he was giving. She would've called his bluff. The woman standing next to her had apparently bathed in her perfume. Charlotte wrinkled her nose and discreetly drew in a breath. It called for another martini. The gin and vermouth would cleanse her nose. A small droplet stuck to her painted lips, but she licked it off. She smiled, batting her eyes so they glittered in the light.

"Margaret it's so good to see you. I'm so glad you made it."

Charlotte waited until her last guest had gone before stumbling into the night. It was eleven o'clock and she was exhausted, but the last stragglers had to be treated with as much courtesy and respect as those who left early, and they all wanted her to have a drink with them. The Chicago River swirled in a rainbow of colored lights that shimmered on the water but she was too tired to notice. What she did notice was the strong scent of diesel fuel which made her stomach slosh and roll like an ocean wave. A water taxi cruised by leaving a small white wake in its passing. She put a hand to her stomach. People on the ferry smiled, lifted their glasses and waved. Their evening had just begun.

She made her way down the steps to the parking garage while trying to search her purse for her keys, tripping momentarily, but righting herself before falling. The cool evening air off the river had helped clear her head, but in the garage the smell of exhaust fumes and engine oil made her nauseous again. She thought about calling a cab, but she would have to leave the car and have someone come for it in the morning.

She put one foot in front of the other, forcing herself to walk straight. She'd been early enough to find parking on the ground floor but the garage had been reasonably empty. Now it was full and there were so many cars she couldn't say where hers had been left. She finished one long row and started down a second. Except for the color, all the backs of the cars looked the same. She could discount the light ones because hers was dark. That much she knew. And she didn't drive a van or a pickup truck so those were out too. A number painted on a pillar jogged her memory. She was in the right row, now she just had to find the right car.

She slid her fingers across the smooth rubbery plastic of the key fob. She'd been holding it since she'd tripped on the stairs. She pressed the unlock button. The taillights blinked on and off, letting her know where her car was parked. *Smart.* She hastened to the vehicle and climbed in, letting the hand still holding her keys drop to her lap. What was Mr. Powers' endgame? What did he hope to achieve? Surely he knew he couldn't win. They'd gone nine rounds and he'd only landed one punch. There she went again, using sports analogies. *Competition.* She'd thought she trained herself better than that, but she was tired and certainly not in her right mind so maybe she had an excuse. She closed her eyes, sitting for a moment to collect her thoughts. She could do this. She slipped the key into the ignition and backed up, but hit her brakes just inches before plowing into the car behind her. Her taillights lit up the paint—a silver Lexus. *Careful.*

She used her restaurant validation to exit the lot and turned to the right, heading for the bridge. The streets were a noisy menagerie of traffic and bright lights. Cars swept up behind her and then swerved around. *Stay in your lane. Beeeeeeep.* A car swung around on her right waving his arm out the window. She swerved back into her own lane and slowed down, but another car came up from behind honking again. *Beeeeeeeeeeeep.* The buildings surrounding her seemed liquid, the streets uneven and it appeared she had more than one line to follow, not a double yellow line, but a quadruple yellow line. She knew she had to cross the bridge, but she couldn't find the entrance. Was that a red light? She started to stop but realized she was already in the intersection so she hit the gas and continued on. Blue flashing lights swept up behind in her rearview mirror. She heard a *whoop whoop. Busted.* The street was crowded with cars lined up along the curb. There was nowhere to pull over. *Whoop, whoop.* "All right, all right! I'm trying." Finally she gave up and stopped in the middle the road.

A uniformed officer climbed out of the car behind her and made his way to her door as she lowered her window. He had his patrol hat on and a gold badge proudly pinned to his chest. On his black leather belt hung the tools of the trade, radio, handcuffs, and a gun. "Driver's license and registration please," he said, stooping over to where he could see inside the vehicle.

Charlotte shook her head. "Look officsur, thish is all a mistake. I need you to escort me home. Juss pull up and I'll follow."

The officer glanced around the front and back seats of the car. "Have you been drinking ma'am?"

"No. Yes. Kinda. I mean I juss came from a cocktail reception but I only had a few."

"Please step out of the car, ma'am."

"I'm not gesshing out of my car."

"Ma'am, please step out of the car." The officer reached to open the door.

"Stop that. Leave me alone!" She smacked his fingers.

"I've asked you twice. I'm not going to do it again." Pedestrians on the sidewalk were stopping to listen.

"Listen, you know who I am?"

"I know you're a woman who's had one too many and that you're driving over the legal limit. Now please step out of the car." Phones with cameras were going up just to make sure the officer didn't get out of line, but the officer didn't mind, he had his own body camera.

"I'm Senator Weise, idiot. Call your Captain and tell him you're trying to arrest Senator Weise and see what happens."

The man took a step back and went around to check the license plate. The cars behind were backing up, frustrated with trying to squeeze between the police car and those parked at the curb. The officer waved them through and went back to Charlotte's door. "I don't see a government plate."

"Ish my personal vehicle." Charlotte drug her purse into her lap and started going through it spilling lipstick, tissues, and a phone onto her seat until she found her wallet. She held it up. "There, see?"

"I'm going to have to call this in. Wait here."

The officer returned a few minutes later and leaned in to hand her driver's license back. "I'm going to ask you to pull your car over there," he said. "It will be impounded. You can pick it up tomorrow. You need to come with me. I'll be driving you home."

"That's wasch I said."

The officer took Charlotte by the arm and helped walk her back to his patrol car. By now a half dozen people were recording Charlotte as she was seated in the back of the patrol car. He went around to the front, removing his hat to lay it on the seat with the brim up as he got in and started the engine, the car roaring to life. The officer felt for his body cam making sure it was there. She hadn't identified herself as a senator and his partner, who'd just ducked out for coffee, wasn't there to witness. A tow truck backed up in front of Charlotte's car with a *beep, beep, beep.*

The officer glanced in his rearview mirror. His eyes were dark and his eyebrows brushy. "I have to make a quick stop to pick up my partner. That okay with you?"

Charlotte stared out the window at the people filming her on camera. Thank God the windows were tinted. She ignored the question.

But the officer continued, "You know, I watched the debate before I started my shift, but there's something I don't get. I heard you say you wanted a world where everyone was treated equal, especially when they apply for a loan or get pulled over for a ticket, but when you get pulled over you want special favors. If you were anyone else you'd be in a cell by now. Instead I have to drive you home because you have privilege. Where's the equality in that?"

Stan picked his paper up off the lawn. After its long winter of dormancy, the grass had sprung to life and would soon need mowing. The dew on the long blades stuck to the cuffs of his suit, causing them to darken. He smacked the rolled newspaper against his palm knocking the loose drops off the plastic bag, but walked back into the house without removing it. He set it on the counter and poured coffee into his travel mug, screwing the lid down tight. He didn't need to read the articles. He wasn't going to like what they said so why bother. He swept the paper up and dropped it out of its protective bag, slinging the blue plastic wrap into the sink. With paper in hand, he grabbed his coffee and headed for the back door. The shades were drawn to keep out the afternoon heat but light filtered in around the sides. The grains of dirt on the worn linoleum crunched beneath his feet. He stepped outside, locking the door and headed for the garage to get his car. The thing he needed to do right now was talk to Bishop Samuel.

The irony of what he'd said to Charlotte dawned on him as he powered down Highway 88 in his polished Lexus. How could he accuse her of hoarding her wealth when he drove such a fancy car?

No one knew where, or how, he lived, they only saw him drive this sleek late-model number with the cushy leather seats and that fancy stereo system he rarely listened to. Maybe he should park it down the block and try to keep a low profile, but it would be pointless. He couldn't keep it up forever. His suit was a medium brown, dark enough to be professional but light enough to herald the coming of summer. Nice suits and fancy cars, but it was all pretense, not the real him. He smoothed his tie and reached for his coffee, flipping the lid open as he brought it to his mouth. Good coffee, and warming to the soul.

His phone rang. He put it on speaker. "This is Stan, how can I help you?"

"Hey boss, it's Bruce. We got a whole lot of people out here looking for you. It's kind of a madhouse."

"Tell them I won't be in today."

"You won't?"

"Maybe later, but if you tell them that now, maybe they'll leave."

"Right. How you holding up?"

"Don't worry. I'm fine. Just get the reporters off my back. I'll try to stop by in a few hours..." He heard a beep letting him know he had another call. "I have to go, see you later." He pushed a button switching him to the call still ringing. "This is Stan, how can I help you?"

"Mr. Powers, my name's Michael Bovine, Pastor Bovine, actually. I pastor MorningStar Church in Peoria. I caught the debate last night and liked what you had to say. It's about time someone had the guts to tell the truth."

"Thank you, sir, but I'm not sure many would agree."

"Perhaps, but enough would. Listen, the reason I'm calling is because I'd like to have you come and speak at our church. We have a good size congregation; the church seats about seven hundred. We'll do it on a Sunday night; I'm thinking the eighteenth. We usually have a smaller service Sunday evenings, but I'm planning to invite the whole community so you should have a full house."

Stan didn't have to think about it. His calendar was clear and he needed to get his message out. "Just so happens I don't have any engagements on Sunday evenings this month. What time would you like me there?"

Stan rolled his window down and stuck his arm out, letting the air rush in. *So they liked what I had to say.* It felt good to hear that. He flipped his blinker on, veering to the right so he could exit at the next ramp. At least his parking space was in the back so he could hide his car. The buildings lining the street were two and three stories high with chipped paint that looked like white petals wilting from a magnolia blossom. Seagulls circled and powerlines buzzed. A page of newspaper tumbled down the street on a breeze. Not a cloud in the sky. He pulled behind a row of buildings to park at the rear of the mission. Another sunny day. He rolled his window up, the warmth coming through the glass easing the tension in his bones. Winter would come again all too soon. He stepped out heading for the door, the screen slamming as he went inside. Several of the parolees were sitting at tables eating Fruit Loops and Cheerios. They jumped up as soon as they saw him and clamored over. One had a milk mustache on his lips which he wiped with a sleeve.

"Great debate last night, Mr. Powers."

"Yeah dude, you nailed it. You got my vote."

They were patting his shoulder and shaking his hand. A man as big as a grizzly, and just as hairy, trapped him in a bear hug.

Stan had to push away to catch his breath. "Thanks guys, I appreciate it, though I'm pretty sure there's only a few who felt that way. Let me grab a coffee and I'll sit down and we'll talk. Samuel around?"

One of the men pointed and Stan turned to see Samuel sitting on stage holding his Bible. The heel of his boot was hooked over the bottom rung of his stool and his cross hung outside his white shirt dangling in the light. He nodded, acknowledging Stan, his white goatee bobbing up and down.

"You know, what you said about our moral breakdown destroying us?" one of the men continued, "I wish others could get that. I mean, we've been there so we've seen it, but everyone around us looked clueless."

"Yeah, man. We should have gone up there and told them what it's like when you start ignoring God. We could tell some scary tales." He looked around and winked, his lips flattening beneath his mustache as he smiled, his long hair and beard hanging below his chin. Others chortled along with him. He swung around and went back to his seat to finish eating before his cereal got soggy.

"Yeah, I'm sure I'd love to hear it." Stan took his coffee to the table and sat down.

Samuel lifted himself from his stool and walked over to take a seat beside him, his boots thumping on the wood floor. "I looked up some verses for you," he said. "Thought you might need them this morning. This one's found in Ephesians 6:12.:

"For we do not wrestle against flesh and blood, but against principalities, against powers, against the rulers of the darkness of this age, against spiritual hosts of wickedness in the heavenly places.

"Kind of fits the situation, don't you think? And this one's found in Peter, 1 Peter 5:8. Be sober, be vigilant; because your adversary the devil walks about like a roaring lion, seeking whom he may devour."

Stan looked up, smiling. "Forgive me, Bishop, but those verses aren't exactly encouraging." He raised his mug, the steam departing as he blew across the rim of the cup and took a drink.

"Devil don't like it much when you speaks the truth." Samuel's voice was scratchy as sandpaper on tin.

"Have you seen the papers yet? I haven't. I've been afraid to look at them." Stan placed his rolled newspaper on the table, watching it unfurl as he let it go.

Samuel closed his Bible. "I saw 'em. That's why I chose those verses. You're definitely under attack, but not by your political adversaries, this one's from the devil himself."

Stan reached over and grabbed his paper, taking another sip of his coffee as he began to read. The photo across the top showed Charlotte storming off the stage. The headline read, 'Senator Weise Livid as Stan Powers Slams Gays.' He folded it again. He didn't have to read the rest of the story to know what it said. They were wrong. He didn't hate homosexuals or transgenders or anyone else in the LGBTQ community. He was simply stating that God had established certain laws and that nations who followed those laws prospered, and those who didn't eventually collapsed.

"Did you see the good news?" Samuel reached for the paper opening it again.

"What good news?"

"You gotta go to the last page of the editorial section," he said sliding the paper in front of Stan. "Apparently you struck a chord." He stabbed the paper with his finger. "While all the polls say you lost the debate, the same polls show you're only thirty points behind Senator Weise. May seem like a lot, but yesterday you were fifty points so that shows a pretty big narrowing of the gap."

Stan took the paper, holding it up to the light to see better. "Well I'll be darned. Look at this, it says many of the people who thought I lost also agreed with much of what I said." He folded the paper and put it down. "Anyway, I don't want to dwell on last night. It's done and gone. It's going to be a long campaign and we're just getting started."

Charlotte squinted, the bright sun throbbing in her eyes. Her head felt like a cantaloupe a couple of kids had kicked down the street. She'd tried to sleep in, but her campaign manager was relentless. The phone's ringing was a bell and clapper in her brain. She was in no shape to be out politicizing, but Bob insisted she get ahead of the damage done last night. She had gone home and passed out, never giving the debate or her encounter with the police another thought. But Bob had gone home and made plans for her to do a meet and greet—not with donors, or even registered voters—but with bums and winos and homeless drug addicts. It was late afternoon before they were able to get everything arranged. She'd taken three Tylenol twenty minutes ago and her head was still throbbing, the sun stretching her forehead like the skin of a drum. The aspirin she'd taken earlier hadn't done a thing.

"Bob, I am never going to forgive you for this."

"Relax, Charlotte. Look around and smile for the cameras. You're here to show your genuine concern for the poor. Mr. Powers painted you as someone who doesn't care. We have to fix this while it's fresh in people's minds."

He took Charlotte's arm and guided her toward the underpass where a few dozen nylon tents were flapping in the morning breeze. Weeds and shapeless plants tried to choke each other out of cracks in the cement, and larger bushes rooted themselves everywhere dirt came to rest. A few people stood watching as they approached. They'd seen the cavalcade of news vans and black limos stopping on the street above.

"How am I supposed to talk to these people? They don't know the issues. I doubt they even care. This is not the kind of publicity I hired you for."

"No, Charlotte, you hired me to boost your popularity. I can't do that when you pull a stunt like the one you did last night. The Internet's gone viral with you being thrown into the back of a police car. That was two strikes against you in one night. I'm trying to deal with the first and show voters how you have a heart for the poor. The other we're treating as fake news. It was dark, so the images of you aren't clear, and we're filling the Internet with the suggestion that it was someone else that looked like you. A case of mistaken identity. Now be a good girl and let's shake the hands of some really unfortunate people and tell them how loved they are."

Charlotte walked into the colorful group of tents that sprouted from the ground like wildflowers. They didn't want her there. She could tell by the way they refused to look at her. She didn't belong. She'd avoided wearing a blue suit with a string of pearls and opted for more casual attire, a thin blue sweater and a pair of gray slacks, but it wasn't enough. These people were dressed in hand-me-downs that draped from their bodies like soiled rags.

She approached what looked like an older woman and introduced herself. She started talking about subsidized housing, but the woman shrank away scratching the gray tangles of her hair. "I don't need no housing. Just leave me be." Charlotte turned, ever pleasant, smiling at the camera. It was all she could do to keep her face on straight. The place reeked like a skunk's vomit. She wrinkled her nose and approached a man holding a frying pan over an open fire. He wore a long sleeve shirt with the cuffs oily and frayed. His pants were threadbare at the knees. The dirt was so rubbed in she doubted it would ever come clean. His hair, wrapped around his face like a lion's mane, was dusty brown. It looked like he was trying to cook a couple slices of Spam.

"Good afternoon, I'm Senator Weise. You know you don't have to eat that. We have programs that provide for people in need. Are you getting food stamps now?"

The man looked up. His baggy eyes were watery and veined with red cords that looked like canals on the surface of Mars. "No."

"No. Why not?"

He picked up a slice of Spam with his fingers and turned it over in the pan, letting it sizzle. "Don't got no address," he said without looking up.

Charlotte nodded, acknowledging her error. You had to have

an address to receive food stamps. "You're right. Maybe we need to draft a measure in Congress that allows people with no home to get food stamps too. You seem to be the only one eating, I'm sure others are hungry. Where are they?"

He shrugged, flipping a second piece of meat over before licking his dirty fingers. "Soup kitchen."

"What soup kitchen? Where?

The man raised a crooked finger pointing down a long row of buildings lining the street above the viaduct. "That way," he said.

Charlotte placed her hands on her hips, blinked slowly, and took a deep breath, sighing. She turned to her campaign manager pulling him aside. Her head was still throbbing, but now she was determined to not waste the day. She wiped her forehead and lowered her voice. "This isn't working. There aren't enough people here. I think it looks more like we're harassing them than helping. Let's relocate to the soup kitchen. According to this guy," she swung her hand around to indicate the man behind her, "that's where the people are. We can go in among them, talk to a few, and then we'll let the people who run the place know I'll be looking for funding to assist them. That'll play well, don't you think?"

Bob puckered his lips and nodded. He raised his eyes and said, "Okay guys, we're going to wrap it up here and reconvene at the soup kitchen. Is there anyone here who knows where that is?"

The people who stared back at him seemed detached. They looked like Holocaust survivors, their eyes unable to see beyond the images in their own minds. No one spoke. A boy Charlotte originally thought was around twenty, but on closer inspection saw was only about fourteen, stepped forward. "Give me five bucks and I'll take you," he said.

The caravan of cars parked on the street outside the Daily Bread Food Bank facing west. Charlotte had to squint against the blades of sun cutting into her eyes. A line of people were huddled along the wall waiting to be let inside. Charlotte turned her visor down and waited in her air conditioned limo until the camera crew had boots on the ground and their cameras hoisted on their shoulders. Then she got out and walked down the line of people, shaking hands and greeting the down-and-outers with the promise of a better tomorrow. "Hello, I'm Senator Weise. I'm here to learn more about your difficulties and see if we can't be of greater assistance." A few smiled deferentially but most kept their eyes on the shoulders of the person in front of them. She couldn't tell if they didn't understand what she was saying or couldn't care less. Charlotte moved to the front and tried to squeeze in but a guy with a chest like rolled leather and a motorcycle skullcap on his head stood in her way. He crossed his tattooed arms and raised his bearded chin. Hey lady, no cutting in line."

"I'm sorry sir, I'm Senator Weise and…"

"I don't care if you're the Pope. Everybody waits their turn."

"We're not here to eat. We just want to talk to the owners."

The man knotted his lips but he stepped aside. Charlotte made space between the people and ushered her campaign manager and the camera crew inside. The newspaper reporter assigned to the story snuck in behind. Most of the tables were full which explained why the people outside were still waiting. Charlotte sat down between two indigents digging their spoons into large bowls of chili.

"You gentlemen eat here often?" she asked.

One went back to eating, shoving an oversized bite into his mouth so that it dripped off his chin. The other looked at her and said, "Some, depends on what they're having."

"Looks a bit meager, but it's good to know you're being fed. I'm hoping in my next term to improve our funding and include soup kitchens so they can provide more and better food. How do you feel about that?"

The man looked at her like she'd just told him he was eating rubber chicken. He shoveled another dripping pile of chili onto his spoon and nodded while taking it into his mouth.

Charlotte looked around to see if her cameraman and reporter were getting this. They weren't behind her. She searched through the crowd to see where they'd wandered off to and found them over by the kitchen. They were talking to someone else. Then she saw who it was and the color drained from her face. *What? What's he doing here?*

Satchel busied himself in the kitchen preparing for the dinner rush. The choices for the evening were pork chops covered with mushroom gravy, served with cut roasted potatoes and petite green peas, or fresh caught trout baked with olive oil, along with baby potatoes and asparagus, or Mama's famous lasagna with a mixed green salad and garlic bread. He looked around the kitchen admiring what Mama had done to get everything working. It was just an old house that she'd had the vision to renovate. She'd put in a commercial ten burner gas range complete with two ovens, a stainless steel sink and commercial dishwasher, and a two door stainless steel refrigerator. It was obvious she'd had to take out a wall to fit everything in. Even then space was tight, but it was big enough to move around in, yet small enough to have most things within easy reach. He sprinkled the pork chops with garlic and onion salt, ground black pepper and paprika and slid them into the oven. The other baking pans held the lasagna.

He would own a restaurant like this someday. At least that was the dream. He grabbed the towel he'd used to wipe down the sink and blotted his forehead. She hadn't upgraded the air conditioning, and in a small room like this with the ovens on it got pretty warm, even with two pole fans circulating the air. Mama hadn't taken the TV back yet so Satchel had it on, watching the news.

"Hundreds of people showed up to hear the debate but few were prepared for what they heard." The scene cut to a reporter with a microphone talking to a woman with a thin face and large black glasses that kept sliding from her nose. Her hair was kinky and parted in the middle, running to her shoulders on both sides. The woman's mouth screwed into a knot. "I never thought I'd hear such bigotry from a political candidate. I think his mother should have washed his mouth out with soap." The scene cut to a second interview, a young gentleman with spiky hair and a two-day-old beard. "Was that a joke? He was talking like someone from another century, no not another century, another planet." And finally an overweight woman in a T-shirt that read, "I just met God and she's black," said, "I came to hear Mr. Powers, to see what he's about. Now I know. He's a pig. Charlotte has my vote."

The camera cut back to the anchor desk where Bill Lawrence pontificated in his custom tailored suit and tie. His eyes cut from the studio monitor to the camera again. "Well, we know one thing, Mr. Powers has an uphill battle ahead of him. Clearly eighty percent of the people we polled said Senator Weise won the debate. For Mr. Powers to win, he's either going to have to sway a lot of people over to his side, or change his way of thinking. Next up we have a story about a couple of local heroes who saved a cat stuck in a tree for three days."

Satchel stooped down to check the oven, making sure the temperature was set correctly. He wasn't a student of the Bible, or of history, so he couldn't speak to anything Stan had said, but it did seem to make sense. If there was a God, and he was now convinced there was, wouldn't He expect people to live virtuously? It seemed to make sense, but what did he know? He reached for a pot and put it on the stove at medium heat to melt the butter for the gravy. Add the mushrooms, onion, and thyme and season with salt and freshly ground pepper. Cook about four minutes, stirring occasionally until the mushrooms are slightly browned and soft. Sprinkle in the flour and mix until fully blended. It was a crazy world out there. Just plain crazy.

He reached over to swirl the pat of butter in the pan. Something else Mr. Powers said had him thinking. "Only those nations are blessed whose God is the Lord." What's with that? Course, Stan had attributed the saying to Abraham Lincoln. Still it had given Satchel pause for thought. Throughout the centuries countries like his homeland of England and all of Europe and America had led the world out of the dark ages into civilization, yet all of these nations had strong Christian roots. Could it be...?

Rachel walked along Lake Michigan picking her way through the pebbles that lined the shore. The waves lapped the hard sand, kissing the earth with tiny foam bubbles, the air pungent with wet moss. Her hair tossed in an evening breeze that also feathered her skin. She was heading toward the Northwestern campus after an hour of reading a book on American history taken from the library.

Last night she'd almost been assaulted by the man who'd killed her mother. He'd stood looking down on her with a grin that sent chills down her spine. She'd narrowly escaped having to introduce herself. That would've been a disaster. And now, adding insult to injury, the blogger world had gone viral with a faux pas by Senator Weise who went to help the needy only to find her opponent already there. She'd seen the video of the soup kitchen on her tablet. She'd recognized it immediately as one of the horrors of her past. If only Charlotte had let her know her plans, she would've warned her not to go. She didn't fully understand how this man could be so evil and look so good at the same time but she knew it was a subterfuge. He was assuming the role of benefactor as a way to assuage his guilt. He was probably the one who'd posted the videos of that woman who looked like Charlotte getting into the police car. That would be like him. If you can't win the debate using logic, have your competition arrested.

She stepped into a forest of oaks sprouting over her head like a great umbrella. They were big trees, well over two-hundred years old, proud and majestic. A Cooper's Hawk cried from a branch and took flight, upset by her sudden appearance. Cardinals, chickadees and robins flittered among the densely leafed maples while squirrels scurried along the ground looking for crab apples and fallen nuts. It was only a few weeks ago that the Eastern redbuds had exploded with tiny pink flowers looking like Fourth of July fireworks bursting in the air.

She kept the book under her arm figuring to read more of it at dinner. She had wanted to prove Mr. Powers wrong. He claimed America was founded by deeply religious men who believed God was responsible for their sustenance and it appeared he'd been right. There were several books on the shelf, a few of which alluded to a desire by the early settlers to worship God in their own way, but the one she'd picked up, and now had in her hand, was a book of their quotes. It was the only way to know what they really thought. As she'd leafed through its pages, it became painfully obvious that these men were, as Mr. Powers said, deeply religious and devout Christian men. They actually expected men to be self-governed, submitting first to the authority of an all seeing God, which aligned with what she'd learned years ago on her trip to Washington DC.

There was one he'd quoted last night who had said it was impossible for the newly formed government to hold sway over anyone but a moral and religious people. Then there was James Wilson, who had signed both the Declaration of Independence and the U.S. Constitution, who'd said, "Far from being rivals or enemies, religion and law are twin sisters, friends, and mutual assistants." And Alexander Hamilton, a founding father and one of America's first constitutional lawyers, who wrote, "For my own part, I sincerely esteem it a system which without the finger of God, never could have been suggested and agreed upon by such a diversity of interests." There were, in fact, so many she'd stopped counting. Even the Continental Congress wrote, "Religion, morality, and knowledge are necessary to good government and the happiness of mankind."

That didn't dissuade her. She knew these men were born in ignorance. They knew nothing of modern science. Their belief in God was an attempt to justify the reason for their existence. Still, she was fascinated by their stringent devotion to an all-knowing God who they readily accepted and wanted to rule their lives.

Several crows were picking at something in the grass, dancing and ducking in and out of a loosely knit circle. She heard a hissing and saw a sprinkler head push up from the ground. The crows took flight. A stream of water erupted from the nozzle, shooting out across the lawn. The founts began to circle. She picked up her pace and ran toward the sidewalk to avoid getting wet.

Watching the faces of the two debaters had troubled her. Mr. Powers, for all his latent evil, looked calm as water in a bowl, while her boss appeared to be standing on an electric wire feeling the joules running through her bones, or maybe that was just an effect she proffered by styling her hair so that it stood up on end. Rachel didn't know contentment, she couldn't even describe what it was. People said she never looked happy, even when she was pleased with the way things were going. She'd tried practicing her smile in a mirror but it seemed so phony, because it was. How do you communicate something you don't feel in your heart? She was glad she hadn't been on that stage. She would've looked more like Senator Weise than Mr. Powers, and that wasn't necessarily a good thing.

The air was warm in her lungs as she caught her breath. It had been an exhausting day. The phones were ringing off the hook with people eager to provide donations for Senator Weise's campaign. Charlotte may have been tense, but she'd certainly wowed her constituents at the debate. Now they wanted to make sure she got elected. The usurper had left the stage humbled and ashamed. *Served him right.* Rachel could not have asked for a better outcome.

The houses along the sidewalk became familiar. She'd been this way so many times she could almost walk it blindfolded. She thought about the families that lived in these homes before they became places of business. Had they been around in the day that Mr. Powers spoke of, where doors could remain unlocked and children could play in the street without fear of being shot? And was the difference really a change in people's attitudes toward God, or was it just that as society evolves it becomes open to new ideas? More importantly, was there a connection between a loosening of a nation's morals and the subsequent collapse of the nation?

She turned and went up the stairs. The room was fairly crowded, but there were several vacant tables. She looked around but didn't see her hostess so she took the liberty of seating herself. She swept a few breadcrumbs off the tablecloth with the back of her hand. The nightly menu was spelled out on an A-frame blackboard in fluorescent pink, yellow, and blue chalk. As she read each entrée she could almost smell their individual juices wafting in from the kitchen; lasagna, pork chops, and trout. A man came out from the kitchen holding plates in each hand with a third one cocked between his elbow and wrist. He placed the plates on the table in front of three people, two of whom appeared to be students. The other was a bit older, perhaps a parent, or maybe a professor.

It didn't take her long to decide. Lasagna was too fattening and pork chops too greasy. The fish looked great. The man approached and stood towering over her table.

"Hello love, Mama had to step out. I'll be doing the duty till she gets back. Can I get you a spot to drink?"

Rachel stared into the man's face, his bulbous nose, his ruddy complexion, the way his lips turned when he spoke with a British accent.

"Daddy?" she cried.

Thirteen

T HE LAST of Mama's dinner guests sauntered out the door and for the first time that evening the room settled into a quiet. It had been a boisterous celebration. Mama had returned to discover the restored-father daughter relationship and planted big kisses on Rachel, and then on Satchel, and then did a three way group hug. Then with her fingers pointed in the air, she began bobbing up and down, saying, "Yeah baby, that's what I'm talking about," as she danced a jig around the kitchen floor. She couldn't entirely grasp that she'd hired the long lost father of one of her favorite customers. Her level of glee was so high the rest of her customers thought someone in the back must be having a birthday party, until Mama let them in on the secret and poured everybody a complementary glass of her own home-brewed apple cider. The entire restaurant applauded and with glasses raised, toasted to a new beginning for Rachel and her father.

Rachel stayed to help clear the tables while Mama did a quick vacuum. She'd already promised to wait until her father finished for the evening so they could have a chance to talk. They needed time to get reacquainted. Mama stayed until she realized she was invading their together time and then took her leave. Rachel leaned against the tall stainless steel refrigerator as Satchel used a yellow, orange, and brown striped cotton towel to dry the last pot. The pans rattled and threatened to come tumbling out as he balanced one on top of another in the cabinet under the sink. The TV was still on, the volume barely audible. An interview with Charlotte Weise was on the set. Satchel wiped his hands on the towel and reached up to turn it off.

"Wait, I want to hear what Senator Weise has to say."

Satchel looked back over his shoulder. He was wearing denims, a white T-shirt that conformed to the swell of his tummy, and tennis shoes, but he had an apron over his clothes. "You look so much like your mother," he said.

"Oh, how's that?"

He turned around to face her, placing the heels of his hands behind him on the sink as he looked her up and down. "I don't know. For starters, she was beautiful. You have the same bright blue eyes and blond hair, I see it in the way your eyebrows lift when you question something, the way your fingers handle things, soft but firm, but it's more than that. It's kind of everything; the way you move, the silkiness of your motions like you could slip through a stream of water without breaking a ripple. Your mother was fluid like that."

Rachel shrugged. "Why did you turn the TV off? I thought you might want to listen."

"Politics? No love, not me. You forget, I wasn't born here. I have no say in your politics." Satchel finished wiping his hands and placed the towel over the handle of the oven door. "Sorry you had to wait so long. I think Mama was just happy to see us together and wanted to let us know."

Rachel strolled back into the main dining area and stood by the door waiting for her father to lock up. She wondered what word she could use to describe the way she felt. Happy, yes, but that didn't do it justice. The last time she'd seen him he was on his way to jail, and before that he was teaching her how to pinch pockets. She'd written letters suggesting that if he wanted to see her again he'd have to turn his life around. She'd always hoped for something like this but never really expected to see it, or that it might even be possible. The debate over whether or not a person with strong predispositions could ever really change filled volumes in libraries. She didn't know if it would last, but just seeing him here plying his hands at a trade instead of using them to steal was enough to make her proud. She had made it clear that there could be no future for them unless he put aside his past, and he had listened.

Satchel opened the door and held it as she stepped outside into a balmy Bahama evening in Chicago. The air was warm, the sky a midnight blue, not completely dark, but with a color so deep it almost looked transparent. A quarter moon rested over their shoulders giving enough light to see as they stepped down to the sidewalk. And there were stars, perhaps not as many as you might see outside the city's ambience, but enough to make the evening seem special. Crickets chirped a sonnet written just for them as they meandered down the street.

"Anywhere in particular you'd like to go?" Satchel asked.

"I thought maybe down by the lake. I was there this afternoon and there was a nice warm breeze and, I don't know, I thought maybe I'd like to see what it's like at night."

"Sounds good to me. You sure you want to carry that book? It looks a tad heavy. We could've left it in the restaurant till we got back."

"I'm fine."

The moon cast faint shadows in front of them as they walked, the sand on the sidewalk crunching under their feet. A car zoomed by leaving a warm breeze tousling their hair in its wake. Rachel reached around, pulling her ponytail to the front. They walked for a while without speaking, each lost in their own thoughts, uncertain about what needed to be said. Satchel finally broke the silence.

"What's it about?"

"What?"

"The book."

Rachel held the volume up to read its title under the dim glow of a streetlamp, but the glare on the glossy cover made it difficult. "Oh, it's American history. I got interested in it the other night at the debate."

"You were at the debate?"

"I had to, I work for Senator Weise."

"You work for her?"

"I manage her Northwestern campaign office."

"Oh, I didn't know."

"How could you? I'd ask you to vote for her, but I guess you can't."

"Even if I could, I probably wouldn't."

Rachel looked at her father, her eyes squinting. "What? Why not?"

"Sorry, luv. I don't mean to be contentious."

"But why wouldn't you?"

They went a few more paces breathing in the heavy lake air before Satchel answered. "I don't know much about the senator so it's not fair to say I don't like her. It's just that I know Mr. Powers, and I like him better."

Rachel reached out to take her father's arm, pulling him around until they were face to face. "Please don't say that."

"Say what?"

"Say you like Mr. Powers. That man is evil."

Satchel shook his head, looking at his daughter. The light from the moon made her face look blue, but the consternation in her eyes let him know her face was probably turning red. He shook his head and shrugged. "Maybe you're talking about someone else. The word evil doesn't fit the bloke I know."

"It does, and he is. You don't know him."

"I know they put me in the slammer for ten years for shooting a man during a holdup. Stan, Mr. Powers, was the bloke I shot. He took a bullet that would've hit a little girl and probably killed her. I wouldn't be talking to you right now if that had happened because I'd still be in jail. Then he came to my trial and begged the judge for leniency, and when I was finally released he took me in, knowing it was me what shot him. I can't name on one hand the number of men I know that would do that. And he recommended me for this job at Mama's, or I might be still unemployed. But the most important thing he did was to help me understand that there's more to this life than just the living. There's a whole world beyond waiting for us. He taught me how to depend on God, and frankly, I can't thank him enough."

Rachel's lips puckered, her eyes firm. The trees overhead were like a parasol blocking the moon's light. "Yeah, so now all is forgiven and Mr. Spiritual gets to walk away free. I don't buy it. Maybe people can change, I hope you have, but it doesn't make up for the people you hurt before your redemption."

Satchel slipped his hands into his pockets and began walking again. "That's a good point. I've often thought about that little girl and what I did that night. I could've killed her. For all I know the trauma screwed her up permanently. How do I make amends for that? How do I make it up to the hundreds, if not thousands, of people whose money I pinched? Christ may have forgiven me, but have they?"

"He killed my mother."

"What? Your mum, Wren? No way."

"I'm certain of it. I can't prove it, it would be my word against his, but I was there when it happened. It was him."

"You saw Stan Powers kill your mother?"

Rachel stepped on a stone sending a jab of pain through the arch of her foot. *Ohww.* She bit her bottom lip and kicked it out of the way limping the next few steps.

"You okay?"

"I'm fine. Just stepped on a sharp rock." She forced herself to walk straight with her shoulders back. "I didn't actually see it. Mom sent me out to get something and I came back and found him standing over her body. The needle was still in her arm. He gave her a hotshot and she OD'd. He killed her."

"Look luv, that's just not possible. You think he did it and then got religion? Nope. He was working at that mission long before what happened to your mum. I hate to say it, luv, but your mum did it to herself. It's one of the things about being a junkie. The more you take, the more you have to take to satisfy the need. You keep building up the high, wanting more and more, until you come to a place where you reach to get the ultimate high, and that's the point of no return. You get that ultimate high all right, but then it's over. You're dead and gone. I watched your mum do that to herself. She stopped caring. Everyone was telling her to back off and get help, but she wouldn't listen. If you saw him that night, it's more likely he was there to help her than put a needle in her arm. What reason would he have for killing her, anyway?"

Rachel shook her head, her lips pressed tight. "Sorry, but you weren't there, I was, and I know what I saw. Let's change the subject. This isn't how I want our reunion to be." They were passing the Cambridge style buildings on the left, tall gray block edifices that looked pale in the moon's light. "Sometimes when I pass by here I imagine myself in the twelfth century. I pretend I'm in Camelot with King Arthur and the Knights of the Round Table." She waved her hand out in front of her, a light hand almost floating like a bird. "Can you see it? The castle's right over there, the river runs through here surrounded by medieval forests, and there, right over there," she said pointing, "the magnificent cathedral, St. Stephen's. I can almost hear the sound of the horse's hooves as they trample the turf under the city gate." She dropped her hand. "I guess that would grow old for a lot of little girls who read about it in fairytales, but I never got the chance so I think about it now."

"You want to see castles? Now you're in my bailiwick. Maybe we could plan a trip and go to England together. It might take me a few years to save enough money but there are plenty of castles there, and the real thing."

They strolled on, wandering through the campus until they reached the lake and walked down along the hard packed sand where small whitecaps lapped up on the shore. The smell of humus filled the air. Rachel rubbed her arms feeling, for the first time, a slight chill. There were boats on the horizon, their lights flickering on the surface of the inky-blue water. Seagulls glowing in the moon's neon white light bobbed up and down on the surface of the sea.

Satchel paused to gaze out over the water. His thoughts appeared to be far away, looking into another place and time. He took a deep breath and let it out with a sigh. "You know, I ran into an old mate of ours last week. Been going through a hard time, riding the needle. You know what that did to your mum, but he's trying to get himself straight. You remember Freddie?"

"Freddie? Of course I remember Freddie. Is he still alive?"

"Alive, and still on the streets. The years haven't been good to 'im but I suspect he's trying to turn it around. At least he's making a go of it. We got 'im in detox, but he's due out this Sunday. That's my day off. Bishop Samuel, one of the blokes what runs the mission, he and I are going to pick 'im up. Think you might want to come along?"

"There you go, a crusader on your white horse riding in to save the day. I always knew you had it in you, Dad." She crossed her arms and leaned in, bumping his shoulder playfully. "Freddie, huh? That does bring back memories, but not very good ones I'm afraid. To be brutally honest, there was a time when I would've been happy never to see either one of you again, but times change, and a girl does need a father. I don't necessarily need Freddie, though. I think he cared for me, but we kind of had a mixed relationship, mostly about him. I don't know, that might be a bit too much, too soon. I think I should focus on getting used to you right now. Tell you what, if you want to start saving for that trip to England, by all means. As long as you stick to the straight and narrow, we'll call it a date."

Dillon McShay hit the send button and eased back in his chair with this fingers interlaced across his bulging stomach. He wore the same rumpled gray polyester suit he had purchased for the Clinton inauguration, though he'd had to let out the waist and could no longer button the coat around his chest. His maroon tie had several small spots embedded in the fabric, hardly noticeable, and the yellow stains under the arms of his white shirt refused to come out even with bleach. He always wore a suit because, unlike the pajama-wearing young reporters in the field today, he was a professional.

He glanced about a room made of shadows. The walls were covered with the framed stories he'd written as a zealous young reporter in the jungles of Korea, but they were barely visible in the dim light. He kept the shades drawn to keep the room dark, not just to keep out the heat, though that was partly the reason, but because he enjoyed the privacy it afforded. Only a single lamp was lit. It glowed on the corner of his desk, a banker's lamp with a green glass shade spilling light from a forty watt bulb. The last thing he needed was yuppie wannabes peering in the windows to see him work.

The only other light came from the dim glow of his computer. Part of him regretted writing the article. He liked Senator Weise, he wasn't out to sully her reputation, but this was news and he had an obligation to share it with the public. It was no one's fault but her own. She'd set out to create a false narrative and it backfired. If she'd wanted to challenge Stan's assertion she could have done something real, like donate a wad of money to the food bank, or something else worthy of merit, but to just go out and have the media do a photo op wasn't kosher. Journalists were not political lackeys. At the very least she should've done her homework. He chuckled. She'd walked right into a soup kitchen run by her political opponent. His arms rode up and down on the rumbling of his stomach. *I'm not that fat.* He reached for the double fudge donut sitting beside the cup of coffee on his desk.

It was a half-page story and one that needed to be told because, as far as he knew, no one else had their teeth into it yet. It was his little undiscovered scoop. He reached for the coffee and took a sip to wash his donut down, *eeewww, tepid.* He wiped his lips with the back of his hand. Stan Powers sure wasn't going to tell it. He'd refused to give an interview, claiming that what he did privately at the mission was separate from what he did publicly on the campaign trail. Then he'd quoted a verse from the Bible, "'When you do a charitable deed, do not let your left hand know what your right hand is doing.' Now if you'll excuse me," he'd said. Then he'd left the building.

He should've known better. Denying a reporter an interview was like throwing a bone to a dog and then trying to take it back. There was a story there, and Dillon knew he was going after it whether Stan cooperated or not. He leaned forward, squinting as he checked the screen. Dang it, another typo his editor would have to catch. He was getting sloppy in his old age.

He relaxed again and continued reading. He didn't need Stan to get what he was after, there were plenty of sources; the people in the soup line, and the people who worked there, and his partner, Bishop Samuel, who didn't at all mind disclosing what this candidate had done to feed so many of the city's poor. Dillon would have liked to have nailed down the amount Mr. Powers gave out of his own pocket, but apparently that figure was unknown. Suffice it to say his partner, Samuel, let him know that the advertising agency owned by Mr. Powers was a primary source of income for the mission.

Dillon continued rocking in his chair. He thought about refreshing his coffee, but was too tired to get up. He patted his stomach and burped. His desk was a mishmash of news clippings, envelopes, file folders, and paperclips. He shoved a stack of paper aside so he could see the red digital numbers on the clock. He had made the six o'clock deadline with time to spare. His article would be in the morning papers. He was probably cutting his own throat, but it was too late to worry about it. He'd already hit the send button. There was no turning back.

It was Charlotte's fault for inviting him in the first place. He was a reporter of the old school. When others said, "Never let facts get in the way of a good story," he said, "Just the facts ma'am, just the facts." Even then he'd shown Charlotte a courtesy by ignoring the fact that she'd been there to boost her image. He left her out of the article completely. He wasn't out to publicly humiliate her. He'd left that to the TV types. But he did believe Stan had an incredible story that needed to be told. A successful businessman who, according to those closest to him, could easily reside in the high-rise districts of River North or the Gold Coast but who chose to live in suburban Oak Park just so he could use his money to help those less fortunate. It was the kind of feel-good story people needed more of.

Dillon reached for his mouse and clicked on the other story he'd written. He could only hope they didn't appear on the same page. Charlotte might be able to forgive his letting Mr. Powers upstage her, but she would never forgive his sidebar. While the Twitter world continued to speculate on whether or not Charlotte had been arrested for drunk driving, he'd settled the issue. He'd gone online and found a video that captured the back of Charlotte's car and had a buddy in the police department run the plates. The smaller article had a photo of the street showing the patrol car with Charlotte's Lincoln in the background, but it also had an inset close-up of her plates. The headline read, "Yes, It Was Senator Weise!" Beneath the photos his article explained how the debate was over, how the woman who looked so much like Charlotte really was Senator Weise. Her car had subsequently been impounded.

Having a story accusing Senator Weise of drunk driving, beside a much larger article of her opponent doing good deeds would constitute an unpardonable sin. He took a bite of his donut and chewed with cheeks bulging. Maybe he would go to hell. He chuckled. But at least he'd go with a smile on his face.

Another beautiful Sunday morning and Samuel was smiling like a cat over a plate full of fish. His fingers drummed the wheel of the old Caddie as he belted out, "This is the day that the Lord has made, I will rejoice and be glad in it." His voice rumbled and roared, loud enough to scare birds in flight. There was barely a drop of light in the sky when he headed out at six a.m., but now the firmament over Lake Michigan was a blush of coral pink. Hallelujah! The sun was getting ready to shine.

He was on his way to pick up Satchel. He took Highway 90 to the 94 heading north toward Evanston. He didn't mind the distance. He liked getting his baby off the city streets once in a while just to clear the carbs. The white behemoth trundled down the freeway like it was made for the open road, smoke and nauseous gases notwithstanding. He had the top up and the windows down with the elbow of his black suit coat sticking out the side. There was no traffic, or at least very little, as he zoomed down the freeway. He liked to think it was because people were in church on Sunday morning, but he knew it was because they wanted to sleep in. Ramp to Evanston. That was his exit. He didn't need a map, he'd been to Mama's before, though not as much as back in the day when her business was on the south side of Chicago. She'd been a washed-in-the-blood, water-baptized, Holy-Spirit-filled member of his congregation back then. He pulled up to the dusty curb in front of Mama's Home-Style Cookin' Restaurant and started to get out, but just as he did, Mama's front door opened so he settled back into the seat.

Rachel came down the steps, lithe and graceful as a doe, followed by Satchel. The lane was lined with shade trees but it was too early to require protection from the sun, though it was now fully visible. A yellow haze had settled on the landscape. A squirrel, paws wet with dew, bounced by leaving tiny tracks on the sidewalk before disappearing into the branches of a sugar maple. Satchel opened the door in a gentlemanly fashion, helping Rachel into the front seat.

"You sit up here too," Samuel said. His hand patted the gray leather. "This baby's plenty big to hold the three of us." He cleared away a pizza box and plastic Coke bottle, tossing them onto the back seat. He was dressed in a black three-piece suit with vertical stripes that shone in the light. His shoes were patent leather and shined like mirrors. His tie had become caught in the wind and though it was pinned down with a large gold clip, it was flipped up backward so that its tip was under his chin. The only silver jewelry he wore was the cross which was now tangled under his tie. Rachel climbed in and slid over to sit next to the bishop and Satchel crawled in beside her, closing the door.

"So this is the daughter you been telling me about. I won't call you a liar but you sure understate the truth. She is one handsome woman, indeed." The bishop thrust a large black hand at Rachel. "Allow me to introduce myself, I'm Bishop Samuel. I'll be doing the preachin' at this morning's service, and I'm so glad you decided to come." Rachel took the hand feeling the calloused dryness of Samuel's skin. A breeze coming in off the lake smelled of decomposing plants. He let go and glanced at a gold watch the size of a river stone, then kicked the shift into drive and roared off heading south. They were going to church.

Rachel looked down at her denims and Northwestern logoed T-shirt. "No one said what I should wear, but a high school friend of mine asked me to church once, and when I went everyone just wore regular school clothes."

Samuel had his arm outstretched with his wrist folded over the arc of the wheel. He looked over his shoulder to his right. "Lord don't care what you wear, he cares what's in your heart. The rest is all for show. I understand you used to know our boy Freddie," he said.

Rachel grabbed her hair to keep it from flying away, and Samuel hit his indicator pulling on to the freeway. She nodded. "That was a long time ago, Bishop. I confess I'm a little hesitant about reconnecting again. I'm just beginning to get to know my father."

"It'll be fine. You'll see. It's all part of God's plan."

They pulled up in front of a church that could have been lifted from a Norman Rockwell painting. It was tall and white with a red brick foundation and five steps with iron railings that led up to the sanctuary. Two flower gardens bursting with roses were on either side of the walkway. The sky was postcard blue which stood out starkly against the building's fresh coat of paint. A bell tower rocketed high overhead, and along the side of the building were four stained-glass windows, all flat on the bottom but peaked at the top, standing in a straight line. "Welcome to my home," Bishop Samuel said.

Satchel brought a hand up over his eyes to block the sun as he looked up to the top of the tower. "I thought this was your church?"

"It is, but it has a rectory around back for the pastor, and that's where I live so it's my home too."

They climbed out of the car and crossed a roadside patch of grass to the sidewalk. The lawn was moist and smelled like it had just been mowed. People were clustered on the walkway talking, every one of them dressed to the nines. Rachel quickly noted that hers and Satchel's were the only white faces to be seen. They were also the only two not dressed in full church regalia, suit, tie and fashionista dress.

Bishop Samuel glanced over and saw Rachel's dismay. "Black folk just love to dress up pretty on Sunday," he said, "but it's like I told you, we're here to worship. It don't matter what we wear.

Come on and let me introduce you around."

Rachel and Satchel spent the next few minutes being glad-handed and passed from one group to the next. The bishop was right. No one seemed to notice the difference in the color of their skin or what they wore. They made their way up the steps to the portico where an usher took Rachel by the arm and, with Satchel following, led them down the red carpeted aisle to their seats. Rachel reached up to receive the bulletins and songbooks the man was handing them. The stained-glass windows glowed with oranges, reds, browns, and blues depicting Christ's birth, His crucifixion, His resurrection from the grave, and His ascension into heaven. Large white fans hung from the vaulted wood ceiling, spinning to circulate the air. A young man bounded up to the pulpit wearing a charcoal gray suit with a red tie, his shoes almost a shiny as those of Bishops Samuel's. "Aren't you glad we're here today?"

"Amens," and "Hallelujahs," and "Praise the Lords" burst from the congregation.

The young praise leader began a routine designed to get folks worked up. He was turning back and forth asking questions and the more questions he asked the louder the shouts from the congregation became until the whole room was filled with an epiphany of sound. "Glory hallelujah. Then let's sing!"

The entire congregation bounded to their feet. Onstage an organ opened its electronic bellows, filling the room with sound. A rim-shot cracked, followed by a roll from the drums and an electric guitar peeled off a low droning riff joining in. Three ladies who were seated in the first row hopped onto the stage and started shouting, "Page three-ninety-six, song three-ninety-six." They all wore purple dresses, though not the same style, with purple pumps, and purple lips, and purple nail polish which could be seen as they flapped their hands. People began flying through the pages of their hymnals while the band continued to play. At the first pause the people began to sing,

"Let it rain, let it rain,
Open the floodgates of heaven,
Let it rain, let it rain,
Open the floodgates of heaven."

People were clapping and shouting. Their exuberance was over-the-top and infectious, motivating both Rachel and Satchel to join in, but they didn't know the words so all they could do was lip-sync while they moved and swayed and clapped with the beat.

It went on for more than thirty minutes before Bishop Samuel stepped onto the stage. It was a subtle change as the song leader handed the reins over to the pastor and the singing became more subdued. Slowly people began taking their seats. The songs wound down, but the excitement never did.

"Who wants to see my Jesus?" Bishop Samuel shouted. "I'm here to tell you, there's only one way you're going to see my Jesus, and that's if you know Him, and the only way you're going to know Him, is if you give Him your heart."

"Amens" and "Glory to Gods" undergirded Samuel's rumbling voice.

"My Jesus. My Jesus left His home in heaven. Glory! My Jesus came to this earth. Hallelujah! My Jesus lived like a poor man, but He died like a king. Do you hear me? My Jesus put his life on a cross that you might live. Can I get an amen? My Jesus gave it all. But my Jesus rose from the grave. My Jesus ascended to heaven. My Jesus lives and reigns on high! Do you hear me? Can I get an amen? Do you know my Jesus." The shouts of "Hallelujah" and "Amen" rose from the pews, thundered through the sanctuary and echoed in the rafters.

They were standing under the shade of a walnut tree waiting as Bishop Samuel said goodbye to each and every last one of his parishioners. Rachel had her arms crossed looking down eyeing a squirrel scavenging for seeds in the grass. She didn't know what to make of the service. It was only the fourth church she'd ever been in, the first being the church her first foster family, the Robinsons, took her to at Christmas. That was a much more sedate and regimented service, with everything organized and done in proper order. The style of dress was more like this church, men wore suits and ties and the women fine dresses. And the people sang, but they didn't jump and shout. An offering plate was passed and the pastor preached and everyone said goodbye and went home. The second was a service the Purveys took her to. It was pretty much the same as the Robinsons' church only the dress was more casual. The third was with her friend, Carla, in high school. They sang a few of the same songs and raised their hands to worship and the parishioners wore street clothes, but the pastor didn't stand behind a pulpit. Instead he moved around on the stage to interact with the people. This one was much more animated than the other three. All four were different, but all were the same in that they all shared an intense belief in some kind of invisible God and in salvation through His Son, Jesus.

Satchel glanced up to see how many people Samuel still had to shake hands with. Not that many, the crowds were thinning. Several had stopped to thank them for coming and wish them a pleasant day, a few even invited them to lunch, which of course they declined because they were on their way to pick up Freddie. It was nice to be in the shade. The warm midmorning sun felt like a wet blanket on their shoulders. Humidity was on the rise.

Bishop Samuel walked over. "So, what did you think?"

"It was an experience," Rachel said.

"I'll bet it was. You go to church often?"

"Almost never."

"I suppose that makes sense. I don't suppose your father ever took you as a child."

Rachel glanced at Satchel then back at Samuel. "No sir, he didn't."

"Well don't take ours as typical." He reached down to pick a walnut from the ground. "Churches are as different as walnuts, we have many stripes," he said pointing to the grooves along the back of the walnut's shell, "but we all hold the same kernel of truth inside." He cracked the shell open and popped the nut into his mouth. "At least as long as we preach the gospel of Jesus." The squirrel darted away as though miffed that Samuel had stolen the very nut he'd been searching for. "Alright now, if you guys are ready, let's go pick up Freddie."

Samuel pulled to the curb. The building was nondescript. Were it not for the paper sign taped to the window, she wouldn't have known it was a clinic. They'd only gone three or four blocks. It made Rachel wonder why they hadn't walked. The three climbed out, feeling the heat rising from the sidewalk. The sun on their shoulders made her glad they'd decided to drive. The car had air conditioning. She could already feel little prickles of sweat breaking out on her arms. They went inside to find Freddie sitting in a dark corner of the community center.

"Hey mate, good to see you," Satchel said. "It looks like you made it, congratulations. Sorry I didn't get out here sooner but did Bishop Samuel tell you I got me a job?"

Freddie was rocking back and forth, not much, but slightly. He didn't answer. Satchel looked at Rachel and shrugged. He placed a hand on Freddie's head and tousled his hair. "Ready to go, mate?"

Freddie jerked back, shaking the hand off. He crossed his feet in front of him then interlaced his fingers backwards so his palms were facing away from each other and tucked his shoulders in. He rocked forward keeping his head bowed. "I'm not ready for nothin'. They're the ones who say I'm drug-free. So how come I

213

keep needing something?"

The lady who originally signed Freddie in said, "Freddie, you know we've explained this to you. You're always going to be an addict. There's always going to be that little voice that pops into your head telling you you need a fix. The only advantage you have right now is that the drugs themselves are out of your system, so saying no should be easier. But only you can determine whether or not you'll start using again."

Freddie was seated deep in the cushions of an overstuffed chair in a corner where the absence of light kept him hidden in the shadows. Rachel couldn't get a good look at his face. It could be the young man who'd befriended her all those years ago, the voice was vaguely familiar, but she couldn't be sure.

"Yeah, and that's why I need Angela," he said. "I told you that. We look out for each other."

"Come on Freddie." The woman reached out and took Freddie's arm, lifting him to his feet. He stood for a moment, teetering, but caught his balance and folded his arms in front of his nearly invisible stomach, still looking at his feet. He was wearing a flannel shirt, old and worn, but clean. It looked a few sizes too big extending over his knuckles, and his pants were bunched up around the ankles of his sneakers.

"You'll see her again. Didn't you both make appointments with our counselor for Wednesday?" The woman straightened his shirt and dusted him off as a mother would a child. "But right now it's time to show how strong you are. You have to be able to stand on your own."

"Who's Angela?" Satchel said.

Freddie continued looking down, leaving the question unanswered.

"Angela is a young lady Freddie met while here," The nurse responded. "They made a connection and got kind of close, trying to support each other."

"When did Angela leave?" Samuel said, looking at Freddie.

"Yesterday," The nurse replied.

"Is anyone looking after her? Did she have somewhere to go?"

"She has family. They weren't able to pick her up because they only have one car and her father had to use it for work. We gave her bus fare. She assured us she knew the route, and her mother promised to be waiting. They'll take care of her."

"What about me?" Freddie's arms were wrapped around himself like he was cold. He shivered, his jaw trembling.

So far Rachel hadn't said a thing. She could now see it was him, same height and mannerisms, but he looked more like a spirit than a human being. He didn't seem to recognize her either. What was there to say?

"You're going home with us," Samuel said. "You can stay at the mission, at least for a while. You'll have people to talk to and keep you on track. And you'll be able to come back here and get counseling when you need it."

A smile played at the corners of Freddie's mouth. He brought the cuff of his flannel shirt up to wipe his eye. The bridge of his nose had more freckles than Rachel had ever seen. She didn't remember noticing them before. "Yeah, Angela and I are going to meet our counselor on Wednesday."

"Okay then, let's grab your stuff. Oh, by the way, I'm not sure you need an introduction but this is an old friend of yours, Rachel."

Fourteen

CHARLOTTE STOOD with her hands behind her back looking out her window on the forty-second floor. The stance she took was that of a navy admiral, an effect reinforced by the outfit she wore which looked almost like dress blues. Miles and miles of cityscape spread before her. It was her realm, her fiefdom, the land over which she was elected to exert authority. People depended on her to make decisions. That was the onus placed on her by the electorate; those who chose to abandon their responsibility either because they lacked the will, or the intellect, to make such choices for themselves. It was an awesome charge and one she took seriously. If men like Mr. Powers were allowed to assume office the nation would regress to a state of primeval anarchy.

She could see into the distance the way a prophet sees into the future, all the way to where the smog erased the horizon. She looked down the backs of seagulls as they darted in and out between the mighty towers of her realm. She had risen above. This was her destiny. No one could take it from her. Nature calls its own to do its bidding. If she had been a bird she would've been an eagle not a sparrow; if a mammal, a lion not a mouse; if a fish, a shark not a guppy. Some were born to rule and others to serve. They were choices made by nature, or at least the nature of man, and could not be thwarted. The people on the sidewalks below, pedestrians that looked like bits of sand, depended on her. She would not let them down.

She turned at the sound of her campaign manager hustling into the room. He looked tatty and harried. He stopped and put a hand to his chest and let out a breathless sigh. He was wearing gray slacks with a shirt the color of a robin's egg and a gray tie with a thin blue diamond pattern. His sandy blond hair stuck up and lay flat at the same time like a field of wheat blown by the wind, and his beard was a yuppie scruffy two-day-old brush of hair. His brown eyes matched his brown belt and the brown loafers with tassels he had on his feet.

Charlotte didn't wait for him to speak. She grabbed a newspaper off her desk and threw it at him. "What the heck is this?"

Bob jumped back, startled, then stooped to pick it up. He had been summoned to her office first thing. He'd barely gotten out of the shower, dressed and sat down with his cup of coffee to read the morning paper when his phone rang.

"You need to get in here fast. Something's got the senator all in a tizzy. She's demanding to see you right away," the voice had said.

Bob knew better than to keep Charlotte waiting. He'd tossed the paper aside and rushed out without even combing his hair. It had that unmanaged look anyway, she probably wouldn't notice. "What?" he said. Charlotte was standing at her desk, never a good sign, standing usually meant she was agitated. He preferred it when she was sitting and relaxed.

"You mean you haven't seen this?" Charlotte grabbed the paper out of his hand and folded it to a page with a three column photo of the soup kitchen they had visited a few days earlier. She thrust it at him.

The bold type read, "Senatorial Candidate, Stan Powers, Spends Spare Time Feeding the Poor." Bob was already scanning the story.

"This was your idea. You're the one who talked me into going out there. They've made him a saint for cripes sake. And look who wrote it, Dillon McShay. He was your pick. You said he was a friendly. And you see what's below it, me, getting arrested for being drunk! So now I'm a drunk and he's a saint!" Her face was hard and, in the light from the window, looked like sandstone fissured by wind abrasion.

Bob shook his head. "You weren't being arrested. The officer just gave you a ride home."

"That's not what everyone sees. I'm being put into the back of a police car. You're the one who's always saying perception's more important than reality."

Bob folded the paper and let it drop to his side. "I know this looks bad, but it'll blow over. There's a long campaign ahead. Mr. Powers doesn't know when or how to shut up. Word on the street is he's speaking at a church in Peoria next Sunday. This will be his first foray into the public arena. It won't take long for people to see his agenda is regressive and oppressive. He'll step on himself and this whole thing will go away."

Charlotte placed her hands behind her back and walked over to face the window again. "I wish I could believe that, but unfortunately I don't."

"You'll have to be patient. It'll all work out. I bet he says something incredibly stupid, and even if he doesn't, in a few days he's due in court over that gay discrimination thing. He's not going to wear that well. By the way, guess who our judge is? Milton Meriwether. Judge Meriwether's daughter is an activist, does parades with signs and posters and all of that, so he's already predisposed to rule in our favor. And he's an old friend of yours isn't he? I think maybe you should call Milton and invite him to lunch. Remind him that you backed him for judge, let him know how a settlement against the defendant would help keep him in your good graces. He'll play along."

Charlotte turned to face Bob again, her face as hollow as the Grim Reaper. "I still don't like it. We need something more. There's a skeleton in that closet somewhere, and if we want to tarnish that halo, we've got to find it."

There were times when Bill didn't like being a chaplain because the burden of carrying other people's secrets was too heavy to bear. This was one of those times. He looked at the scrap of paper in his hand. It was the soullessness of the facility that road roughshod on a man's sensibilities. The only way to get here was to break the law in one form or another, so collectively the population was composed of miscreants who had defied the norms of society. It was easier on the outside where a man's personal misconduct was masked by the pervasiveness of the good around him. But inside, the concentration of evil was so prevalent it could be felt as surely as a man feels his clothes touch his skin. There was no escaping it. This note, however cryptic, was proof.

Bill understood the evil. Conrad's novel, *Heart of Darkness*, exposed how men, left in a jungle where the laws of society did not apply, returned to the evil that resided in every man's soul. Golding's, *Lord of the Flies*, did the same wherein innocent boys became ravenous killers when loosed from societal restraint. It was the nature of man, its roots going back to Genesis, at the fall, when man resisted God's plan. It was a primal instinct, a flaw rooted in the will, that caused men so often to make the wrong choice.

Being good is so much harder than being evil. Take a child and put him in a room full of toys, and tell him to play with any of the toys in the room except the one which you say he's not allowed to touch, then leave the room, close the door, and watch through the window as that child begins playing with all the approved toys until eventually his eyes drift to the forbidden toy and he slowly works his way over until he has it in his hands. Theologians liked to refer to this phenomenon as, "man's sin nature," but regardless of what it was called, it was in the heart of every man to rebel.

Inside the walls of the system were perpetrators of crimes so nefarious Bill couldn't bring himself to discuss them out loud, but in God's eyes the sins of a chainsaw murderer were no worse than those of a man who cheated on his taxes or stole from his employer. Any time man stepped outside the will of God, he was in trouble. Bill hoped to be a light shining in that darkness, hopefully like a candle drawing one or two of the hopelessly lost into its light.

He didn't know why, at this moment, someone had chosen to slip him the note he now held in his hand, but he knew what he had to do about it. He looked at the note again.

"They're going to punch Satchel's ticket."

The inference was clear, someone wanted Satchel dead, but Satchel had already been released. Crimes of revenge usually took place within the prison walls.

Bill reached into his drawer for a sheet of paper and pen. Sliding the piece of paper up under the light from his desk lamp, he clicked the pen open and wrote:

> "Satchel,
>
> It has come to my attention that your life may be in danger. I am enclosing a short note I received, probably from a former inmate, or maybe one of the guards, many of whom are as corrupt as the people they oversee. I have no information other than this, and I'm telling no one other than you. I would admonish you to keep an eye out for trouble. "Be sober, be vigilant, for your adversary the devil walks about like a roaring lion seeking whom he may devour." *1 Peter 5:8*
>
> I trust you're continuing to read your Bible daily and are remaining strong in prayer. I spoke with

Bishop Samuel last week and he assured me you're doing well. I thank my God for the progress you've made and trust whatever the future may bring we will one day be reunited in God's kingdom. I pray for you continually.

Soldier on, my friend.

Bill Stokes,
Chaplain, Dixon Correctional Facility.

He folded the sheet of paper with the note inside and slid it into an envelope. There wasn't much more he could do. The police would not take action on such a glib, unsigned, note but at least Satchel was informed. The rest was up to God.

Time in a correctional facility moved as slow as the shadow of a sundial. The minutes crept into hours that bled into days, and months, and years, bringing little fulfillment or sense of purpose. The men in the yard were gathered in groups of twos and threes, some shooting craps for cigarettes, some arm wrestling for duty swaps, and some just whiling away the time in idle conversation. The sun was high over the yard, beating down on the prisoners with blistering heat. A game of hoops was in progress. A jumble of glistening bodies streaming sweat were mixing it up, the sound of their shoes trundling on the asphalt, balls smashing against the backstop and swooshing through a hoop without a net created a rhythmic pattern as constant as a train clacking down a track. Black gangs strode across the blacktop doing the low jailhouse shuffle, a slouched way of walking with their knees bent and their arms swinging as they moved.

The bodybuilders were doing chin-ups and tummy crunches,

but Skinhead Jack was pumping iron. He hefted two hundred and fifty pounds. His face was red and saturated with sweat, his teeth gritting like rocks slammed together, his cheeks quivering, his mouth emitting a sound like air passing through the pinched neck of a balloon. The *clank* of the metal bar hitting the rack gave him pause. His arms relaxed as he emptied his lungs in one swift breath. *Whew!* He used the bar to pull himself up, his biceps looking like footballs under his reddened skin. He swung his feet around and sat on the edge of the bench.

Four of his brothers were standing around paying homage. Jack put his hands under the hem of his sleeveless shirt and brought it up to wipe his face. "Hail the AB," he said as he stood, putting his fist forward.

"Hail the AB," the others responded, each butting his fist off of Jack's in a show of solidarity. Jack moved away from the workout station followed by his minions, heading for the interior of the yard where they could talk without being heard.

"Today's the day," Jack whispered. He brought his hands up with enclosed fists and butted them together.

"You sure you want to do this?"

The look from Jack sent chills up the questioner's spine.

"I just mean you might be released at your hearing without having to take any risks."

Jack shook his head, his lips pursed, looking at the man like his head wasn't screwed on straight or the left side of his brain wasn't working. "So what's the plan?"

"We've got a crew ready," Digger said. "They'll hit the van on the way to your parole hearing. Everyone knows what to do. The screws got their money so they won't give us no trouble. Ain't nobody gonna touch you."

"What about a weapon?"

"All good. Bomb Squad's got you covered. He'll hand you a piece, soon as you're out."

Skinhead Jack pulled his elbows in with his fists still clenched and rotated to the left and right, then punched the air a few times for good measure. "I'll be wearing a blue teardrop tat in the corner of my eye when I return."

"If, you return. The regular cops orders will be, shoot to kill."

Freddie woke up at five a.m. to the sound of muffled snorts, heavy breathing, and the smell of unwashed clothes on unwashed bodies. He turned toward the wall and closed his eyes but he couldn't get his thoughts off Angela. She was ruining his sleep. He was in a room with three other men, two of whom worked in the kitchen and one who just got out of jail on an early release. And all three were Bible thumpers. Two days of hearing nothing but Jesus. It was enough to drive him crazy.

It was Wednesday. He'd made it two whole days on the outside without a fix. He brought a finger up and used his thumbnail to scratch paint from the cuticle. That was their strategy. Keep him too busy to notice. "Idle hands are the devil's workshop," Samuel said. It was an overused cliché but had merit. Samuel had him painting the building, changing its sickly green pallor to a nice warm tan. He brought his hand up to look at his fingernail. His arms were sore, all those brushstrokes and heavy rolling were hard on his atrophied muscles, but he found he had a knack for it. Samuel had come outside to inspect his work and told him that he was doing a fine job. Apparently the last guy who painted got as much on the asphalt as he did on the walls, much of which could still be seen on the edge of dirt that bordered the parking lot. Freddie was being careful not to drip or spill anything. Finding an occupation he was good at was rewarding. He was almost tempted to go outside and start again, but not today, today was special. Today he had an appointment with the counselor at the detox center. Today he would see Angela again.

He listened to the grunting of the men around him. They were sound sleepers but thankfully didn't snore heavily. People usually got up around six. Everyone would be out of bed and downstairs eating by seven. He rolled over to face the window. A thin film of light made the glass appear luminous. He rolled out of bed and grabbed his pants, shirt, and shoes and headed for the shower. One thing about rising early was you didn't have to wait your turn. His clothes were still clean. Samuel had given him a pair of old dungarees to wear while painting. He cranked the rust pitted taps, the sound of their screeching echoing off the chipped tiles of the bathroom as water flooded the stall. He waited for the right temperature and stepped inside. Samuel had promised to give him a ride back to the detox center around ten o'clock. He would be looking his best long before then.

Stan was in his office going over the books. They had picked up three new accounts; Riley's furniture, a five store chain serving the greater Chicago area, Northern Moped who had previously wanted to use the agency but couldn't because of a possible conflict with Kosner Motorcycle, and 24-hour Pick and Put, a regional courier company going head-to-head with the nationals for local business. Billings were up. Stan held a pencil between two fingers, letting the eraser drum against his desk. It seemed Kosner's leaving hadn't hurt them at all.

The phone rang. Stan reached to pick it up, "This is Stan how can I help you?"

"Stan, I'm glad I caught you. This is Michael over at MorningStar. I want to let you know how excited we are about having you here on Sunday, but there have been some changes."

"Okay."

"I told you I planned to let the community know about your speaking at our church and, to be honest, the response has been overwhelming. We've had too many people register for us to accommodate, so we've had to move the venue. We're now having the event at the Embassy Suites in East Peoria. They have a conference center that holds fifteen hundred, which I hope is enough because we're already over twelve hundred and there's still a few days to go."

"You're kidding?"

"No, I'm happy to say I'm not. What you said at the debate must've really struck a nerve. It did solve one problem for us, though. It's about a two and a half hour drive out here, and I was already uncomfortable with having you come that far and not stay overnight. Aside from having a conference center, Embassy Suites is a hotel so we booked you a room. That way you can come out early and just relax and, after you make your presentation, know you have a place to rest before going home the next day."

"I appreciate that, but who's paying for all this?"

"The church. We have a budget for conferences and guest speakers. I'm told we'll be able to handle it without having to juggle our budget. You just be there. Don't worry about anything else. Oh and, is there a Mrs. Powers?"

"No, my wife passed on several years ago."

"Sorry to hear it. I'll make the reservation in your name alone. Anyway, I look forward to seeing you on the eighteenth. The program starts around seven. I'll probably be there early helping get set up so if you want to tee up before that give me a ring and we'll put something together."

"Thanks Michael, I'll do that." Stan hung up the phone. Twelve hundred people? It seemed like a lot but he shouldn't be surprised, when God makes a plan He makes a way. Or, as he liked to think, "Stan's the man for God's plan."

Freddie walked into the detox center feeling alive for the first time in years. There was an awareness about him, the smell of the coffee in the kitchenette, the scraping of metal as a chair was unfolded, the feel of the breeze from the overhead fan as the air rushed down his back, sensations denied him as an addict. He walked down the hall toward the community center, his stomach simmering in a bath of caffeine from his morning breakfast. Only a few days ago he would've watched others coming in for their once a week group therapy. Now he was one of them, a soldier who'd fought the battle and come out victorious. His eyes roamed side to side wondering if anyone remembered him, noting the same vacuous look on their faces he'd probably had when he'd first arrived. He was by no means cured, but he felt a heck of a lot better than they looked. He found the group seated in a circle with their counselor, Jim Pauly, waiting for the last few chairs to be filled. He didn't see Angela.

Freddie took a seat, looking around the room. He recognized several who'd started the program after him and were still awaiting completion. There were also a number of new faces. The circle was composed mostly of new graduates like him, as well as a few he suspected had been coming for a long time. Sunlight streamed through the window with specks of micro dust floating in the light.

Jim looked at his watch. "All right then, I guess it's about time we got started. My name is Jim and I'm a recovering addict."

"Hi Jim," group said in unison."

Freddie's hand shot up.

"Yes,"

"There's someone coming who's not here yet. I was supposed to meet her."

"That's all right. We'll start by doing introductions. When she arrives she can jump right in."

But forty-five minutes passed with junkies telling stories of their individual struggles to control their demonic thoughts and Angela still wasn't there. The detox center was a ship that provided shelter from the storm, but the siren's call was always in their ear, luring them back onto the rocks. Freddie shared his struggles, and praised Bishop Samuel for keeping him busy and for watching over him to make sure he didn't drift off course. He understood the benefit of living through everyone else's difficulties and the consolation it provided, but he was too distracted to listen in detail. Angela hadn't shown up. His thoughts were occupied with figuring out why. He kept one eye on the door hoping she'd step in at any moment. At the end of the session, Jim asked for those who needed one-on-one to stay behind and talk with him privately. Freddie waited until the group dismissed and while everyone else was getting up and heading out, he went looking for Jennifer Mitchell.

He checked the main centers of activity and finally went down the long dimly lit hall. The walls were pale yellow, the ceiling tiles were chipped around the edges and coated with ochre water stains, the carpet was worn and encrusted with ground-in dirt. He knew counseling was good for him, being around others engaged in overcoming the desire was therapeutic. But if he had his druthers he'd never come back again. He found Jennifer in her office. He tapped on the door, easing it open just enough to stick his head in. "Hi, Mrs. Mitchell, remember me?"

"Of course I remember you, Freddie." She was wearing a black skirt with a white blouse and a three inch wide belt that formed a barrier between the two. Her lips and fingernails were lacquered pink. "What can I do for you?"

Freddie brought a hand up to scratch the back of his neck. "I was supposed to meet Angela. You remember? The lady I kind of hung out with? We were supposed to meet here today."

"She didn't show up for counseling?"

"No. You think she's okay? What if something happened? She was supposed to be here."

Jennifer stood, gathering the papers in front of her into a pile and slipping them into a folder. "As I recall, they only had one car which her father drove. Maybe she couldn't get a ride. Thank you for letting me know. I'll look into it. It's important she attend these counseling sessions."

Freddie brought his hand around to scratch under his chin, then slid it down to scratch his thin stomach. "You think you could let me have her number? They have a telephone over at the mission. I'd like to give her a call." He brought his finger to his mouth and bit the edge of his cuticle.

Jennifer was already shaking her head "We can't give out personal information, but if you want to wait outside maybe I can give her mother a call right now. As long as it's nothing private I'll let you know what I find out."

Freddie stood in the hall looking back toward the community room. No wonder the hall was so dim. A few of the fluorescent tubes were burned out and one flickered, ready to go. He had heard Samuel say most of the people who worked here were volunteers. They obviously worked on a small budget with little for maintenance and upkeep.

The door to Jennifer's office opened. She stood there, her hair shining with a high gloss luster. She had one hand on the knob and the other on the frame. Her unsmiling face said it all. "Angela never made it home. Her mother says she waited. Said it broke her heart when she didn't show up. She's been missing for three days. I suspect she walked out of here and went straight to her pusher. A lot of our graduates do that. They like the idea of getting clean, but when it comes to facing the world outside they cave under pressure."

"I've got to find her."

"I doubt you'll be able to. If she's gone back into the life, it's likely she doesn't want to be found."

Freddie didn't wait for Samuel to pick him up as agreed upon. He left on foot, heading west into the darker more nefarious region of Garfield Park. The sidewalks and walls bathed in the sun were soon emitting a radiant heat that baked his skin like a microwave. Sweat poured down the sides of his face, running underneath his shirt collar and down his chest. They'd spent hours talking. He'd shared what it was like living in the tent city under the bridge with the homeless and unemployed; and she had explained the difficulty of surviving on death row—the 4400 block of West Monroe. Everyone she knew was there. It was where she would go to acquire drugs. It was reputed to be the most dangerous block in the city. He approached the two-story building with caution. He knew if she was anywhere this was where she would be.

He made his way down the hall. He had never seen so much filth. At least the people living under the bridge used the open fields behind the railroad tracks to relieve themselves. The floors were covered with garbage and the smell of human waste permeated every room. People, the very dregs of humanity, either sat with their backs against the walls smoking or lay on sleeping bags and filthy mattresses passed out. A guy over in the corner was plucking a ukulele with only three strings. It wasn't music, just random notes. No luck on the first floor. He made his way up the flight of stairs and began searching again. He found her lying on her side in a squalid pile of rags. It was obvious she'd puked on herself. The smell was rancid, but at least the window was broken letting in a modicum of fresh air. She smelled like rotted eggs. He got down on his knees and nudged her elbow. "Angela, Angela wake up."

She didn't respond and for a second he thought she might be dead. But then he saw her chest rise as the mechanics of her body took an unconscious breath. "Angela, come on, we need to leave."

Angela's eyes opened, but only halfway. He could see only part of her iris with the pupil large and dilated. The entire orb looked cloudy, like an eye of someone blind. Apparently she didn't have the strength to open her eyes fully. "Fredd...ie?"

While Freddie made his way to the apartment complex, one of his thoughts was that he would see these people in their element and be tempted to take a spike for himself. Looking at Angela made him realize that was the last thing he wanted. She looked like living death. "Come on Angela, I've got to get you out of here."

"Where we going?"

"Back to the detox center. You had a relapse. You need to get straightened out."

"No. *Uhaaaa.* This is home."

"But your parents... Your mom wants to see you. She was brokenhearted when you didn't show."

"My mother?" Angela twisted around as though looking for something. She found a dirty spoon with metallic burn marks in its bowl. "This is my mother; she gives me life." She smiled, but it faded immediately as she plopped down again.

"Come on Angela, you gotta come with me."

"Hey cracka, she wants to be left alone."

Freddie looked up to see a large black man standing behind him. The guy wore bib overalls with no shirt, the sweat on his skin glistening in the light from the window. The handle of a pistol protruded from his pocket. His arms were as big as hams. "I just want to help her."

"She don't want your help. Now boogie."

"Sure she does, she just doesn't know it. Maybe you can help me get her up. Once she's on her..."

But before he could finish his sentence the man reached out and grabbed him by the collar and the seat of his pants and half picked him up and half pushed him out the door. They got as far as the staircase and Freddie found himself airborne. He somersaulted the first eight steps and came to a stop with his head below his feet. One shoe was underneath him and the other tangled in the iron baluster. The man at the top the stairs was glaring at him. He reached for his gun.

"Get the hell outta here."

Freddie reached around to feel the back of his head. When he brought his hand back there was blood on his fingers. He tried to push himself up but his arm wouldn't cooperate. He pulled his foot free and rotated his body to get his feet beneath him.

The man raised his weapon and pointed just above Freddie's head. He pulled the trigger. Freddie flinched as the bullet went whizzing by. "Next time you're dead."

Freddie felt the adrenaline surge through his body. He pulled himself together and ran.

Friday morning Charlotte Weise called her entire staff in for a meeting. Rachel had come in early hoping to catch a glimpse of the view afforded by the wall-to-wall windows, but a heavy heat clouded the air. She could only see about a mile beyond where she stood. The nearby buildings looked like a watercolor rubbed with a thumb before it was dry. She took a seat at the table with her cohorts, wondering why they were there. What could be more important than raising the money Charlotte needed to fuel her campaign? Charlotte was pacing back and forth at the front of the room beating a rolled newspaper against the palm of her hand. She hadn't smiled or greeted anyone.

"You all know why you're here," she said abruptly after everyone was seated.

But Rachel didn't. She only knew she'd received a call urging her to attend an emergency session. She assumed the details would be explained after she got there.

"I'm sure you all saw the newspaper." Charlotte plopped her copy down with enough force to drive it to the center of the table. It unfurled to the front page. Rachel tried to read the headline but it didn't seem to have anything to do with Senator Weise. "Scandalous. And it hit us hard. Polls show I've dropped five points, and the story was fake news, I was never arrested. I politely asked that officer to give me a ride home because I knew I shouldn't be driving. The whole thing's been blown out of proportion. And now the national news is picking it up. Stan Powers' numbers, on the other hand, continue to rise. People read all that nonsense about him running a soup kitchen and suddenly he's God's gift to mankind. It looks like he's picked up the constituents I've lost, and gone up five points. We've only got a ten point spread between us, and the polls are trending in the wrong direction. He was supposed to be speaking at a church this weekend, but the word is they had to move it to a convention center because too many people wanted to attend. I want this man stopped."

A hand went up on the other side of the table. "Yes, Gloria."

"Isn't he being sued by a gay couple? What's happening with that? That should be enough to destroy him."

"Yes it should, and I have it on authority that that decision's in the bag. The case is being handled by Judge Meriwether, whose daughter happens to be gay. He's not going to let this slide, but the world is full of nutbags who seem to like the stance Powers is taking. We can't leave it to chance. We're going to sit here and brainstorm until we figure out a way to stop him. And remember, no idea is too lofty or low. I want to hear every thought you have on how to bring this fascist down."

Fifteen

S TAN ATTENDED his own church Sunday morning. It surprised him how much things had changed. A week before he was greeted by his usual group of friends, but today the whole congregation claimed to know him. He was patted on the back and ushered to the front, where the pastor anointed him with oil and the deacons prayed over him—a ceremony he considered a bit peculiar since the Baptist church he attended generally frowned on excessive displays of faith.

He arrived in Peoria in the early afternoon and was checked into the Embassy Suites by three o'clock. The plan was to go over his notes, take a shower, and get some dinner before the evening started. He removed his jacket and laid it over the back of a chair. His accommodations were far more than he anticipated. They had him in a two room suite with a full bedroom and a nicely appointed living room complete with a large screen TV. There was a couch and chairs, a desk and a small kitchenette with a microwave, refrigerator, coffee pot and sink. He walked to the window and pulled back the curtain, admiring the view which from his room on the fourth floor had a nice overlook of the Illinois River. He yawned and checked his watch. Plenty of time for a short nap. He kicked off his shoes and went to the bed to lie down.

The room phone awoke him with a high-pitched shrill. *Bleeeeeepppp, bleeeeeepppp.* He rolled over fumbling for the receiver, for a second wondering where he was. His watch said six o'clock. *Oh no.* He let a hand flop over his forehead as he brought the phone to his ear.

"This is Stan."

"The front desk said you'd checked in but I hadn't seen you yet. I thought I'd better check and see how you're doing."

"Hi Michael." Stan drew in a breath to stop his heart from pounding. "Yes, I was taking some time to go over my notes. I just want to make sure I have everything down pat."

"No worries. Glad you arrived safely. How's your room? Everything okay?"

Stan swung his feet around to sit on the edge of the bed. "First rate, thank you. You didn't have to put me up in such nice accommodations. I'm only staying the night."

"No, no, don't mention it. Have you been down to the conference center yet? They've got it all set up. Final number of confirmed attendees is fifteen hundred and fifty-seven. That's a bit over what the room will hold, but I'm sure we'll have some no-shows. And if not we'll just have to squeeze them in."

"Wow, that many? Look, I really appreciate what you're doing. I haven't even started my campaign and you've already got me an audience."

"It's not you I'm doing it for, it's God and country, in that order. What you said is exactly what people need to hear. Listen, I won't keep you, just come down when you're ready."

"I'll do that. See you in just a bit."

Stan pushed himself off the bed and stood arching his back with his fist held tight as he yawned. He shook his shoulders and limped to the bath, his stockinged feet feeling cool on the tiles. The purple balls of soap stacked in a pyramid on a dish gave the room the scent of lavender. He ran his fingers through his hair and it bounced back into place. He'd been sleeping in his clothes. Fortunately he'd taken off his jacket so it would still look pressed. His shirt was a bit wrinkled but it would be covered by his coat. He looked at his watch again, six fifteen. He barely had time to go over what he planned to say.

Stan took the elevator down, appreciating the glass doors that allowed him to look out over the atrium below. A series of monolithic square cubes formed a fountain in the lobby surrounded by palm trees and ferns. The guests were already arriving. Hundreds of people were wandering the halls, forming into groups, or resting in comfortable chairs positioned around the expansive foyer. He paused to listen to a couple who were asking the concierge for directions to the conference center. As they ambled off he fell in behind them and followed discreetly. Once again he felt humbled by the size of the crowd he'd drawn, and let there be no mistake, this time they were there to see *him*. The place was packed. If all fifteen hundred seats weren't already taken, they soon would be. He made his way to the front and approached the first man he saw that looked important enough to be in charge.

"Excuse me. I'm looking for Michael Bovine."

"That would be me," the gentleman said extending his hand. "And you must be Stan Powers."

Michael had a firm grip that exuded confidence, but Stan was a bit taken aback by his overall appearance. His voice over the phone was a strong baritone which had Stan thinking he was tall and lean. But he was in fact, rather short; five seven or eight, balding, and a tad on the heavy side. He had a round face and a small nose that supported a pair of round wire spectacles. His suit was brown with a maroon tie and his brown wingtips were scuffed like they hadn't been polished in a few months. "Guilty as charged," Stan said.

Michael looked at his watch. "You're just in time. We're starting in a few minutes. I've got a place for you right here in the first row. Just wait for me to introduce you, and you're away to the races."

Stan took a seat subconsciously feeling he had let Michael down. Courtesy would've dictated he be there early so they'd have time to become acquainted. Clearly his host had wanted that. He could tell the man felt slighted. He sat down, feeling the eyes of a thousand people on the back of his head. Stan reached into his coat pocket and removed the three-by-five cards that contained his notes. He didn't figure he'd need them, what he had to say was common sense, but he went over them all the same. He was reading the last one when he heard Michael at the podium tapping the mic, *pop pop pop.* He slid the cards into the cover of his Bible.

Michael wasn't completely bald, but his hair was light colored and thin enough for the skin to show through, leaving the impression he was balder than he actually was. As he turned his head, his glasses reflected overhead lights. "Okay, we're just about ready to get started here. Looks like we've got a fantastic crowd this evening. As you all know, our speaker tonight is Stan Powers, a Chicago businessman who recently decided to throw his hat into the race for Senator. I'm sure most of you heard his debate with Senator Weise, or if you didn't, got told about it by someone who did. So we're here to hear firsthand what Mr. Powers has to say. I'm not going to waste your time telling you about him, I figure he can do that himself. So without further ado, I give you Mr. Stan Powers. Stan." Michael extended his hand as though receiving an old friend.

Stan marched to the front, keeping his limp to a minimum, his notes concealed inside the flap of his Bible. He reached the podium, opened his Bible to a preselected verse and laid it flat on the podium.

"Thank you, Michael." Stan looked out over a crowd four times bigger than he'd had at the debate. His heart was thumping like a metronome set on high. He felt his fingers tremble. His only disappointment was the demographic. The group seemed to be composed mostly of seniors with gray being the predominant hair color. When he looked closely, he could spot black and brown faces sprinkled into the mix but they were few and far between. His message was for all people.

"I want to begin by reading a verse from Scripture. I'll probably do that several times tonight, so I apologize in advance if some of you go away thinking I'm a preacher. I'm not. I'm just a regular guy. But I believe the Bible is God's word and the manual by which we should conduct our lives, so I like to refer to it often. The verse I want to read is found in the book of Proverbs, chapter fourteen, verse thirty-four. Here it is, 'Righteousness exalts a nation, but sin is a reproach to any people.'

"That single verse pretty much sums up everything I want to say. When we as a people or a country or a nation live righteously, we are exalted in the eyes of God. But when we sin, when we step outside the laws God has established, we become a reproach and loathsome in the eyes of God.

Stan looked out over his audience. He'd hoped to receive a murmur of response, something that signaled their affirmation, but they remained silent as a room full of mannequins.

"Michael mentioned that you've already heard what I had to say in the debate so I won't bother repeating it. Well, maybe not all of it."

A wave of polite laughter rolled through the auditorium. Stan smiled. At least they weren't dead.

"But history does have a way of repeating itself. If you heard that speech, you heard me say we're on the same path other nations have taken on the way to their demise. Historically, we find most powerful nations begin with a strong ideology or belief system, centered around the social structure of the family and an adherence to law and order. But over time, we see them abandoning these principles and as they do, they begin to disintegrate. This is what we see happening in America today.

"The framers of our Constitution believed that in order for

this nation to exist the people would have to be governed, not by man, but by God. This is something that's made clear in all their writings. And for a hundred and fifty years that's just how it was. Not everyone believed, but certainly the majority did. People went to church, kids prayed in school, we sang hymns at public gatherings and our nation prospered like no other nation before.

"But over the last fifty years all that changed. Almost every law God has given us we have broken. When God said to Jeremiah the prophet, 'Before I formed you in the womb I knew you, before you were born I sanctified you; I ordained you a prophet to the nations.' He left no doubt that He sees a child as a person before birth. David, through the Holy Spirit, said something similar, 'For You formed my inward parts; You covered me in my mother's womb. I will praise You, for I am fearfully and wonderfully made.' And Isaiah said, 'Thus says the Lord , your Redeemer, and He who formed you in the womb, I am the Lord who makes all things.' God knows every soul He puts in a mother's womb and for the first century and a half our country acknowledged that fact and respected the sanctity of life. It wasn't until 1973 that we, as a society, determined to go our own way and so with the decision made by the Supreme Court on Roe V Wade we became a nation that has slaughtered fifty million babies, children God had a plan for and expected to be born.

"God also established that we should govern our bodies and keep them holy. Sex is a wonderful thing and God made it enjoyable, but He also laid out certain rules He wants us to follow. Why He did that, I don't know. You'll have to ask Him. But I do know when we start to do things our own way and ignore His instructions, we lose our connection with Him. This wasn't a problem for the first hundred and fifty years of our national existence. Adultery and sodomy were illegal in every state. As time passed we gave up trying to enforce laws against adultery. Men were too carnal and we couldn't throw everyone in jail. Now we're normalizing homosexuality as well. Right here in Illinois, in 1962, our state sought to decriminalize sodomy. We were the first state to do it. The trend grew, and as more and more states jumped on board the Supreme Court in 2003 made it a right for men and women to engage in homosexual activity nationwide. Since that time we've been sitting like a frog in water that's slowly being heated. Sodomy is no longer just legal, it's virtually illegal, and certainly politically incorrect, to speak out against it. Kids today are taught to explore different sexual avenues. If you don't feel comfortable as a boy, you're advised to consider becoming a girl. Now most of us can see a litter of puppies and discern which ones are male and which ones are female. We just can't tell the gender of human beings. In today's crazy world you can look at your own biological organs, know they tell your one thing, and honestly believe you're something else, and be commended for it. And slowly the water in the beaker is heating up.

"For our first century and a half people had the common sense to know that feeding yourself mind altering drugs wasn't a good idea. But in the 1960's we sought to reverse that way of thinking. Today smoking pot is either legal, or socially acceptable, in every state in the union. When I was young I was told the reason we wanted to keep marijuana illegal was that it was a gateway drug that would inevitably lead to the use of harder, more addictive opiates. The youth of that day said the argument was nonsense. Yet here we are today suffering what's being called an opioid epidemic that kills tens of thousands of people every year while addicting hundreds of thousands of others. So in hindsight, I guess you'd say our failure to enforce our drug laws did lead to the use of harder drugs.

"And so it goes. And I'm only talking about some of the more obvious aspects of our rebellion against God. Everywhere we turn we try to thwart God's laws, even in simple things like cheating on our income taxes, or flirting with someone else's spouse, or lying to avoid having to pay a traffic ticket.

"Without God, we're hopeless. It goes all the way back to Genesis where the Bible says, 'Then the Lord saw that the wickedness of man was great in the earth and that every intent of the thoughts of his heart was only evil continually.' Maybe God doesn't see America as quite that bad yet, but we're certainly on the path, and perhaps even beyond the point of no return. That's the world we live in. We're on a downhill slide.

"It's not like we haven't been warned. Before the children of Israel went into the promised land God told Moses, 'But it shall come to pass, if you do not obey the voice of the Lord your God, the Lord will send on you cursing, confusion, and rebuke in all that you set your hand to do, until you are destroyed and until you perish quickly, because of the wickedness of your doings.'

"But God also said. 'Now it shall come to pass, if you diligently obey the voice of the Lord your God, to observe carefully all His commandments…that the Lord your God will set you high above all nations of the earth, and all…blessings shall come upon you and overtake you, because you obey the voice of the Lord your God.'

"And that, my friends, is the choice we face in America today. So the question then becomes, how can we turn it around… ?"

Stan couldn't see the expressions on people's faces, whether they were receiving what he had to say, or not. He was standing, while everyone else was seated, but he wasn't on a platform or raised dais so his ability to gauge the crowd's reaction was limited. There was certainly no emotional response, no vocal outbursts or spontaneous applause. That was left for the protesters outside. He'd learned that about thirty activists had shown up and tried to block the front doors carrying signs and shouting, "Racist, sexist, anti-gay, born again bigot go away," but they'd been restrained by hotel security and hadn't caused a problem.

What Stan would like to have seen but couldn't, because they were seated way in the back and hadn't let him know they were coming, were three people very interested in what he had to say:

Samuel, because they were brothers in the faith and of like mind, Satchel because what he'd heard before seemed to make sense and had left him with a desire to learn more, and Rachel because Satchel had talked her into coming and she wanted to spend time with her father on his only day off. She also knew Mr. Powers days of making speeches were numbered, and she thought it prudent to hear his point of view while she still could.

Stan was exhausted. The meeting had ended with a standing ovation putting to rest his anxiety over what people thought. Apparently they'd agreed with him. He ended up spending an hour shaking hands and signing autographs, an event that would've gone on till midnight if hotel security hadn't needed to clear the building. He was on his way back to his room when he was approached by a young woman in the hall.

"Oh, Mr. Powers, please, I'm so glad I caught you." She held out her hand. "My name is Marianne Waters. I flew all the way out here from California just to get an interview."

Stan took her hand and shook it politely. She looked to be in her mid-thirties, tall and slim with a slinky blue dress that emphasized her curves in all the right places. Her long brunette hair was tied in a knot with a ponytail sticking through that swung back and forth as she turned her head. Her skin was tan with high cheekbones, her eyebrows heavy with just enough makeup for her dark brown eyes to look alluring. Her lipstick and nail polish were a dark shade of pink. All in all, the look was attractive. "From California, I'm sorry, I wish you would have called first. I don't give interviews. I've decided to make all of my views known in person. The media always seems to get it wrong and I'm tired of being misquoted or misunderstood."

"But I came all this way. I…"

"I'm sorry, I'm tired of being misconstrued."

Her head was shaking, her ponytail swinging back and forth. "But I won't, I promise. I represent The Shepherds Network. We're a nondenominational affiliation of pastors across the United States. Our members represent some of the largest congregations in the nation. We work with pastors across interdenominational lines to keep them informed, especially on political issues. We have a quarterly newsletter, which I happen to be the editor of, and your story about how to change America is perfect. These are men you need to reach…"

"Sorry, but I hardly think pastors in California or Idaho care who gets elected in Illinois."

"To the contrary. A lot of these men have radio and television ministries, and they talk to each other. If they agree on a candidate, they'll use their influence from their home states to make sure the vote goes well for you here in Illinois. You'd be surprised at the effect that can have. Please, it's only an interview. I'll even let you see the article before it gets published and let you make any changes you want."

Stan looked at his watch; it was getting late. "I'm sorry, but I'm exhausted. I really need to be turning in."

"Have you eaten? Because I haven't. My plane arrived just in time for me to get here before your presentation and I'm starved. How about you let me buy you dinner? They have a lovely café here and it has patio seating outdoors. It's such a lovely evening. How about we grab a quick bite and you can tell me your story over dinner. You'll still be in bed by eleven. That's early. Come on, what do you say? Please."

Stan felt the grumbling of his stomach, and if he had to admit it, a tug on his heart. The woman was quite attractive. He needed dinner, and she might be pleasant company. If she was willing to let him read the article before it went to print, why not? "Alright, a quick dinner, with emphasis on the quick. And it will have to be Dutch."

She smiled. "Have you been here before?"

"No, can't say that I have."

She put her arm through his and began walking with him as he sucked it up and put on a good face to keep his limp from showing. "That's okay, I know where it is."

They entered through the lobby, which was much emptier now, though a few people still lingered, down past the fountains and palm trees and out the doors to several tables set on a patio that bordered the river. The air smelled sweet, like fresh cantaloupe. The lighting was subdued and the atmosphere warm. A server found them a table and handed them two menus. "Can I get you something to drink?" she said.

Stan looked up shaking his head. "No, nothing for me, thank you. Just water."

Marianne looked up and said, "Water's fine for me too." She reached into her purse and pulled out a recorder, laying it on the table. "I'll use this to make sure I get what you say right. I think we should decide what we're going to eat before we get started. Otherwise, we might be here all night."

Stan looked at the menu and Marianne did the same. Their server returned with two glasses of water and their cutlery and napkins which she laid in front them.

"Are you ready for me to take your orders?"

"I think I'm ready." Stan looked at Marianne.

"I'm fine, I'll have the herb roasted chicken with potatoes and vegetables."

"And I'll have the Greek marinated salmon."

They folded their menus, handing them back to the server who walked away leaving them alone.

"If you don't mind, we should probably get started because it's hard to talk while eating and I have a lot of questions to ask."

"Sure, that's fine, fire away."

"So, Mr. Powers...

"Stan."

"Okay, Stan. What made you decide to get into politics?"

Marianne wasn't exaggerating when she said she had a lot of questions. It seemed like they'd only just begun when their server set their plates in front of them. "That's really quite a story," she said. *"Uhmmmmm, this looks delicious."* Marianne left the recorder running and continued the interview, but she made her inquiries feel more like conversation during dinner, kind of like two old friends catching up after being apart for several years.

For his part, Stan found the dinner relaxing. Marianne seemed like a good reporter, interested in truth, not fiction. He had a good feeling about the interview, and the idea of connecting with some ten thousand pastors across the United States, if indeed it happened, was a real coup. The moon rose in the sky, full, bright, and banana white, shimmering on the Illinois River like the tail of a kite. He felt their spirits lifted on the breeze and the music of the river soothing. By the time they finished dessert, he was slouching in his chair ready for a good night's sleep. He yawned but tried to hide it.

"You think you have enough? I'm just asking because I don't imagine what more I can tell you and frankly I'm ready to hit the hay."

Marianne reached out and clicked her recorder off. "Sure, I think I've got everything I need." The waitress stopped by to ask if they wanted dessert and when they declined, left their check on the table. Marianne reached for her purse and pulled it into her lap. She brought her wallet out and rifled through it. "Oh dear, I need to ask you a favor," she said, still looking into her wallet.

"What's that?"

"It seems I'm a little short on cash, and I'll need a few dollars in my wallet for my trip home. I can put the meal on my room and if you pay me your part in cash it will save me a trip to the bank in the morning."

Stan shrugged. "Why don't you just let me put it on my credit card?"

"Absolutely not. I invited you to dinner. You were the one who insisted on going Dutch, I'll be darned if I'll let you pay. Besides, it doesn't solve my problem. I don't like not having cash in my wallet when I travel. I never know what incidentals I might need."

"Fine by me." Stan reached into his wallet and passed several dollars to Marianne. "That should be enough to cover my dinner and the tip."

Marianne put the money in her purse and wrote her room number on the bill. "I'll put the tip on my room too. It never hurts to have a few extra dollars in my wallet. Where are you staying?"

"Here in the hotel, you?"

"Me too. It's a bit expensive but I convinced my boss the convenience was worth the extra money."

Stan stood and went around to pull the chair back for Marianne. "Thank you, sir."

"Come on, I'll walk you to the elevator."

They strolled back through the lobby which was quiet now and almost empty. The fountain gurgled in a never ending cycle of running water. A black custodian was sweeping the floor with a three foot wide dusting broom. An elevator car was already waiting with the doors open so they stepped inside. "What floor?" Marianne asked.

"I'm on the fourth."

"Me too."

The elevator carried them up while they watched the lobby disappearing beneath them. When the doors opened they stepped out together into a long hallway. They looked at each other, "Which way?"

"I'm in 422 to the right."

"Small world. I'm in 432 just a little further down. Come on I'll walk you to your door."

They walked along the carpeted aisle with Stan thinking about how his leg was going to pay him retribution when he got back to his room. They reached Marianne's door. She turned facing Stan and took his hand. "Thank you so much. It was pleasure getting to know you, Stan. You're going to make a fine senator." She wrapped her arms around his neck and reached up to kiss him on the cheek but then, as an afterthought, kissed him full on the mouth. "Oh, sorry, I don't know why I did that. It was just an impulse. I shouldn't have."

Stan glanced to the side. A few doors down a maid stood beside her roller cart stacking towels. It was a harmless indiscretion.

"Nothing to be sorry for. If I were to be honest, I'd admit to having similar thoughts but long distance relationships rarely work and frankly, I'm preoccupied with my campaign for the next few months."

Marianne nodded. "Of course." She turned, and opened her purse and retrieved her key. She swiped the card and waited for the light to turn green, then stopped. "You think you could do me one more favor?" she asked.

"Sure, what's that?"

"My toilet was sticking earlier. I couldn't get it to stop running. I was going to call maintenance but I was running late, and if I call them now I'll be up all night waiting until they come. You think you could look at it for me?"

"Sure, no problem."

She took his hand and pulled him inside, leading him to the bathroom. He noticed hers smelled like oranges and the balls of soap were yellow. He would've preferred that scent for himself. He went over and jiggled the toilet's handle. "Seems fine to me. I don't hear it running."

"Really? Great. I was worried it would keep me awake all night."

"Glad to be of service." Stan reached into his wallet and removed a business card for Powers Advertising. He handed it to her. "Call me when you get your article done and I'll let you know where to send it. I enjoyed the evening, Marianne. If our paths don't cross again it was a pleasure meeting you."

"It was nice meeting you too. I'd offer to buy you breakfast but my plane leaves at five a.m.. That's a joke, by the way, breakfasts here are free."

Stan shook his head. "And I thought I had to get up early. Good night Marianne."

"Good night, Stan."

Sixteen

S TAN MADE a pot of coffee and went to the window with a fresh cup in hand. He was wearing his skivvies with a towel draped across his shoulders, but he couldn't be seen from where he stood so he wasn't shy. Clouds had overtaken the sun painting the sky gunmetal gray. The wind whipped down the Illinois River creating whitecaps on the normally smooth current. The tempest had the flags on the shore stretched out stiff as cardboard. Stan brought the cup up to his lips and blew across the surface making a circle of steam on the glass. He hoped it wasn't as cold outside as it looked. He took a sip, appreciating the warmth it brought. Mark Twain had said, "If you don't like the weather in New England now, just wait a few minutes." It was true of Illinois as well. Yesterday warm and sunny, today cool with clouds. He turned away, rubbing his scalp with the towel.

Marianne said the breakfast in the cafeteria was free. He went to his closet and took down the suit he'd worn the day before, slipping into the same pants and shirt again. He hadn't brought a suitcase with a change of clothes, only a shaving bag. He stepped back into the bathroom and wiped steam from the mirror. His hair was still moist from his shower. He reached for the hairdryer and blew it dry, rubbing his scalp to make the job go faster. He wasn't in a hurry, he had nowhere to be. Unless she'd missed her flight, Marianne was already gone. He stood by what he'd said, there was no point in starting a long distance relationship, so there was no reason to be thinking of her this morning.

He went for his shoes and sat on the edge of the bed putting them on. The phone startled him. *Rrriiiinnnng. Marianne?* He reached out and tucked the phone under his chin as he continued tying his laces. "This is Stan."

"Stan, this is Michael. Look, I'm already getting calls from people who heard you last night and they're very upset. Just tell me you didn't do it."

"Do what?"

"You haven't seen the papers? Rats, I want you to do me a favor. Get your stuff together and get out of that hotel. You're about to get a flood of reporters. Try not to talk to anyone and if you do, leave us out of it as much as possible. Our church has a good reputation. We don't need it sullied by bad press. It's better if we try and straighten this out later."

Stan pushed himself up and removed his tie from the back of the chair, looping it around his neck. His leg wasn't hurting him as he'd thought it might after all the stress he'd put on it the day before. "You're not making any sense. What did I do?" He went to the mirror with the phone propped under his chin.

"I don't have time to go into it. Grab a newspaper from the front desk on your way out, but please go now. We don't need a media frenzy here, and frankly I'll be able to handle this better at arm's-length."

Stan heard a click and the line switched to a dial tone. He took the phone away from his ear and stood staring at it blankly. *What was that about?* Why would Michael call in such a flap? Whatever it was, it sounded serious. He stood and grabbed his coat, slipping it on. He didn't need a tie today. He slipped it off his neck and folded it into his pocket. He went to the bathroom and checked behind the shower curtain to make sure he wasn't leaving anything behind. His overnight bag was on the bathroom sink. He tossed in his shaver and toothbrush and headed for the door.

He exited the elevator heading straight for the front desk. Complimentary copies of the *Journal Star* were in a stack on the edge of the counter. His bill had been prepaid. He slid his key toward the woman behind computer terminal and said, "Checking out," as he reached for one of the papers. The headline screamed back at him."

"Stan Powers Caught In Dalliance With Hooker." The photo was a picture of him kissing Marianne in the hall outside her room.

Stan's stomach was queasy. *Too much caffeine,* he thought, as he barreled down the freeway. The clouds had gone from a whitish blue to a deep gray, and trees along the road were bending in the wind. He could feel his car wanting to change lanes with each new gust. He fumbled with the radio, trying to find a station that was broadcasting the news. His phone had started ringing shortly after he'd hit the road. He'd turned it off. He wasn't ready to talk to the media yet. What could he say? He found a talk program and paused to see what they were discussing. No surprise, the subject was him.

"And you were there last night?"

"Yes I heard him firsthand. He sounded sincere, I actually liked him. Frankly, if I had to bet, I'd wager this is fake news. We get so much of that these days. Mr. Powers was dead set against our moral decline. I can't believe he was out carousing with a hooker right after he finished his speech. That just doesn't compute."

"Okay, thank you Susan, and on line three, we've got Don from Elmwood. Don what's your take on the story."

"I have a problem with all these holier than thou types. I quit going to church when I was fourteen because our pastor was caught in an affair. I was sitting in the pew feeling guilty because I'd just lost my virginity to Carmine Holsted, and trust me I wasn't the only one who lost their virginity to Carmine. Then this deacon comes

250

up and announces how the pastor has resigned because he's been diddling another deacon's wife. And there's me sitting there worried about going to hell. I mean, come on, how many times do we have to hear about another self-righteous saint falling from grace. These guys are all a bunch of hypocrites wearing fancy frocks and telling everyone else how to live when they can't do it themselves."

"That's a good point Don. And we have Alberta on line four, Alberta what do you have to say, is Mr. Powers guilty or innocent?"

"I was always taught you're innocent until proven guilty, but when you catch a man standing over a dead body with a smoking gun there's not much left but for the man to sign a confession. Look at the pictures. You got him in a restaurant giving the hooker money, then they kiss just outside her room, and she takes his hand and they go inside. I don't need to see pictures of them in the sack together. She said they did it, the photos back up her story, all we need..."

"Hold on a minute. Alberta, I hate to break in but I'm told we have our female escort on the line. And your name is, Marianne Moss, is that correct?"

"Yes it is, Bert."

"And you claim Stan Powers paid you to have sex with him last night?"

Stan's heart stopped beating. A chill ran from his shoulders down his back as goosebumps rose on his flesh. That was Marianne's voice.

"No, I'm not saying that all. That would be illegal. I'm an escort, and I do charge for my service, but it doesn't necessarily include sex."

"So you're saying you didn't have sex with Mr. Powers last night?"

"No, I'm not saying that either. We did end up in bed together, but it was consensual."

"So, what was the money for?"

"I think it would be better if I just told you what happened."

"By all means, go ahead, shoot."

"I met Mr. Powers in the bar of the Embassy Suites Hotel. It's not a place I frequent often, but I have been there before. And I want to be clear about this, I wasn't there trying to meet anyone. As I say, I am an escort, but my business comes through my office and all appointments are scheduled in advance. When I do have a client, say an out-of-town businessman or diplomat or just someone who feels the need for female companionship, I'm very clear about letting the gentlemen know I'm there to provide company, nothing else. So anyway, Mr. Powers sat down beside me at the bar and we start talking, and he mentions that he hasn't eaten dinner yet and asks me if I'd like to join him. I explained to Mr. Powers what I do for a living, just as I told you, and he says fine, so that's why he paid me. He just wanted some company. Later, we went back upstairs and I felt sorry for him. As a few of your callers already said, he is a very nice man, and he seemed lonely, so I invited him in. And the rest is history. Frankly, I had no idea he was there to speak to some religious group about morality."

"But you're saying you did have sex with him?"

"I thought I'd made that clear."

Stan was sweating, drops swelling and rolling down his chest, his stomach constricting under his skin making him queasy. His ears had to be lying because what he heard made no sense. It was a combination of half-truths and out-and-out fiction meant to make people believe he'd engaged the services of a prostitute. Her voice was calm and sincere, without a hint of impropriety. She demonstrated the very kind of character failings he'd spent the evening warning people about. How could she sound so genuinely heartfelt knowing it was all make-believe? And not just that, it was a set up. The whole thing had been staged. They'd taken pictures. There had to have been a camera somewhere. And to think he'd seriously considered asking her for a date. It was like she'd had her conscience lobotomized. It was a perfect example of what he'd said about a society so embedded in evil it could no longer see right from wrong. He tried to loosen his grip on the wheel. He was holding it so tight his knuckles were turning white.

Samuel's fingers twiddled the envelope on his desk. The return address was from the chaplain at the Dixon Correctional Facility, but it was addressed to Satchel. The problem was, he hadn't seen Satchel and probably wouldn't until Satchel made a trip to the mission. The cat jumped into his lap and walked up on his desk, sniffing the envelope. Samuel stroked it's head and set the envelope down, turning his attention back to the phone conversation he was having with Andy Whitmire, head of their mission board. He'd already had a half dozen calls from media types wanting to get his perspective, and now Andy was putting pressure on him to have Stan take a step back from the ministry, at least for the short term.

The voice was hesitant with just enough warble in it to connote it was elderly. "You know our association with him is going to cause a dip in our donations."

The room was cool because they'd shut the heating system down to save money. Specs of sand tossed by the wind pelted the window. The sky outside looked like a sheet of tin. Samuel was sitting upstairs in his office where he'd gone to pray, his Bible lying open in front of him on his desk. He placed a hand on the book and silently turned the page. "The Lawd's always taken care of us in the past. He'll take care of us now, and in the future."

"But the Lord doesn't reward sin, or those who patronize sinners."

"All a us are sinners, Andy, and if you mean Stan, he didn't do nothin'." The cat stepped off the desk and put his paws on Samuel's chest. Samuel pulled him into his lap.

"Did he tell you that? How can you be sure? All men have failings. The Bible says the heart of man is desperately wicked. You and I don't know what goes on in Stan's heart. All we know is what we see, and what we see is him handing money to this…woman, and then kissing her and going into her room."

Samuel paused. He rocked back in his chair. The cat continued to purr as he stroked its back. The wind outside howled. His eyes went to the window. A small branch with leaves still clinging to its stem flew by. "You don't know Stan like I do."

"Even King David fell. A good man can still make mistakes."

"And a person can be falsely accused. They called our Lawd a glutton and a wine bibba. They accused Him of telling people not to pay their taxes. They said He was about to lead a revolt against Caesa. None of that was true, no, but they made it look like He was guilty, 'nough to get Him hung on a cross." He set the cat on the ground and leaned forward with his elbows on the desk, one hand rubbing his forehead, the other holding the phone to his ear.

"Doesn't matter if it's true or not, they'll always be a certain number of people who believe it. I'm just saying as long as we're associated with Stan our revenues are going to suffer. All I'm asking is that we cut ties with him until this thing blows over. Then if you want to bring him back, fine."

"And I'm saying Christ's disciples never forsook him, no. They knew the truth and stuck with it even at the cost of their own lives. God 'pects us to remain loyal to the truth, but I hear what you're sayin'. We haven't heard from him yet. If he walks in here and confesses and says he made a mistake, I'll forgive him, but I agree it's probably best to disassociate ourselves for a time. But if he maintains he's innocent, and I'll know when I looks him in the eye, then this mission will back him even if it runs us into the ground. Now, I'm gonna hang up this phone 'cause all this talking ain't doing nobody no good. What we needs to be a doin' is prayin'."

Samuel hobbled downstairs, his alligator boots leaving tracks on the linoleum as he shuffled through the dining room. His denims were hitched up around his waist with his rodeo belt, and his white shirt was open at the collar with the cuffs folded back on his wrists. His cross hung from his neck like a dragonfly flitting back and forth. The room looked empty. He'd hoped to find a few of the staffers so he could gauge their reaction to the news and hopefully get them engaged in prayer. He headed for the kitchen and then out the back door to see if they were outside. No one was around, not even Freddie, who was supposed to be painting. A sealed can was on the ground along with a brush wrapped in cellophane. A gust hit Samuel, causing him to bring an arm up to protect his face from flying dirt. Freddie couldn't be expected to paint in this wind. Where had everyone gone? *Strike the shepherd and the sheep will be scattered.* What if this challenge to their faith caused them to abandon ship? He dismissed the thought. These men had given their hearts to Jesus Christ, not to Stan.

He walked over to the stage and picked up his guitar, feeling the worn frets under his fingers. The scratched box still had enough lacquer to shine in the light but it had definitely seen better days. He sat down on the stool and ran his finger across the strings, then reached out and cranked the pegs until they struck a harmonious chord. He began to sing a hymn taken from a medieval poem describing how Christ's body suffered during His crucifixion. The last stanza, which was borrowed for the song, addressed Christ's head. The weight of the message took on more gravity with the raw grating of his voice.

> "O sacred head, now wounded,
> With grief and shame weighed down,
> Now scornfully surrounded
> With thorns, Thy only crown.
> How art thou pale with anguish,
> With sore abuse and scorn?
> How does that visage languish,
> Which once was bright as morn."

Stan pulled into his parking spot behind the mission and staggered out of the car. The wind pummeled his hair, puffing his jacket up at the lapels. Bits of sand stung his face. He pulled his coat in and reached for the door, holding on tight as he pulled it open to keep it from being ripped from his hand. He could hear the music. He went inside and secured the door without letting it slam.

"What now, my Lord, has suffered,
Was all for sinners gain.
Mine, mine was the transgression,
But Thine the deadly pain.
Low, here I fall, my Savior,
'Tis I deserve Thy place.
Look on me with Thy favor,
Vouchsafe to me Thy grace."

Stan felt his whole body tremble, moisture building in his eye. He spent much of his life as a warrior. He'd seen the destruction of battle, the suffering caused by man's lust for power and insatiable cruelty. He'd had wounds inflicted on his body and had bled for things he thought he believed in, but never once had he cried. He thought of a line from another hymn, *Jesus paid it all, all to him I owe, sin had left a crimson stain, He washed it white as snow.*

"What language shall I borrow
To thank Thee dearest friend.
For this Thy dying sorrow,
Thy pity without end.
O make me Thine forever,
And should I fainting be,
Lord let me never, never,
Outlive my love for Thee."

It felt to Stan like someone had packed sand bags on his shoulders as he limped around the corner. Except for Samuel, sitting on a stool on the makeshift stage, the one they'd worked to build together, the room was empty and strangely quiet. Samuel had stopped playing, there was no one in the kitchen juggling pots and pans, even the overhead fans with their whirring motors were silent. Samuel took a sip of coffee from a mug that had the words "His Mercy Endures Forever," printed on it. Stan felt his shoulders rise and fall as he sucked in his breath, his mouth filling with mucus and his chest coughing up phlegm.

"Hey, Samuel, I guess you heard. Heck of a night, huh? Look, don't stop playing on my account. I love that song. It's kind of what I needed to hear." A tear wound its way down the side of his face, catching on the corner of his mouth. He sucked it in, tasting the salt. "I'm sure you know what's going on. None of it's true, but that doesn't matter, it still feels like I stepped on a Bouncing Betty, like my legs and arms have been ripped from my body. I want to cry, 'Why me Lord? Why me?' Funny how easy it is to feel sorry for yourself. I was driving back from Peoria having a pity party in my car, not even thinking for a moment what Christ suffered for me, and then I walk in here and you put it all back into perspective. 'Mine, mine was the transgression, but thine the deadly pain.' I didn't do anything with that woman, it was a complete set up. I should be laughing about it, but I can't. All I can think of is that I'm on trial for something I didn't do, and then you sang that song. My Savior died for me without doing wrong. Samuel, just what the heck is going on?"

Samuel placed his guitar back on its stand and stepped down from the podium. He placed his broad black hands on Stan's shoulders and looked him in the eye. "I told ya the devil was out to get ya. We don't wrestle with things of this earth, not with that woman, not her false accusations, no, we wrestle with spiritual forces of darkness in high places. You stepped into his territory now, you gotta 'spect to get attacked. I read it to you just the other morning. Satan's on the prowl looking for someone to devour."

Stan swallowed and took a deep breath, clearing his throat. "I know, but sometimes I have to hear it. You get weary fighting the battle, you know? But I'll be okay, especially if I can get some of that coffee. Any more of that around?"

Samuel took Stan by the sleeve and turned him toward the kitchen. "Fresh pot, right over here."

A light was on over the stove, but the room was dark. Several bowls were in the sink, rinsed but not washed. An empty jug of milk was left on the counter along with two spoons with white puddles beneath them. "Where is everyone?"

"Good question. I haven't seen…" A thump echoed down from above. Their eyes went to the ceiling. "I was gonna say I haven't seen 'em but I guess they's upstairs."

Samuel and Stan plodded their way up, their feet thudding on the wood staircase. The walls weren't wide enough to walk side-by-side so Stan followed Samuel until they were standing on the second floor. The carpet was worn, but clean. Samuel flicked on the hallway light. "I think the sound came from the bunk room," Samuel said.

They treaded down the hall to where the men had their sleeping quarters. The door was closed but voices could be heard on the other side. Samuel leaned in turning the knob, letting it fall open. Five men were sitting in a circle, their heads bowed, elbows on their knees with hands folded. They looked up at the intrusion and then rose in unison grabbing Stan and pulling him to the center of their circle. The room was moist and smelled like heated bodies. Samuel went to the window to open it a crack and let in some fresh air but saw the wind gusting through the trees, a newspaper rolling like a tumbleweed down the alley. A pigeon seemed to be having a hard time finding purchase on the branch of a tree. He turned around and found the men placing their hands on Stan's shoulders.

"So glad you made it, brother."

"We didn't know what to do, but Jason said we should pray so here we are."

"Yeah dude, we've been going at this for more than an hour, except when we stopped to listen to the bishop's music. That was awesome, man."

Freddie didn't say anything, but Stan could see red imprints where his hands had pressed against his forehead as he knelt in prayer.

Samuel stepped into the circle. "Don't let us interrupt, no." He laid his hands on Stan's head. "We in a spiritual battle here. We gotta keep fighting. Lawd God Almighty. This is your servant Stan. Now I know you sees from heaven above, and I know you knows what's going on down here below. That old devil monster is a tryin' to kick the stilts out from under our brother, but your word says, 'Resist the devil and he'll flee.' So I'm praying right now Lawd, that you give my brother, Stan, the power to resist. And Lawd, there are some people out there who think the world would be a better place without You. You think you can show them different?"

As if it wasn't enough to have his name sullied by the nonsense printed about him in every newspaper in the land, Stan had to wake up Tuesday morning to stand before a judge of the human rights commission. The trial date had been set before he'd received his invitation to speak, but he'd never considered how one might impact the other. His body felt stiff as he crawled from bed, afraid to retrieve the morning paper. If it had his picture in it, he didn't want to know. He reached for his tan slacks, struggling to get a leg up over the waist to slip them on. His light blue shirt sat on shoulders that ached, his fingers feeling knotted as he tried to do up the buttons. He stood thinking about it, realizing his thoughts were more about Marianne's ruse than what he should wear. She'd played him. *So what? Get over it. Live to fight another day.* He selected a blue sport coat, hoping it would make him appear respectful without looking pretentious, as he feared he might in a posh business suit. He closed the closet without selecting a tie. For this engagement an open collar should do fine.

It would be another sweltering day. The sun was wrapped in the clouds, looking like a infant's head peeking out from its blankets. There would probably be thundershowers in the afternoon. The car's comfy interior was a welcome relief after hours of stressful rolling from one side of the bed to the other. His sheets had been damp when he rose, the fan barely cooling his moist skin. The car's air conditioner was so much better. He melted into the cushy leather and drove into the city with a travel mug in hand, but no newspaper.

He parked and headed for the front of the building, his limp more pronounced than it had been in some time. Art Stone was waiting for him as he pushed through the doors.

"Looks like you've already had a bad week," he said, as he thrust a copy of the Tribune at Stan.

Stan looked down and saw his face filling the front page, just as he'd feared.

"I guess if you were looking for publicity you got it, but I can't say this is going to help our case."

"Good morning to you too, Art." Stan paused, placing a hand on his lumbar and arching his back. "I hope you know that's nonsense. The woman and I had dinner because she said she wanted to interview me for an article she was writing. Her room was on the same floor as mine and when I stopped to say good night she kissed me. It was a set up. End of story."

Art brought his arm up to check the time and swung around, his briefcase nearly clipping Stan's leg as they headed into court. "All well and good," he said, "but the judge is going to see this as defining your character. If you're a philanderer you're probably a bigot too."

They stepped into a room already filled with people. Art took his arm. "Don't worry, we're first on the docket."

Stan looked over his shoulder scanning the crowd and recognized, much to his chagrin, the faces of several reporters. *How did they hear about this?* They took seats at a table set aside for the defendant and his counsel. The air conditioner didn't seem to be working. Stan tried to get comfortable, but the warmth made him feel itchy. He reached around to scratch his back with a thumb refusing to take off his coat and appear too casual, like he wasn't taking the proceedings seriously. A podium stood in front of their table. A second one was positioned across the aisle where the plaintiffs were seated. Stan recognized the two young men, Thomas and Marty, if memory served. Just the two of them. They didn't appear to have a lawyer. He tried to read their faces. Thomas looked angry, his face hard with lips pressed flat and eyes narrow, while Marty looked sad. His lips were pouty and his eyes appeared to be tinged with water. Marty looked over at Stan, his eyes furtive and veined with red. He shook his head and shrugged.

Art leaned in to say something, and Stan bent forward to meet him halfway. "I'm glad they agreed to have this litigated before an administrative law judge. I assume they couldn't afford a full-blown jury trial, but it works to our advantage because juries in human rights hearings have consistently favored the plaintiff."

"All rise."

Stan looked up as their judge entered from stage left. He and Art Stone slid their chairs back and stood, as did his accusers on the other side of the room. The judge was short with a full head of wavy brown hair, a round face and rouge cheeks. He had a pair of reading glasses perched on the tip of his nose and looked like he'd rather be at home drinking tea with a cat in his lap, than making punitive decisions. His plump hands had short fingers. He picked up a file folder which he opened and began to read.

"This hearing before the Illinois human rights commission is now in session. The Honorable Judge Meriwether, presiding."

Judge Meriwether dropped the folder and lay it flat on his bench, looking down on those standing before him.

"Sit down, sit down," he said waving a pudgy hand up and down. "I do things a bit differently in my courtroom. Were going to keep these proceedings informal. I will listen to each side state their case and ask any questions I find necessary for clarification. Then I'll make my decision. Keep it simple, that's my motto. However, my decision will be binding. Any appeal of my judgment must be filed with the Illinois Circuit Court. The Illinois Human Rights Act generally defines unlawful discrimination as discrimination on the base of race, color, religion, national origin, ancestry, age, sex, marital status, and sexual orientation. I gather this first case is about discrimination with respect to sexual orientation." The judge glanced over at the plaintiffs table. "You already filed a charge with the human rights commission, which was investigated and deemed credible, and passed to me for litigation. I'm not going to call you up to the witness box," the judge reached around and rubbed the back of his neck," I have a kink that makes it difficult for me to turn to the side, but we have these two podiums here and I would ask the plaintiff and the defendant to come forward and stand behind them. Come on boys, now," he said waving his puffy hand toward himself as though drawing them in. "Let's get this show on the road."

Stan looked at Art, who nodded and leaned in to whisper, "I've never been the defense at a civil rights tribunal so I don't know what to expect. Just do as he says."

Stan rose from his seat and went to the podium pressing a hand against his thigh to keep his limp from showing. He wanted justice, not sympathy. His shoulders felt heavy, but he pulled them back and stood erect like a SEAL honoring the flag.

From the bench Judge Meriwether said, "Let's begin with the plaintiff. Please explain to the court the nature of your claim."

The young man who had taken the stand was, as was to be expected, the more hostile of the two. He was the one Stan thought was Thomas. He glanced to the side at Stan with a look that could only be described as disdain. It was too bad, too, because other than that he was a good looking youth with medium length brown hair streaked with blond highlights that swirled over the top of his crown in long waves while being cropped short along the sides. His cheeks were covered with a two-day-old beard and his lips, though firmly pressed together, were full and red. His eyes were blue. His long lashes fluttered as he began to speak.

"Your honor, as you probably already know, my partner," he looked over to include the man Stan thought looked sad, "and I are gay. We are also citizens of the United States of America where all men, according to our Constitution, are supposed to be equal. Unfortunately, in reality, that's not the case. Marty, that's my partner, and I are forever running into people who see us as being less, or somehow inferior to themselves, people like Mr. Powers here, who can't accept us as we are and refuse to acknowledge us as decent human beings.

"This is why we're here, today. On May 14th of this year, my partner and I approached Mr. Powers with the prospect of doing an advertising campaign for our new business, a cocktail lounge we're calling, The Silver Slipper. But he refused us. He said he couldn't, in good moral conscience, advertise a club that promoted deviant behavior..."

"He actually said that?" Judge Meriwether interjected. He leaned forward with his elbows on the bench and hands folded, his eyes wide behind their shields of glass, looking incredulous.

"Well, maybe not in those exact words, but that's what he meant. We were left to feel like the genuine love we have for one another is, in his view, somehow immoral, like there's something broken in us that needs to be fixed. We were humiliated."

Judge Meriwether looked at Stan, the once playful clown-like face now red and humorless. "Did you say that?"

"Your honor?"

"I want to know if you told these young men you couldn't advertise their club because you felt their lifestyle is immoral."

"Not exactly. And certainly not in those words. But I am a man of faith and to the best of my ability I try to live by the tenets of the Bible. The Bible calls homosexuality a sin, not any worse than any other sin, but a sin nonetheless, so I can't allow myself in good conscience to promote something I know God says is wrong..."

Judge Meriwether brought his gavel down hard on the bench, *Bam!* "That's enough, Mr. Powers. I don't need to hear anymore from you. I saw enough of that on your televised debate with Senator Weise. And now, of course, you're being accused of entertaining prostitutes. We know what kind of man you are. But none of that, I assure you, has any bearing on this case. My only interest here is that you've been accused of discriminating against these young men for their sexual orientation, and since you've just admitted to doing that, I'm ready to make my decision."

Art Stone jumped to his feet. "Your honor! You need to listen to my client's side of the story. There are other issues to consid..."

The gavel came down again, *Bam!* "Sit down, Mr. Stone. If a man tells the court he murdered someone, the court is under no obligation to listen to why he chose to do it. The man is guilty and the court has every right to pronounce sentence."

"But, your honor..."

"Sit down or I'll hold you in contempt."

Stan turned to look at Art, who appeared completely flummoxed. He shrugged in resignation and sank down to his chair. "We'll take this up on appeal," he said, more to himself than the court.

"What was that you said?"

Art looked up, his face muscles tense, his eyes buzzing like they were receiving jolts of electricity, "Nothing, Your Honor."

"Not one more word or I'll hold you in contempt."

Stan could see Art was grinding his teeth, his cheeks twitching, his lips pursed. He turned back to judge Meriwether. "But, Your Honor, doesn't the Constitution guarantee me the right to the free exercise of my religion?"

Judge Meriwether placed his elbows on the bench and interlaced his fingers, twiddling his thumbs. "You bet it does. You have the right to worship however you choose, whenever you choose, wherever you choose, and whatever God you choose. You do not, however, have the right to hurt others when you exercise your freedom of religion."

"But, Your Honor, I didn't set out to hurt anyone. These men came to me, I only..."

"You insulted them by making them feel unworthy of benefiting from your professional expertise. Mr. Powers," Judge Meriwether continued, "my ruling is that you will complete this advertising campaign, and you will not only do it to the best of your ability, using your best copywriters and artists, but you will do it at your own cost. I am setting a budget of fifty thousand, which you must use to purchase ad space, or airtime, or whatever other media your clients choose to promote their business, and you will advertise for them using art and graphics of which they approve until this budget is spent."

"But, I can't..."

"You can, and you will."

"No, your honor, hear me out, please. Our business is based on a charter which clearly states if the company is ever found engaged in anything contradictory to biblical teaching, the company is forfeit and must be sold or cease operations."

"That is your choice, then. Either run this campaign, sell your company, or shut it down. You decide. I give you thirty days at which time I want to see you back here with copies of your first ad for the Silver Slipper, or documents showing you have either divested yourself of Power Advertising, or it is no longer in business. I suggest you consider running the ad. Thirty days." The gavel came down one final time, *Bam!*

Stan blinked and stood there motionless, stunned. It felt like his chest had just been blown open by a mortar. He looked over and saw Thomas. The grin on his face reminded him of a little boy he'd known as a child. The boy had poured gasoline on a cat and set it on fire and then sat grinning as he watched the animal turning in circles while burning alive.

Seventeen

TWO DAYS later Charlotte assembled her troops again. It was Thursday and they were gathered in the tower to go over the latest polling results. Charlotte had held back the fact that she had a surprise for everyone. They'd thought they were coming in to work, but she'd brought them in to party. Faithful service deserved reward. She pulled a large green bottle from a silver bucket, spilling ice on the table as she handed it to Bob. "Would you do the honors?"

She had a reason to celebrate. On the boardroom table were several newspapers. Pollsters were quick to jump on the turn of events and get people's reaction. Charlotte was back in her old spot with Stan trailing far behind.

Her staff stood around the room holding plastic flutes, waiting for Bob to pour the champagne. The cake had already been cut, the words, 'Thank You For a Job Well Done' written in scrolling letters, now separated into dozens of two-inch squares and placed on paper plates with plastic forks.

Bob twisted the tab of the muselet, freeing the plastic cork from its wire cage. Using his thumbs, he began prodding it up until, *POP*, it rocketed to the ceiling. Several of the staffers had to duck to keep from being struck by the flying projectile. Everybody gave a lighthearted laugh.

The champagne bubbled through the neck of the bottle onto

Bob's hand. He grabbed a champagne flute and held it underneath
to catch the overflow but most of it missed and landed on the floor.

"Don't worry about it, it's just champagne; it doesn't stain." Bob
set the bottle down and scurried to grab a half-inch thick stack of
napkins to blot up the mess he'd made.

Rachel stood with her back to the room staring out the window.
The wind had blown the clouds out over the lake, leaving behind
a pristine sky. For the first time she was able to see what captivated
Charlotte nearly every day. Only a few buildings attained to the
height at which she stood. It was breathtaking. A slight burning
sensation arose in her chest. She knew the glass was unbreakable,
but it still bothered her to look down. She turned back to face the
group again.

Bob was walking around the room filling glasses. She of course
would refuse. She was only seventeen. She suspected a few of the
others weren't twenty-one yet either but they were allowing their
glasses to be filled. Maybe protocol called for lifting a full glass up
for the toast and then setting it down. Bob came by and filled her
glass without asking, and she didn't decline.

When all the glasses were full, Bob set the bottle on the table
where it made wet rings on the bright mahogany wood. He looked
back at Charlotte.

She looked remarkably composed. Her white pantsuit was
custom tailored and fit her small frame with elegance and style. The
deep lines of her face looked like they'd been sanded smooth, and
her previously straw-like hair now had a soft moisturized quality to
it. She raised her glass. "A toast," she said. "Here's to Stan Powers."

There were groans and guffaws throughout the room.

"No, I mean it, you couldn't have a better fall guy. When you set
yourself up on a pedestal you're easy to knock down. He's not going
to recover from this. The churches that supported him are going to
throw him to the wolves. The media will hound him for months,
digging into his background to see if they can't find something

else, and by then he'll be so far behind there'll be no chance of catching up. And the really good news is, I didn't have anyone to run against before. Now they can't say I won uncontested. And after this, I doubt anyone will ever run against me again. So, here's to you, Stan." She extended her hand out to all those in the room. "Thank you."

In unison the entire room brought their glasses to their mouths and took a collective sip, all except Rachel. She brought the plastic flute to her mouth but didn't drink. She looked around to see if anyone was watching and finding them preoccupied, set her glass down. She turned to the window again. *"And the devil took Him up on an exceedingly high mountain, and showed Him all the kingdoms of the world and their glory. And he said to Him, all these things I will give You if You will fall down and worship me."* Where had she read that? Then she remembered, it was in her room, the one with the frilly bed and stuffed toys she'd had while staying with the Robinsons. They'd bought her a Bible for Christmas. She ended up reading it because it challenged her reading skills but why had she recalled this particular verse right now? *All the kingdoms of the world, hum.* And then there was the one that said, *"What does it profit a man if he gain the whole world and lose his own soul?"* She knew that one in particular because she'd pondered the question long and hard. The two verses seemed like a logical pair, but she'd never put them together before.

She should talk to her father about it. He'd been trying to pique her interest in Jesus. Maybe he'd know why these two verses weren't written side-by-side. *All the kingdoms of the world.* That wasn't what Senator Weise was after, she only wanted to make the world a better place, and that meant getting reelected to serve another term. Perhaps tracking Mr. Powers' every move the way they had was unscrupulous, but it was effective and Mr. Powers had only himself to blame for his demise. They had caught him with his pants down, fair and square. Charlotte said keeping this man out of

269

office was paramount. She didn't know the half of it. The last thing people needed was to be governed by a philandering homophobe who thought he'd gotten away with murder.

Stan had to drag himself into the office the next morning. He'd seen the papers. Everyone already knew what he had to tell them, but that didn't make the job any easier. He pulled into the parking garage and stepped from his car, feeling about a hundred years old. He stooped over, barely able to lift his briefcase from the seat.

People on the elevator pretended not to know him, though they were faces he recognized and had said good morning to him dozens of times. They stood looking straight ahead with their hands folded around their briefcases and purses. He felt like he was standing in a room full of mannequins.

The door opened and he made his way down the hall, through the lobby and into his office without a word to anyone. He shut the door, laid his briefcase on his desk and removed his coat. The day outside was gray as steel wool, the clouds scouring up against the sides of the building. *It never rains, but it pours,* he thought. He reached for the phone and used the intercom button to connect with reception.

"Hi Maria, could you assemble everyone in the work room? I have an announcement to make."

"Yes, of course, sure boss. I'll do it right away."

Stan placed the receiver back in the cradle and leaned back to sit against the edge of his desk. He folded his arms and took a deep breath, bowing his head. "Lord, You gave me this agency, and now it appears You've taken it away. Let me be like Job, Lord, and bless your name even when things don't make sense. But most of all, Lord, I want to pray for those who will be affected by this change, some even more than I, that they'll be able to find new jobs and won't lose hope, and Lord, as I put my trust in You, let my example be a witness that they'll see my faith and maybe learn to trust in You as well."

Stan took a deep breath and opened his eyes. He slipped a finger up to loosen his tie and unhook his top button. It was time to face the music.

Thirty people were assembled in the back part of the building huddled around the artist's work stations and copywriters desks. Stan walked in holding the newspaper and held it up. "Anyone not seen this?"

A peal of thunder shook the windows and water poured from the sky, bouncing off the sills like the deluge of Noah.

"Well I guess that about sums up how I feel," Stan said. Chuckles came from all around the room.

"Anyway, you all know I was accused of engaging the services of a prostitute. I want you to know that never happened, but I'm hard pressed to prove it so you're just going to have to take my word for it, or not. And you also know that our company was taken to court for my refusal to run a series of homosexual ads." Stan looked at Julie. "Please don't say I told you so," then he looked at Bruce, but Bruce crossed his arms and looked away nervously shuffling his feet. "This is on me, the fault is mine. Sometimes standing for what you believe comes at great cost. In this case I've lost the agency, and I apologize deeply for how that affects you."

"Can't you just do the ad? Step down off your high horse for a moment. Doesn't God tell you to obey the law?" It was Julie, standing there in her slim fitting black one piece with a pattern of white feathers. She had her arms crossed and her right toe tapping in a show of defiance.

Stan bit his bottom lip to keep it from quivering. "Yes, Julie, He does, but when that law comes in conflict with the rules he's established, I choose to follow Him. Anyway, I've made my decision. This agency will be closing within thirty days. Julie, you mentioned you had an offer from another agency, I would suggest you take it and invite as many of our customers as you can to go with you. I'll personally be working with the rest to find them a good home. As for all of you, I've gone over our financials and we have enough in the bank to pay each of you a one month severance. You can stay for the entire thirty days and apply for jobs while you continue to work and then take your severance when you're ready to leave, or leave now and collect your severance immediately. If anyone needs a reference, I'll be happy to give it. I just want you to know it's been an honor to work with each and every one of you."

"You can't just give up, boss, that's not like you. Really." Stan was surprised by the sincerity in Bruce's voice, though it held a tremor. His eyes looked glassy, like they were about to rain. He had no cause for concern. With talent like his he should have no problem securing another position. The newspapers were full of articles proclaiming this as a victory for gay rights. He, of all people, should be happy.

"Believe me, it's not my choice, Bruce. I'll probably put the agency up for sale, but I've only got thirty days and that may not be enough time to pull something together. Other than that, I'm out of options."

Lightning flashed, flickering in the windows like a gigantic strobe. Rain fell in a torrent so thick you couldn't see through the glass. Thunder bounced off the walls.

"For those of you who stay, I would ask that you continue working on the commitments we have with our clients while you seek out other opportunities, but if you feel you must leave at any time, I'll understand."

Stan pulled his Lexus into his parking space behind the Daily Bread food bank. He'd gone from his office to the parking garage without getting wet, but the way the rain was coming down, there was no chance of that between here and the back door. He waited for a moment, mustering courage, then swung the door open and ran into the building. He dusted his shoulders, the water rolling off in waves.

"I was wondering when you was gonna show your face around here," Samuel said. "Not that I needs an explanation, no suh, but you surely do need prayer."

Stan removed his coat and walked around the corner where Samuel was seated on a stool with his guitar in his lap. "How'd you know it was me?"

"Who else would be coming through the back door in a storm like dat."

"Right. Well, I guess you heard I've lost the agency." The cat trotted over and began doing figure eights, weaving in and out around Stan's legs.

"So how you takin' it?" Samuel slipped his pick in between the strings and put his guitar back on its stand, the strings twanging against the metal frets.

"I'm fine. My main concern is the drop in revenue this is going to mean to the mission." Lightning flashed in the window, the sky a bit darker than before. A rumble rolled through the room.

Samuel scratched his bald head and stood. His hand fell to his cross which he tucked inside his shirt. "Now don't you be fretting about that, no suh, we're in the Lord's hands, always was, always will be."

Stan nodded. Samuel had always been a great man of faith, a solid example of what it meant to trust God for everything. "I appreciate that, but I also know things around here are going to be tight, at least in the short term."

"That may be so, but God never closes a door without opening a window, so I say let those blessings come pouring through."

Stan laid his coat on the table and turned a chair around, sitting down with his elbows on his knees and his fingers interlocked in front of him. The cat tried to jump into his lap. He leaned back to receive it, but thunder boomed and the cat hopped back down and scampered off toward the kitchen.

"I saw on TV where that hustler lady is still goin' around saying you solicited her. That's the one that's got me bothered. The other's just about money. This one's about spoiling your good name."

Freddie came trundling down the stairs, the rain having brought his work to a halt, his bib overalls covered in drips of tan paint. He saw Stan and swung around cupping his mouth. "Hey guys, Stan's back." And before Stan could think to say anything he found himself surrounded by men with their hands on his shoulders, petitioning the Lord for mercy and grace.

Eighteen

SUN POURED through the windows of Stan's room like a beam of light at the mouth of a mineshaft. It was a nice hotel, not as swank as the Embassy Suites but clean and well appointed. His computer was open on the coffee table. His eyes went back to his work, his fingers striking the keys preparing the statement he would soon release to the media. He was dropping out of the race, but he would go on his terms. The rectangle of light on the carpet, emanating from the window, held the shadow of three flags flapping in the wind.

He glanced over at the bed, a mountain of mattresses so high it required a footstool to ascend. The bedspread was a glossy maroon with two broad gold leaf stripes running top to bottom with matching pillow shams. Several smaller maroon pillows, made of some kind of velveteen material, were stacked in front along with a rolled pillow that looked like a large sausage. A large piece of commercial art was mounted above the headboard depicting a deeply wooded meadow with frost on the ground and a grove of maples with leaves of red and gold.

He was tempted to go lie down. He hadn't slept in several nights. Maybe a different bed with a different pillow and a different set of sheets would help him find rest. He sure couldn't find it at home. Reporters were camped in his front yard, maybe not in tents, but in cars and news vans. It appeared they were there to stay. So far he'd refused to give a single interview. He wished he could turn back the hands of time and refuse to meet with Marianne. Be that as it may, he owed the public an explanation. He stared at the computer screen praying for the right words.

His Bible sat beside him on the couch. God's instruction manual—operating procedures for the maintenance of life on planet Earth. He picked it up, smelling the leather and feeling the smooth cover as it flopped open, his fingers flicking through the pages with their gilded edges. God could never put the sum of his knowledge into one small book, but every question man needed an answer to was there.

Stan stared out the window into the blue haze. He might have understood, in a tacit sort of way, that men were evil. But not like he knew it now. He'd lost his business, and been run out of public life, and had his reputation sullied, all for what he believed. He had seen the vice of man's heart firsthand.

All he wanted to do was warn them of what was coming. The world was about to be shaken and it would eventually fall, as forewritten in prophecy. When Jonah prophesied to Nineveh about their coming destruction, they'd repented and stalled God's judgment another four hundred years. That's what Stan hoped for, a delaying of God's justice. He'd been called, like Jonah, to warn the people, but his message had been cut short. Maybe God would send someone else.

His head turned at the tapping on his door. He quickly read the last few lines he'd written. They weren't good, but he could rework them later. Everything was set. He got up and shuffled across the carpet to let his guest in. He would exit on his own terms, he reminded himself. He opened the door.

"Hi Marianne," he said. "Come on in." She was wearing a trim fitting black dress hemmed just below the knee with arms cut just above her elbows. Her brunette hair was long and hung over her shoulders in front. He suspected she'd just placed it there to look more provocative. There were gold hoop earrings dangling from her ears and a gold necklace around her neck with a single pearl at the end. Her high heels were made of glossy patent leather, as was the small purse she held in her hand.

"You!" she said.

"Yes me," he pulled the door open, stepping back so she could enter.

"I…I think I'd better go."

"Too late. I already paid for your service."

A smile crept across her face. She took a step inside. "So… What? You figure as long as everyone says you're sleeping with me you might as well do it?"

"No, nothing like that. You can put your purse over there," he said, indicating the bed with a wave of his hand.

Marianne went over and set her purse on the comforter, the spikes of her high heels leaving divots in the carpet. "What then? You want to have another dinner?"

"No, I've already eaten. Please, sit down." Stan waited till she found a place on the couch and sat down beside her.

Her eyes went to the computer.

"It's my resignation speech. I'm withdrawing from the race. You can tell Senator Weise it worked. She'll be happy to know she got her money's worth. But that's not why I had you come."

Marianne leaned in so she could read what he'd written, then pushed her hair back over her shoulders and sat up straight, crossing her hands in her lap. "And why would that be?"

"That's the question, isn't it? Why? Aside from the money, I mean. Why would you purposely try to destroy my life? You don't know me. I've never done you any harm."

Marianne stared at him and for a moment her face was blank, an unwritten sheet of rose colored paper. She placed an arm across her torso and propped her elbow on it with the back of her hand under her chin like Rodin's thinker. She shook her head. "Like you said, I got paid. That's how I make my living. Someone wants to hire me for my time, I really don't care how they use it as long as I get paid."

"I thought you'd say something like that, but it still troubles me. You must know it's wrong. Do unto others as you would have them do unto you. That's the golden rule. Actually Christ was the one who said that. You wouldn't want to be treated the way you treated me. Imagine what it would be like if the whole world had an attitude like yours? Would that be a world you'd want to live in?" The screen on Stan's computer faded to black, the sleep mode kicking in. He reached for it but stopped. She'd already seen what he wanted her to see.

"I really don't think about it. Is this what you want to do all night? Because I think I'd prefer to have my office refund your money." Marianne uncrossed her arms and began tugging on the sleeves of her dress.

"So the bottom line is, you have no conscience at all. It doesn't matter who you hurt or what damage you do, as long as you get paid. The problem is the world's becoming full of people like you, and people like Senator Weise who hired you."

Marianne wiped her hands on her lap, her shoulders rolled in, a sign of nervous agitation. "Senator Weise just wanted you out of the way, but I guess you're right, she is a lot like me. She has an agenda. Mine is making money, hers is getting elected, but both of us are willing to do what's necessary to get what we're after. If I'd known it was you who hired me tonight, I would've had them charge you double."

"You should've come to the presentation I made just before we met. You would've heard me say that kind of self-centered attitude is leading to America's downfall. The only hope this world has is Jesus. That heart of yours may be hard as stone but He can turn it into clay, something He can mold into…"

Marianne slowly rose to her feet. "Okay. That's it," she said.

"I've got your business card. I'll have my office send you a refund. Every once in a while I run into a creep I just can't stand, but I always refund their money. See I have ethics. You want me to make the check out to Roy Morgan, that's who I was supposed to be entertaining tonight? Which only proves you have a little deceit in your heart as well."

"You don't know the half of it," he said.

"Don't get up. I'll show myself out."

There was a bounce in his step as Satchel hopped down from the porch into a day made by God for worship. The air smelled of the crocus and grape hyacinth and lily of the valley. Mama had planted a small garden along the sidewalk that bordered her lawn. The sky was a hazy blue and striated with clouds that looked like beach sand rippled by the ocean, the trees lining the sidewalk held a bounty of leaves that twittered with birds, and a light breeze, warm and soft, feathered his skin. He passed the small store owned by the Indian couple where he bought most of his groceries. He was allowed to use restaurant supplies for his staples, like milk, eggs, sugar, and butter, but the restaurant wasn't open for breakfast so for things like cereals and pancakes, and of course his toiletries, he was on his own. The ad from the newspaper taped inside the window said they had cantaloupes two for a dollar and bananas ninety-eight cents a pound. He made a mental note to remember. He hadn't seen cantaloupes that cheap in a long time.

Only a few cars congested the street, but people were prone to sleep in on Sundays, which made it nice for people who wanted to get out early and take a stroll. He had vowed to start looking for a church to attend, but Sunday was his only day off and the only day he could see Rachel because her office was closed on the Lord's day too. *Forgive me, I will start going to church. I promise.* At least he'd taken time to read his Bible and commune with the Father in prayer.

One of these days he was going to get Rachel on that subway and take her to the mission. Mama allowed him to use the restaurant's phone to keep in touch with Samuel. He was encouraged to know they were praying for him. The television reported daily on the demise of Stan's campaign. If they were to be believed, Stan was a bigot and pervert. He deserved to be abandoned by his constituency. The Christian community, his strongest base, had disavowed him, calling him a wolf in sheep's clothing. Samuel said he believed Stan was innocent, that he'd never had a relationship with that strumpet who claimed he did. And if Samuel believed it, that was good enough for Satchel.

The light at the corner turned green. Satchel picked up the pace. It would be close, but he could make it. The light blinked yellow as he entered the intersection and hustled across, hopping up the curb on the other side just as the light turned red. A car zoomed by spinning up road dust and filling the air with the fumes from its exhaust. He faced the park, according to Rachel, one of the most beautiful places on earth. He was inclined to agree. When you stepped onto the lawn of the Northwestern campus you left the world behind and stepped into Sherwood Forest in the realm of Nottingham. Rachel was quick to point out that that might change in the fall when the school filled with people, but at least it seemed that way during the summer when the campus was empty.

Satchel cut across the grass, waving at a man on a riding mower who waved back with a gloved hand. Lancelot with a floppy gardening hat mounted on his green steed. A robin flew off with a worm that made the mistake of tunneling out of the ground to avoid being drowned by the sprinklers and a squirrel skittered across the lawn with its cheeks full of nuts as it bounded into a tree. "Summer and winter, springtime and harvest, sun, moon and stars in their courses above, join with all nature in manifold witness, to thy great faithfulness, mercy and love," Satchel hummed. He'd never been a man of music nor could he say he knew the words to any songs except those he played on the radio while cooking. But those songs now filled him, warming his insides and often caused him to swallow a tear. *God is so good!* God had brought him out of prison, and taken him off the streets, and given him a fine job, and reintroduced him to his daughter. He brought him from death back to life. What more could he ask?

The newly mowed grass stuck to his tennis shoes. He stopped at a peat garden filled with ferns and used a rock to scrape the bulk of it off, then stepped onto the sidewalk and stomped his feet, shedding the rest. It wouldn't do to meet Rachel with his shoes covered in grass.

It was a routine. Every Sunday for the last four weeks they'd met on a garden bench in the center of campus and then taken a walk. He honestly felt he was getting to know his daughter, and while there wasn't much they agreed upon, they were having good discussions, though he wasn't looking forward to what she'd probably say today. He saw her up ahead sitting alone on the cast-iron park bench they used for their meetings. His heart turned to jelly. She was reading, as she always did whenever she had to wait for him. Her legs were stretched out in front of her, the book in her lap. She wore tightfitting denims, dark in color, that matched the blue of her T-shirt, which like most of her shirts, had a silkscreened imprint of the Northwestern logo. The clouds had just parted enough to let in the sun, but the beam was broken as it filtered through the overhead branches of the trees. A single ray shone directly on Rachel, lighting her blond hair which was pulled back in a ponytail. The illumination had the effect of putting a halo around her head.

Rachel failed to look up. She rubbed her arm, enjoying the sun, and turned another page.

"Hi muffin," Satchel said. "Must be a good book. You didn't hear me coming."

"Sorry Dad. Yeah, I'm kinda into it."

Satchel sat down feeling the warmth on his shoulders. "Lovely day, eh?" Shards of light were breaking through the trees creating yellow puzzle patterns on the lawn. The breeze lifted his thinning hair. He brought his arms around and laid them over the back of the bench and crossed his legs at the ankles, then leaned forward to wipe a few remaining blades of grass off his tennis shoe. "Anything special you want to do today?"

Rachel closed her book and looked over at her father, "No, I'm happy just to have the chance to talk."

"So a walk around the campus and down to the lake then. Well it's a blooming lovely day for it. Come on then, might as well be going."

Rachel put the book into a small lightweight backpack and stood, slipping it over her shoulders. They turned and started walking. The tree leaves rustled in the breeze. An elderly woman crossed their path pushing a baby stroller with a Chihuahua inside. Two young boys kicked a soccer ball across the lawn.

"So what's new in your life this week?"

Out the corner of her eye Rachel caught Satchel's grimace, apparently sorry he'd asked, and for good reason.

She looked over. "Yes, we had a celebration in Senator Weise's office. I guess you know your boy's history. I hate to say I told you so—but I told you so."

Satchel shrugged and turned his arm over to scratch his elbow. "Told me so? How?"

"I told you your man Stan likes prostitutes."

"That's what the newspapers say, but I still don't believe it," he said, letting go of his arm.

"Oh come on, Dad. It's one thing to say you don't believe me when I tell you he killed my mother but you can't deny this. They've got pictures."

They traveled a few more paces before Satchel responded. He paused and turned to look at her. "I can't explain the pictures. I just know he says he didn't do what they're saying, and I believe him."

"Willful blindness. I'd hoped for better of you." They began walking again. A gaggle of geese flew by in a perfect V formation heading back to Canada from their winter abroad. They began a series of honks signaling they were about to descend on the lake. "I thought maybe once you saw the evidence you'd admit you were wrong." Rachel raised a hand over her eyes to watch them land.

"Wrong about what?"

The air bore the scent of time immortal, like an odor that had been there since the dawn of creation. The lake was the color of indigo. An Eastern breeze brought small waves in to lap against the shore. The sand upon which they walked was wet and hard, and strewn with shiny black pebbles.

"You said he wasn't a customer, that he only wanted to get my mother off the street. Why can't you accept the fact that he was just another one of her johns?"

They were walking side-by-side, shoulders almost touching. Rachel could feel the heat of his body, a kind of connectivity shared between a father and daughter, and yet somehow it wasn't.

"It's kind of sad in a way. I was there the other night and I enjoyed listening to him, not that I agreed with what he had to say, but at least I thought he was sincere. Then he goes to the bar and finds a hooker and proves everything I thought about him was true. What's your answer to that?"

Satchel shook his head. "Can't say I have one, luv. Sometimes you have to walk by faith, not by sight."

"What's that supposed to mean?"

"It means you can't always believe what you see, and sometimes should believe what you can't." He placed his hands behind his back and walked a little further. "All my life I would've said God didn't exist, that all religions were inventions of man created for the purpose of assuaging guilt or to give hope of a life after death. Now I believe that God is real, not because I can see Him or have any proof, but because I feel Him on the inside and I see the things he's doing in my life. I walk by faith not by sight. Same thing goes with Mr. Powers. Sight would tell me he went into that bar to find someone to cozy with, but faith, what I feel in my heart, tells me he didn't do it."

"Yeah, and one night a guy named Mark Chapman heard a voice from God telling him to kill John Lennon. He believed in his heart he was doing the right thing. You can't always trust what you feel in your heart."

Satchel sighed. He stopped and turned to face her. "I think you need to be careful. I'm a little closer to this than you are. I'm British don't forget. Turns out David Mark Chapman was deranged. He took massive quantities of LSD, which made it hard for him to separate hallucinations from reality. It wasn't God he heard, it was the manifestation of specters he'd created in his own mind."

A figure approached them jogging down the beach, though he didn't look like a jogger because he was wearing denims, a T-shirt and tennis shoes. He had a man bag over his shoulder that bounced along beside him as he ran. As he got closer he slowed his gait and slipped his hand into the bag. Rachel, just to be friendly, brought her hand up to wave, but then something strange happened. She heard a spurt, like the sound of someone easing pressure off a leaky faucet, and saw her father grab his chest. "Skinhead Jack," he said. Then she felt a pain and looked down to see a patch of red quickly pooling into her T-shirt. She saw her father drop to his knees and buckle over onto his side. Her legs felt like rubber-bands as she collapsed beside him.

The man stood over her father. "Told ya you weren't getting out alive," he said. "I'll see you in hell." Then he turned to Rachel. "Sorry lady, I've been tracking Satch, but you're always with him. Consider yourself collateral damage." He turned and raced off down the beach to a motorcycle parked on the bluff.

Rachel stared into her father's eyes. They looked glazed, like whatever thoughts were behind them had faded into the ocean of time. "Don't! Don't you die!" Satchel's fingers curled like he wanted to hold her hand. She reached out and squeezed his fingers but they felt like mush.

She saw him shake his head. "I won't," he said, his voice as soft as a whisper. "I'm going to live." He tried to smile. "I'm sorry. You don't…don't deserve this. Such…such a bloody rotten father. Call upon Jesush. Pleash. Do it *nowww.*" His words came out gargled by the liquid collecting in his larynx. He closed his eyes and then opened them again. A trickle of blood came up through his throat and drained from his mouth. He squeezed her fingers and let go, his eyes veiled as though covered by a shroud, seeing nothing.

"Dad? Dad? Please, God, no!" Rachel felt a surge of pain shoot from her spine to the top of her head. Her world went black.

Nineteen

THE AMBULANCE screamed down the highway blowing its foghorn at anyone who refused to get out of the way. The sirens were blaring with the blue and red lights bouncing off the hood of the van. The driver had his foot to the floor while his partner, also a registered EMT, took an address from the dispatcher and plugged it into the GPS. They were local boys, familiar with Evanston and its medical community, but they needed a clinic with a level one trauma center. Hospitals able to handle gunshot wounds were mostly downtown.

They pulled into the emergency bay of Northwestern Memorial and hopped out of the cab, sliding Rachel's gurney from the back and rolling it onto the trauma center floor. "Victim has sustained a gunshot wound in the abdominal area. Bleeding stabilized, blood pressure 85 over 55, heart rate 115, respiratory rate 32."

"Okay guys, thank you. We'll take it from here." A trauma team of six medical personnel took up stations on both sides of the cart, wheeling Rachel into a room with glass walls and floor to ceiling curtains. "Watch that BP, it appears to be falling. Let's get her off this cart. On my count, one, two, three," and the six people hefted Rachel off the gurney and onto a hospital bed. The doctor cut the straps of her backpack, pulling it free as it dropped to the floor. The EMTs had already sliced away her shirt and patched her wounds on both sides to stop the bleeding. "Looks like a clean through and through, but I'm concerned about the location. The anterior portion of the kidney may have sustained damage, and she appears to have a scar on her left from a previous nephrectomy. I'm going to need a transabdominal ultrasound, stat."

A nurse rolled a portable machine in, and after covering Rachel with gel, gently moved a small handheld transducer around her abdomen. The sound waves created a picture of her pelvic organs on a small TV monitor. "Just as I thought, the patient already had one kidney removed and her second is severely damaged. There may be thoracic and abdominal injuries as well, but we won't know until we get in there and do an exploration. At this point I don't see any uncontrolled bleeding or symptoms of hypovolemic shock. Call Doctor Ravensbrook and get him to the O.R., and have this girl prepped for a nephrectomy, stat. Oh and start a doner search. Unless we can get a transplant ASAP this poor kid is destined to live the rest of her life strapped to a machine."

Doctor Ravensbrook removed his mask and gown and hung them in the prep room outside the OR. Rachel's case troubled him. He pondered what her life would be like as he slogged back to his office. She'd survived the surgery, but she needed a kidney. According to UNOS, the current transplant wait time was three to five years. Compounding matters was her blood type. She was AB negative, very rare. They'd had enough supply on hand to complete the operation, but not enough to do a transplant, so even if they found a donor her chances of getting her kidney replaced was slim. It just didn't seem fair. A young lady like that had so much to live for.

He made his way back to his office and snapped his computer on as he sat down. He could only recall being in a situation like this one other time, another gunshot wound where the patient was AB negative. He'd recently seen the man on TV debating the state senator. He didn't pander to watching the news but he'd heard there was some kind of controversy surrounding his former patient. The man could probably use some good press. Maybe he was looking for a way to redeem himself. It was worth a shot. He logged on to the main hospital database and searched the file with his patient's records. Stan Powers, easy name to remember. They did share the same blood type. Good. Contact information, all there. He picked up the phone.

Stan tried to ignore the ringing but it was incessant. They never quit. They all swore they would tell his story fairly, but he'd been that route before. The story would come out, but in his way, and in his time. He glanced at the display. Northwestern Memorial Hospital? Stephen Ravenbrook? Huh? He reached for the phone.

"This is Stan, how can I help you?"

"Stan this is Doctor Ravensbrook, the surgeon who pieced you back together after that holdup."

"Yes, Doctor, I remember. Kind of hard to forget. How have you been?"

"I've been fine. Maybe we can catch up sometime but right now I'm on a mission of mercy, and trust me this is not something I do every day, but I have a young lady here who needs blood. It's a special circumstance. It looks like she lost one kidney several years ago, and this morning I had to remove the other. She needs another kidney, but right now the main problem is we don't have enough blood here in the hospital to keep her going. It's kind of a rare blood type, the same one you have, and I was wondering if you'd be willing to come in and make a donation."

From the outside, Northwestern Memorial looked like the juxtaposition of two separate worlds in a confluence of space and time. From the left, the building's architecture was tall and gothic, with castle-like arches and towers, a form that would have been disparaged by Howard Roark, Ayn Rand's protagonist in her book, *The Fountainhead,* but from the right you saw a more modern structure, a building that resembled a Rubik's cube made of glass.

Stan rode the elevator up, stopping frequently to let off and take on nursing staff and visitors. When he reached his floor he exited to the right, following the instructions given him by the receptionist at the information desk on the main floor. He had an appointment with Doctor Ravensbrook, but that wasn't for another fifteen minutes. He felt compelled to seek out the young lady he was being asked to help. The Doctor said her name was Rachel Carter. Satchel's last name was Carter, and he had a daughter whom Stan was almost certain he'd called Rachel. It was a mystery he wanted to solve before committing his blood to her rescue.

He found the room and peeked in. There were four beds, each surrounded by a privacy curtain hanging from a channel track. Only two of the room dividers were open to viewing. One of the beds was empty. The other was occupied by an older woman, perhaps in her eighties, whose whitish skin and bluish lips made her appear to be already deceased. He could tell she was alive by the rise and fall of her chest and because she was snoring softly. That narrowed it down to the two patients he couldn't see.

A nurse walked in and pulled back the curtain on one of the cubicles. Stan crept around to sneak a peek at the person lying on the bed. He shook his head and took a step back. That couldn't be Rachel. The doctor had described his patient as young, with her whole life ahead of her. This woman was mid-fifties with a mat of red hair and two inches of gray roots showing. Her face was a network of veins. Both her legs were raised and suspended by chains, and both were encased in casts. Rachel was supposed to be suffering gunshot wounds. That left only one cubicle.

He slid the curtain back enough to creep inside and ducked

behind it so he couldn't be seen. Monitors with wavy lines and graphs and numbers blossomed like red and green fruit growing on a stainless steel tree. He was looking down at a young lady in her late teens, blond with high cheekbones. He'd seen her before. She'd been there the evening of the debate. He thought back on that night, remembering how she had almost bumped into him as she exited the conference center, how she'd looked startled, and then afraid, and then fled. Small world.

Her eyes popped open. For a moment she stared up at him like her brain was foggy and working through the process of identifying where she knew him from, then her eyes filled with recognition. She rolled onto her side with her back to him and drug her pillow over her head.

"Sorry, I didn't mean to startle you."

Rachel pulled the pillow tighter, her elbow winging out in a manner that suggested she was also trying to block sound from reaching her ears.

"I have a friend, Satchel Carter, I just wondered if you two were related." He waited but the girl didn't move. "I'm almost certain he has a daughter named Rachel. If that's you, does he know you're here? Maybe I can get word to him. Or if he already knows, I'd like to talk to him. He may need a friend right now." There was no movement. Stan could see he was upsetting the young lady, which was the last thing he wanted to do. He took a step back. Perhaps Doctor Ravensbrook would know more about the girl's father. He looked at his watch and turned to go.

Stan was stretched out on a hospital bed with a tube inserted into his arm. The flow of blood leaving his body was monitored by a lab technician. Doctor Ravensbrook, who now insisted Stan call him, Stephen, had wasted no time in getting Stan to the lab. They'd barely shaken hands when Stephen took him by the elbow and started guiding him down the hall. He'd insisted that Rachel was in no immediate danger, but they never knew when something might go wrong. Stan's blood could be needed at any time.

Stan had allowed himself to be escorted through a labyrinth of corridors ignoring the sound his Hush Puppies made as they squeaked on the linoleum. He wore a pair of denims and a white shirt with the tail out and a tan corduroy jacket. It was the first time he'd allowed himself to be seen in casual dress since the start of his campaign. Doctor Ravensbrook, wrapped in a white cotton smock with the name of Northwestern Memorial stitched above the pocket in blue, walked beside him.

Doctor Ravensbrook looked smaller, and his hair thinner, than Stan remembered. Of course his own operation had been ten years ago. "Perhaps I shouldn't have, but I stopped in to see your patient. I was curious because I know a man whose last name is Carter who has a daughter named Rachel and I wondered if they were the same. Do you know who this girl's father is?"

They continued down the hall. Doctor Ravensbrook used a finger to slide his glasses back over the bridge of his nose as he pondered the question. He seemed hesitant to speak but finally said, "What your friend's first name?"

"Satchel. You'd know him if you saw him, big guy, speaks with a thick British accent."

Stephen stopped and waited for Stan to stop also. Then he closed the gap between them and shook his head. "I'm afraid the girl's father is down in our morgue. I don't know what happened, but they were both shot and he was brought in DOA. If he was your friend, I'm sorry."

Stan swallowed, the lump in his throat sliding down like a rock. That wasn't what he was prepared to hear. "Yes, he was. A very good friend." He turned and began walking again. *Satchel gone? Impossible,* and yet true. He suddenly realized Rachel was now his responsibility. Satchel would want it that way. "So what happens

291

now? Will the girl receive a new kidney?"

"We're looking into it but frankly the odds aren't good. Her blood type's rare, as you know, and even if it weren't, typical wait times can be as much as five years, especially with someone who's young and otherwise healthy. Available kidneys go to those who are facing death and need one quickly."

"You said she'd had both kidneys removed. How can a person live without kidneys?"

"Well, it's certainly not ideal, but life does go on. She'll have to have dialysis three times a week, which takes about five hours per session, that's where we remove the blood from her body and run it through a machine that takes out all the impurities and then pumps it back into her system. And she could end up taking as many as 20 different prescription drugs to help control her blood pressure and heart rate and lower her levels of phosphorus and potassium. She'll probably suffer a few side effects too, like constant itching and stomach aches from trying to digest so many pills, but the main thing is, she'll live, if you call that living. Sooner or later we'll find a donor and hopefully, if it's not too late, her life will return to normal."

Stan paused. He placed his hands in his pockets, bit his bottom lip, and rocked back on his heels. "What about me?" he said.

Twenty

RACHEL STARED up at the TV mounted high on the wall. She'd never been a fan of television and rarely watched it, but it was a distraction and she needed something to keep her mind off the pain. She'd asked for her backpack; she wanted the book she'd been reading. The nurses said they were trying to locate it but so far hadn't had any luck. Nor had she received any answer to her question about what happened to her father. They either didn't know or were unwilling to say. She wanted to believe he was alive, but couldn't stop dreading that he was dead. She tried to adjust her position to ease the pressure on her backside but it made her wince. They had her on Percocet to reduce the inflammation and ease her discomfort but it only worked to a degree. As far as she was concerned, her life was over. The doctor had explained what life was like for someone on dialysis. She wouldn't be able to go to school. All she'd worked for had been trashed in a single moment. She wasn't showing up for work. Charlotte would more than likely fire her, but that was okay since she couldn't work while going through dialysis three times a week. Satchel had laid there telling her to call on God, but God had taken his life, and hers too. Even if she wasn't dead, she might as well be. She was a vegetable unable to work and contribute. Why go on? She flicked the remote to change the channel. *Him again!* Mr. Powers' face appeared on the screen.

A voiceover gave the picture context. "…apparently the video was sent to more than fifty news agencies, so we apologize for our original report saying this was a major exclusive. For those who haven't seen it yet, this constitutes a real eye opener, a sharp contrast to stories reported earlier about Mr. Powers and his liaison with noted escort Marianne Moss."

"Apparently, Mr. Powers turned the tables on Ms. Moss and Senator Weise by setting up a camera and inviting the escort in to have a conversation about what really happened that night. In the clip Ms. Moss not only admits to having faked the story, but goes further to implicate Senator Weise in the deception. A spokesperson for Senator Weise denies any wrongdoing, but sources tell us the police have obtained a bank statement which shows a check in the amount of three thousand dollars made out to Marianne Moss on the same day the story broke. We want to note that this clip may be disturbing for young people to watch, so if you have children in the room you may want to ask them to leave."

Rachel tried to sit up, but her stitches were raw and the pain sharp. She relaxed her head against the pillow and turned up the volume of her headset. Her stomach turned, the pain raking her gut like the stabbing of a knife.

Rachel awoke to her arm being nudged. It felt like she'd only just fallen asleep. She opened her eyes to see two blurry figures standing beside her bed. They wore suits, one blue, one gray, with ties. The taller man had on a blue shirt. The shorter man's shirt was white. The taller man opened his wallet and proffered a badge.

"Hi Rachel. My name is Detective Tooley and this is my partner Detective Burke. We were wondering if we could ask you a few questions; I mean, about how you got here."

Rachel pulled the covers up under her chin and nodded.

"Maybe you could start by telling us in your own words what happened."

She blinked. Every word she said caused a rise and fall in her abdomen which increased the pain of her injury. "I'll try," she said. "But first maybe you can answer a question for me." She placed a hand over the patch and applied pressure to keep it from moving. "What happened to my father? I keep asking, but no one will tell me anything."

The two detectives looked at each other, the taller one shaking his head and the shorter one nodding in agreement. "That information hasn't been released yet, so we're not at liberty to say."

Rachel exhaled with a grimace and slowly drew her breath back in. "Then I also have nothing to say."

Once again the detectives looked at each other, then the taller one, detective Tooley said, "They don't want us to say anything because they don't want you becoming distraught. You need to focus on your recovery, but saying that is pretty much the same as saying he didn't make it. I'm sorry, but your father's gone."

Rachel had promised herself she wouldn't cry. She tried to stare at the ceiling, but her eyes began to burn and then to water and suddenly she found herself in tears.

Detective Strokes reached for a box of tissue and handed them to Rachel. "That's okay, go ahead and let it out."

Rachel told them everything. She let them know what the man was wearing, but they were sure those clothes would be gone by now. She gave a description of the man but it was vague, except for the fact that his head was either shaved or bald. She wasn't looking at his face, but she did feel she might be able to point to him in a lineup and thought she might recognize his voice, if it ever came to that. The best lead was when she told them her father had cried, "Skinhead Jack," before crashing to his knees. Detective Tooley knew Skinhead. He was a lifer who'd recently escaped. There was an APB out on him. He went to his phone and scrolled through wanted posters until he found Jack's image.

He turned the phone in Rachel's direction. "This him?" He said.

Rachel's eyes went wide, the color draining from her face. She nodded. "Yes, that's definitely him."

Detective Tooley put his phone away. It just didn't get any better than that.

Rachel wanted to open a window. The room had a ubiquitous odor of bandages, antiseptics, and body creams. It was disquieting, but she couldn't get out of bed to do it herself and the nurse she'd asked didn't want to bring discomfort to others in the room. She was tired of being here. It had been three days already. She felt claustrophobic, like the walls were closing in. Her first dialysis was scheduled for today and she was nervous.

It hurt to know she had argued with her father and that he'd been right. She wished she could've had the chance to tell him how she'd started exploring the claims of the Bible, or at least had begun reading it. It was the book she'd been reading when he'd found her in the Park but she hadn't wanted him to know. She'd found a hard bound version and used a brown bag to make a book cover so he couldn't see what she was reading. She didn't want him harping on her about getting saved. Now she hoped he was right about that too. She had to remember to ask the nurse about her backpack again.

She looked up and saw Doctor Ravensbrook enter the room. He walked over to her bed-side and took her hand. "You're looking good, Rachel. Good skin color, warm hands, indicates good circulation." He looked up at the monitors. "Good heart rate, blood pressure, your vitals are all in good order. Are you ready for your treatment?"

She stared at him, her blue eyes looking like they were receiving shocks from tiny wires inside her head. "No," she said."

"You'll do fine. And I have good news. We've found a potential donor, so if things work out you'll only have to go through this a few times."

Rachel's face visibly brightened but then froze as her head sank back down into the pillow. "Who?"

"Actually, at this point the donor would rather remain anonymous."

Rachel stared up at the ceiling giving no indication that she'd heard. "I saw that man, Mr. Powers in here a while ago. He's been hanging around outside my room. Just tell me it isn't him."

The Doctor sat on the edge of her bed, still holding her hand. He stroked it affectionately. "Why does it matter? You need to think about living. If someone offers you a kidney, you should take it. You're facing dialysis three times a week for the rest of your life and a whole lot of issues that go with it. With a new kidney, all that goes away and you live a normal life." He patted her hand and let go, standing again. "We still have to make sure we have a good match, but I put a rush on it and so far it looks promising."

Rachel turned her head away from Doctor Ravensbrook. A tear fell from her eye and slid down her nose. All things being equal, dialysis three times a week, as opposed to having a killer's kidney, was an easy choice. "You do what you got to do, but if the kidney's from that man, I don't want it."

Twenty-One

RACHEL WAS having trouble breathing. It wasn't a respiratory problem, her lungs were fine, the problem was her stomach. She felt nauseous, like she wanted to throw up. She felt if she took in too much air too fast she might heave. Her nurse had told her she'd probably feel sick after her dialysis, and as usual her nurse was right. She placed her hand on her stomach and took a few slow deep breaths.

The procedure had gone smoothly. She had laid there hour after hour with a needle in her arm while blood flowed from her body and went down a tube into a machine. The nurse said to think of it as a washing machine because it was washing her blood and getting rid of any impurities. Then the blood was sent back through another tube into her body again. In essence, the machine was replicating the function of a kidney. This would be her life from now on. She couldn't think of anything less appealing.

Doctor Ravensbrook stood at the door. He tapped the frame lightly with his knuckles just to let her know he was there and then entered.

"So how does it feel to have fresh clean blood?"

Rachel's lips were pressed together tightly. She looked peeved. "Awful," she said.

Stephen walked over and sat on the corner of the bed. "The nurse tells me you did great." He brought the clipboard up and flipped through a few pages. All your vitals are normal. I'll be starting you on a new drug regimen to reduce the chance of infection.

"I never want to go through that again."

"Was there a problem?" He said, looking up.

"No, the process was fine. It's the way you feel afterward. I think I want to puke."

Stephen nodded. "Well the good news is, you don't have to. Our donor checked out. He's not only a good match, he's a paternal match, which is perfect."

Rachel pushed herself up on her elbows, trying to raise her head. "What did you say? What's that mean?"

"It means the man who wants to donate his kidney to you is your father. And yes, it is Stan Powers, the man you've been refusing to see."

"That's impossible. My father was Satchel Carter. He showed me my birth certificate. His name was on it."

"You need to hear me out. Satchel Carter was brought in DOA but since this was a shooting, I was asked to draw a sample of his blood. The police like to get a jump on things when they can. They wanted to see if drugs were involved. Their thinking was that maybe you both were shot in a drug deal gone bad, but it turned out that wasn't the case. I did find something interesting though. Turned out Mr. Carter's blood type was O."

"So?"

"A father whose blood type is O can't produce AB offspring. You're AB negative. That set off all kinds of bells and whistles. I admit, I'm not much of a sleuth, but every doctor has to be an investigator of sorts. Getting to the cause of a problem often requires a knowledge of the patient's genetic background. You get used to looking into things. I tried to locate the hospital you were born in…"

"I wasn't born in a hospital."

"So I found out. Turns out you've had an interesting life. You were born in a pizza pub. I had to track down the ambulance company that responded. The technician who delivered you is retired now, but he remembers the incident quite well. He said the manager was the one who made the call. Your mother's water broke while they were sitting there having drinks and she's acting flabbergasted. She swears she never knew she was pregnant. You were crowning by the time the ambulance arrived. People were circling around trying to get in close to see. It was a real three ring circus. But my ambulance guy said when you were lifted from between your mother's legs and handed to her, it was almost mystical. Your mother literally glowed, physically I mean. He said he's never seen anything like it before or since. Anyway, the technician who was with him was the one filling out the paperwork. When she asked who the father was, the guy your mother was with raised his hand. That, of course, was Satchel. The funny thing was your mother shook her head but Satchel shrugged and told the technician that your mother slept with a lot of men and couldn't know who the father was, but that nine months earlier he'd been the only man in her life. So Satchel's name was put on the document and he became the father of record. Quite a story, huh? And it solves the mystery of how Satchel came to think he was your father. And I guess he died still thinking it, which isn't a bad thing. It would've been hard on him if he found out otherwise."

"But...Mr. Powers?"

"Ah, well, to tell the truth, the only thing I had to go on there was your common blood type, which is rare, but not *that* rare. I did notice you both had the same eyes and fair complexion and I saw a resemblance in other areas as well, enough to make me suspect you might be related down the line somewhere. So, nothing ventured, nothing gained. I had them run a paternity test and it came back positive.

Rachel's face clouded like a storm brewing on a distant horizon. She turned her head away, her tears disappearing into the soft cotton pillowcase the way rain disappears into a soft bed of loam.

The Doctor placed a hand on her shoulder. "Rachel, I can't pretend to understand what you're going through. It's obvious you have an issue with Mr. Powers, but I would counsel you to try and get past it because he is your father and right now he wants to give you a kidney." He stood holding his clipboard to his chest. "Frankly, it puzzles me. I would think you'd be overjoyed just to know there's a kidney available. From everything I know about Mr. Powers he seems like a decent man, and if you're thinking about all that stuff that's been in the news recently, he's been cleared of all that. Anyway, I'll leave you to think about it." Dr. Ravensbrook took one last look at her bedside monitors, made a note on her chart, and sauntered out of the room.

Rachel didn't want to cry. She sniffed and wiped her eyes. She had to stop, if for no other reason than it hurt. Each sob caused a pounding of her solar plexus that wrenched her gut and tugged at her stitches. She rolled onto her back looking for her tissue box, but it was out of reach. That was so unfair. She had enough problems without her doctor adding more. She couldn't fathom having Stan Powers as a father. She sniffed again and wiped her nose with the back of her hand. She closed her eyes and rolled back onto her side, facing the wall. Her mind wasn't working. All that Percocet was inhibiting her ability to think. She had just returned from foraging food and found him standing over her mother's body. He didn't have a knife or a gun, he was just standing there, but her mother was blue and had that needle stuck in her vein. That was weapon enough. She'd never seen them together, not in that way, but her mother never let her see her with anyone. And he was there frequently, just like most of her regular customers. And they always argued. Her mother may have kept her out of sight but she was never so far away that she couldn't hear them fighting. He was always trying to get something from her, something she was unwilling to give. And when they weren't fighting he was bringing her money. If not for services rendered, then what? But when the coroner came the next day, Mr. Powers was with him. It wasn't like he was on the run, or had something to hide. It was all so confusing.

She felt, more than heard, someone at the door clearing their throat. They were trying to get her attention. She didn't have to roll over to know who it was. Doctor Ravensbrook would have given him the news. "Go away," she said.

"Rachel...I"

Rachel rolled over. Her eyes were buckets of water, blurry and out of focus. She used the sleeve of her hospital gown to pat them dry. "You really think this changes anything?"

Stan stepped into the room. He was wearing tan slacks and a white polo shirt. His eyes were blue as the flame of a gas fire, just like her own. He moved to where he could stand beside her bed.

She looked up at him unblinking, her eyes, blue eyes, sandy brown hair—*like looking in a mirror.* "Why did you do it? Just tell me that. Tell me why you killed my mother."

"What?"

"I was there that night. I saw what you did. You gave my mom a hotshot. I saw the needle in her arm and you standing there. And then you chased me because I was a witness."

Stan was shaking his head, his sandy hair somewhat darker than her own. "I...I guess I can see how it might appear that way, but that's not what happened."

Rachel rolled toward the wall putting her back to him again. Her words were slurred by the tears clouding her throat. "You and she always argued. All these other men would pay their money and go but that wasn't enough for you. You'd get what you wanted and throw your money at her feet like she was some kind of trash and then scream and yell at her to make her feel worse."

"Boy, I don't know what you saw, but that wasn't me. We did argue some, that's true. Would you like to know what we argued about?" Stan waited but Rachel didn't respond. "We argued because

I wanted her to come home. I loved your mother, Rachel. Truth is, she's the only woman I've ever loved. But I wasn't one of her tricks, I was her husband. We were married, but your mother was schizophrenic. We didn't know it at first, but over time she began acting strange, like she was losing touch. I felt like she was slipping away, like I was losing her—because I was. She became disorganized. She stopped doing things that were part of her regular routine. We talked about it and she agreed. She was having difficulty concentrating. We went to several doctors and ultimately she was diagnosed with schizophrenia and that's pretty much where our marriage ended, not because I wanted it to, I was in it for the long haul, but because she refused to take her medication. I was in the military and got deployed so I couldn't watch her all the time. She began running off, only for a few days at first, but eventually for weeks at a time and I wouldn't know where she was.

Someone, somewhere, introduced her to oxycodone. She was open with me about it. She said it released her from all her anxieties and all that pent up tension associated with schizophrenia. I tried to get her to stop. I loved her, Rachel, but the more I pushed the more she pulled away. She finally stopped coming home. I went looking and found her living on the streets. By then she had already turned to prostitution to pay for her growing habit. I tried to bring her back but she refused. Then she went into hiding and for about a year I didn't know where she was. That must've been around the time you were born, but she never told me about you.

That night you saw me, it was because another street person came by the mission and let me know where she was. I had gone there to bring her back. It was forecast to drop to way below zero and I felt if she stayed outside, she might freeze to death. I got there only a few minutes before you showed up, but she was already gone. I saw you, and I did chase after you. I even looked for you for several days afterward. In fact I didn't stop until child services told me they'd picked you up and found you a good home. But

I thought you were someone else's child. I didn't know anything about us until this very morning."

Rachel's sobs were muted by the pillow but Stan could hear them nonetheless.

She raised her head slightly, strings of saliva breaking on her lips. "So where's my mother now?" she said.

"She's resting at Oak Woods under a headstone that reads, Karen Powers."

Rachel twisted her head on around, a look of disbelief breaking through the wet shine of her cheeks. "Karen? Her name was Wren."

"No, that was just her street name. Your mother was Karen Powers, and I loved her very much."

Epilogue

The morning grass smelled fresh and green. Rachel walked across the lawn holding a bouquet of yellow daisies, relishing the sun on her shoulders. A few of the trees were wearing fall colors, but not many, not yet. It would be hard coming here once it started to snow.

She was thankful for Chicago's rapid transit. If it weren't for that she couldn't come at all. She still didn't own a car, and had no plans to buy one. Most students didn't find it necessary. Filling the atmosphere with carbon monoxide was frowned upon, and she couldn't afford a hybrid. She did have a bicycle now, an old ten speed she'd found in pretty good shape at the White Elephant resale store. She used it to get around campus, and for transportation to Mama's where she now worked as a server.

Mama had taken her fa… Satchel's…death pretty hard. Funny how she still thought of Satchel as her father even though he wasn't. Ten years of living with a false assumption made the image hard to erase.

Mama had hosted a memorial service for Satchel. It had taken place while Rachel was supposed to be recovering from her surgery, but Doctor Ravensbrook had permitted her to attend as long as she promised to stay in her wheelchair and didn't try to get up and walk around. Samuel and the crew from the mission were there. No one had known Satchel long enough to write enduring eulogies or deliver humorous anecdotes. Freddie tried, but he'd mostly stood there choking down his tears while stammering unintelligibly. All had tears in their eyes and respected that Satchel had given his life to Christ. He was heaven-bound even before Skinhead Jack sent him to meet his maker. All would remember Satchel with fondness.

As for Jack, he'd gone down hard. A captain in the Aryan Brotherhood had fronted him two-hundred and fifty dollars' worth of methamphetamine, and when he couldn't pay, sent an enforcer to collect. The altercation took place at Chain Shakers, a local hangout the feds had had under surveillance for over a year. When shots were fired, the agents had run in and found Skinhead lying on the floor in a puddle of blood. His hand held a Bowie knife pulled from a sheath strapped to his ankle. The blade had blood on it, but the enforcer was nowhere to be found.

And Freddie? Freddie was now part of a paint crew operated by a contractor who, as a former inmate, specialized in helping people get a fresh start. He thought about Angela often but hadn't been to see her since being thrown from her 4400 block apartment. He refused to go back, not because of the danger, but because its proximity was too close to a life he no longer wanted to live.

Rachel felt a breeze coming in off Lake Michigan, cool at this time of year. It would've been nice if Satchel could have been buried there too. Oak Woods had been established in 1854. Five thousand Confederate soldiers who'd been imprisoned and died at Camp Douglas were interred there, along with Chicago's prominent rich and famous. There were numerous large monuments. One she passed was constructed of black granite and covered an area the size of a small backyard. The words, "Jesus is Lord" were engraved in the stone, to which she said, "Amen."

Rachel approached a small lake, a reflection pond really, but it did add an element of serenity to her mother's resting place. She stood looking down on the polished slab of stone. "Karen Powers." It seemed strange that she hadn't even known her mother's real name. She placed the yellow daisies on top of the stone and sat down to bask in the sun.

The lines outside the mission were getting longer as cooler weather set in. The days were growing shorter, making the windows dusky even at the five o'clock hour. Stan grabbed a large vat filled with noodles that had been boiling for about fifteen minutes. He placed a strainer in the sink, slipped on a pair of potholder mittens, and tipped the vat up, letting the water run through while capturing the noodles. Then he repeated the process with a second vat and strainer.

Two days after he'd made his announcement to his staff they had come back to him with a proposal offering to buy him out. The logic was simple. The company name would stay the same to prevent client migration. Customers would be assured that little had changed and, as far as they were concerned, it was business as usual. Stan would remove himself from the company's day-to-day business operations but would become Chairman of the Board, overseeing major shifts in policy and direction. He would comply with the edict of the court by divesting himself of the corporation. From a legal standpoint, the case would be settled. Power Advertising hadn't signed a contract with Thomas and Marty, so the new owners were under no obligation to promote the Silver Slipper. And during the period of restructuring, they would not be taking on new clients.

Thomas, who brought the original lawsuit against Stan, was facing bigger issues than the loss of free advertising. He now found himself being sued. While partnered with Marty, he had begun a fling on the side with a contractor named Barry, who in light of their budding romance provided a crew to renovate the building Thomas had leased for the Silver Slipper. After leading Barry to think they would both own the lounge as equal partners,

Thomas abruptly ended their relationship, leaving Barry to pay the cost of the renovations. Barry filed a suit against Thomas for fraud, and Marty, when he discovered Thomas had been cheating on him, packed his bags and left. Thomas promptly emptied his and Marty's joint bank account and disappeared. He hadn't been seen since.

Stan insisted, if his name was to remain on the door, that Power Advertising continue to operate under the guidelines of its original charter, a stipulation to which everyone agreed. His refusal to back down, regardless of the cost, had Julie and Bruce and several others looking in earnest at what he believed. Besides, they were getting the company for half its value, a deal too good to pass up. Stan had requested the money he received from the sale be directed to the Daily Bread food bank.

No longer employed, Stan had to put his house on the market or risk falling behind on the mortgage payments. He now occupied the prophet's chamber upstairs, but he liked it because it allowed him to be closer to the people they were trying to help. The car, too, was gone, but that wasn't a problem. It seemed he'd garnered a following and now had people standing in line to chauffeur him around. And when he didn't, he had access to Samuel's Caddy, though when he drove the behemoth it felt more like he was piloting a boat.

Behind him, a new parolee stirred several pots of meatballs bathed in marinara sauce, his arms streaming with tattoos. The new recruit had taken cooking courses out at Dixon and was anxious to demonstrate his culinary skills. Another man pulled the oven door open to see how the garlic bread was coming along. The long loaves were sliced in half lengthwise and looked to be bright yellow with an edge of golden brown. *Perfect.*

The five o'clock news was about to start. Stan reached over and turned the volume up on the small TV he'd recently installed in the kitchen.

"With only a month to go before the election, it's still too close to call. Polls show Senator Weise still slightly ahead, but it appears Powers has the momentum."

"That's right, Bret. Funny how the tables have turned. Only a few months ago, Weise held an impregnable lead. Mr. Powers was embroiled in controversy and was ready to drop out but his constituents rallied behind him and convinced him to stay."

"They did, and his base has been growing ever since. Odd too, because his message isn't particularly attractive. But it looks like more and more voters are buying into it."

"And Charlotte thought she'd walked away from the scandal unscathed, but it continues to haunt her campaign."

"It didn't hurt that the GOP gave Powers the nod and gave him financial backing."

"Or that his daughter, who originally worked for Senator Weise, left to become his campaign manager..."

Stan clicked the TV off. He'd heard enough. America's forefathers had expected people to be governed by God, not by men. If the message rang true, it was because it was part of America's heritage. Israel frequently wandered from God, and when things got bad, returned to Him. But always, even after God restored their blessings, they ended up wandering again. He was glad the people were ready for a change, but it wasn't likely to last. At least not until Christ came to establish His throne. He looked at the clock. "Okay guys, it's time to open the doors."

The bodies trundled in like one fat centipede with a hundred arms and legs, grabbing up plates, cups, and cutlery. Stan and his crew began dishing out bowls of noodles smothered in the new parolee's meatball sauce, and slices of hot golden bread. The room filled quickly.

Up front on the stage, a bald black man in a white shirt and alligator boots with a huge shiny cross around his neck picked up a guitar and started to sing.

"Amazing grace, how sweet the sound,
That saved a wretch like me,
I once was lost but now I'm found,
Was blind but now I see..."

Stan looked up in time to see Rachel coming through the door. She had to squeeze through the people standing in line, elbowing her way past dozens of hungry guests. She headed straight for the kitchen and picked up an apron which she slipped over her head and tied around her back. Reaching into her pocket she pulled out a hairnet and then caught her father's eye. She went over to kiss him on the cheek. "Better get a move on, Dad. We've still got a hundred mouths to feed." Then she turned to look at all those they were trying to help, her eyes blue as the ocean, her smile shimmering—*from sea to shining sea.*

Also by Keith R. Clemons:

If I Should Die

Above the Stars

These Little Ones

Angel in the Alley

Mohamed's Moon

Mohamed's Song

Stretching Heaven

One Pair of Shoes